Alone in the Woods

Alone in the Woods

Charly Cox

hera

First published in the United Kingdom in 2021 by

Hera Books
28b Cricketfield Road
London, E5 8NS
United Kingdom

A CIP catalogue record for this book is available from the British Library.

Print ISBN 978 1 80032 515 9
Ebook ISBN 978 1 912973 29 3

This book is a work of fiction. Names, characters, businesses, organizations,
places and events are either the product of the author's imagination or are
used fictitiously. Any resemblance to actual persons, living or dead, events
or locales is entirely coincidental.

Look for more great books at www.herabooks.com

Printed and bound in Great Britain by Clays Ltd, Elcograf S.p.A.

1

This one's for you, Melissa Naatz, for all the reasons. That includes, of course, but is not limited to, keeping me sane – or sometimes going nuts with me – and making me laugh while you do it.

And:

For all the readers out there who welcomed Alyssa Wyatt, along with her family – both work and home – into their lives; I've loved having you along on this journey.

Chapter One

Addis Penn Kensington pounded on her mother's chest in a vain and misguided attempt to get her to breathe. Misguided because it was obvious from the bullet hole in her mother's forehead that chest compressions would get her nowhere. Still, she continued beating despite the vacant eyes staring up at the ceiling tiles as if her mother had been counting them, or more likely, wondering who she should scream at for the grime that coated the paint.

It was only when a low, keening wail coming from across the room finally penetrated that Addis was able to drag her numb brain away from the state of her mother's corpse long enough for her mind to accept the reality of the bloodbath surrounding her. Fighting to keep the contents of her stomach inside, along with the scream clawing at her throat, she knew, as much as she wanted to pretend she'd done nothing more than stumble into a bad Halloween movie, she had to face what was right in front of her.

How could she not when the final nail in the coffin of deniability happened to be lying not ten feet from where she'd been working frantically at reviving her mother? Her father's death had been far more savage than a bullet hole to the forehead.

1

Tears streaming and gasping for breath, Addis abandoned her efforts and pushed herself to her feet before collapsing against the stove, squeezing her eyes tight against the carnage as she fumbled for her phone. Though she tried, she couldn't ignore the distinct coppery odor of blood that rushed in through her nostrils. Gagging, she barely turned to the trash can in time. Trembling as her knees threatened to give way, she averted her focus away from her parents and latched tightly onto the counter, as inch by slow inch, she staggered toward her best friend who was propped up against a wall, muffled, wheezing sobs bursting from her throat as she rocked back and forth, one arm wrapped protectively around her stomach while the other covered her nose and mouth.

When she and Emerson had walked through the door that evening, she'd been expecting the inevitable explosion of anger for taking off when her mother had forbidden her to leave her room, much less the house. She was even prepared for the required silent treatment that would surely follow, something that was never the punishment her mother believed it to be. But that wasn't the point. The point was: she'd been expecting *that* – not this carnage.

Even after stumbling upon this horrific scene, her brain had refused to grasp the veracity of what she was seeing, and she'd stood frozen, unable to do or think about anything other than: *It's still three and a half weeks from Halloween*. That thought had still been swirling in her mind when Emerson's ear-piercing scream ripped through the room, her feet backpedaling as if she'd just encountered a diamondback rattlesnake, stopping only when she'd backed into the wet bar where her dinner made a return trip. Seconds later, Em's legs had given out, and she'd collapsed against the nearest wall where she remained.

From that moment to now could've been minutes or hours. And though Addis knew she and Emerson needed to get out and call for help, the weight of the horror instead had her collapsing down beside her friend. Gripping Emerson's hand in her own, her voice thick with fear and disbelief, she whispered, 'We have to call the police.'

Temporarily releasing her grip, Addis, hands shaking, retrieved her phone from her pocket, dropping it twice before she was finally able to unlock the screen. Three numbers, that's all she had to push – nine-one-one – but getting her brain to coordinate and cooperate with her fingers was far more difficult than it might seem. Especially as her eyes refused to stop darting her father's way. A clawing pressure to crawl to him and curl herself into his side ripped through every fiber of her being.

Emerson's fingernails bit into her forearm, halting Addis as her body subconsciously gravitated toward her father. 'Ad, we need to go.'

It wasn't Em's plea that breached the recesses of Addis's terrified mind; it was the musical chime above the front door, the sound chilling and ominous in a way it never had been before. Her heart jackhammered, making it even harder to breathe. 'Oh my God. Someone's in the house!'

Emerson's head jerked up as Addis's eyes flickered to the patio door. Could they cross the room, unlock the metal bar, and slip out without being noticed?

Footsteps sounded in the foyer, coming closer.

No, they didn't have time. Addis forced herself to her feet, wrenching Em up with her.

As they skirted past her father's corpse, she ordered herself not to look, but her head and limbs had a mind of their own because her chin dropped, and her eyes darted down to the tattered mess of his chest, causing her to sway unsteadily.

As she regained her balance, the unmistakable echoes of someone else's footsteps on the tile floor drawing closer to the kitchen propelled her forward. Quietly and urgently shushing Emerson's bubbling hysteria, she hauled her best friend past the carnage and down the hall to her father's office where they could hide beneath his massive desk as she called for help.

But the moment she stepped through the doorway and saw the upended mess of files and papers, it was instantly clear that this might not have been the best choice. Keeping her grip tight, she turned to head back out, to run to her bedroom instead, but then a shadow darkened the wall at the end of the hall near the kitchen.

Whoever was in the house was coming this way. They were out of options.

Gasping for air through the sudden tightening in her chest, Addis gestured frantically toward her father's desk before shoving Emerson in that direction. The second her friend was tucked into the small space, she squeezed herself in beside her, making sure their feet weren't poking out before issuing a silent prayer that the intruder wasn't close enough to hear her voice as she called the police. Except instead of dialing 911, she tapped the contact image of the one person she trusted most in the world besides her best friend.

'Hello?'

Addis's vocal cords froze, unfreezing only when her aunt's worried voice came over the line once again.

'Hello? Addis, are you there?'

Barely breathing, she whispered, 'Aunt Grace—'

The sudden appearance of a man's booted feet had Addis snapping her mouth shut even as, beside her, a shrill cry escaped Emerson.

Seconds later, a man's blood-spattered face appeared in front of them, his cheeks flushing a ruddy red as he latched onto Addis's wrist and yanked the phone from her hand. Screeching, she kicked out at the tall, muscular guy as he dragged her from beneath the desk. Just as she yelled out for Emerson to run, a fist connected with her temple, making Em's horrified screams the last sound she registered before her world went black.

Chapter Two

The house on Apache Ridge Place was ablaze with lights, making it appear there was a festive party taking place within the swanky neighborhood as opposed to the dramatic tale Detective Alyssa Wyatt knew was unfolding inside. Just as she hunched down to duck under the crime scene tape, headlights illuminated the area in front of her as her partner Cord Roberts parked behind her government-issued Chevy Tahoe. As he unfurled his tall frame from his car and headed her way, she noted his rumpled shirt, his uncombed hair, and the new lines decorating his face.

'You look like demons dragged you through hell and brought you back. Is everything okay?'

There was a slight tremble to Cord's hand as he tunneled his fingers through his hair, tugging at the ends. 'Sara was having a bit of a rough night. Just as I was heading out, she got sick again, so I stuck around to make sure she was okay.' He drew in a ragged breath and released it. 'She is.' In May, in the midst of a particularly heinous case, they'd learned his wife was pregnant with twins, and last month they'd had quite the scare when the doctor couldn't detect one's heartbeat only to have it reappear, weak, but present.

Cord eradicated further discussion by shifting his attention past the mobile crime scene van and along the long walkway before landing it on the house. 'Why don't you give me the condensed version of what happened here?'

Trying not to be too alarmed, Alyssa studied her partner's profile before she finally accepted the dismissal for what it was. If Cord suspected Sara wouldn't be okay, he wouldn't be here. 'All I know for sure is that Grace Burgess is the one who called Dispatch after she discovered her brother and sister-in-law, Gabriel and Lydia Kensington, dead, and their daughter, Addis, and Addis's best friend, Emerson Childress, missing.' Her footsteps quickened as they hurried up the walkway, her mind automatically conjuring up the young female victims – one of them being her daughter's friend – of the sex-trafficking ring she and her team had broken up less than five months ago.

Before stepping through the doorway, in an effort to brace herself for what she knew she was about to encounter, Alyssa inhaled deeply through her nose, knowing it could be hours before she'd be able to breathe the fresh outside air again. Beside her, Cord's frame stiffened as he, too, sucked in a breath.

Once inside, vomit mixed with the tangy, metallic odor of blood and death permeated every molecule of space around them, and Alyssa had to suppress the impulse to cover her nose and mouth to combat the overwhelming stench. Then, recognizing the voice of one of her team members whom she had thought was still out on vacation, she moved briskly through a dim formal dining room and around the corner into the kitchen where the rotting odor of death took on a whole new level of assault on the senses.

'Holy Christ,' she and Cord breathed out at the same time.

Less than five feet in front of them, Gabriel Kensington lay in a pool of blood. With one side of his skull caved in and his chest showcasing a multitude of stab wounds, he bore no resemblance to the man Alyssa had occasionally assisted on some of his cases.

She directed Cord's attention to the pulpy mess of the man's hands where his bones had clearly been shattered. The sight of the marble rolling pin covered in blood lying not far from Gabriel's body near two overturned chairs depicted a picture of animalistic rage in the killer. Unfortunately, she could too easily envision Mr. Kensington's last moments, and the graphic mental image sent chills rippling down her spine.

She'd seen pinatas that were less beaten.

And now it was quite possible, probable even, that the same killer had taken the girls, a thought that iced Alyssa's blood.

One of their teammates, Officer Tony White – whose name was a perfect descriptor for his pale skin – turned when he heard her voice. His right eye was dotted with color, and down the side of his face was a nasty scratch, as if a large cat had dragged its talons across his skin. Alyssa wondered when he'd returned and why he was here at all since, avid hunter that he was, he'd taken time off as he usually did this time of year to head out to his cabin for a week of hunting. Unless she was misremembering, he wasn't supposed to return for a few more days. Maybe he *had* tangled with a cat.

Tony grabbed one of the technicians with a camera and pointed to something Alyssa couldn't see. Then, barely slowing his stride, he motioned for her and Cord to follow. 'Grace is this way.'

In a seating area off the kitchen, Bernalillo County's district attorney sat perched on the very edge of a cornflower-blue sofa, eyes shimmering with unshed tears, her face pale save the red splotches on her cheeks and forehead. It was a far cry from the fierce, sophisticated attorney Alyssa held in such high regard.

'She insisted on waiting for you.' Though Tony didn't whisper, his voice was lower.

Not wanting to startle the other woman, Alyssa, too, spoke quietly. 'Grace?'

Almost as if she couldn't process Alyssa's greeting, Grace stared vacantly into the space between the detectives before recognition set in. Then, pressing the heels of her hands against her eye sockets, she rubbed. 'I— I don't—I can't—I need—' Grace's voice was gravelly, edged with fear, sadness, and disbelief. Her head swayed back and forth as if she was still in denial of what had taken place in her brother's home.

Referred to by some as 'the ice queen' because she never flinched or backed down as she went toe-to-toe with some of the worst, most evil predators the state had ever known, Grace was one of the toughest women Alyssa knew, and so it was more than a little jarring to see her sitting here broken and traumatized, her usually impeccable appearance now disheveled as she clearly tried to absorb the shock of what was happening around her.

Alyssa shifted until she was directly in Grace's line of sight. 'We're going to do all we can, but I'm going to need you to focus so we can do that.' Though she tempered her commanding tone in light of the district attorney's state of mind, she knew they didn't have time to wear kid gloves when the lives of two teenagers were on the line. 'Now, start from the beginning, and walk us through how you ended up here.'

A tear trailed down Grace's cheek. 'I was having a glass of wine while I studied the case file for my upcoming trial when Addis called.' She bent forward, releasing the necklace she'd been twisting in favor of pressing her hands down on her bouncing knees.

'What time was that?' Alyssa prodded.

'Close to ten. Maybe a little after.' Her phone was sitting on the sofa beside her, and she picked it up, tapping the screen a few times. 'Ten-o-five. She didn't answer right away when I said hello, and I thought maybe she'd accidentally dialed me.' Eyes flickering toward the kitchen, her voice wobbled when she said, 'But then I heard her whisper my name.' Her gaze focused on something just past Alyssa's shoulder as if she were envisioning the scene in her mind before she dropped her phone to the side so she could wind both arms around her waist. 'And then she screamed... so loud... That's when I heard her yell for Emerson to run.'

Grace's dark, frightened eyes lifted. 'There were a few grunts and what sounded like scuffling. And then... silence. The call ended.' Her words sped up. 'I called right back, but she didn't pick up. I don't know how many times I tried, but I finally gave up and tried Gabriel, and then Lydia's phones. When I got no answer there either, I grew concerned and jumped in my car and drove straight over here. I didn't think—'

Alyssa knew what Grace couldn't say – she hadn't thought she'd be walking into a slaughterhouse.

Blinking rapidly, Grace tried to stem the flow of tears that now ran in a steady stream. 'The door was open when I arrived. That's when I found Gabriel and Lydia. I thought—' Squeezing her hands into fists, she pressed them against her sternum as she tried to get her breathing back under control. 'I thought she, Addis, was—' Grace's head whipped violently back and forth. 'I ran through the house to find her. I needed to find her.'

When her pained stare finally found its way back to Alyssa, she was no longer reliving what she'd stumbled upon. Speaking more clearly, she whispered, 'I didn't find them, but I found Addis's phone in Ga—Gabriel's office. And Emerson's phone near the wet bar.' Her face twisted in torment. 'Oh God, Alyssa, please, you've got to find them; they're only seventeen.'

Chapter Three

Nearly thirty minutes after walking into the Kensington house, Alyssa had gotten as many details out of Grace as she could. 'Can I call someone to drive you home or at least be with you?' she asked now.

'No, thanks. I prefer to stay here until you're finished.'

Because the two were similar in so many ways, Alyssa understood Grace's need to oversee what was happening. They were both strong women, used to protecting others, and it didn't sit well when outside influences threatened their inner sanctuary of security. She also knew through personal experience how nearly impossible it was to release the reins of power to someone else, regardless of who that person was or how much she trusted her. Knowing and understanding that, however, changed nothing. 'Grace, you know I can't allow you to remain in my crime scene while it's being processed.'

Grace opened her mouth to argue, but when her eyes strayed toward the kitchen where her brother and sister-in-law still lay, uncovered, she cast her anguish-fueled gaze in Alyssa's direction. 'Find who did this, Detective. And bring Addis and Emerson home,' she choked out before allowing herself to be escorted out by an officer Alyssa didn't immediately recognize.

With Grace's final words ringing in her ears, she headed back to the kitchen where her eyes traveled along the wall before settling on a phone encased in pink rhinestones with decorative lettering down both sides – *Emerson* on the left, *Childress* on the right. Splatters of partially digested food smeared the screen. According to Grace, she'd been frantically searching for Addis when she'd heard what she thought sounded like a text message notification. Racing back to the kitchen, she'd spotted Emerson's phone.

To Cord, Alyssa said, 'It's eight minutes after eleven right now. If Addis called Grace at five after ten, then the girls have been missing just over an hour.' Alyssa's stomach twisted itself into a knot. Even a minute in the hands of an obviously sadistic killer was too long for *anyone*, much less two teenage girls. She forced herself to stay focused, knowing she'd do no one any good if she allowed her mind to fixate on the vile kinds of things that could be happening even as she stood here.

She pointed at Tony who stood off to her left, waiting for her direction. 'I need you to get Addis and Emerson entered into NCIC.' The National Crime Information Center was a database that could be accessed by virtually every law enforcement agency nationwide, twenty-four hours a day, three hundred sixty-five days a year. 'When you're finished, head over to the Childress residence and notify Emerson's parents about what's going on. I'd say if we're super lucky, both girls will be there, safe and sound, but I know that's only wishful thinking on my part.'

As soon as Tony hurried away to do as she'd asked, Alyssa pulled Cord off to the side, knowing what she was about to propose was risky. 'I'm going to call Hammond to request two Amber Alerts be issued immediately.'

Unsurprisingly, Cord's eyebrows shot up. 'You're not worried that might be a little premature? We don't even have a description of what the girls are wearing or who may have taken them.' He hesitated a fraction of a second before adding, 'Or even if they're actually missing – though all signs certainly point in that direction.'

Alyssa was undeterred. 'I understand that, but we can't chance waiting or wasting another second because if we wait and something happens… Needless to say, I'd rather risk my own image – and the department's – than gamble against the lives of two girls.' She looked pointedly in the direction of the kitchen. 'Especially in light of that grisly crime scene.' Furthermore, she knew their captain, Guthrie Hammond, would back her decision since he'd always regretted hesitating when it had been her own son who'd gone missing six months ago, especially after discovering he'd been kidnapped by a serial killer with a personal vendetta.

Cord glanced at the carnage then back at her. From the look in his eye, Alyssa knew he, too, was remembering Isaac's ordeal. 'On the mantel in the living room, I noticed a photograph of the two girls impersonating *Charlie's Angels* that looks recent. We can use that to base the description. If there's fallout, we'll field it together.'

Alyssa nodded and retrieved her phone from her pocket. She hadn't doubted it, but it was always nice hearing that her partner had her back, no matter the situation. She placed the call, and as she suspected, Hammond more than trusted her judgement and promised to issue the Amber Alerts as soon as he hung up.

With that out of the way, she and Cord moved over to examine the area surrounding Gabriel Kensington's body. Resting just beneath his right ribcage was a knife;

its handle, like the rolling pin, was smeared with blood. Alyssa lifted her gaze and spotted the wooden butcher block with its one empty slot sitting on the blood and tissue-sprinkled counter.

Studying the pattern of blood spatter flung high onto the ceilings, walls, and counters made it abundantly clear they were dealing with a crime of passion, whether that was love, hate, anger, or an amalgamation of all of them. In the end, they all equaled the same outcome – a murderous rage.

In order to understand the motive, Alyssa knew it was often imperative to first try to understand who the victims were. But despite the story the gruesome scene conveyed, she found it difficult to believe Gabriel was the type of person who might warrant such fury, though granted, her only dealings with him had been on a purely professional level. As a private investigator, he'd contacted her a few times in order to inquire about a case or ask what she could share with him regarding certain individuals, and he'd always been cordial and polite.

His public persona was more of the same – friendly and outgoing, something that wasn't always easy since the citizens of Albuquerque tended to either love or hate the Kensingtons. Gabriel's great-grandfather was rumored to have been an outlaw – and not the Hollywood heroic type – who'd used ill-gotten means to amass the Kensington fortune. His grandfather, tired of the tarnished name, invested his money wisely and became wealthy in his own right. Choosing to use his riches to help the less fortunate, he launched numerous charities, several of which were shut down when Gabriel's uncle decided to both skim money from the top, as well as ignore that pesky requirement of paying taxes. Of course, the coup d'état was when he'd avoided jail time only to turn around and scam hundreds of thousands of dollars from unsuspecting citizens, dying before being forced to pay retribution.

Years later, after his own parents had died, Gabriel had stepped in to run the few remaining charities. Though he'd only been a teenager when his uncle had made front page news every day for months, Alyssa knew there were still people out there who held a grudge against the Kensington name. It was plausible Gabriel and Lydia's murders were a result of misplaced revenge.

Careful to skirt away from the body so as not to contaminate evidence, she moved around the island to Lydia Kensington's body. In stark contrast to her husband's death, Lydia's appeared far less vicious, though no less disturbing. In fact, if it weren't for the light pink silk blouse that bore small, smudged, bloody handprints, and the one neat bullet hole that decorated the woman's forehead, it might've appeared that she'd simply chosen an odd place to take a nap. Based solely on the vastly different styles of killing, Alyssa speculated that Gabriel had been the main target.

Cord, who had stopped to talk to one of the officers recording the crime scene, came to stand beside her. 'Think this might have to do with one of Gabriel's investigations?'

Tuning out the racket of voices of people milling about collecting evidence and snapping photographs, she squatted near Gabriel's body, careful not to get in the way of the technician placing plastic bags over his hands. 'It certainly crossed my mind. It might explain why his murder was more brutal than his wife's.'

Rising back to her feet, she angled her body so that she could take in the kitchen, the wet bar, and the patio door at the same time. 'Or maybe it's the fallout from a burglary gone bad, or it could have something to do with the Kensington family name.'

'Ah, the *Kensington Swindle* story heard around the country,' Cord said, quoting the infamous headline. 'That was before my time.'

Alyssa snapped a hair band on her wrist while she filtered through her thoughts. 'If it was misplaced revenge, a burglary gone bad, or something pertaining to Gabriel's work, why take Addis and Emerson instead of killing them, too?'

'That's a good question.' Cord pointed to Lydia's chest. 'There's another. Looks like someone tried to resuscitate her, so was Mrs. Kensington still alive when Addis and Emerson walked in? And if she was, where was the killer at that time?'

Alyssa didn't have an answer, but unfortunately, she could imagine the terror Addis must've felt at realizing her parents' murderer was still in the house. 'Grace said she found Addis's phone in Gabriel's office, which tells me the girls went there to hide. But if Addis was trying to revive her mother when she realized she and Emerson weren't alone in the house, why wouldn't they just try to slip out the patio door?' She felt there was something obvious she was overlooking. 'Maybe Gabriel's office will offer more clues,' she said abruptly, already shifting course to follow the voices down the hall.

As soon as she stepped through the doorway, a young officer with smooth skin and a long, wet braid that left a dark mark on her uniform twisted around and introduced herself. Alyssa recognized her as the same one who had escorted Grace out earlier.

'Sandra Falwin,' she said, extending her hand first to Alyssa then to Cord before turning back with a sigh as she waved her arm toward the chaotic mess that was Gabriel's office. 'What a wreck, right?'

A black leather sofa had been dragged away from a wall and placed in nearly a forty-five-degree angle. The drawers on the expensive teak filing cabinet were pulled out with several of its files strewn about on the floor. Similarly, the doors from the desk were all flipped upside down, their contents scattered across the carpet. A storage closet containing reams of paper and other office supplies was ajar but otherwise undisturbed.

Alyssa rotated in a slow circle, her eyes appraising the destruction. Near a clean spot on the desk where it appeared a computer usually resided was a pair of gold and diamond cufflinks, and behind that, on one of the built-in bookshelves, was a woman's diamond-encrusted Rolex. Both items would rack up more than a few pretty pennies if fenced. She directed Cord's attention to the jewelry. 'It's beginning to look less like a robbery gone bad.'

Next, she focused on a coffee table with a dark spot marring its corner. On the carpet next to it was what appeared to be blood, smudged into a long line as if the bleeder had been dragged away. Spotting a lone sandal near the office doorway, Alyssa moved further into the room, locating its partner peeking out from beneath the desk. If she closed her eyes, she could envision Addis screaming for her best friend to run, to save herself, all while struggling to get away from the man who'd just brutally murdered her family. She shook her head to clear it. Imagining the terror both Addis and Emerson must've felt wasn't going to get her any closer to locating them.

Giving the office one final glance, she and Cord left the technicians measuring, recording, and collecting evidence and moved down the hall to the master bedroom.

Clothes were strewn from one end of the room to the other, with a silky blouse decorating a large potted fern in the corner, the weight of it forcing the leaves down. Items from the bureau were scattered throughout the room. She turned to Cord. 'This kind of reminds me of Holly's first date.' Her daughter had nearly emptied her closet by grabbing clothes at random and tossing them behind her without a backwards glance, muttering the entire time that she had nothing to wear.

Cord chuckled and then almost instantly paled, and Alyssa knew he'd momentarily flashed forward to his own future, if he and Sara were to have girls. She tugged at his sleeve. 'Let's go check out Addis's room.'

It was a typical teenager's room with a hastily made bed and jeans and blouses draped over the footboard, as well as the chair in the corner which also happened to be harboring five mismatched shoes beneath it. Photographs tucked into the mirror's frame drew Alyssa's attention. Moving closer, she studied each image. Most were of Addis and Emerson, but what she found most telling was the series of professional eight-by-ten glossies consisting of Grace, Gabriel, and Addis arranged in a floral pattern on the wall. Missing from all of them – and in fact from any picture in the room – was Lydia Kensington. She pulled out her phone and opened her camera, hitting record as she slowly captured a video of all the pictures, unable to stop wondering if she was wrong, if it was Lydia who'd been the intended target.

Regardless, there was one thing Alyssa kept coming back to. Based on the macabre scene in the kitchen, it was clear Addis and Emerson were likely in the hands of an unpredictable killer, meaning it was imperative they find the girls before the man snapped again.

If he hadn't already.

Chapter Four

Thursday, October 3

Adam Campbell paced from one end of the bedroom to the other, alternating between pulling at his hair, wringing his shaky hands, and wiping the sweat rolling down his neck and soaking the back of his shirt, all while trying to ignore the throbbing pain in his swelling wrist where he'd caught it on the table in Gabriel Kensington's office. From the second Alex had dropped him off with the order to shower and go to bed, he'd fought back against the rising, suffocating panic.

He was a football player with a promising career in front of him, not a criminal. Now, he wasn't just a criminal, he was an accomplice to a double homicide.

Alex had insisted over and over that there was nothing to tie either one of them to the crime, but what Adam hadn't been able to confess was that he was missing his favorite red beanie, the one with the initials A.C. sewn into the front right next to the university's howling Lobos logo. For the life of him, he couldn't recall if he'd been wearing it at the Kensingtons', or if he'd left it in Alex's truck, or if he'd just managed to misplace it somewhere completely unrelated.

And as much as he wanted to, he couldn't just pick up the phone and admit that they might have left something behind, something possibly swimming with DNA from the hairs on his head. He might not understand how these things worked, but he'd watched enough television to know the police could get some kind of genetic footprint from the craziest things. He could already hear Alex berate him for being so stupid, so careless and foolish.

To make matters even worse, Adam had neglected to admit where the gun had come from. Alex had said to bring a gun and Adam had dutifully obeyed, no questions asked, like the idiot he was. And that had brought up a new fear. Had they remembered to snatch the gun from the kitchen counter when they left? If he closed his eyes, he thought he could picture Alex placing it in the glove box of the truck as they hightailed it out of there. But what if he was wrong? What if he was only 'recalling' what he wanted to believe, and they'd actually forgotten it? Now, with the possibility of his DNA being discovered at the crime scene, along with a weapon easily traced back to him, there was no doubt Alex would allow him to hang for everything that went down.

It wasn't like it would be the first time. He swallowed the bile that rose up to meet the raging paranoia he was trying unsuccessfully to tamp down.

That's when it had come to him. He'd go back to the Kensington house without Alex just to make sure nothing had been left behind. In and out with no one the wiser. That was his plan, anyway. At no point had he anticipated running into anyone – at least no one who was still breathing. So, when he'd heard voices coming from down the hall in the private investigator's office, he'd assumed a television had been left on, and that he simply hadn't noticed earlier. Understandably, since people were being murdered.

Frayed nerves already on edge, he'd decided to shut the television off. Averting his gaze away from the massacre in the kitchen, he'd made his way down the hall, baffled not only because there was no television in the room, but also at the sudden silence that invaded the space. And then he'd heard it, a faint noise – a voice – coming from beneath the desk. Ignoring the pulse of rushing blood swooshing through his ears, he'd tiptoed into the room, cocked his head, and listened.

Seconds later, a mere whisper of sound had sent his heart thumping in its race to escape the confines of his chest. Quickly, he'd moved over to the desk, leaning down only to discover two girls hiding underneath. But it was the realization that one of them was on the phone that had sent him into a full-fledged panic before his natural instincts on the field kicked in, and he'd simply gone with his gut reaction with no thought of the possible consequences.

So now, along with murder, he had two new problems who were currently huddled together in the corner, their hands and feet secured, and their mouths covered with disintegrating duct tape he'd found stashed in the back of the old junk drawer.

While the tape managed to keep them from hitting and kicking and kept their muffled cries to a tolerable level so he could think, it did nothing to hide their wild, fear-filled eyes from following his every movement or their tears from falling every time he shouted. But more than anything else, it was the accusation in their eyes and the dried blood on the side of the one girl's face shouting *Stupid* at him that threatened to hurtle him the rest of the way over the edge.

He halted his pacing and planted himself in front of them, jabbing his finger in the air and waving it between the two of them. White flecks of foaming spit flew from his mouth as he roared, 'You shouldn't have made that call. Why did you even have to be home? This is your fault, and now what am I supposed to do?' His hands flew up to yank two handfuls of his hair. Watching the tremors wrack their bodies from head to toe, he knew his unwanted prisoners had no conception that his exploding rage stemmed as much from fear of being caught as it did from anger and frustration – not to mention dreading what might happen if Alex were to find out what he'd done.

With each shouted word, the girls shrank further back, their shoulders inching up around their ears as they dragged their tethered legs up even closer to their bodies, causing his tightly coiled nerves to finally unravel. Unable to stop the eruption of fury, he punched his right fist into the wall already riddled with holes he'd put there over time, ceasing only when the burning pain from his scraped and bruised fist penetrated his brain.

Stumbling backwards, panting, he whined, 'All I wanted was to make sure I hadn't left anything behind. In and out. I'm supposed to be going pro, not to prison. I'd never survive there. Even Alex said so.'

A ringing from inside his pocket drew him back from the brink of a complete meltdown. He didn't need to see the screen to know who it was, and even as he considered ignoring it, he jerked the phone out, knowing he wouldn't dare. Whirling around to face his unwanted prisoners, he placed a finger over his lips, shaking his head in warning at the same time.

He depressed the button that would answer the call, but remained silent, unwilling to be the one who spoke first.

'Adam?'

'I'm here.' Even to his own ears, he sounded weak and pathetic, not at all how he knew the rest of the world saw him. His face paled as another horrendous thought occurred to him. Would the girls recognize him from the few times he'd been unable to dodge the media after a game? He didn't have time to dwell on this new concern because Alex was talking again.

'I'm just checking to make sure you're all right.'

'I'm here,' he repeated.

'Everything's going to be all right. I've already got everything all figured out.'

It was the calm, cajoling tone that reignited Adam's panic. 'You said you just had to talk to him! To convince him to hand over whatever he'd found out. That's all. Why'd you have to go and kill anyone?' Despite knowing how it made him look, he couldn't reel in the whimper that escaped.

'Adam, you need to calm down, do you hear me? We're in the clear. Trust me.' A long pause followed, then: 'Do you have classes tomorrow?'

Confused by the question, Adam nodded once, then remembered Alex couldn't see him. 'Yes.'

'If you haven't got your emotions under control by morning, you need to stay home, and I'll check on you in the evening after I get off work. Okay?'

Of course, Alex would be able to return to work as if they hadn't just murdered two people.

A low groan rumbled from deep inside Adam's chest. 'Why'd you shoot that lady? You went too far this time. I don't know how you think you're getting us out of it.'

Alex hissed out an exasperated sigh. 'I had no choice. You understand, right?'

Adam knew the rage his next words would cause, but he said them anyway. 'You *slaughtered* that man. It was a bit of overkill there, so to speak, wouldn't you say?'

Too late he remembered the girls were there and listening to his end of the conversation, and he swung around, his gaze connecting with first one, then the other. One of the girls leaned back as if she could somehow escape into the wall while the one with blue and brown hair widened her eyes at his words even as her chin fell toward her chest, her shoulders dropping as if he'd placed a ton of bricks on them – or murdered her family.

A chill, angry laugh drilled into his ear. 'Adam, don't be so naïve. Do you think he was going to just let us walk away after giving us what we wanted?'

The way Alex had grabbed the marble rolling pin before bludgeoning the private investigator was still stuck in his head, the sight of mangled flesh playing in Technicolor in his memory. And all he'd done was stand there, stunned and terrified as he watched, wincing as blood sprayed everywhere, peppering his face and arms, remembering another time when Alex's anger had taken over.

Goosebumps and a cold sweat broke out over his skin, and his insides roiled. He rattled his head back and forth in an effort to scrub the images from his brain, both the hopelessness in the girls' faces and that of the murdered Kensingtons. It didn't help, so he stepped over to an old coffee can that had once been used as a spittoon and

26

kicked it across the floor, watching as it hit a closet door, rust sprinkling off the sides.

One of the girls whimpered loudly, the end of her pink nose dripping as she wiggled her body so close to her blue-haired friend, a sheet of paper wouldn't slide between them.

'What was that noise?' Too late, Adam realized he'd made a mistake, and when he didn't answer right away, Alex's voice rose, shrill in its demand. 'Adam? What. Did. You. Do?'

He opened his mouth to lie, but the truth tumbled out before he could stop it, even admitting he hadn't located the beanie.

'You *idiot*! What the—what were you even *thinking*?' The hissed response was akin to having a snake embedded in his ear, sending a shiver down his spine. 'Shit!' Adam heard a *thump, thump, thump* as Alex pounded on something, probably imagining it to be him. 'Damn it! Stay put. Do not go *anywhere*. Adam? Are you listening? I'll be there as soon as I can get away, and then I'll take care of the problem. Again.'

The words *I'll take care of the problem* echoed in the silence of the abruptly ended call and looped like a roller-coaster in Adam's already addled thinking. But Alex's intention was clear, and a new surge of adrenaline raced through him.

Sprinting down the hall to his bathroom, he yanked open his medicine cabinet, tossing items aside until he found what he needed. Pressing his palm to the top of the bottle, he wrenched it open and dropped four tablets into his palm, grateful he hadn't tossed the fentanyl after his surgery for a torn meniscus.

His next stop was the kitchen, where he grabbed two whiskey glasses and slammed them onto the counter. Using a mortar and pestle, he ground two of the tablets and dumped the powder into one of the glasses. Then he repeated the process with two more pills, finally adding water.

Carefully, he carried his concoction down the hall. His voice pitched high as he approached the girls, knowing they had no reason to trust him, but knowing if they didn't, they were as good as dead.

You are, too, a voice whispered in his ear.

'Drink this or die.' He let them think he would be the one to kill them if they disobeyed. He set both glasses on the windowsill before lowering himself to his knees. Then, reaching out, he grabbed a corner of the duct tape and ripped it from the blue-haired girl's mouth, slapping his hand over her lips before she could scream. He didn't need a degree in psychology to dissect his reasoning behind choosing her first. He needed to stop her knowing, accusing glare from seeping into his brain, and the sooner he got the fentanyl down her throat, the faster that goal would be accomplished.

Gripping her jaw tightly so that she had no choice but to open her mouth, he dumped the contents of the glass down her throat, clenching his jaws as he made sure she swallowed before releasing his hold. Whether it was the menacing glare he shot in her direction or seeing what he'd done with her blue-haired friend, the other girl was more compliant, her quivering mouth falling open as he brought the drugged water to her lips. He wasted no time before replacing the tape, just in case, and then headed to his own bedroom where he grabbed his wallet and a few extra blankets. Thirty minutes later, his car loaded, he checked on the girls, relieved to see the drug had taken effect.

After covering their mouths with fresh pieces of tape, he lifted the blue-haired girl into his arms. Checking outside his door, he made sure no one was lurking about, and then scurried to the back of his car, hitting the remote that would pop his trunk, and slid her all the way back before returning for her friend.

Five minutes later, he was on the road, heading to the only place he could think of, hoping Alex wouldn't think of it, too, after discovering the girls were no longer at his house.

Chapter Five

Just before six o'clock Friday morning, Alyssa pulled into the precinct seconds ahead of Cord. A huge travel mug of strong, black coffee in hand, she waited beside her car for him. She was running on less than three hours of sleep because every time she'd closed her eyes, images of Addis and Emerson being slaughtered or abused like the girls they'd rescued back in May wormed their way into her brain, taking up refuge. When she'd finally given up any pretense of rest, she'd climbed out of bed and done her best to cover the dark shadows under her eyes. One glimpse in the mirror assured her she'd been far from successful.

She didn't think it was possible for her partner to look worse than she did, but she was wrong. Much like last night when he'd first arrived on scene, his shoulders were bowed down, and the black circles under his red eyes reminded Alyssa of the grim reaper. All he was missing were the black hooded cloak and the scythe. Unable to mask her concern for two of her favorite people outside her family circle, she asked, 'Sara?' as soon as Cord was within a few steps of her.

Fixing his eyes straight ahead, his voice was almost flat as, wearily, he answered, 'Rough night, rough morning.'

His chest expanded as he sucked in a deep breath. 'Rough week all the way around. She's staying home today. I mentioned staying with her, but she pretty much kicked me out the door, complaining that she was beginning to feel a bit claustrophobic by my constant hovering before kindly reminding me she was a registered nurse and knew what to do and who to call if something happened.' He frowned. 'I don't hover.'

Alyssa highly doubted that, especially since she'd witnessed it firsthand, and that was before Sara's pregnancy had turned from this miracle of joy into something that had her partner perched on a precipice, afraid of losing the love of his life and their children, too.

Never having experienced a rough pregnancy like Sara's, the words to comfort eluded her, so she did what she could; she stopped him with a hand on his forearm and waited until he brought his gaze down to hers. 'I wish I could say it will all be okay, and even though I believe it will—' She shook her head. 'That's not the point. Remember, you don't have to suffer your fears alone. I'm here anytime you need to get it off your chest. And before you argue, I'd like to remind you that you would and *have* done the same for me. So, no pressure, just a reminder.'

Cord dipped his head in acknowledgement, his soft, 'Thanks, Lys, I appreciate it,' barely audible, as they headed inside and walked into her team's usual commandeered incident room.

Flipping on the light, she set her coffee aside and booted up the computer. Just as she was opening the file on the Kensington murders, Hal Callum rolled in wielding his usual good-natured grin, greeting her and Cord.

'Morning lady and gent.'

Alyssa glanced up, noticing right away that something was different about the department's most favored advice-giver. 'You're sporting a new chair!' Her smile stretched from ear to ear.

A few months ago, Hal's wheelchair had begun showing its age, squeaking and squealing with every inch of movement. Everyone, especially his wife, had hounded him about purchasing a new motorized one, but he'd dug his heels in. One night while celebrating with drinks at a local brewery after successfully locating a missing three-year-old, Alyssa had asked him what was up with his stubborn refusal to ditch the old chair.

He'd chugged half his Blue Moon and then stared off into space, uncharacteristically quiet before finally answering. 'When I was shot, lots of folks told me I'd never work in law enforcement again. Even more told me I was stupid for wanting to. This ole gal' – he stroked the chair's arm the way someone might stroke a lover – 'became a symbol of my determination. Giving her up when she's the one falling apart feels like a betrayal somehow.'

Alyssa had nodded and then asked one simple question: 'If the tables were reversed, and it was me in that chair, what sage advice would you give me?'

He hadn't answered, but the next day she'd walked in on him checking out wheelchair websites. It might've taken him a while to settle on one he liked – he still refused to roll around in a motorized chair, much to his wife's dismay – but apparently he'd found 'The One,' and despite its shiny newness and the brilliant purple seat, it looked much like the old one, which was probably why he was looking pretty pleased with himself.

Cord whistled and walked around the chair, eyeing it up and down like he might the fancy sports cars he coveted. 'Nice wheels there, Hal.'

Eyes twinkling, he replied, 'You can call me Your Highness.'

Alyssa barked out a laugh. 'Let me guess: it's *royal* purple?'

They were still chuckling when Officer Joseph Roe walked in carrying a large brown bag of bagels in one hand and balancing a wobbly takeout tray of drinks on his shoulder, grumbling, 'Ten more days of this.' Cord leaped over to rescue the cups before they could tumble to the floor.

With no other context than that, Alyssa knew Joe was referring to Albuquerque's International Balloon Fiesta. The official first day wasn't until tomorrow, but the streets were already clogged with travelers from every state and a multitude of countries, which added at least twenty-five minutes to her commute.

By the end of this year's run, Fiesta officials predicted that close to nine hundred thousand people would hit the field as they oohed and aahed over the hundreds of hot air balloons gracing the city's skyline. Alyssa's gaze shifted outside where a few of the colorful balloons already dotted the morning sky, casting shadows over the ground. Immediately, her mind jumped to Addis and Emerson. Instead of sipping on steaming cups of hot chocolate with melted marshmallows and scarfing down one of Golden Pride's famous breakfast burritos while enjoying the show, the girls were out there somewhere with a sadistic killer, terrified and probably confused. And that was if they were still alive.

33

Just as she opened her mouth to rally the team to get down to business, Tony wandered in, the dull, faraway look in his eyes indicating he might be present physically, but mentally, he was anywhere else. Not usually the most exuberant – that often fell to Hal – he still enjoyed sharing stories about his hunting adventures when he returned from one of his trips. But this morning, instead of launching into an exciting narrative, he simply nodded a greeting and took a seat.

A feeling of helplessness washed over Alyssa. Ever since the team had busted up the deviant sex trafficking ring – dubbed *The Toybox* by the media – back in May, Tony had been in a dark, unreachable place. Even though Captain Hammond had insisted on each of them attending personal counseling sessions, they hadn't helped Tony as much as they had everyone else. She'd been harboring hope that his annual hunting trip, something he always looked forward to with childlike glee, would bring him back, but it seemed that wasn't to be the case.

Joe stopped bragging about his daughter Hailee issuing her first words last night – Dada – to cast a concerned gaze his best friend's way. In the last several months, even he hadn't been able to get his best friend to divulge what it was about that particular case that had burrowed in to affect him so deeply, and it certainly wasn't from a lack of trying. They had all tried.

The touch of Cord's hand on her arm took Alyssa's attention away from Tony's state of mind and put it back on their current case, where it needed to be. She cleared her throat, waiting until everyone trained their eyes on her before cutting straight to the heart of the matter. 'I think it's probably safe to assume that the key to locating Addis Kensington and Emerson Childress will be in finding out why Gabriel and Lydia were murdered. If we can get the *why*, we'll be closer to revealing the *who*. And the *who* will hopefully lead us to the *where*.'

She nodded to Hal who had already wheeled over to the computer. A few key taps later, the graphic crime scene photos were projected onto the white wall across the room, splashing the space with garish colors, evoking an eerie vibe that the brutal murders had taken place in this room instead of across town.

Alyssa turned away from the image of Lydia lying on the kitchen floor, her right arm bent backwards while one finger on her left hand pointed outward in a jab as if she'd been poking her killer in the chest. 'Okay, here's what we know; Grace Burgess received a call just after ten last night. She heard her niece, Addis, whisper her name followed by a scream. A few seconds later, she heard Addis yell for her best friend, Emerson Childress, to run.' Her gaze drifted around the room, making eye contact with each member of her team. 'And then there was nothing.

'Grace tried calling back, but when she received no answer from either Addis's phone or her brother's, she drove over to his house where she discovered both Gabriel and Lydia dead in the kitchen. She was searching the house for the girls—'

Joe interrupted. 'Wait. Hold up a sec. Did I hear that correctly? The *district attorney* walked into a crime scene and didn't *immediately* call 911? What the hell?'

Cord jumped to Grace's defense. 'Under normal circumstances, I'd agree. But look at those pictures.' His head swiveled toward the images cast on the wall. 'There's no way to describe that scene other than *slaughter*. Now, she'd just received a frightening call from her niece, and then finds her brother and sister-in-law swimming in their

35

own blood. In light of that, I think it makes perfect sense that her first thought would be to save her niece.'

The way Joe pursed his lips told Alyssa he wasn't entirely convinced that was a good enough reason. 'If she was that worried, then why didn't she dial 911 before leaving her house? Or hell, while she was driving?'

'I think I can safely say,' Alyssa said, 'that when it comes to our own families, we – even those of us in law enforcement – don't always react logically.'

This seemed to appease Joe, and he dropped his chin in a quick nod. 'Good point. Sorry for the interruption.'

Alyssa walked over and tapped her fingernail on one of the projected images. 'I was about to say Grace was searching for Addis when she heard a text notification alert. Emerson's phone was discovered here against this wall. It wasn't pin or password protected, so we were able to see that close to ten-thirty, her mother sent a text to ask when she'd be home.' She gestured toward Tony. 'Why don't you go ahead and fill everyone in on what you found out when you met with Emerson's parents.'

Tony plowed his hands through his hair, giving Alyssa a glimpse of scraped knuckles and several deep scratches down his arm. They looked as painful as the one on his face. When he saw her staring, he yanked his sleeves down. 'According to Jill and Jeffrey Childress, Addis arrived at their house around three-fifteen, three-twenty yesterday afternoon, angry at her mom.'

Joe held his palm out to interrupt again. 'Did they say *why* Addis was so upset with her mom?'

'Emerson's younger sister, Hannah, said she overheard Addis say her mom was, quote, "wigging out again." Apparently, Lydia Kensington had a frequent and nasty habit of misplacing items that she then falsely accused her daughter of swiping.' Tony's tone switched from matter of fact to one of bafflement. 'In this case, according to Hannah, it was some kind of designer make-up. What the hell is that, even?'

Alyssa knew he didn't really expect an answer, which was good because she didn't have one. Designer make-up, designer handbags, designer shoes – she didn't get the appeal of any of it. 'Speaking of expensive items, last night while we were combing through the house, we discovered enough jewelry to make any robber worth his ilk salivate. In light of that detail, along with the fact that we found close to six hundred dollars in cash between Gabriel's wallet and Lydia's handbag, I think we can safely rule out a burglary gone wrong.'

Tony nodded his agreement. 'Makes sense. Getting back to what I was saying: At twenty minutes to eight, the girls decided they were hungry and headed out for a bite to eat. A little after eight, Emerson sent her mom a text to ask if it was okay for Addis to stay a few nights with them. Mrs. Childress responded immediately with a "yes, of course."' He glanced up, catching Alyssa's eye. 'That should be pretty easy to verify since we have both the girls' phones.'

'I do remember seeing those texts, but we should probably double-check the time stamps, anyway.' Alyssa randomly grabbed a dry erase marker and began scribbling out the timeline as they discussed it. 'Last night – or rather quite early this morning – we were able to use the phones' GPS systems and the cell tower pings, to track their movements.' She twisted around so she could see Cord. 'What time does it show the girls left Little Anita's?'

Cord ran his finger down the page in front of him. 'Quarter after nine. It would seem they drove around for a

37

bit before actually heading to the Kensington house which is next pinged at nine-forty. From there, the phones' location remains static.'

'We know Addis drove because her Chevy Malibu was in the driveway with the key still in the ignition, which makes sense if they were just planning on grabbing some clothes or schoolbooks or whatever girls snag for a sleep-over,' Tony threw in for Joe and Hal's benefit. 'And aside from a take-out bag of sopapillas, there was nothing in the vehicle, at least nothing that sent up any alarms.'

'Or gave us anything else to go on,' Cord added, nodding.

'I want to add one more thing real quick,' Tony's shoulders drooped, and he stared down at his empty hands as he spoke. 'When I arrived, Emerson's parents had just received the Amber Alert notification, so Mrs. Childress was already on the phone with Dispatch. When she saw me at the door, man, she crumbled. It was bad.'

Alyssa understood all too well the horror and help-lessness of realizing your child was missing, so she didn't have to imagine what Mrs. Childress had been feeling or thinking because she already knew.

She also didn't need to turn her head to know Cord's penetrating stare was drilling into her. He knew her well enough to guess where her head had gone. Forcing her mind away from that point in her history, Alyssa reminded herself what was at stake – Addis and Emerson's lives.

Tony reached into a folder to grab a five-by-seven photograph. He set it on the table for the rest of the team to look at. 'Mrs. Childress said this was taken a couple of months ago during Emerson's senior photo shoot. She wanted us to have an updated picture to release to the media. She also told me what the girls were wearing when they left the house last night.' His gaze drifted around the table. 'You all probably got the updated Amber Alerts?' At everyone's nods, he turned to Alyssa. 'And I was able to update NCIC, as well.'

Joe twirled a pen between his fingers like it was a baton as he asked, 'Can we back up a second? Seems we've got quite a bit of information from Emerson's phone log. What about Addis's? Were you able to go through hers, as well? And if so, was there anything in there that might point us in the right direction?'

'Addis's phone – which, by the way, showed finger-prints, but from their placement, I'm guessing probably belong to her – had a lock screen, but Grace easily guessed the passcode. It was her – Addis's – birthday, so not at all difficult or original. So, to answer your question, we can verify that around the same time that Emerson sent a text to her mom asking if Addis could stay with them, Addis sent one to her father asking the same thing. He responded with a yes, so, we know at a few minutes after eight last night, Gabriel Kensington was still alive. We also noted the phone call to Grace and the numerous missed calls from Grace to Addis.'

Alyssa's gaze traveled the room, connecting with each of her teammates. 'So, between the call logs and tracking the girls' movements, I think we can safely assume the murders occurred after eight but before nine-forty when Addis and Emerson arrived at the Kensington house. Does everyone agree?'

An echo of yeses filled the room, so she continued. 'One of the things bothering me is that neither Gabriel nor Lydia's phones turned up either in a search of the house or in their vehicles, despite both of them pinging the Kensington residence as their last known location.

Let's assume the killer took both phones. If that's the case, it's possible – probable, even – that he was knowledgeable enough to know he needed to power off the phones so that the GPS couldn't track them.'

Hal shrugged. 'All he'd have to do to know that is watch any true or fictional crime show on television. Doesn't really help us narrow down the field of suspects.'

'That's true. There's something else, though. Last night, Cord noted there were no signs of a forced entry, making us wonder if either Gabriel or Lydia knew their killer and allowed him inside. Add that to the fact that just before we left, we learned the Kensingtons' security system had been tinkered with – or hacked, to be more specific – so whoever we're after is clearly tech savvy.'

The team grew quiet, the only noise coming from Hal's drumming fingers until he finally broke the silence with, 'If the Kensingtons allowed their attacker entry into their home, maybe it was someone who knew them well enough to know they needed to disable the security system beforehand? So, we could be looking at someone close to the family, perhaps?'

'It's definitely one angle we need to consider,' Alyssa agreed. Joe raised his hand as if he were in a classroom, and she couldn't help but chuckle. 'Yes, Officer Roe.'

Joe smiled and lowered his arm. 'I know this seems like an obvious question, but I'm assuming the neighborhood was canvassed last night. The Kensingtons live in a pretty affluent area, so it stands to reason that at least *one* of their neighbors had a working security system. Did any of them pick anything up?'

'The area *was* canvassed,' Cord said, 'but it was late, and a lot of the neighbors either didn't answer the door at all or claimed not to have seen or heard anything. With the acreage between the houses, that makes sense. It also explains why, of the security cameras we were allowed access to, none picked up any suspicious activity – that we noticed anyway.'

'Well, that just sucks.' Joe wadded up a piece of paper and tossed it across the room into the wastebasket.

'Can't disagree there,' Hal said. 'But can we take a few minutes to focus on the oddity in the different modes of death.' He moved his mouse, enlarging the photo of the area surrounding Gabriel's body. 'The rolling pin and the knife from the Kensingtons' own kitchen hint at this being an unplanned attack – whether the Kensingtons knew their assailant or not. On the other hand, that bullet plus a disabled security system hint at premeditation. We could be dealing with anything from someone who was burned by the Kensingtons in the past to something more current, like one of Gabriel's cases or anything in between. What isn't making any sense to me is what was the purpose of kidnapping Addis and Emerson? The Kensingtons are dead, so holding the girls captive in the hopes of getting revenge or something in return is off the table.'

Tension crackled in the air, and Alyssa knew everyone's thoughts had turned to the sex trafficking case, the same one that had altered Tony's personality.

Shoveling his hands through his hair, Cord was the first to voice out loud what none of them wanted to consider, even if they had to. 'As much as I don't want to put this out there—' He huffed out a puff of air. 'Unfortunately, we're all aware that there are some real sick bastards in this world, and we don't know for sure if we rounded up everyone involved in May's sting. It's possible some of the players are still out there' – his jaw clenched as he continued through

41

gritted teeth – 'and we all know that two cute teenage girls equal more money.'

One glance at her partner was all it took for Alyssa to know that Cord had been transported back to a dark time in his own past, one that involved his younger sister. Beneath the table, she stretched out her leg to nudge his foot, dragging him back before he could get lost in the agony of remembering. Shaking his head, he threw a grateful but sad smile her way.

Tony cleared his throat, and his gaze dropped to his hands now curled into fists. 'What about that case a couple years back when Orlando Griego murdered that twelve-year-old girl's entire family and decided at the last minute to keep her instead of killing her along with the others?'

Cord's lips flattened into a frustrated scowl. 'Yeah, and as soon as she turned thirteen, what did he use her for? So, that just plays back into the theory the girls were taken for sexually sadistic purposes.'

Tony's face flushed a rainbow of colors. 'Maybe that wasn't the best example,' he mumbled.

'Regardless,' Joe said, his eyes trained on his friend and partner, 'whatever the reason our killer took Addis and Emerson, my gut tells me they're alive.' He pointed to the graphic images of Gabriel and Lydia. 'He's clearly not afraid of the violence. Or maybe he's a killer with a conscience.' He snorted as if the very concept was ludicrous.

'Yeah, well, that still leaves him with two eyewitnesses, so he's gotta do something with them, doesn't he?' Hal asked glumly.

Alyssa's phone chimed with a text message stealing her attention away from the possible motives and theories being batted around. She peeked down and saw it was from Liz Waterson, forensic artist and a member of their team.

> Hey Lys, just dropping a quick line to tell you my services have been requested down in Cruces. 23yo female was attacked in her home, sexually assaulted, shot, and left for dead. Miracle of all miracles, she survived and was able to give a complete description. I'm heading out now. Not sure when I'll be back.

Alyssa wasn't the least bit surprised that Liz had jumped on board to make the three-hour trek. After all, their paths had crossed when Liz's sister, Amanda, had been attacked in a remarkably similar fashion. Unfortunately, her sister hadn't survived the ordeal. Within a week of being handed the case, Alyssa had hunted down the killer, and shortly after, Liz had requested to be transferred to the same precinct. They'd been teammates and friends ever since. Alyssa hit reply.

> Thanks for letting me know. I'll tell the team. Good luck, stay safe, and keep me posted.

> Will do.

When she looked back up, the team was staring at her expectantly. 'Liz got called to Las Cruces to assist with a sexual assault case. She won't be joining us as planned.'

She turned to Hal. 'I think we need to dig into Mrs. Kensington's background, as well, see if anything sends up a red flag.' She quickly filled everyone in on the fact that there were no pictures of Lydia in Addis's room. 'It could mean nothing more than Addis and her mother had a troubled relationship, but we still need to check into Lydia's history. Hell, maybe she was having an affair that went south.'

Hal's fingers flew over his keyboard as he jotted down some notes. 'Lover could've come to the house, killed her with a bullet to the head and took his anger for not being able to hold onto her out on Gabriel. I'll dig in and see what I can find.'

'While you're at it, I'm going to need you to order a search warrant for Kensington Investigations, too.'

'You got it.'

Joe scratched his head. 'I can see why a scorned lover or even someone hell bent on revenge might show up on the Kensington doorstep, but it doesn't make sense if it's related to Gabriel's business. I mean, why not confront him at his office instead?'

'Maybe he thought there was a better chance of getting what he was after if Gabriel's family was in danger?' Cord threw out the theory.

For the next twenty minutes, the team reflected on the evidence they did have while batting around possible motives. But Alyssa knew that while they could sit here and toss around ideas all day, it would get them nowhere. At least now they had a starting place, and anxious to get moving, she waited for Joe to finish up what he was saying, and then she began issuing directives.

'Tony, Joe, get started on pulling financials and phone records. Hal, you start digging into Gabriel and Lydia's backgrounds, maybe their latest charity events. See if anyone remembers the two of them acting out of character in the past few weeks, or if they've been approached by anyone that stood out. We'll all meet back here later this afternoon.'

Before the words were fully out of her mouth, everyone except Cord was moving. As soon as the door closed behind Tony, Joe, and Hal, she turned to her partner. 'All right, spit out whatever it is that you're thinking.'

Cord shoved back from the table and began pacing. 'What if we're looking at this the wrong way? What if it has nothing at all to do with Gabriel and Lydia and everything to do with Grace and *her* career? Convicting people to a lifetime behind bars tends to piss off some people. And it might explain why Gabriel and Lydia were murdered while the girls were kidnapped. It might even explain why Gabriel's death was more brutal since he's her brother.'

'I can see that argument, but if the purpose was to get to Grace, to really hurt her, wouldn't our perpetrator have killed Addis, too, to really twist the knife, so to speak?'

Cord was already shaking his head. 'Not if he wanted to drive her insane with worry.'

'Okay, well, here's where your theory gets murky for me. *If* this was about Grace, and the girls were taken for the purpose of driving her "insane with worry," then wouldn't the guy have found a way to taunt her already, to show her he had control? And something tells me if Grace had received any threatening or concerning messages lately, she would've brought it up immediately last night.'

Cord's fist banged against the table. 'Where are they?'

Alyssa wanted that question answered as much as the next person. An idea occurred to her. 'I know Tony already interviewed Mr. and Mrs. Childress, but I think I'd like us to speak to them ourselves. Maybe we'll learn something new that will help.'

'It certainly can't hurt,' Cord agreed, grabbing his phone off the table and heading toward the door, but before he had taken two steps, they were interrupted by a loud knock a split second before Ruby, the department's brusque and surly secretary, thrust it open hard enough that it banged against the wall. Poking her head in, she pointed at Alyssa. 'For as often as you're in this space, Hammond ought to just slap a plaque with your name on it and call it done.'

Alyssa agreed.

'Grace Burgess is here to speak to you.' Ruby delivered her message and then turned on her thick-wedged heels and stalked back to her desk without waiting for a response.

Alyssa darted a questioning glance toward Cord whose expression, aside from the scowl still lining his lips, mirrored her own. 'Let's go see what's she's got,' she said, following Ruby out to the main room of the precinct.

Around the corner and standing near the front was Bernalillo County's district attorney, her face devoid of make-up, her hair dragged back into a messy ponytail, her eyes glassy, haunted, and just plain lost, looking as out of place as Alyssa had ever seen her.

'Grace?'

'I think I have an idea who might've killed Gabriel and Lydia.'

Chapter Six

Friday, October 4

The one-window, cramped cabin was the stuff of horror flicks with its rotting wood smell, dead rodents, the skeletal remains of some kind of small animal, and humid air. With a sluggish brain and partially closed eyes shimmering with tears, Addis followed their kidnapper's erratic movements as, mumbling something to the effect of 'no way, never finding them here,' he scurried between the popped open trunk of his car and back to the "living" area of what amounted to an oversized ramshackle shed with a kitchen sink and bathroom that, from the inside, at least, seemed to be barely standing.

The throbbing pain on the right side of her face from where he had punched her in her dad's office brought a fresh round of silent tears. In a matter of hours, she'd gone from being a normal teen angry at her mother to an instant orphan, robbed of parents who hadn't just died but been brutally slain. And then, as if the universe hadn't thought that was enough for one person to deal with, she and her best friend had been kidnapped by the murderer and brought to God only knew where.

Woken when their captor had dragged her from the trunk of his car and tossed her over his shoulder to carry her inside, Addis tried to see where he'd brought them, but all she could see beyond the door he left ajar when he went to retrieve Em was darkness, and beyond that, more darkness. And that was only when she could keep her heavy lids from slamming shut. The sensation of being weighted down with dozens of wet, woolen blankets coupled with Emerson's too-still form was all she needed to convince her that the foul-tasting water the kidnapper had forced down their throats earlier had been drugged with something powerful.

Squinting through half-slitted eyes and chomping down on the scream that rested in her throat a mere breath and a tug of tape away from being released, she tried to focus on Emerson. Only the very slightest rise and fall of her chest assured Addis that her best friend was still alive. Feeling selfish and guilty, she simultaneously wished Em would wake so she wouldn't feel so alone while also hoping she'd stay knocked out for her own sake.

The metallic echo of a trunk being slammed drew Addis's attention back to the door, though it was still an effort for her to lift her head. At the sound of their kidnapper's footsteps crunching across the debris covering the creaky wooden porch, she suddenly found herself praying for the drug to drag her back under. If this was where she and Emerson died, it was probably better if neither saw it coming.

And then he was in front of them. One boot inched forward, nudging Emerson in the side. 'She's not dead.' It was a statement made as blandly as if he was stating *the leaves are falling*, and Addis wasn't sure if he was speaking to her or himself.

Yanking a dusty beer bottle off the warped crate that doubled as a coffee table, the man scooted it so that it was positioned in front of them but far enough away that their feet couldn't knock it over if they kicked it. Then he turned and walked back to the door, closing it and shutting out the inky blackness of the night. The click of the lock was thunderous in its implication of what was to come.

Evidently satisfied they were secure for now, he returned and sat on the crate, leaning toward Addis as his eyes shifted away from Emerson and settled on her. She recoiled when he moved his right hand toward the blossoming, throbbing bruise on her face, and even though she wanted to look away from the evil in his eyes, she was too frightened, especially when he growled out his warning. 'If you scream… Just don't.'

What happened next wasn't at all what she expected. With two fingers he tugged at the corner of the tape, wincing along with her as she involuntarily flinched against the pain. Each centimeter of sticky adhesive removed took another layer of skin with it, and she had to bite down on her tongue to stop herself from crying out, his warning ringing loud and clear in her mind.

When he switched his angle to face Emerson, Addis realized her friend was finally coming out of her drug-induced slumber, though the way her head flopped to the side hinted that she was still fighting the effects. Aside from a slight squeak, she, too, remained quiet as her tape was removed.

Then – nothing.

For what seemed like forever, the guy sat there, twisting a blue-stoned class ring around one of his fingers. Every few seconds, he'd sit up straight, run both hands through his hair and then return to fiddling with the ring. Addis was afraid to exhale, terrified of drawing his attention back to her. Carefully, she formed a small 'o' with her lips, releasing the air from her lungs bit by tiny bit, all the while keeping her eyes on the myriad of expressions crossing the guy's features. On her last exhalation, he heaved a deep sigh and cocked his head to the side, mouth sagging open, staring, his face scrunched into a mask of confusion, almost like he'd forgotten they were even there.

It was in that moment that the realization of how young he truly was slammed into her. Her terror had kept her from noticing before now, but he couldn't be more than a few years older than her and Emerson.

But that wasn't all that constricted her breathing. No, that came from the absolute certainty that she recognized him. Keeping her eyes trained on his movements, she skimmed through her memory files as she tried to place where she'd seen him or how she knew him. Had he been at one of the numerous barbecues her father liked to host? Had she spotted him at one of the rare parties she and Em had crashed, the ones where college-aged boys were a dime a dozen? Her chest constricted as a wave of dizziness sent all her nerve endings rushing to the surface, heating her skin. What if her face gave her away? She'd read enough true crime books to know that being able to identify one's assailant was the surest way to a death sentence.

Instinctively, she shrank back when he suddenly bolted up and began pacing, mumbling something about 'Always acting without thinking it through,' followed by knocking his knuckles against his head as if trying to jar loose some kind of solution. It took her several seconds to convince herself he hadn't guessed what she'd been thinking.

Abruptly, he came to a halt, and his head snapped around, concentrating on something behind them before moving in that direction. There was a skin-tingling creak as a door with squeaky hinges opened. Addis couldn't see, but she heard rustling and scraping. When he was finally back in her line of sight, he held a wickedly long knife and a length of dirty rope which he sawed in half. Mumbling and grunting, he leaned over and pressed her arms down before coiling the length of one section around her arms, securing them to her sides. Then, without any warning, the knife snaked between her wrists and ankles, slicing the tape away so he could tear it off, along with several fine hairs, before wadding it up and tossing it behind him. After repeating the process with Emerson, he stepped back, eyeing his handiwork. Then he reached into his jacket pocket and produced a clear sandwich bag containing four white pills and a half-empty bottle of water.

Squatting down so he was slightly above eye level with them, he made a simple demand. 'Open.'

Tears blurring her vision, body quaking, Addis obeyed, gagging when the powdery pills hit her tongue.

'Swallow.'

Addis swallowed.

Moving over to Emerson, he simply stared until her mouth fell open enough for him to place the drug inside.

Then, before Addis could process what was happening, he pulled her to her feet, slapping his hand over her mouth when she cried out. 'Don't,' he warned as he nudged her forward until she stood in front of a three-by-three-foot door, behind which loomed a dark crawl space that caused cold fingers of dread to prickle along her skin.

Her grandmother's old house used to have one of these. It was where she kept her burlap sacks of potatoes. Once, when Addis had used it as her hide-and-seek spot, someone had accidentally placed something heavy in front of the door, but she hadn't realized that until she'd tried to get out. She probably hadn't been in there long, but it had felt like a lifetime as she pounded and screamed until her father had come running from outside and rescued her, pulling her into his arms, comforting her as sobs and hiccups tore through her. When she'd finally released her hold on him, it had only been so she could clamber up onto Aunt Grace's lap where she'd burrowed her face into the crook of her neck as Aunt Grace murmured softly that she was safe now.

So, when she realized the kidnapper's intentions were to force her and Emerson inside, her muscles practically liquefied.

And then his hands were on her shoulders as he pushed her down to her knees. 'Inside,' he ordered. Like she had regressed back to the place of her childhood trauma, her sobs choked her, cutting off her air, but she did as he said, knowing her dad would never again be able to come to her rescue. A few seconds later, Emerson was crammed in beside her. Surprised when he left the door open and walked away, Addis prayed he wouldn't actually lock them inside.

Em's head dropped to her shoulder, her body trembling so violently, it made Addis feel like she was bouncing down a bumpy road. 'What's going to happen to us, Ad? I don't want to die.' Her gravelly whisper was outlined in terror.

Even if Addis had known the answer, she couldn't have spoken it out loud because a crippling panic attack had wormed its way through to the surface, and she struggled to concentrate on anything else. It was clear she'd lost the battle as her own baying pleas to let her out pierced the air.

How much time passed before the man's form darkened the doorway once again was a mystery, but he was suddenly there, leaning down as he peered inside, swiveling his head back and forth between her and Em before rising back up and walking away, repeating this strange behavior over and over. With each trip, the man, the room, and everything else became one giant fuzzy blob as Addis felt herself tip to the side, the weight of her body held up by Emerson's.

Just before everything became nonexistent, the door dropped closed. The last thing she remembered before the darkness welcomed her back was a damp, earthy odor tickling her nose as she pushed four words past her numb lips and foggy brain. 'Daddy, please save us.'

Chapter Seven

Friday, October 4

Coming toward Alyssa, Cord, and Grace was Officer Falwin who offered up a warm smile and a good morning before continuing on her way. Alyssa absently nodded her greeting, but before she could usher Grace much farther past the conference room door, a booming voice demanding to speak to the persons in charge of the Kensington case came from near Ruby's desk.

Beside her, cheeks flushed with color, Grace's steps faltered, confirming Alyssa's suspicions.

When the man bellowed, 'Do you have any idea who I am?' she decided she should go rescue Ruby, though the precinct secretary would likely skin her alive if she knew Alyssa had thought she needed rescuing.

Mack Kensington. Even if he hadn't resembled his older brother, she would've recognized the wildly unpopular criminal defense attorney from the southern part of the state. In recent years, his ruthless reputation had grown exponentially – as had his already overflowing coffers – by his decisions to defend some very controversial, very high-profile cases. In fact, he was currently representing a prominent, wealthy senator accused of selling and obtaining child pornography on the black market.

Now, here he was, dressed in a button-down shirt with the sleeves rolled to his elbows, towering his frame over both Ruby and Hal, who had wheeled out to see what the commotion was. Neither seemed the least bit fazed at the man's brutish behavior. Ruby had her arms crossed over her chest with one eyebrow arched in a way that could've meant she was irritated, amused, or bored. With her, it was often difficult to tell.

'If you're quite through with your temper tantrum, young man, I'll be glad to direct your attention behind you,' Ruby said drily.

Mack swung around, his eyes narrowed into snake-eyed slits as his gaze slid past Alyssa and slithered onto Grace.

'Why didn't you answer any of my calls last night?' Grace demanded before her brother had a chance to speak.

'I was busy, and my world doesn't revolve around you.' Before Grace could lob any more questions at him, Mack moved his stormy expression onto Alyssa. 'I assume you're in charge. If you don't mind, I prefer to talk somewhere there's not an audience.'

Alyssa had her doubts as to the veracity of that statement since wherever the man stood seemed to be his stage as was evidenced through his well-documented show-boating ways. Still, in order to stop this collision course of hostile sibling discord from spiraling out of control, she turned on her heel with a barked, 'Follow me,' expecting everyone would follow. Except for the heavy exhales from Grace and the no-nonsense treads of a man used to being in charge, their short trek to an open interrogation room was silent.

After ushering everyone inside, Cord closed the door, and Alyssa turned to Grace. 'What do you mean you

have an idea who may have killed Gabriel and Lydia?'
Already she was wondering if she'd too soon dismissed
Cord's theory about Grace being the motivation behind
the murders.

Mack visibly stiffened as his head snapped in Grace's
direction. 'What? Why the hell didn't you leave *that*
information on my voicemail? You sure as hell didn't mind
leaving a message telling me Gabriel and Lydia had been
slaughtered and that Addis was missing. Don't you think
this bit of news was also noteworthy?' His bellows seemed
to shake the very walls of the room.

Grace barely spared a fleeting glimpse in her brother's
direction before focusing her attention between Alyssa
and Cord. 'I'm afraid I misled you when I came in. At
least in the sense that I don't actually have any specific
names.' Either tired of standing, or the exhaustion of the
last several hours finally catching up to her, Grace, with
her unsteady hands, grabbed one of the chairs in the room
and collapsed into it before she began.

'This morning, I remembered that Gabriel called me
early yesterday because he wanted to discuss a case he'd
undertaken.'

Mack, standing with his back against the wall, feet
crossed at the ankles, arms across his chest, snorted as he
shot daggers at his sister. 'Gabriel didn't talk about his
private cases.'

'Just because he didn't trust *you* didn't mean he felt the
same way toward me.' Grace poked her thumb into her
chest. '*I* can be discreet. *I* know how to keep my mouth
shut. *I* get child perverts locked behind bars where they
belong, not thrown back out into society where they can
continue devastating lives!'

Feeling like she was refereeing Holly and Isaac in their younger days, Alyssa thumped her fist onto the table, successfully gaining everyone's attention. Seesawing her hands in the air between them, she snapped, her voice growing louder with each word. 'Do you want to find Addis and Emerson and figure out why your brother and sister-in-law are currently residing in the morgue, or should I just bring you both a pair of boxing gloves and leave you to it instead of allowing you to waste my time? Because if *you* don't care, my team sure as hell does!'

Skin flushed with guilt, at least in Grace's case, the siblings silently shifted their bodies away from each other. 'I'm sorry. You're right. Tensions are high, but that's no excuse.'

Alyssa didn't have time to soothe ruffled feathers, so she brushed the apology aside and bit out, 'Just continue.'

Grace nodded. 'Gabriel wanted to discuss a case he'd recently taken on, but all he would say when I asked was that he really needed to see me because he wasn't comfortable hashing out the specifics over the phone. He had something he wanted to show me, but again, he refused to say what that was, only that it pertained specifically to the case he'd mentioned to me a few weeks ago. Thinking back, I realize he sounded nervous, but I was so preoccupied that it didn't register.' Her voice cracked, and she had to swallow several times before continuing. 'Until it was too late.'

She lifted her tear-filled gaze to Alyssa, silently pleading for understanding. 'I've been buried with the Clay Timberton murder trial coming up, so I asked Gabriel if we could meet up Saturday. He said it was too urgent, that he didn't want to wait, but I really didn't have much wiggle room in my calendar. He finally muttered something about it being "this long already, so a few more days couldn't hurt" before he reluctantly agreed, and we tentatively made plans to meet at Weck's Saturday at seven.' Yanking a tissue out of the box situated in the center of the table, Grace roughly scrubbed at the tears spilling down her cheeks.

Nearly two years ago on Christmas Eve, Clay Timberton had allegedly broken into his ex-wife's house in the middle of the night and brutally slit the throat of all eight people inside, including that of her elderly grandparents and her youngest child, a three-year-old. So, Alyssa understood exactly why Grace hadn't felt like she could take the time to meet with her brother. From the moment the Timberton case had landed on her desk, Grace had been like a pit bull, making sure there were no legal loopholes that would allow the man to get anything less than the absolute maximum.

Because the two of them were so similar, Alyssa knew that she, too, would've carried such a burden on her own shoulders, just like she knew there would be no reason valid enough to stop the district attorney from teetering on the ledge of guilt or beating herself up over the 'what ifs.'

Grace's voice was full of torment when she spoke again. 'And now he and Lydia are dead, and Addis and Emerson are missing. Surely, I could've spared fifteen minutes to—'

From the corner of her eye, Alyssa watched Cord and Mack shift, and she darted a quick look in her partner's direction before leaning forward, her pulse kicking into high gear. 'Grace, you don't know that you could've prevented this, and you can't think that way. So, I need you to focus. Addis and Emerson's lives may depend on it. Now, I need you to think back. I know you said you were distracted, but did Gabriel hint at what his concerns were, aside from them involving one of his cases?'

After several steadying breaths, Grace answered, her courtroom persona finally seeming to kick in and take over. 'Not exactly. But here's what I do know. A few weeks ago, Lydia was out of town, and Gabriel invited me to dinner. Over dessert, he confided that he'd been approached by a woman in her mid-twenties hoping to uncover the truth about what had happened to her high school sweetheart. He wanted to pick my brain since this wasn't anything like his typical cases.'

Alyssa fought the need to drum her fingers on the table, unused to the non-direct approach the district attorney was taking.

'The woman claimed that seven years ago, she and the father of her unborn baby had planned on running away and hiding out until she turned eighteen so they could legally marry before she gave birth. According to Gabriel, the woman's parents were quite zealous in their religious beliefs, as in borderline Puritanical – so finding out she'd been having an illicit relationship before a proper marriage – the client's words, not mine nor Gabriel's' – she rolled her eyes and shook her head – 'would've sent them over the top. They figured if they married before she gave birth, it might soften the blow, so to speak.'

Mack interrupted, the tone of his voice similar to what Alyssa had seen on sound bites when he was in the midst of cross-examining a witness he didn't believe or who threatened to damage his client's chances of an acquittal. 'And do tell, what was this mysterious woman's name? Or for that matter, her missing boyfriend's?'

The same question had been on the tip of Alyssa's tongue, so she was quietly glad he'd asked.

Grace didn't hide the fact she was rolling her eyes. 'In order to maintain confidentiality on the slight chance he agreed to take her case, he never gave either name. Anyway, the night of their "great escape," as Gabriel called it, the boyfriend never showed, and in fact, was never heard from again. Unable to locate his vehicle and with no evidence of any criminal wrongdoing, the authorities closed the case and ruled that he'd voluntarily disappeared, hinting that he probably realized he hadn't wanted to be saddled with a wife and kid at such a young age.'

Grace paused to take a breath. 'Initially, Gabriel tended to agree with the authorities' ruling and tried coaxing his potential client to either accept that or at least find someone more experienced in her type of case.'

Alyssa frowned. 'Skipping out and cutting off all contact with your family to avoid taking responsibility seems a bit drastic, even for someone that young and possibly not thinking clearly,' she argued.

Grace shook her head. 'I agree, so I assume there must've been something else his client said that led him to agree with that finding. Regardless, he asked the woman how she'd feel if it turned out that her son's father had really skipped out after all. She said it didn't matter, that her son was at that age where he was beginning to notice he was the only one amongst his group of friends without a dad in the picture, and he was starting to demand answers. So, she wanted the father found, if for no other reason than to give her and her son some type of closure. And since she'd done her research, she knew Gabriel was the best private investigator in the state, and according to him, the woman was insistent on hiring him specifically for that reason.' Again, her gaze met Alyssa's. 'What if he discovered something that got him killed?'

'I'm curious or maybe just confused,' Alyssa said, 'about why Gabriel felt compelled to ask your advice. Was this something he normally did?'

Grace's chin lifted proudly, and her eyes flashed in a way that hinted at the strong woman Alyssa knew her to be. 'Because he knew there was a time I struggled whenever I had to explain the Kensingtons weren't my birth parents. He was concerned about damaging the young boy for life with what he might uncover, and so he wanted to know what my reaction would've been to different scenarios. I explained that it was impossible to know since my situation was so different.'

Though it was in no way a secret, Alyssa knew Grace didn't openly discuss that, at the age of ten, she'd been adopted by the Kensingtons after her parents and a much older sister died after contracting a deadly virus while serving overseas with Doctors Without Borders. Mary Kensington, Gabriel and Mack's mother, was Grace's school counselor at the time, and had taken her in, refusing to risk her falling through the cracks of an over-worked foster system.

Alyssa's earlier excitement at a possible lead deflated like a balloon pricked with a needle. She supposed it was possible Gabriel had been killed by a father who hadn't wanted to be found. But a pissed-off baby daddy who'd never wanted to be located didn't explain two missing teenage girls. Before she could voice her concerns out loud, Cord beat her to it.

'Okay, Grace, let's say you're right, and Gabriel's case had something to do with his and Lydia's murder. That doesn't explain why your niece and her best friend were kidnapped after the fact.'

Uncharacteristically quiet in a way Alyssa hadn't expected, Mack finally spoke up again. 'Not all who kill are evil through and through. Some actually have some good in them.'

Alyssa was unable to hide the disbelief that flashed across her face. She knew the man was a criminal defense attorney, but was he seriously defending his own sister-in-law and brother's murderer? When he noticed her bug-eyed stare, he shrugged. 'Maybe he didn't kill them because he didn't think they knew anything. Still, he couldn't let them go because then he faced the possibility that they could and would identify him.'

Grace exploded out of her chair, and before either Alyssa or Cord could react, she was across the room and in Mack's face. 'You really are despicable, you know that? Gabriel is dead! Lydia is dead! Murdered, Mack. Addis and Emerson are missing and in danger, possibly dead, for all we know' – her voice broke – 'and all you can think to do is defend the person responsible? God, no wonder no one ever wants you around.'

Instead of responding, Mack, drilling a laser beam of anger into his sister, pushed away from the wall, forcing Grace to back up out of his space. Without a word, he retrieved a rectangular case from his shirt pocket and clicked it open so he could grab one of his business cards. His eyes darted around the room, landing on a pen, which he snapped up, scrawling something on the back before thrusting it at Alyssa.

'Clearly, your department has nothing of substance yet regarding what took place at Gabriel's house. I maintain a residence here for when I'm in town. Since I was already in Albuquerque, I'll be working remotely until my brother's case is solved, so I'll be around. I assume *you'll* keep me apprised of what's going on with the investigation.' The dig toward Grace was obvious.

Alyssa shoved Mack's business card into her back pocket, nodding to Cord to open the door. 'Thank you both for coming in. My team will look into what you've told us, and I'll try my best to keep you apprised on things.'

Mack whirled around, glowering at her. 'Do more than *try*, Detective.' Without another word, he turned on his polished leather shoes and stalked off.

As much as she didn't like him, Alyssa had to admit that if their situations were reversed, her reaction would've been the same.

Chapter Eight

Weak, shaky, terrified, and cold, Addis tried to keep her head from flopping back to the side by pressing it against the dirt and cobweb-infested wall. Pinpricks of pain stabbed at the back of her neck as tiny splinters from random pieces of wood shaved off and needled themselves into her skin like little cacti. Wetness trailed her cheeks as she whispered Emerson's name, her only reply the deep breaths of someone sleeping heavily.

A lump wedged in her throat as the familiar panic of being trapped in this crawl space cloaked her. How had her life turned into this nightmare? What could she have done in her past that was so evil it produced this kind of karma?

It was as if Aunt Grace could hear her thoughts because Addis heard her response through the fog in her brain as clearly as if she were sitting beside her. *You're being silly. This isn't some cosmic force paying you back for something you've done. You're stronger than this, Addis.*

'I'm not,' she whispered to the invisible specter of her aunt. But even as she said it, she found herself tilting her head up and then from side to side, squinting through the eerie shadows cast from the faint circle of light from a hole cut way above her head in the hopes of finding something

64

that might help them escape. As her eyes darted around the cramped space, her mind raced. Their kidnapper had freed their mouths but had still tied them up. The only reason she could think of for that was because wherever he had them stashed, he was worried less about someone hearing their screams and more about their ability to escape. Her chin wobbled as she forced herself to face the truth – that this could very well be the place she and Emerson died.

If she'd only kept the New Year's resolution she'd made back in January – it had lasted less than a week – not to let her mom's never-ending false accusations get to her, then she would've never stormed out of her house, thus dragging Em into this nightmare – both of them waiting to be slain just like her parents had been. How would Emerson's parents go on? How would Hannah?

'Please, Em, you have to wake up now.' The pressure behind her rib cage increased as she tried to convince herself that the rising and falling of Em's chest was not her mind playing cruel tricks, punishing her.

Outside, the howling, screeching wind rocked the place on its decrepit foundation like mini earthquakes. And no matter how hard she tried, she couldn't distinguish between the blustery weather versus the creaking floor-boards that would alert her to their kidnapper's presence beyond the walls of their enclosure.

'Ugh—'

At Emerson's muffled groan, Addis jerked her neck to the side, scraping her bare skin against something sharp sticking out of the rough wall. She closed her eyes and breathed through her nose to stave off the blurry vision and the wave of dizziness. 'Em? Please be okay. Don't leave me alone here, and I promise we'll find a way out.' A clap of thunder drowned out her words, but she continued the litany of lies until finally, blessedly, her best friend lifted her chin the tiniest bit, enough to assure Addis this wasn't merely a figment of her imagination.

For several heartbeats, Emerson did nothing more than smack her lips together and run her tongue over them.

'Ad, my head hurts, and I'm so thirsty.'

'I know,' she whispered.

'Oh God, I really don't want to die.' Emerson struggled to breathe.

Like razor wire, her friend's fear sliced through her. 'We won't. Aunt Grace probably already has the National Guard out searching for us right now.' Addis prayed she was telling the truth.

Emerson sniffled, lowering her head enough to wipe her nose on the upper sleeve of her shirt. 'Is it weird that I think I recognize him, like I've seen him before?'

'No, it's not weird. In fact, I thought the same thing.' What she kept to herself was the dread that if their kidnapper knew they recognized him, he'd have no choice but to kill them. Through the sudden silence, Addis couldn't tell if it was her own galloping heartbeat she was hearing, or Emerson's.

When her best friend started plucking at her pants – a habit she had when she was too nervous to say what was on her mind – Addis nudged her. 'Em, don't shut me out. Whatever you're thinking, you have to tell me.' Even as she whispered the words, Addis was afraid that what Em didn't want to say was that all of this was Addis's fault. And she'd be right.

'Whoever he is,' Em finally stuttered, 'he didn't act alone.' She leaned her head onto Addis's shoulder.

Remembering how their kidnapper had discussed the cold-blooded murder of her parents with the person who'd called him sent a crushing pain rocketing through Addis, and she doubled over as she gasped for breath.

She and Emerson weren't dealing with one murderer; they were dealing with two – one who remained faceless. One who slaughtered her father either before or after shooting her mother. A vision of their kidnapper and his unidentified accomplice doing the same thing to her and Em snapped her back to reality, spurring her into action.

Unless she found a way out of here, she would be responsible for her best friend's murder. Ignoring the fact that her shirt was ripping, ignoring the blistering pain of splintered wood slashing against her arms and back, Addis tugged against the binding rope, sweat pouring off her in rivulets. She screeched and kicked out when one of the bugs crawling around on the floor skated over her legs. It took no time before she was zapped of energy.

Extending her legs flat out in front of her, she arched one foot, wiggling her toes until they touched the tips of Emerson's. With a catch in her throat, Addis admitted what scared her the most. 'Em, I can't watch him kill you.' Her head swung back and forth. 'I just can't.'

'I can't watch you—either.' Emerson's toes tapped the top of Addis's foot, the pedestrian version of squeezing one's fingers. 'So, let's make a pact that we'll get out of this. Together. Pinky-toe swear?'

'Pinky-toe swear.' They tapped their little toes together, and with a conviction she didn't really feel, Addis said, 'Aunt Grace will know how to find us.'

Chapter Nine

'Is it me, or is there a lingering chill in the air?' Cord asked as he watched Grace and Mack exit the precinct, doing their best to pointedly ignore the other.

'It does seem a bit nippy, all right,' Alyssa agreed before switching mental gears. 'While we're waiting for that search warrant, let's head over to speak to Jill and Jeffrey Childress. And if there's still time, we can try the Kensington neighborhood again. Maybe someone will have remembered seeing or hearing something they didn't think important last night.'

Alyssa's mind wandered to the wealthy subdivision. Most of the houses in the area were situated on three to five acres and surrounded by massive privacy walls that shielded them from passersby. A rock band could be playing inside one of the homes, and the neighbors would be none the wiser, so she didn't truly hold out much hope that they'd get much more than the officers who'd canvassed the area less than twelve hours ago. But she also knew they had to try.

'It's worth a shot anyway,' Cord said, echoing her thoughts. 'If we get the same results, then we're no worse off.'

An hour later, Alyssa and Cord said goodbye to the Childresses and climbed back into her Tahoe. As she pulled away from the curb, she darted a quick glance at her partner. 'You're awfully quiet all of a sudden. What are you thinking?'

Cord tapped his fingers on his thighs, something he tended to do when he was trying to get his thoughts in order. 'If Mr. and Mrs. Childress are to be believed, Lydia Kensington didn't bother hiding the jealousy she harbored for her own daughter – which, for the record, makes absolutely no sense to me. Why the hell would a mother be jealous of her own daughter? But I digress. According to them, she also didn't have much in the way of friends or interests outside her husband's dealings, which would put a hole in our theory of a possible affair. Of course, she could've just been good at keeping it hidden. But I've gotta be honest; as unlikeable as the woman sounds, I just don't get that gut feeling that these murders came about because of a twisted love triangle.'

Alyssa flashed her lights at the driver in front of her who was too busy texting to realize the light had changed to green. 'I agree. What I *did* find interesting, however, was that Mack showed up uninvited to the last barbecue his brother hosted. Too bad Mr. Childress couldn't hear what their heated exchange was about.'

'Of course, Grace would pick that weekend to be late to the barbecue,' Cord threw in. 'If only she'd known in a month's time we'd need her as a witness because her oldest brother would be dead and her niece kidnapped.'

Though Alyssa knew Cord was being sarcastic, she said, 'Maybe she knows something anyway. She and Gabriel seemed to confide in each other, so it's possible he shared with her. Wouldn't hurt to call and ask.'

Cord picked his phone up out of the center console where he'd thrown it, but before he could dial Grace, he received another call. 'Hal,' he said.

'Our search warrant?' Alyssa could hope.

'Hey, Hal. Have you got something for us?' Cord asked.

'Sure do. Your search warrant is here waiting for you.'

Alyssa turned on her blinker and made an illegal U-turn in the middle of the road after making sure traffic had cleared. 'We'll be there in fifteen minutes. Thanks, Your Highness.'

Hal chuckled. 'I think I like the sound of that. Hey, if you've got a few minutes while you're driving, I can tell you what I rounded up regarding Lydia Kensington's background.'

'Shoot.'

'It's pretty basic, so if you need me to dig further, just say the word.'

Alyssa already knew if Hal was sharing his findings, there was probably a reason he didn't think he'd uncover much that wasn't more of the same. 'Let's see what you've got first, and then we can decide.'

'Short version: she hails from Ohio from a lower middle-class family, and she was the only child born to Oscar and Lisa Penn. When she was five, her mom died. At the age of eighteen, she moved here to attend the University of New Mexico, which is where she met Gabriel Kensington. Ten years ago, her father, who was the sheriff in a town of about four hundred, died of lung cancer. From what I could gather from online articles and local newspapers, Lydia allowed the Fraternal Order of

Police to arrange the services. She showed up – alone – the day of the funeral, attended, and then hired an estate sales company to liquidate her father's meager holdings before flying back the next day. If she has social media accounts, I've found no evidence of them. Almost all her public appearances seemed to be linked to her husband's dealings, charities, et cetera. Besides that, adding my own opinion, based on everything I've read, Lydia Kensington acquires acquaintances rather than friends.'

Alyssa trusted Hal's instincts – she couldn't think of a time when he'd failed her in that respect – but she asked for verification anyway. 'What makes you say that?'

'Because she's rarely photographed with anyone other than her family, and that's usually just Gabriel. Of those very few pictures that I came across where she posed with other women, she always stood just a hair farther back, and her smile appeared forced. But again, this is me injecting my opinion.'

'Your opinion is usually pretty spot on, but don't let me saying that go to your head.'

'Too late,' Hal joked.

Both Alyssa and Cord chuckled. 'If there's nothing else, I'll let you go, and we'll see you in a few minutes.'

'Nothing from me. Joe and Tony might have an update by the time you arrive, though. I'll see you when you get here.' Hal ended the call without waiting for a goodbye.

Alyssa glanced at Cord. 'Looks like speaking to the Kensingtons' neighbors will have to wait.'

'Looks like.'

With most of the hot air balloons down, people were either crowding the field, the art festivals, or partaking of a late breakfast in any of the numerous restaurants around town. Because of that, traffic was kind, so it only took

71

them eight minutes to arrive back at the precinct. 'I'm almost afraid to say it out loud,' Alyssa said as she and Cord headed across the parking lot, 'but I sure hope that's a sign that things are going to go smoothly for us on this case.'

Cord barked out a laugh. 'You're funny. And you've also probably just jinxed us. So, thanks for that.'

'Oh, shut up.' She was only half-kidding, especially since she was superstitious that way, but she didn't have time to dwell on it since Hal rolled up with the search warrant in hand, presenting it to her like he was serving high tea at noon on a silver platter. She couldn't help but chuckle.

She snatched the paperwork and turned toward Captain Hammond's office so she could give him an update, but she didn't get far before she saw a woman stroll up to Ruby's desk, demanding to speak to someone about 'that poor man, Gabriel Kensington.' Garbed in a flamingo-patterned dress, wearing rollers in her hair, and lugging a none-too-pleased-looking lavender-colored poodle tucked beneath her arm, she continued, 'I heard it on the news just this morning. Dreadful what happened to him.'

Alyssa noted Cord's expression, and she wondered if the inquisitive look on his face was because he, too, detected how the woman had neglected to mention Lydia. Or Addis and Emerson, for that matter. She extended her hand. 'I'm Detective Wyatt. How can I help you?'

The flamboyant woman's gaze bounced right over her as if she were invisible and landed directly on Cord. After a once-over – or twice-over, in this case – where she openly admired Cord's physique, as most women did, she shuffled the poodle to the other side and extended her hand. 'Barbara Carpenter. And I believe *I* can help *you*.'

Her words practically dripped in syrupy sweetness, and Alyssa had to turn her head to hide the fact that her eyes had nearly done a three-sixty in her head. She coughed to cover the chortle that bubbled up. Cord tended to have that effect on women – and some men, too. In the end, she didn't care who Ms. Not Subtle spoke to if it helped them find Addis and Emerson or locate the person responsible for making Addis an orphan.

Cord offered his most charming smile, the one he reserved for women like Ms. Carpenter. 'I certainly hope you can. Did you see something last night that might help us?'

Barbara Carpenter lowered her voice to a loud whisper, making it obvious she wasn't really trying to be discreet. 'Yes. It was shortly after four, and I was out walking Lucious.' She ran her fingers through the curls on the dog's neck.

Momentarily distracted when the young officer from last night strolled up and stood off to the side, Alyssa almost missed Ms. Carpenter's next comment.

'When I passed by Mr. Kensington's house, he was in the driveway arguing with some man. I only noticed because the guy's vehicle blocked the sidewalk, and I was forced to walk in the street to go around it. Pfft. It makes me so angry when people are inconsiderate that way.'

Alyssa straightened, and from the corner of her eye, she noticed the young officer do the same.

'Can you describe this person?' Cord asked.

'His back was to me, so I didn't see his face, but he was tall' – she blinked in a manner Alyssa could only assume was intended to be flirtatious – 'about as tall as you, but not as broad-shouldered.' She reached out and touched

Cord, her manicured fingernails playing with the hairs on his arms.

Alyssa wondered if anyone else noticed how Cord stiffened before he smoothly removed his arm by shifting his stance.

'Okay, tall like me. What about his hair? Was it dark? Light? Do you remember what he was wearing?'

'Dark brown hair, like Gabriel's. And his clothes were business attire.'

'You said this man's vehicle was blocking the sidewalk,' Alyssa said, ignoring the way the woman's nostrils flared before shooting daggers her way. 'Did you happen to notice the make or model or maybe catch a glimpse of the license plate?'

'No.'

Alyssa didn't let the sharp, one-word response rattle her or stop her from forging forward with her questions. If Ms. Carpenter had information that might help them solve this case and bring the girls home, she was going to pry it out of her one way or another. 'Did you overhear what they were arguing about?'

This time Barbara Carpenter huffed out an insulted breath of air. 'I'm not into *eavesdropping*.'

Methinks you protest too much, Alyssa thought. It was what her husband always said to the kids after they got busted and refused to admit to whatever wrongdoing had been discovered.

'Of course you're not. That's not what my partner was implying.' Alyssa recognized Cord's tone; it was the one he used when he was trying to charm someone into taking the irritation down a notch. As usual, it worked. 'Is there anything else you can think of that might help us?'

'No, I don't think so. But I do hope you'll find whoever did this. I won't feel safe until you do.' Ms. Carpenter actually fanned her face like an old-fashioned damsel in distress. If it weren't for two missing girls' lives being at stake, Alyssa might've found it amusing.

'I appreciate you taking the time to come in. I'm going to have Ruby' – he tipped his head – 'take down your contact information before you go.' Ms. Carpenter's face lit up like a Fourth of July finale when he pulled a business card out of his pocket and handed it to her. 'In case you think of anything else that might assist us.'

Alyssa didn't bother to give her card to Gabriel's neighbor because she doubted it would make it farther than the nearest trash can. After Ms. Carpenter left – with a hopeful and suggestive peek back at Cord – she turned to the young officer who still stood patiently off to the side. 'Sandra, right? Did you need to speak to me about something?'

'Yes,' Sandra said, nodding a little more enthusiastically than Alyssa thought the situation called for. 'Captain Hammond wants me to assist with the Kensington case because he appreciated how I helped the gang unit solve a string of burglaries.'

Ah. That explained why she'd been so interested in what Ms. Carpenter had to say and why she'd waited so patiently. 'Yeah? How'd you do that?'

The color from Sandra's nose stretched across her cheekbones. 'It was nothing really. One of the victims managed to snap a picture and hide his phone, and I spotted the reflection of the getaway driver in the side mirror of the car. When they blew the picture up, someone recognized the guy from past arrests. The rest, as they say, is history.'

'Good eye,' Alyssa offered.

'Thanks. Anyway, the captain thought I'd learn a lot and get more experience by shadowing you because it's my goal one day to make detective.' Her gaze shifted slightly before adding, 'I've heard all kinds of stories about you, Detective Wyatt, so I'm excited to be given this opportunity.'

Alyssa grimaced. 'Do me a favor – if you hear anything spectacular, let me know, and I'll tell you if it's true or not.'

Sandra's head bobbed up and down, and when she spoke again, her words ran over each other in a way that reminded Alyssa of an auctioneer. 'Captain said to go see him if you have any concerns.'

Sandra's eagerness reminded her a lot of herself when she was in her first years on the squad. She'd been like a sponge in the ocean, soaking up as much information as she could, packing her brain and memorizing techniques and skills she hoped to one day master.

Alyssa fixed her with a pointed stare. 'It'll be a lot of long hours and a lot of tedious leg work,' she warned.

There was a slight pitch in the tone of Sandra's voice as, eyes glowing, she said, 'I'm not afraid of hard work or long hours. Hit me with it. I'm a firm believer that complete immersion is the best way to learn.'

'Well, a fresh pair of sharp eyes never hurts. In other words, welcome to the team. I'll let Hammond know we spoke.' She retrieved her phone from her pocket and shot off a text, envisioning the captain's scowl as she did. The man lived in the stone ages when it came to text messages. He stood firm on the hill of talking to someone on the phone, claiming if he'd wanted to read every damn communication, he would've picked a different career.

'All done,' Alyssa said, unable to hold back a grin as Hammond bellowed from his office that he was less than twenty feet away. Similarly, Sandra's wide smile showcased two rows of perfectly straight teeth that had to have required years of dental work.

'Thank you so much, Detective Wyatt.'

Hal chuckled when Cord said, 'You might want to hold back on that thank you until your first day on the team's in the history books. Lys here can be a real taskmaster.'

'Bite me,' Alyssa retorted.

'Point...' Cord wisely allowed his comeback to trail off when Alyssa's glare threatened retribution if he completed it.

'Well, you've met Cord. This is Hal Callum, everyone's go-to guy, from advice to anything research-related. You'll meet Joe and Tony as soon as I track them down.'

'Tony White? I think I kind of indirectly met him last night at the Kensington residence,' Sandra said.

As Alyssa was saying, 'Then you'll meet him officially,' Joe and Tony rounded the corner together, and she couldn't help but notice Tony looked much more like his old self as he described how he had tracked an elk through the woods in the early morning hours of his last day of hunting, having it charge, and then losing it altogether when he tripped over a tree root poking out of the ground.

'Hurt like hell when my face scraped down the side of that damn tree,' he said, pulling up short when he spotted Sandra. His normal white pallor flushed such a bright red he appeared to have a third-degree sunburn, as if he was embarrassed to admit to someone not on the team that he'd been so ungraceful.

'Just the people I needed. Joe, Tony, this is Officer Sandra Falwin. She'll be joining our team for this case. Cord and I just spoke with one of Gabriel Kensington's neighbors, a Barbara Carpenter, who may have given us our first glimpse of a possible suspect, so I'm going to need you both to canvass the neighborhood once more, see if anyone who has a security system will let you take another look. Gabriel and an unknown male had some type of verbal altercation yesterday in the driveway around four or shortly after. If we're lucky, someone will recognize Gabriel's visitor. Or at the very least, maybe someone's camera will have captured the guy's car driving up, and we can at least release something to the public.'

'We can head over there right now, unless you've got something else you need us to do,' Joe said.

Alyssa held up the search warrant for Kensington Investigations. 'Actually, I do. I'd like you to accompany Cord and me to serve this warrant. But before we head out, where are we on the phone records and financials?'

'Still waiting,' Tony said. 'Sorry, I know that's not what you want to hear.'

'True. What I'd like to hear is that the girls have somehow found their way home and were never in danger, but since the chances of that happening are less than slim to none, let's get this show on the road.' She turned to Hal. 'Could you light a fire under the tech team regarding those prints found on Addis's phone? Even if we rule it out as hers...'

'Consider it done.'

As they headed for the door, Alyssa realized Sandra was still standing in the same spot she'd been earlier, unsure what she was supposed to be doing, and gestured to her to come on. 'You can ride with Cord and me.'

Their newest team member wasted no time catching up.

Chapter Ten

Friday, October 4

Kensington Investigations was housed in a quaint brick building nestled at the end of a commercial cul-de-sac that was tucked between two quiet residential streets. According to Grace, Gabriel had taken great care in choosing this location. It gave the respectability of being in a professional area while still giving the privacy many of his clients craved.

Armed with the search warrant, Alyssa climbed out of her Tahoe, taking note of the black Escalade with gold-colored trim and shiny rims parked in the space designated *President*. It made the powder blue Prius parked next to it look like a toy. 'Wonder who's here.'

Cord tapped the hood of the Cadillac as he moved past it, hurrying forward so he could hold the door open for her and Sandra, something she was finally getting used to. It had only taken five and a half years. 'Whoever it is can't have been here too long. Engine's still warm.'

Inside, the first sounds that greeted them were snuffles from a copper-haired woman perched behind a desk with a placard that read *Marnie Hanson*. When she heard the chime above the door, her head jerked up, putting her red-rimmed eyes and cherry-tipped nose on full display.

In front of her stood Mack Kensington who spun around when they entered. If the expression on his face was anything to go by, he was less than thrilled to see Alyssa and her team. Which was fine because she was less than thrilled to see him, as well.

'I—I'm sorry. I'm afraid we're closed right now,' Marnie said, yanking several tissues from the box near her phone, blowing her nose into one, blotting her eyes with another, and dabbing her cheeks with the final one before tossing the lot into the wastebasket.

From her jacket pocket, Alyssa retrieved the search warrant and handed it over to Gabriel's secretary. 'Albuquerque Police Department. We're here to search the office.'

Marnie dropped her gaze to the badges clipped at their hips, the sight of them reigniting the stream of tears she'd just finished wiping away. But it wasn't the crying that had Alyssa nervous; it was the way the woman's sudden hysterical gasping breaths turned her face purple, making Alyssa fear Gabriel's secretary was about to pass out – or worse, puke.

Clearly impatient with the display of emotion, Mack snapped. 'Marnie, for God's sake, I told you to go—'

Alyssa interrupted his tirade. 'Exactly what are you doing here?'

Mack's left eyebrow arched high, the sneer on his face depicting a level of superiority he felt over her. 'Not that it's any of your business, Detective, but I'm getting my brother's things in order.'

His opinion of her mattered not in the least. As long as he didn't hinder her investigation, he could think she was the Great Pumpkin for all she cared. 'Coming from you, that's an asinine comment. Considering your line of work, *Counselor*, I'm sure you know exactly why it's my business,' Alyssa countered. 'Especially with respect to the conversation that took place at the precinct not too long ago.'

Cord stepped forward. 'Have you taken anything or gone through any of Gabriel's files, paper or electronic?'

Mack leaned back and perched on the edge of Marnie's desk in a show of confidence, but a furious tic at the corner of his eye suggested he wasn't as unaffected as he pretended to be. 'Just walked in two minutes before you, so no.'

Alyssa peered at Marnie who nodded her confirmation of Mack's claimed timeline. 'What things are you trying to get in order when you yourself claimed Gabriel didn't speak to you about his private practice?'

'Gabriel was my brother, and someone has to take care of it. Grace is busy with other things, I presume, so I took it upon myself to handle this side of the estate.'

Alyssa didn't believe for a second that was all there was to it, especially as it appeared Mack had been trying to talk Gabriel's secretary into leaving, which would've left him alone in the office. She leveled a narrow-eyed, penetrating glare at him. 'Mr. Kensington, even a civilian would know that tinkering with anything regarding your brother's estate while we're still investigating his murder is cause for concern. Do the words *obstruction of justice* ring any bells for you?' She ignored Mack's flared nostrils and intimidating posture as she issued her command. 'Stay out of my team's way.' She tipped her head toward the search warrant still clutched in Marnie's grasp. 'Feel free to look over the warrant while we go about our business.' She gave the go-ahead to Joe, Tony, and Sandra who stood just inside the doorway. To Marnie, she said, 'Is Gabriel's door locked?'

Voice thick with emotion, Marnie whispered, 'Yes,' before bending to open a drawer, and coming back up with a key that she handed over.

Alyssa cocked her head for Cord to follow but stopped when Mack's arrogant demand followed her down the hall. 'I'll expect a complete inventory of what you've taken, Detective.'

'I know how to do my job, Counselor. And for the record, you're not in the courtroom right now, so the sooner you stop your theatrics, the sooner we can discover what happened to your brother and his wife and locate your niece and her friend. I assume that's still your main goal?'

A storm of anger flashed in his eyes at her sarcasm. 'Careful there, Detective. I'm smarter than most people you badger on a daily basis. You really don't want to tangle with me.'

'Nor you me,' Alyssa promised before turning her back on him once more so she could get busy with the reason she was there.

Just as Alyssa stepped into Gabriel's office, Cord's phone rang, and he excused himself to take the call. Because she was wondering what the true purpose of Mack's premature efforts of getting his brother's affairs in order might be, what he was clearly afraid her team might uncover in their search, she missed the way her partner's face drained of color as he brushed past her into the hallway.

–

Surrounded by scores of boxes removed from Gabriel Kensington's office, the team, quiet as the afternoon wore on, methodically scoured the contents of each one in hopes of finding a red flag that might point them to a killer, but more urgently, help them locate Addis and Emerson. Situated around the table and on the floor, Joe, Tony, and Sandra divvied up the files alphabetically while Hal, mumbling under his breath, was singularly focused on the laptop in front of him as he searched through Gabriel's online files, payment schedules, invoices, calendar, and anything else that would give them a name to go on.

Much to Alyssa's surprise, Mack had left the premises before her team had completed the search, which gave her the chance to question Marnie, not that his presence would've stopped her. Unfortunately, Marnie's husband had had a heart attack, and so she'd been out of the office for the past several weeks while he recuperated. During that period, the only times she spoke to Gabriel had been when he called to inquire how her husband was doing, and according to her, she never detected anything off, though she admitted to being distracted with worry over her husband's health.

She explained her absence was also the reason Gabriel's online calendar was so empty. Without her entering his appointments, she confessed her boss had a tendency to jot things down on sticky notes whose information occasionally made its way into his phone's calendar before being tossed in the trash. In fact, though Marnie wasn't officially returning until Monday, she'd dropped in just to try to get a jump start on reorganizing the mess she predicted Gabriel had left her. But she'd been pleasantly surprised that the office had been less cluttered than she'd anticipated.

When Alyssa had asked about the case Grace had mentioned, Marnie apologized for not knowing anything about it, going on to explain that if Gabriel had taken on a case, the client's number would likely show up on the phone bill, which prompted Alyssa to inquire about the business phone.

Marnie waved her hand in the air to dismiss the idea. 'Oh, that's just for me to field calls and take messages. Since he's always on the move, Mr. Kensington prefers to use his cell. In fact, I think the only reason he keeps an extension in his office is for me to talk to him without having to get up.'

So now, while her team was busy searching boxes and computers, Alyssa was systematically going down the list of numbers from a cell phone bill left opened on Gabriel's desk. Immediately, she'd recognized Lydia's, Grace's, and Addis's numbers and crossed those off. There was one ninety-six second call to Mack which she guessed was a return call from a twenty-second message he'd left ten days earlier. If nothing else, the phone records showed that Gabriel was in touch with Grace far more often than he was with Mack.

For the briefest of moments, she wondered what her relationship would've been like with her own brother if he hadn't been ripped from their lives when he was four. But that wasn't only a dangerous path of 'what if' to travel, it wasn't where her head needed to be, so she shut it down before it got a toehold and distracted her from her job of bringing Addis and Emerson home alive. She refused to accept the possibility that her team may be on a recovery mission as opposed to a rescue. She'd learned early on in her career to focus on the positive or she'd easily lose her mind to the darkness that often stole into the lives of those in law enforcement.

Now, as she disconnected from a paper supply company, Alyssa jotted a note and moved on to the next number, watching as Sandra, with a grunt of frustration, shoved aside her first box and pulled another closer to her. A small smile tugged at the corners of her mouth as she recalled how their newest team member had insisted on carting two of the heavy boxes in one load.

Joe had given her a hard time. 'You know you're just making Tony and me look bad, right? Now we're going to have to haul in extra boxes so we don't look weak next to you.'

Huffing with every step up the stairs, she'd said, 'I'm a weightlifter, so I'm a lot stronger than I look.' Then she'd set her boxes down and flexed her biceps, earning a chuckle from Hal and a whistle from Joe. Earlier in the afternoon, Tony had returned to his inner shell, so he'd remained quiet and unaffected by the team's easy banter with Sandra and amongst each other. More than once, Alyssa had caught Joe and Hal sneaking concerned looks beneath lowered lashes. She'd been doing the same thing. Once again, she wished she knew how to reach him. She could only hope that he'd come around in his own time and in his own way, and she hoped it would be sooner than later.

Alyssa's phone rang, putting her head back where it needed to be. But when she checked the caller ID, her palms became slippery with moisture. It was Cord. She punched the green icon and answered. 'How's Sara? How are you? The babies?'

All activity in the room ceased as everyone's heads snapped up, Tony's included. They froze, their hands in various degrees of hovering as the lot of them, wide-eyed, stared openly.

The phone call Cord had received earlier had been from a panicked friend who'd spontaneously dropped in to check on Sara only to find her collapsed on the kitchen floor, bleeding. She'd immediately dialed 911 and followed the ambulance to the hospital, calling Cord on the way to inform him of what was happening. When he'd raced back into Gabriel's office, visibly shaken, moisture turning his eyes glassy, and uttered 'Sara,' Alyssa had tossed him her keys, no questions asked.

'Go,' she'd ordered, ignoring her own wash of fear for her friend and partner.

Catching the keys mid-air, he'd rushed out, the squeal of tires as he left the parking lot a clear indicator of the terror that had to be nearly paralyzing.

That had been hours ago, and the only thing keeping Alyssa and the team from storming the waiting room in a show of moral support was the fact that they were still searching for Addis and Emerson. They hadn't wanted to intrude with a phone call. If the news was bad, Cord and Sara would need their privacy as they tried to come to terms with whatever had happened.

The lightness in Cord's voice, as much as his words, forced a loud expulsion of relieved air from Alyssa's chest. The nervous energy in the room instantly evaporated.

'We're all fine. They're still running some tests, but the bleeding's stopped, and despite Sara being annoyed about being placed on complete bed rest for the duration of the pregnancy, both she and the babies are resting but safe.'

'Hold on a second. The team's all here, and they've been waiting to hear word, so let me fill them in.' Alyssa knew the smile in her heart was evident on her face, as well. 'Mom and Dad-to-be and twins are doing fine. They're still running tests, and Sara's confined to bed rest, but everyone's good.'

Cheers and thunderous claps of high-fives erupted before Sandra awkwardly hugged Hal with one arm. Joe, as usual, grimaced hearing the word *twins*, and Alyssa imagined he was reliving all the sleepless, colicky nights his Hailee had brought him and his wife and thinking how much more exhausted Cord and Sara would be with two.

'We all wanted to be there—'

Cord interrupted her. 'I know every single one of you would've dropped everything if you could've. Speaking of which, any luck so far?'

Alyssa sighed and rubbed her temples with her free hand. 'Not yet. But we've only been at it for a few hours. However, the team's managing just fine, so I don't want to see you until tomorrow – at the very earliest. And if you need more time... Well, Sara and the babies come first. Understand?'

Chortling, Cord agreed. 'Understood. And speaking of, Sara's awake now and mouthing "Say hello from me."'

'Hello from all of us. Now all *four* of you get some rest and check in again later if you get a chance.' They spoke another minute before Alyssa ended the call.

Adrenaline still high but waning now that she knew everyone was fine, she pushed back her chair, wound her hair into a ponytail, grabbed her empty mug, and said, 'I'm going to get a refill. Why don't we take ten to rest our eyes and then get back to it?'

'Don't have to tell me twice,' Hal said, whirling his chair around and rolling himself out behind Alyssa while Joe, Tony, and Sandra scattered in different directions in search of food, drink, and whatever else.

–

It was nearing four-fifteen, and Alyssa was bone-weary and frustrated that in the nearly five hours that they'd been fine-tooth combing through Gabriel Kensington's records, they'd accomplished little more than reaching dead end after dead end. Going back over the call log, her last hail–Mary attempt was to try phoning the numbers again where no one had answered, even though she'd left a message on each one. A throbbing in her temples warned of a bitter headache, and she knew if Cord had been here, he would've harangued her for not eating when the others had.

On the other end of the line, a female with a warm, husky voice answered. 'Hello?'

Wiping one palm over her tired eyes, Alyssa said, 'Hello. This is Detective Alyssa Wyatt with the Albuquerque Police Department. We're investigating the deaths of Gabriel and Lydia Kensington. To whom am I speaking?'

'Elizabeth Monroe.'

'Ms. Monroe, were you a client of Mr. Kensington's?'

A gruff, humorless laugh hit Alyssa's ears before the woman answered. 'Yes. I asked him to look into the disappearance of my high school boyfriend and the father of my child.'

Recalling Grace's visit and her fear that Gabriel had discovered something that might've gotten him killed,

Alyssa's adrenaline kicked back up a notch. 'Ms. Monroe, I need to ask you a few questions about that case. Would now be a good time for you to come by the precinct?' She purposely didn't pose her question as optional.

An audible sigh sounded over the line. 'Detective Wyatt, you said?'

'Yes.'

'I have a young son I'd rather not take to the station, so is it possible for us to meet at my home instead?'

Alyssa was already gathering her things. 'Tell me when.'

'Is quarter to five too soon?'

'Not at all.' After getting Elizabeth's address, Alyssa turned to Sandra. 'Unless you've latched onto something that will lead us to Addis and Emerson, why don't you come with me?'

Comically, Sandra's thumb jabbed her own chest as her mouth dropped open. 'Me?' The rest of the team chuckled as she scampered to her feet.

Chapter Eleven

Friday, October 4

Enough light trickled in from the hole high above their heads that Addis could just make out the large roach-like bugs that scuttled about in the cramped space. When one decided to take up residence on her exposed leg, its antennae tickling at her skin, she kicked out, trying to dislodge it, whimpering when it didn't move. The thunderstorm seemed to have driven them in by the dozens.

She tilted her head up with her mouth open when a drip from above splattered onto her arm. The hole wasn't large enough to have allowed the torrential downpour inside, but it had provided the girls much needed moisture for their dry mouths.

'Ad, how long have I been out? And *where* are we?' Emerson's hoarse, scratchy voice coupled with her stuffy nose made her sound like a decades-long smoker with laryngitis.

'I don't know,' Addis croaked. 'We could be in the middle of town or up in the mountains. Whatever he drugged us with is messing with my head, so I don't even know if we've been in here for hours or days.'

'It doesn't really matter, though, because it already feels like forever,' Emerson whispered.

'Em, I'm so sorry. If you hadn't been with me, then—'

Emerson didn't let her finish. 'Hit the brakes! It's not your fault.' Labored breaths filled with fear stretched across the claustrophobic space between them.

An explosive clap of thunder buried Addis's response and shook their prison's foundation. After her heart stopped climbing the walls of her throat, she forgot about the insects, the smell, the dampness, and everything else except this horror show she and her best friend had a starring role in. 'Em, listen to me. Someone's going to come for us.'

'Yeah, but what if that someone is *him*? What if he's still here? Or what if he's gone, and he's never planning on coming back? We'll either starve to death or the animals will eat us.' Loud groans filled the air. 'I don't want some giant rat to eat me. What if I'm still alive, and I feel all of it?'

Addis wished she could clap her hands over her ears. She needed Em to stop not only because those were her fears, too, but because she was afraid she'd fixate on the images being planted in her head.

'Em, you know Aunt Grace isn't going to rest until we're back home, even if that means she has to personally search under every rock and inside every cave in this country. And there's Uncle Mack, and even if it's for no other reason than to make him look good to the outside world, he'll hire an army if that's what it takes.' She prayed her declarations weren't merely empty promises. 'We can help them if we can find a way to get loose and get out of here.'

Emerson's sobs turned into hiccups as they slowly ebbed. 'Do you really believe that?'

No. Maybe, Addis thought to herself. 'Yes,' she said out loud.

When Em finally spoke again, determination replaced the tremor in her voice. 'Okay then. Can you wiggle around so your back is to me?'

'I think so.' Addis was already shifting her weight as nerves comingled with hope at the thought of escaping before they suffered the same fate as her parents. Yet, despite her resolve to stay strong, her mother's still form and her father's shattered skull, his mutilated body, the lake of blood that had littered the kitchen floor flashed in her mind, and several seconds ticked by before it registered that the mewling howls echoing around them were coming from a dark cavernous abyss within her chest. Her parents couldn't be gone, especially not her dad; he just couldn't. It wasn't possible. How could she be a daddy's girl without a daddy?

This time, it was Emerson who tried to soothe *her*.

Five seconds or five hours later, the ache deep inside subsided to a dull throb, and she dropped her head onto her raised knees. 'God, Em, the last thing I said to my mom was that she was a delusional nutjob who needed some serious psychiatric help.' She struggled for air to breathe through the pain of repeating those words out loud.

'Addis, stop! You couldn't have known what was going to happen. And let's be honest, your mom was always accusing you of stupid shit. That doesn't mean she deserved to die the way she did, but you can't own this guilt. Besides, we can deal with that later, after we get out of here. But we'll do it together, just like we do everything else. Right now, you have to keep it together. Do you hear me?' Emerson's sharp tone bit through the devastation and despair, but it did nothing to erase the truth of what Addis's future held – death or loneliness.

As Emerson struggled to untie her hands, Addis saw something glint in the trickle of light coming in through the hole, and she twisted in an effort to see what it was. 'Wait,' she whispered, kicking her leg out to try and drag the object closer.

'What are you doing?' Em asked.

Addis's response was a series of grunts as she maneuvered the object enough to lean over and pick it up. Her heart raced as she held it in her palm, running her thumb carefully over the pointed, sharp edge. 'I think it's a piece of glass or broken pottery. Maybe we can use it to try to saw through these ropes.' The possibility of escape edged closer than she'd allowed herself to hope.

However, her tiny drop of optimism was short-lived when the hair-raising sound of grinding gears reached her ears. A wave of nausea gurgled up her esophagus, their aid to freedom slipping from her hand as the vehicle's approach grew closer.

Chapter Twelve

Friday, October 4

A woman in a dusty rose A-line dress and with long, wavy mahogany hair pulled up into a high ponytail answered the door.

Alyssa extended her hand, mindful of the nervous energy emanating off Sandra beside her. 'Detective Wyatt. We spoke on the phone.' She tipped her head. 'And this is Officer Falwin.'

Elizabeth gripped Alyssa's hand, then Sandra's. 'Of course. Please come in.' After closing the door, Ms. Monroe led them into a spacious room with a colorful burgundy wall. Scattered in a circle around a young boy were hundreds of Legos. His tongue poked out one side of his mouth as he studied the model in front of him.

'Brandon, honey, my company's here, so it's time for you to head over to Nate's now.'

Brandon's head snapped up, his eyes brightening as he jumped up, whooping as he did. 'Can I—'

Elizabeth's smile removed five years from her face as she interrupted whatever her son was about to ask. 'You cannot.' She wagged her finger at him. 'You're eating dinner at home, so don't go getting yourself invited over there.'

The freckles sprinkled across his cheeks and nose were accentuated by the way he crinkled his face. 'Aw, Mom, it's fish sticks Friday,' he moaned.

Elizabeth raised her hand, stopping his protest. 'It's that or don't go. You can always just take your Legos up to the loft to play.'

Brandon scuffed one foot, then perked right back up when a notification chimed on the phone that had magically appeared in his hand. 'It's Nate.' He flipped his phone around for his mom to see.

'Remember what I said, Brandon.' This time Elizabeth's voice carried a hint of warning as her son raced across the room.

'Got it. Eat here not there. See you later, alli-greater!' he hollered just before the front door slammed.

Elizabeth laughed as she moved to the front window, flicking the curtains back to watch her son run across the lawn to his friend's house. 'As a toddler, he could never pronounce alligator, and over the years, it just kind of stuck with us as our own inside joke.' A few seconds later, the curtain fell back into place, and she turned back to them. She waved her hand to a navy-blue sofa. 'Please have a seat. Is there anything I can get you to drink?'

Alyssa settled next to Sandra. 'No, thank you.'

Simultaneously, Sandra shook her head. 'You've got a handsome little boy there. You're a single mom?'

A curtain fell over Elizabeth's eyes as she answered. 'Yes, I am. And thank you.'

Alyssa waited until Ms. Monroe settled onto a loveseat across from them. 'I'd like to talk to you a little about the reason you hired Kensington Investigations.' From the leather bag beside her, Sandra retrieved a notebook she'd snatched on the way out of the precinct, bringing a smile to Alyssa's face because it reminded her not of herself this time, but of Cord.

Shifting just the tiniest bit, Elizabeth linked her fingers together, settling her hands into her lap. 'Do you mind if I ask a question of my own first?'

'Of course, go ahead.'

'What does my case have to do with yours?'

'We don't know that it does,' Alyssa answered honestly. 'But we're investigating every avenue because not only do we have a double homicide' – she didn't miss the way Elizabeth winced at her blunt words – 'but we also have two missing girls we have reason to believe could very much be in danger of meeting the same fate.'

Shoulders slumping, Elizabeth stared down at her linked hands, sucking in a deep breath and exhaling loudly. 'I'm not sure how my information will help, but I guess it doesn't hurt for you to know.' Her humorless laugh fell flat. 'With Mr. Kensington's death, it's not like I'll be getting the answers I'd hoped he'd find for me anyway.' One hand flew up to cover her mouth as she gasped. 'That sounded so callous. I'm sorry. I didn't— Please forgive me. This is all—'

Alyssa held one palm up to halt the onslaught of Elizabeth's apology. 'I understand.'

Elizabeth released her breath and settled her hands back in her lap. 'Three weeks ago, I approached Mr. Kensington about finding out what had happened to my high school sweetheart. Seven years ago, I got pregnant, and he and I were going to run away. My eighteenth birthday was coming up, and so we planned to hide out until we could legally marry, and then we'd return home and tell our parents.' She blinked moisture from her eyes. 'We weren't so concerned about his parents, but mine, well, that was a different story altogether.'

'Tell us a little about them, your parents, I mean,' Alyssa suggested, remembering Grace's claim that Gabriel's client had Puritanical parents.

Elizabeth twisted so she could scan the room behind her. When she caught herself doing it, she wiped her palms on her dress and laughed nervously. 'Clearly, my mother and father still have an unhealthy hold on me. My parents belonged – belong – to an extreme fundamentalist group who follow the strictest parts of scripture. Primarily, anything that places women in subservient positions and elevates men to near godlike status, they believe. Dating before marriage – and that includes even holding hands with someone – is a very slight step below adultery. Needless to say, they never knew I had a boyfriend, much less one I was having a "sinful" relationship with.'

'How did you manage to keep your pregnancy a secret from them?' Alyssa asked.

'Baggy clothes.' Elizabeth covered her middle as if she were still protecting her unborn child, and Alyssa wondered if the woman was aware that she was doing it.

'I also made sure they saw me "eating more" even though I wasn't.'

Alyssa's eyes were drawn to Elizabeth's hands. She pointed to an angry, red gash with a blue tinge around it in the space between Elizabeth's thumb and forefinger. 'Do you mind if I ask what happened?'

An indulgent smile changed the planes of Ms. Monroe's face. 'I was cutting up chicken for dinner when Brandon decided to show me the toad he'd caught. It leaped from his hand onto the counter, scaring the hell out of me, and the knife slipped. I was going to put a Band-Aid on it but got distracted. It is rather nasty-looking, though, isn't it?'

'I think stitches might've been a good idea,' Alyssa agreed, an image of Gabriel's chest popping into her mind. But if Elizabeth Monroe was responsible for his death, the rage and destruction wrought upon his body probably would've created more severe cuts than just that one. Still, she made a mental note to add the observation to her write-up of the interview.

'Tell us a little bit about your boyfriend,' Alyssa said, still trying to determine if Grace's fear had merit. But so far, nothing she'd heard convinced her that the case of a missing boyfriend had spurred the hatred that resulted in the deaths of Gabriel and Lydia and the kidnapping of two teenagers.

'His name was Joshua Benson, but everyone called him by his middle name, Hayden.' Alyssa could practically see floating hearts hovering over Elizabeth's head as her eyes became distant and fixed. A soft smile teased the corners of her mouth as she mentally returned to the place of her memory. 'That's why he always used to call me "Beck" because my middle name is Rebecca.'

Alyssa followed Elizabeth's gaze where it had drifted to a photograph on the mantel.

Sandra pointed at the image. 'Is that the two of you?'

'Yes, it is.'

Already standing, Sandra asked, 'Do you mind if I take a closer look?'

If Cord had been with her, Alyssa would've been able to tell by his body language or by the tone of his voice that there was more on his mind than mere curiosity, but with Sandra, she couldn't discern if the young officer was simply interested or if there was another reason she wanted a closer look.

Elizabeth waved her hand. 'Of course.'

Sandra returned to her place beside Alyssa, studying the picture before handing it to her and asking, 'What happened the night you were supposed to run away together?'

Elizabeth plucked at the fabric on her love seat. When she spoke, her words were hushed. 'I waited for him at the library where we were supposed to meet – that's where we most often met up, unless it was at his house, where we mostly hid out in his room – but he never showed. At some point, his parents reported him missing when their calls went unanswered, and none of his friends, myself included, knew where he was.

'His car was nowhere to be found.' Here, Elizabeth closed her eyes and breathed in through her nose once, twice, three times before reopening them. 'When the police searched his room, they found a partially packed suitcase on his bed. That's when his parents noticed two other suitcases missing, along with most of his clothing. The police asked his parents if he had a reason to run away, and when they eventually showed up at my house, I had to admit to what we'd been planning. Soon afterwards, they closed the case, insisting he'd run off, having decided he was too young to be, quote, "saddled with a wife and kid – especially with such a promising future in front of him." Those were their exact words, by the way.'

'What promising future were they referring to?' Sandra asked.

'Baseball, but what they didn't know is that while Hayden loved the sport and had even been offered a scholarship to play for some college in Cali, he had no intention of making it his career. He was far more interested in architecture at the time.'

'I see. Please go on.'

Elizabeth's hand dropped to a throw pillow beside her as she absently twirled the lace edging between her fingers. 'None of Hayden's friends, no one in his family, and certainly not me believed for a second he would do something like that. Hayden was simply not the type of person to shirk his responsibilities. And we were in love. Anyone could see that.'

Sandra cocked her head to the side at Elizabeth's proclamation that 'anyone' could see how in love she and her high school boyfriend had been, and Alyssa wondered if it was because, like her, she couldn't tell if Elizabeth was a woman remembering or a woman forcing herself to believe what she wanted to be true.

'I understand that most teenagers believe their high school love is *the* everlasting one,' Elizabeth said as if Alyssa's thoughts had been spoken aloud. 'And maybe Hayden and I wouldn't have gone the distance, but there's no way he would've missed the birth of his own child. Not after what he'd seen his own sister go through when her fiancé abandoned her before her first baby was born.' Elizabeth stood and moved across the room to a built-in bookshelf where she reached up and pulled down a year-book, flipping it open and removing a loose photograph. She turned it over and read aloud:

"*Beck, here's to our forever future – together. Everything is going to turn out exactly right, just you wait and see. My love for you will stay true to the day I die.*" Running her fingers over the words, she whispered, 'That doesn't exactly sound like someone who's about to take off because he's afraid of settling down.'

Alyssa shifted, and the high-pitched squeak of the sofa's legs against the tiled floor as it moved startled Elizabeth. It was like watching a curtain go up at the beginning of a play. 'Are you still in contact with your family?'

A flash of pure hatred stole across Elizabeth's face. 'No. Aside from calling me some pretty nasty names when they learned I was pregnant, they also spewed some pretty hateful comments about my unborn child. When my father yanked his belt from his pants so that he could "beat the devil out of me," I ran to my room, barricaded my door, grabbed my suitcase, and snuck out my bedroom window.'

Alyssa couldn't say she blamed her.

'I haven't seen them since, though I did call them after Brandon was born in case there was any part of them that had thawed, that might've wanted to know their grandson. It was instantly clear their opinions about either of us hadn't budged a bit, so that conversation lasted less than thirty seconds.'

Alyssa couldn't imagine not wanting to know one's grandchild. Even though she and her own mother-in-law had once had a tumultuous relationship in which Mabel consistently insulted and undermined everything Alyssa said, the woman was convinced Holly and Isaac hung the moon and scattered the stars, and she would – and did – bend over backwards to be there for them.

'What about Hayden's family? Do you keep in touch with them? Do they have a relationship with Brandon?' Even as Alyssa asked, she wondered if it was because she was drawn into the saga of this woman's past or if there was some instinct holding her captive, telling her if she waited long enough, she'd have what she came for.

'Not as much as when he was first born.' Elizabeth stroked the photo in her hand as if the glossy paper was truly Hayden's skin. 'Brandon very much resembles his father, and I think it's just too much for Hayden's mother. His father was killed in an industrial accident six years ago, and his brother moved to Montana. But I still see his sister Rosalyn. In fact, I told her I was hiring Gabriel to look into Hayden's disappearance, and while she wasn't thrilled at bringing all that pain back to the surface, especially because of her mother, she also understood why I was doing it.

'I know Mr. Kensington set up a meeting with Ros, but I never got a chance to ask how it went. This past Wednesday, he left me a message saying it was urgent he speak to me right away, that he had some promising new information and wanted to get together so he could show me some pictures. His voice was, I don't know, excited but frantic, maybe? Because I didn't want the boys to overhear our conversation, I sent him a text telling him I'd taken Brandon and Nate down to Carlsbad Caverns to see the bats for fall break, and I'd call when we returned so we could set up a time to get together, but by the time we got back, I was already rushing to make another appointment I had.' A strange expression flitted across Elizabeth's face, there and gone so quickly that Alyssa wondered if she'd only imagined seeing it. 'By the time I finished up with that, it was too late to call. And then the murders were all over the news this morning…' Her voice trailed off.

Her head reeling with this new information, Alyssa played out the scene in her mind. *Gabriel speaks with Hayden's sister, who from Elizabeth's account, appeared none too happy that the case was being looked into, then he comes across some pictures, and then ends up murdered.* It was eerily similar to what Grace had told her this morning, and that was more of a coincidence than she was comfortable with. 'Do you still have the message Gabriel left?' She didn't bother to mask the urgency in her voice when she asked.

Elizabeth pressed her finger onto the biometric scanner of her phone and swiped across the screen until she found her voicemail and hit play. Gabriel Kensington's booming voice burst into the room from beyond the grave.

'Elizabeth, this is Gabriel Kensington. Call me back as soon as you receive this message. I've uncovered some – disturbing – information, and I'd like you to take a look at some photographs that have come into my possession. Hayden could—Just call me.'

Grace's suspicion that this case may be connected to her brother's murder was beginning to make more sense than Alyssa had originally thought. 'I'd appreciate it if we could get Rosalyn's number.'

After writing down Rosalyn's contact information, Elizabeth ripped off the piece of envelope she'd randomly grabbed and handed it over.

'You said none of Hayden's friends believed he'd run off, either. Did you ever talk to any of them about that night?' Sandra asked.

'Yes, a couple of them, anyway. To be honest, I was so paranoid about keeping our relationship a secret, I didn't actually hang out with them much. I can't even remember most of their names. So, I met up with his best friend Marcel and his partner Thad, and the general consensus was that the police believed we were all in denial due to hero worship.' It wasn't physically possible for Elizabeth's eyes to roll any further back into her head.

'Would you have a way for us to contact either of them?' Alyssa asked.

'Actually, Ros told me Marcel died from cancer a few years back. As for Thad, they broke up, so no one really knows what happened to him. The only other friend of Hayden's I can recall was Al. If Hayden was late for one of our dates, which was frequent, it almost always had to do with Al. I actually never met him, so… Sorry, I know that's far from helpful.'

'In my career, you never know when the tiniest bit of information that seems like nothing at the time cracks a case wide open.' Alyssa stood, indicating the interview was over.

At the door, she thanked Elizabeth for her time and offered her a card. 'Please call me if you think of anything else.'

Chapter Thirteen

Whipping her SUV around a slow-moving Chevy Spark, Alyssa mulled over Gabriel Kensington's message to Elizabeth Monroe. More importantly, she wondered what and where were the photographs he'd mentioned because, as of yet, none had been discovered in their search of either the Kensington home or office. It seemed the most likely person to answer that question was Rosalyn Benson, Hayden's sister, since Gabriel's message came on the heels of his meeting with her.

Sandra pulled at her left ear lobe, a trait Alyssa already recognized as something she did when she was thinking. 'Is it just me, or does it seem a little odd to you that Hayden Benson's family wasn't overly thrilled to have Monroe hire someone to look into his disappearance? If that was my brother, nothing would stop me from getting to the truth. Also, let's just say he did run off because he got cold feet about becoming a daddy so young. Don't you think at some point over the past seven years, he would've reached out to his parents at least? Reading between the lines here, of course, but Monroe made it sound as if he was close to his family. Walking away and never contacting them again just for the sole purpose of making sure he doesn't have to take responsibility for knocking someone up seems like a pretty far stretch. Two plus two is not equaling four in this instance.'

While conducting an interview with Sandra had been a far cry from the smooth system she and Cord had worked out over the past five and a half years, Alyssa still found the young officer to be amazingly astute. 'That pretty much sums up my thoughts, too,' she said.

When Sandra remained quiet, Alyssa darted a quick glance her way. It was immediately clear to her that her newest team member was preoccupied as she studied the image of a smiling Hayden Benson leaning up against a tree with his jacket casually hooked over one finger so it draped over his back. In the picture – the same one that he'd written his message of devotion to his future with Elizabeth on – he appeared ready to take on the world.

How long before he discovered he was going to be a dad had the photograph been taken, Alyssa wondered.

'You know, I'm looking at this picture Elizabeth loaned us, and Hayden Benson seems to have it all – looks, and from that smile, charm. I just can't get over the Bensons' lack of interest in their son's disappearance. It doesn't make sense at all. I mean, I can't even imagine the helplessness and the horror I'd feel if I had a child who suddenly vanished without a trace, not knowing if I'd ever see him again. Can you?'

Sandra's words brought to the surface memories of Alyssa and her family alternately pacing the floors or curling up on Isaac's bed all while checking the phones glued to their palms every thirty seconds in case they missed that one call that would tell them where he was, or better yet, bring him home. 'Actually, I don't have to imagine. It's a feeling I'm more than familiar with.'

Sandra's hand flew to her mouth, the clap loud in the small confines of the Tahoe. Eyes wide, she pried her fingers open enough to whisper a choked apology. 'Oh. My. God. I can't even believe I said that. Of course, you'd know. I mean, holy hell… I heard about how Evan Bishop—Wasn't he…' Her words trailed off into an incomprehensible mumble.

'Yes, he was.' Not wanting to delve into the personal nature of the Bishop case, Alyssa turned the subject to Sandra's family. 'You said earlier that if Hayden had been your brother, nothing would've stopped you from finding him. You have siblings then?'

An awkward silence filled the space between them until Sandra, staring down at her lap, finally responded. 'I did. My brother died from SIDS. It changed my mother. As a result, we weren't very close while I was growing up. And I didn't have the best relationship with my dad, either. I admit I became a bit of a wild child during my teenage years – until a high school resource officer got tired of hauling me out of class for whatever stupid thing I'd done that day and instead stepped in and pulled me to safety. She's the reason I decided to become a police officer, actually. She was the first person to truly believe in me, you know?'

'Yeah, I get that. We're similar in that way. After my brother was kidnapped' – Alyssa paused at the familiar tightening in her chest – 'my own parents stopped paying attention to me.' A memory of her mother as she lay in her bed day after day, ignoring Alyssa's achievements or missteps flashed in her mind. No matter how hard she'd tried, she'd never been able to penetrate that shell her mom had placed around her fragile heart. 'That's why I've made certain that my family, especially my children, know they can always come to me for anything any time. They will always come first.'

'Remember what I said this morning, that I'd heard a lot about you? Well, not to embarrass you or anything, but your devotion to your family – and your team, actually – are legendary.'

Alyssa was more than a little uncomfortable thinking she and her family were a frequent enough topic of conversation that they had become "legendary."

It was time to steer this conversation away from her and back to the case. 'We need to meet with the team and find out what, if anything, the pictures Gabriel Kensington mentioned have to do with his murder and Addis and Emerson's kidnapping.' She flipped a quick sideways glance in Sandra's direction as she added, 'But more than anything, we need to keep Addis and Emerson in the forefront of our minds. While we can find Gabriel and Lydia's murderer and bring that person to justice, we can't bring the two of them back to life. But hopefully, it's still possible to save the girls.'

Sandra stared at the Sandia Mountains as she asked her next question. 'Do you really believe after what we saw at the Kensingtons' that they're still alive?'

It was a good question and one she'd asked herself more than a dozen times, giving Alyssa a good feeling about Sandra's potential as a detective. 'I have to believe that. It's the best way for me to stay focused. If I allow myself to think the worst, I'm not as effective because the way I see it, my subconscious has already decided there's not quite as much urgency.'

Alyssa had never tried to explain this before because she and Cord – and the rest of her team, too – had always just been in sync that way. 'It might sound silly or even superstitious, but it's the urgency that sometimes illumin-ates the path we need to take in any investigation. And what we must never lose sight of is that every moment counts.'

From the corner of her eye, she noticed Sandra's tight grip on the 'Oh shit' handle, and Alyssa realized that while she'd been explaining why she refused to think Addis and Emerson were lying dead somewhere, her voice had risen, her hands had tightened on the wheel, and her foot had pressed down on the accelerator, hurtling them even faster down the road.

Chapter Fourteen

Friday, October 4

At home later that night, Alyssa ignored the vegetables waiting to be chopped for the salad as she scoured the Kensington notes. With her team ascending the ladder of the twenty-four-hour mark concerning the murders and Addis and Emerson's kidnapping, and knowing the chances of locating them alive dropped dramatically with every passing hour, it just wasn't possible for her to think about food right now.

While she tried dissecting the case, Ghost – so named because, according to her son, the pup blended into the darkness, rendering him invisible – leaned against her left calf with one paw pressed on her foot as if holding her in place. When he dropped his head onto her lap and whined, she reached down, absently rubbing his ears. Technically, Ghost was Isaac's Black German Shepherd – his therapist had suggested it would help with his healing after the trauma of being kidnapped – but there was no denying the dog had decidedly attached itself to her, becoming her shadow whenever she was home.

In fact, the only time he preferred Isaac to her was at bedtime. With Ghost curled protectively around him every night, Isaac's nightmares had all but ceased entirely, allowing him to sleep more peacefully throughout the night.

She'd just read through Barbara Carpenter's statement for the third time, trying to decipher what about it made the back of her neck itch, when Ghost's head popped up, ears perked forward, with his tail thwapping against the floor. She didn't have to turn around to know Holly had arrived for dinner.

Knowing she'd be bringing them back out later when the house was quiet again, Alyssa swept the Kensington case notes into a folder and moved them off to the side. 'Hi sweetie.' She tilted her face to the side so her daughter could peck her cheek.

'Hi.' Holly nodded to the abandoned vegetables. 'Were you hoping those veggies would chop themselves?'

'Yes, but they obviously refuse to cooperate.'

Holly moved to the sink, rolled up her sleeves, and washed her hands. 'Where's Dad?'

'In the living room with Grandma.'

'Speaking of which, when can Grandma start driving again? Next week?'

'Two.' Alyssa's mother-in-law, Mabel, had had foot surgery four weeks ago, and so Brock had been escorting her everywhere she needed to go while still keeping on top of his own job.

Holly changed subjects. 'So, Nick sold his sports car.'

Isaac, who had exited the cave known as his bedroom, skated into the kitchen with his best friend Trevor behind him. Overhearing his sister's comment, he swung around so fast, he tripped and fell into a barstool, nearly toppling it over. 'But, but... but *why*? Why would he do that?' he sputtered. He had the look of a teenager who'd just been informed he'd only be allowed to ride a bicycle for the rest of his life.

Since he was a mere three months away from that magical moment in a teen's life when he'd be allowed to get his permit, placing him one step closer to that little slip of freedom called a driver's license, Alyssa knew he'd been pondering the best way to broach the subject of Holly's boyfriend allowing him the use of his car for the driver's test. Now that dream was inexorably crushed.

She had to bite back amusement at her son's reaction, and from the laughter that shined for just a moment in Holly's eyes, she did, too. 'He just did,' she said in answer to her brother's question.

It wasn't her daughter's response so much as the smile that immediately fell from her face that alerted Alyssa that there might be more to the story than she was saying. She waited until Isaac, muttering about dumb adult choices, headed back upstairs with Trevor – who appeared equally traumatized at the news – before she asked Holly what was on her mind.

Holly tilted her head back so that it appeared she was speaking to the ceiling. 'I don't suppose it matters if I say I don't really want to talk about it right now?'

'It matters. But I'm not sure if I believe you. Otherwise, why would you have mentioned it at all?'

Holly rolled her eyes. 'You know, sometimes it just plain sucks having a mom who's good at reading people.'

'Thank you.' Alyssa waited, knowing Holly was gathering her thoughts.

'He sold it because it was a gift from his *mother*, and he and Rachel have both said they want nothing from that woman.' The way Holly sneered the word *mother*, it was clear she wanted to tack something to the end of it.

Alyssa understood where her daughter – and Nick and Rachel, his twin – were coming from. After Rachel had been rescued from the sex trafficking ring, Nina Otis had insisted to Nick that Rachel was to blame for having been taken based purely on the clothes she wore and the parties she attended. At the time, Alyssa had been sickened and appalled at the woman's cold attitude and all-around lack of compassion. Evidently, so were her children, as they should be.

Alyssa peeled the outer skin from the onion she held. 'How are Jersey and Rachel doing anyway? They haven't been over here in a few weeks.' Jersey was another one of Holly's friends who'd been trafficked. She was also the cousin to Holly's best friend, Sophie. The four girls, Holly, Sophie, Jersey, and Rachel, were all renting a large duplex near the university, thanks in great part to Mabel's help, as well as Sophie's parents, Jersey's mother, and Rachel's father all pitching in.

As she studied her daughter's profile, Alyssa found it nearly impossible not to compare what she'd learned about Addis and Emerson's relationship to that of Holly and her friends, or even Isaac and Trevor's.

Once again thinking of the kidnapped girls, Alyssa's mind automatically flashed to the pictures the team had posted on their briefing board, a visual reminder of what was at stake. And along with that came the knowledge that Grace and the Childresses were likely at home battling that ever-present sensation of nerves shredding while waiting for word – praying that word would not be the worst they'd ever receive.

The thought of what horrors the girls could be enduring right this minute distracted her, and she just barely avoided chopping her finger off, instead nicking it. 'Ouch, damn it,' she swore as she turned on the faucet and ran her hand under water. 'I'm sorry. I asked you a question, and then I didn't listen to your answer. I was lost in my case.'

Holly nodded her understanding. 'I figured when you didn't say anything. But to answer your question – again – Jersey's doing okay. She's found a way to avoid going near the duck pond to get to her psych class, which has helped a lot.' It was near the duck pond on campus that Jersey had been drugged, thus beginning her week-long traumatic ordeal. 'She and Rachel still have to leave all the lights on in the house.'

'I imagine that'll take some more time and a lot more healing.' Setting down her knife and wiping her hands off on the dishtowel, Alyssa framed Holly's cheeks in her hands. 'I'm glad you girls have each other.' Silently, she prayed that, somehow, Addis and Emerson were also able to find strength in each other wherever they were.

'Me, too,' Holly said, and it took Alyssa a second to realize her daughter hadn't just read her mind but was talking about her own friends. 'And I'm glad those girls have you and Cord on their case. They have the best. What are their names again?'

'Addis and Emerson.'

'That's right. The district attorney's niece, right? I heard that on the news.'

The conversation dropped when Brock walked into the kitchen, his hand gripped beneath his mother's elbow as he helped her to the table. 'I thought I heard my girl in here.' He kissed the top of Holly's head, then slowly turned in a circle. 'No Nick?' There was only the slightest tightening to his voice, and Alyssa had to duck her head to hide her smile. Her husband was having a little bit of trouble these days adjusting to sharing his 'baby girl's' time with another man.

Holly rolled her eyes good-naturedly. 'No, Dad. He had other plans tonight.'

Just like that, Brock's face lit up. 'Good. That means we get you to ourselves for a while.'

'Yes, you do.' The twinkle bounced back into Holly's eyes as she and Alyssa silently shared their amusement with each other.

–

Nearly two hours later, dinner had been eaten and the dishes cleaned up. Isaac and Trevor had retreated to Isaac's room, still sulking about Nick selling his sports car, and Brock had taken his mother home, leaving Alyssa and Holly alone once more.

Holly tipped her head to the folder Alyssa had been studying when she'd come in. 'I know you can't really discuss the particulars of the leads you have, but if you want to talk things out, I can listen – and be discreet.'

Alyssa knew she was asking not only because she was genuinely concerned, but also because her daughter had decided, after what had happened to her brother in April and her friends in May, to stay in Albuquerque and study criminology, following in her mother's footsteps.

Alyssa sighed. 'I wish I could.'

Holly patted her mom's hands before gathering her keys. 'Just so you know, the offer's not going any place; it's always there – even if you won't take me up on it because you "can't." No matter what, though, I have faith in you, Mom. You'll find them and bring them home to their families.' She kissed Alyssa's cheek. 'I'll text you when I get home. Love you.'

She squeezed her daughter's hand once before releasing it. 'Love you right back.'

Chapter Fifteen

It was nearing ten p.m. Friday night, and Alex counted the steps it took to traverse from the refrigerator to the front door and back again, the fire burning inside growing hotter with every trip. When the key sounded in the lock almost an hour later, the explosion of anger burst through.

'Didn't I tell you last night to stay put? I told you I'd come by as soon as I could and take care of the problem, but when I get here, not only are you not here, but I also haven't been able to reach you all damn day! Where are they? What the hell did you do?' Two fists pummeled Adam's chest before he could fully step through the front door. A sense of satisfaction flowed through Alex when Adam winced and reached up to rub the spot.

Of the two of them, Adam was clearly by far the physically strongest, yet he was too weak mentally to stand up for himself – at least most days. But when Adam spoke calmly through clenched teeth, it became clear that Alex's influence on him was waning. And that couldn't happen. Especially not now.

'I'm not telling you. You'll just have to trust that I' – this time it was Adam's own thumb that jabbed repeatedly into his sternum – 'took care of the problems myself. And

I did it my way.' Uncharacteristically, he refused to avert his gaze, refused to back down under Alex's lethal glare.

Frustration boiled over. 'How? How did you "take care of it," Adam? Are those girls still breathing? Because if they are, you not only didn't take care of a damn thing, you just made the problem one hundred percent worse!'

When Adam remained stonily silent, showing no evidence of a fracture in his steady resolve, Alex whirled around, searching for something to break that wasn't Adam's fool neck.

A rainbow-colored bowl Adam had made for a glass-blowing class was the first casualty. Alex hefted it high before hurling it against the far wall, the shattering sound fueling a more intense rage. Within minutes, an entire cupboard of assorted dishes littered the floor, shards sparkling like glitter under the glow of the kitchen light.

The peace that came from causing the destruction of someone else's belongings lasted only until it was over, and then Alex, nostrils flaring and heaving in great gulps of air, whirled on Adam once again, this time shocking both of them by shoving a gun into his face. The menacing sound of the gun being cocked echoed throughout the room.

The tic in Adam's left eye pulsed rapidly as his face paled and he stumbled backwards, trembling hands raised in surrender. 'Man, what are you doing?'

For several seconds, Alex stared coldly at Adam, then clicked on the safety before setting the gun down. 'I'm sorry. I shouldn't have done that.' Hazel eyes implored Adam to understand. 'I just want to make sure nothing happens to you. Or me. I don't want to go to prison, and you have your NFL career to think about. So, tell me, Adam. Where did you take them? Let me help.'

Chapter Sixteen

Saturday, October 5

Bright and early Saturday morning – well, early, anyway – Alyssa was back at the precinct, along with Cord, Hal, Joe, and Sandra.

At ten after five that morning, when her phone had jolted her awake from a troubling dream in which Sara was desperately treading water and begging Cord to save her, she'd expected her partner to be on the other end, and she'd subconsciously braced herself for bad news. So, when it was Tony's voice in her ear, it had taken her a moment to swim through the confusion of her sleepy brain.

'Hey, Lys. Did I wake you? I'm sorry. I just figured you'd be up already because I know you're an early riser—'

'No problem,' Alyssa said while stifling a yawn. 'I needed to get out of bed anyway. What's up?' Her head had still been muddled from her dream, so it hadn't immediately dawned on her that it wasn't the hour of the phone call that was strange, but that Tony was phoning her at all instead of waiting until he saw her at the station.

'Well, um, listen. I won't be making it in today. I, uh, have a couple things I need to take care of. It's urgent. I called Hammond before calling you, and we agreed that since you've got Falwin, the team won't suffer without me there. I'm real sorry about this, Lys.'

Concern that Tony was calling in during a high-profile case – something he had never done in all their years working together – combined with the tone of his voice had alerted Alyssa that he was keeping something from her. 'Is everything okay, Tony? Do—'

'I'll get in touch later. Again, I'm really sorry.' And then he was gone, leaving Alyssa to stare absently at her screen, consumed with a fresh wave of worry for her teammate.

Swinging her feet to the floor, she'd slogged her way to the bathroom. A quick shower and a to-go cup of java later, she was ready to head to the station, even though she didn't expect the others until six.

However, thanks to Balloon Fiesta traffic, it had taken an extra half an hour to get there, so she'd pulled into the precinct parking lot just ahead of Cord – and the storm that seemed to roll in out of nowhere. The dark clouds hovered menacingly, and she tried to shake the feeling that, coupled with her dream and Tony's phone call, they were a bad omen. No sooner had she climbed out of her SUV and slammed the door, than the first rain pellets hit the top of her head.

'If there's a single guarantee in Albuquerque,' Cord said as the sky suddenly opened up, and the two of them raced up the steps, 'it's that it's going to rain at some point during the first week of October.' Water sprayed everywhere as he shook the wetness from his hair.

He definitely wasn't wrong. 'Like clockwork,' she agreed, leading the way to the conference room where she wasn't the least bit surprised to see Hal already setting up. 'I bet you twenty bucks the storm moves out within the hour and mass ascension will go off without a hitch.'

Cord bent and peeked out the window. 'Nah. Sucker bet.' Then turning to Hal, he said, 'Morning. Can I help?' He pointed to the photographs lying in Hal's lap.

Hal didn't stop pinning the pictures to the bulletin board, simply speaking around one of the pushpins in his mouth. 'That'd be great. Thanks.'

Less than five minutes later, Joe and Sandra joined them. A quick scan of everyone's bleary eyes and slack expressions was enough to tell Alyssa none of them had gotten much sleep last night, and if she understood her team like she thought she did, she knew much of that reason stemmed from a driving desire to locate Addis and Emerson and bring them safely home. Until they did, it was unlikely any of them would be getting much meaningful rest.

Sandra moved to the conference table and pulled out a chair. 'Looks like we're just waiting for Tony, right?'

Alyssa glanced up from what she was doing. 'Actually, Tony called me this morning. He's got some personal things to take care of, so we're it for now.' Mutual concern snaked across the room as Hal and Cord peered at each other before transferring their gazes to Joe. Tony was more than a partner to him; he was his best friend, and the fact that even he hadn't been able to breach the brick wall that had been erected since May was just another reason to add to their worry.

Knowing there wasn't much she could do for Tony until he was ready to share the demons he fought, Alyssa took a drink of her coffee, then cleared her throat. She needed everyone's head in the here and now. 'So, Elizabeth Monroe.' Wanting Sandra to feel like she was definitely part of the team, she waved her arm in the young officer's direction.

Not that she expected anything less, but Alyssa was pleased and impressed by how Hal, Joe, and Cord instantly shifted their attention from her to Sandra expectantly, as if they'd been doing it for years instead of one day.

More exciting was how Sandra smoothly transitioned from observer into informer, as if she, too, had been briefing the team for years. 'We all know Grace Burgess believed one of Gabriel's cases might have led to his murder, and at first, at least where I was concerned, I had my doubts, but what we learned from Elizabeth Monroe *may* support that theory.' For the next twenty minutes, Sandra fielded questions as she gave a rundown on the Monroe interview, ending with, 'Both Lys – sorry, can I call you that? I heard the others, but if you prefer—'

Alyssa was so used to hearing the shortened version of her name that she hadn't even noticed when Sandra did it. 'You're fine. Go on.'

'Anyway, Lys and I both thought it awful peculiar that Hayden Benson's family was none too keen on Ms. Monroe hiring Gabriel Kensington. And soon after he met with Rosalyn Benson, a massacre and a kidnapping take place? Seems a little too coincidental.'

Without looking away from the notes he was scribbling, Cord said, 'We can head out and interview Rosalyn Benson today.' Alyssa wasn't sure if he was referring to the two of them, or if he was including Sandra in the 'we.'

Hal waited to make sure Sandra was finished before jumping in with his own update. 'First of all, Marnie Hanson was right as far as Gabriel's online appointment calendar goes. The last entry I saw on there was for September seventh, and that was just a note for his annual Labor Day barbecue. So, I spent most of last night scouring the financial records on Gabriel Kensington's laptop – good call including that in the search warrant – but so far, I don't see anything out of the ordinary, business-related anyhow. No deposits or massive withdrawals that would raise a red flag. I'll keep digging, just in case. And as far as online footprints go, I'm not getting many hits outside of Mr. Kensington's charities and his private investigation practice.' He tilted his head Joe's direction. 'You're up.'

Joe straightened a pile of papers in front of him. 'I'm afraid I don't have much to add. You know Tony and I went back to recanvass the Kensington neighborhood yesterday evening while Lys and Sandra interviewed Elizabeth Monroe, but we basically got back the same information the officers got Thursday night.'

'What about home security systems?' Cord asked.

'Same. And none of the residents who allowed us access to their footage have cameras directed at the Kensingtons' house. So, that's basically a bust, at least for now.'

'Where are you on getting access to the phone records?' Alyssa asked.

'Still waiting,' Joe growled. 'It's like the phone company doesn't care that we have a double homicidal maniac who likes to kidnap teenage girls running around. I'll contact them again, see if I can light a fire, but so far, they're demanding a warrant for those records, which, as we all know, can take weeks. So, it's a good thing we've at least got the one left on Kensington's desk. Of course, that doesn't really tell us anything about Lydia Kensington's contacts. Regardless, I've already put a call in to Judge—'

Alyssa's phone rang, and she peeked down to see who would be calling before seven in the morning. 'It's Dr. Sharp,' she informed the team as she answered. 'Good morning, Lynn, what have you got for us?'

Across the line, Lynn sighed, and Alyssa could picture the medical examiner's trademark expression of pinching the bridge of her nose with her thumb and forefinger. 'I don't know how much it's going to help. And I want to caution you that these are still preliminary findings.'

'Preliminary, possibly not helpful. Got it. Go. No, wait. Let me put you on speaker first. That way nothing gets lost in the translation.' She pulled the phone from her ear, tapped a button, then leaned it against the whiteboard. 'Okay, you're up.'

Sandra tapped Cord's arm and pointed to one of the yellow legal pads in the center of the table, mouthing a 'thank you' when he scooted both the tablet and a purple pen in front of her. The way her hand whistled across the page reminded Alyssa of her college years when she'd tried to get every single word down that the professor spoke. Thank goodness her roommate had surprised her with a mini recorder and saved her wrist.

The others noticed, too. Hal and Joe both boasted proud smiles as if they'd taught her themselves. As for Cord, he watched momentarily, nodded once, and set his own pen back on the table, content to listen to Lynn and allow Sandra to do the writing. Still, Alyssa would bet a week's supply of her favorite java that he'd be double-checking to make sure she got all the pertinent details.

'Well, Lydia Kensington's death was clearly from the nine-millimeter bullet to her head,' Lynn said.

This wasn't case-breaking info for Alyssa, and by the lack of reaction on everyone else's faces, it wasn't too earth-shattering for them either. Assuming the medical examiner wouldn't have wasted her time calling unless there was something more important to share, she waited.

'Cause of death for Gabriel Kensington came in the form of stab wounds to his chest, in particular, the one that pierced his right lung. However, when I got him on the table, I noticed that the majority of his defense wounds were on his hands and forearms. Now, when a person is stabbed that many times, some of the knife wounds glance off the body as the victim is fighting for his or her life. With Mr. Kensington, there were none of those types of wounds. All the stabbings were pretty straightforward, in and out, center mass with a few exceptions below the ribcage and into the stomach.'

Speaking of stomachs, the contents in Alyssa's swirled in a violent rush as she envisioned Grace's brother lying on the cold kitchen tiles, not yet dead, helpless to do much more than raise his hands in defense.

'So, you might be wondering, why would someone just lie there and allow himself to be stabbed to death? Even in shock, a person's natural instinct would be to fight back. But in Gabriel's case, it's entirely possible he was barely conscious when the knife attack began. And that, Detective, is because he'd also been shot with one nine-millimeter round in the back.'

Alyssa's eyes shifted to the crime scene images still projected onto the wall of the conference room, trying to envision the scenario in her mind. Without asking, Hal zoomed in on Gabriel's corpse. 'So, Gabriel turns to flee after witnessing his wife's murder and is shot in the back for his efforts?'

Cord intuitively picked up where Alyssa was heading. 'Furious, our killer grabs the first thing he can get his hands on – in this case, the marble rolling pin – and bashes Gabriel's skull with enough force that it nearly caves in part of his face.'

Sandra winced but impressed Alyssa when she, too, grasped the thread of the narrative. 'He collapses but is surprisingly still alive and somewhat alert. The killer becomes so enraged at this point that a bullet will no longer suffice, so he grabs a knife from the butcher block on the counter and begins stabbing Mr. Kensington until he's killed him or until the anger fizzles out, whichever comes first.'

'Sounds reasonable. But if you're going with that scenario, I'd say Gabriel's heart stopped long before the stabbings ceased,' Lynn agreed. 'There are still a couple more things I wanted to share with you before I go. After examining the contents of the Kensingtons' stomachs, I can state with a fair amount of certainty that their deaths occurred within an hour or two of what became their last meal. And not to be crass about it, but at least it appeared to be an appetizing one. Steak, broccoli, and some form of berry I'm guessing was either strawberry or raspberry were apparent in both Gabriel's and Lydia's abdomens.'

Alyssa recalled her initial reaction upon entering the Kensington residence Thursday night. The only lingering odor in the air had been that of death. If the Kensingtons had eaten at home, the meal hadn't been prepared there, she was sure of it. Which meant if they could track down a receipt from a restaurant, they could not only narrow down the time of death, they could also potentially review the restaurant's security cameras in case the murders and Addis and Emerson's kidnapping had nothing to do with Kensington Investigations at all. She knew it was a long shot, but crimes had been solved on far less in the past.

'I don't suppose you found a receipt tucked into Gabriel's pocket or wallet, did you?' Alyssa asked Lynn now.

A light chuckle tickled her ear. 'If only it were that simple, right?'

'If only,' Alyssa agreed.

'Before I go, there's something else I want to share. And this is something that *might* be helpful, at least when you begin to gather your list of suspects. In my professional opinion, I believe it's a safe bet that whoever killed Gabriel is either female or a shorter male due to the angle of the blow to Gabriel's head. It came from below which would indicate someone with a smaller stature as opposed to coming from above or level with, which would hint at someone of similar height or bearing.'

Alyssa's gaze swung over to Sandra as she thought of Elizabeth's bandaged hand. She remembered thinking there would likely be more damage if she was the one responsible for the Kensington murders, and while her instincts shouted that Ms. Monroe wasn't personally involved in their deaths, she allowed that she'd been fooled by greater actors in the past.

'Thanks, Lynn. I appreciate the call. Keep us posted, will you?'

'I always do,' Lynn said, 'but I do have one more thing. I pulled several blue strands of hair off Mrs. Kensington, which I assume belong to her daughter, but I'll be sending them off for DNA testing anyway.' She hesitated just a second. 'I'm afraid the lack of physical evidence indicates you're looking for someone experienced in making sure he leaves no DNA behind, which tells me he might've killed before.'

Sandra's head snapped up, her mouth gawping as she shifted her gaze around the room to see if her reaction was out of place. It wasn't.

Though everyone sat up straighter, it was Cord who asked what was on each of their minds. 'Are you suggesting we might be searching for another serial killer?'

Even though she hadn't been the one who'd said it, the words still left a nasty taste in Alyssa's mouth.

Lynn sighed heavily before responding. 'No. But I'm not discounting the idea, either. I'm just sharing my thoughts. But if you care for my opinion, most serial killers are more methodical in their killings, and there's nothing even remotely methodical in the way the Kensingtons were murdered. But then again, I'm a doctor, not a detective. And on that note, I'm going to go. As soon as I have anything else, I'll let you know.' And then she was gone.

It took Alyssa several seconds to gather her thoughts and then prioritize and compartmentalize them before she could share with the others what she was thinking. 'Yesterday, when Sandra and I were speaking with Ms. Monroe, there was a large gash on her hand between her thumb and forefinger.' She pointed to the spot on her hand. 'She explained it away by telling us she sliced it open making dinner. And while I believe there'd be more damage if she was responsible for the carnage in the Kensington home, maybe we should head over there with some follow-up questions.'

'Why not call?' Sandra wanted to know.

It was Joe who answered. 'That's a good question. Short answer is that it's easier to tell if someone is lying or possibly stretching the truth if they're standing right in front of you.'

Alyssa didn't miss the way Sandra's face flushed before she lowered it, mumbling, 'Of course. It's obvious. I should've thought of that.'

Hal patted her hand. 'It's only obvious because you know now. Nothing wrong with asking questions. It's how we all learned.'

Cord pushed back from the table, and catching Alyssa's eyes, cocked his head to the side. She nodded once, and he turned to Sandra. 'Why don't you come with?'

He didn't have to ask twice. Sandra was on her feet and across the room almost before Cord was to the door.

Before they left, Alyssa asked Hal to contact Grace. 'After we meet with Ms. Monroe, we're going to see if we can meet up with Rosalyn Benson. In the meantime, could you see if Gabriel or Lydia had anything to celebrate or if they had a favorite steakhouse they enjoyed. If she can think of one' – she pointed to Joe – 'head over and see if they'll let you go over their security footage from Thursday evening.'

She turned back to Hal. 'Also, see if we can get credit card statements. Or see if you find something in that box of evidence pulled from the house that shows a restaurant receipt. And if none of those options turn up anything, then I guess we'll start checking out all the steakhouses within a fifteen-mile radius of their home and branch out from there if we need to. If anyone gets a hit, call me.' And then she disappeared through the door with Cord and Sandra trailing behind her.

Chapter Seventeen

Saturday, October 5

It was immediately clear to Alyssa when they finally pulled up – Balloon Fiesta traffic was still horrific at this hour of the morning – that Elizabeth wasn't home. Still, the three of them got out and rang the doorbell, but after waiting five minutes, they returned to the vehicle. Undeterred, she tapped her built-in Bluetooth, scrolled through her call log, and dialed Elizabeth's number, listening to it ring five times before going to voicemail.

'Ms. Monroe, this is Detective Wyatt. We've uncovered some important information, and we need to speak to you, so please contact me as soon as you receive this message.' She rattled off her number, tapped the end call button, and pressed her head into the SUV's headrest.

With every possible lead ending in some type of roadblock, the ticking clock in Alyssa's head grew louder as the pressure to find the girls intensified. She knew all she needed was one small crack, just one, and she'd be able to pry the case open. And then she'd be able to bring Addis and Emerson home to their families. She shook her head to erase the idea her team could be bringing home the girls' bodies.

'Could we go interview Rosalyn Benson and then try Elizabeth again afterwards?' Sandra suggested from the back seat.

Cord tapped the side of his head. 'Great minds. I was just about to suggest the same thing, but you beat me to it.'

Alyssa didn't say it, but the thought had also crossed her mind. 'Why don't you give her a call, then? I'll start heading in the general direction of Del Luna, and that way we'll have a head start on getting there.'

'If she agrees to see us,' Sandra said.

Alyssa backed out of Elizabeth's driveway. 'Even if she doesn't. If she's home, we're heading that way.' She hoped Sandra realized her snippy tone was directed at the situation, not at her.

Nearly fifteen minutes later, Rosalyn Benson had yet to answer her phone or call back, and as Cord's finger hovered over the redial button to try again, Hal's name popped up on Alyssa's Bluetooth.

'Hey, Hal. What did you find out?'

Crackling static made him sound like he was talking to them from a spaceship, and she checked to make sure her signal strength was still good. It was, so it had to be on Hal's end.

'Talked to Grace. She gave me the name of two restaurants. One was Gabriel and Addis's favorite; one was Lydia's, so I decided to contact that one first and hit pay dirt. The manager confirmed that the Kensingtons were frequent patrons at their establishment, and they definitely dined there Thursday evening from seven to eight-fifteen. When I asked if he was sure, he said that Gabriel and Lydia came in at least twice a month, always on Thursday. Since he's known them, they've never wavered from that time frame. He said to give him some time to clear it with the owner because they're not actually open right now, but he didn't foresee any issues with us going over their security footage. I wanted to let you know before I sent Joe out.'

'Thanks, Hal. By the way, what restaurant was it?'

'The Ranch Steakhouse.'

'Oh,' Alyssa said. 'We're about three minutes away from there, so we'll just save Joe a trip since Elizabeth wasn't home anyway. Could you go ahead and text me the manager's contact information?'

'You got it. I'll let Joe know.'

After Hal ended the call, Alyssa glanced first at Cord then in the rearview mirror at Sandra. 'Looks like a slight change in plans. Let's go see what we can find out.'

–

Exactly three minutes later, Alyssa parked her Tahoe beside a dark blue Mercedes sporting one of New Mexico's 'Green Chile Capital of the World' license plates. Before she turned off the ignition, she used her Bluetooth to dial the restaurant. The manager answered on the second ring.

'The Ranch Steakhouse, Christopher speaking.'

'Christopher, this is Detective Wyatt with the Albuquerque Police Department. You spoke with—'

'Officer Hal Callum. Yep, yep. You're hoping to check the security footage from Thursday, October third, right?' He didn't wait for a response. 'I just got off the phone with the owner, so give me two minutes, and I'll come unlock the front door for you.'

It only took one before a heavyset man with a balding head and a bad comb-over pushed open the thick wooden door to the restaurant, the lingering scent of garlic and butter flowing out as he did. Nodding to each of them, he invited them in, where Alyssa made the introductions.

Christopher's appreciative perusal of Sandra's body caused two splotchy red circles to bloom on the young officer's cheeks, but Alyssa couldn't tell from her expression if it was from pleasure or disgust, though she could certainly guess. In any case, the man had to be at least two and a half times her age.

After relocking the door, he said, 'Follow me,' and then led them to the back of the restaurant where his office was located. Moving behind his desk, he muttered, 'This'll only take… a… few… seconds.' His fingers flew over the keyboard, typing in some lengthy password that he had taped beneath a paperweight. 'A-ha. There, I'm in.' He thumped his fist on the desk and backed up. 'There you go. If you don't mind, I'm going to grab these receipts and head out to the dining room.' He tossed both hands in the air as if they'd just informed him he was under arrest. 'Unless you need me to stay for legal purposes?'

'That's okay. We'll come get you if we have any questions.'

After another quick scan of Sandra's body, Christopher backed out the door, leaving it ajar, and headed down the short hallway.

Cord was already settling into the chair in front of the computer, his index finger clicking on the mouse as he navigated through the video feed in front of them until he'd rewound to the time Gabriel and Lydia pulled into the parking lot. There he hit pause and waited as Alyssa and Sandra dragged the visitors' chairs around and settled in beside him. But before they could get started, Christopher poked his head back in. 'Sorry to interrupt already, but can I get anyone some coffee?'

Huh. Sleazy or not, maybe the restaurant manager had a few redeeming qualities, after all. 'Please, black,' Alyssa said.

As usual, Cord declined, but when Sandra said, 'Same, thanks,' his eyes practically rolled back in his head. 'No wonder you're both short.'

'Careful there, partner,' Alyssa retorted before she turned to Sandra. 'I knew there was a special reason I liked you.'

When Christopher backed out again, Alyssa cast all joking aside as Cord hit play again.

After parking the vehicle, Gabriel climbed out and moved around to open his wife's door. Though the image was grainy, Alyssa could clearly see Gabriel's lips flatten into a thin line when his wife angrily jabbed the air, almost connecting with her husband's chest. He didn't appear to reply as, grasping her elbow to hold her steady when she wobbled on her high heels, he ushered her to the front door.

Inside the restaurant, the unhappiness etched across their features abruptly morphed into enormous, toothy smiles as they greeted the maître d' who took their coats and led them back to a table in the center of the dining room against a far wall.

Within moments a waiter appeared, a bottle of wine already in hand. Gabriel quickly scanned the label before nodding his head in approval, giving Alyssa the impression that the waiter was familiar with the Kensingtons' choices. After filling their glasses, he placed the bottle near Gabriel's elbow and gave a quick dip of his head before disappearing again.

Neither Gabriel nor Lydia opened their menus, instead pushing them aside, as once again, left only to themselves, their faces returned to the scowls of displeasure they'd been wearing when they'd first arrived.

Christopher cleared his throat, and Alyssa, Cord, and Sandra snapped their necks around. Two steaming cups of coffee sat on a silver tray next to a carafe and a bottled water, presumably for Cord. 'Thank you,' the three of them said in unison as the manager retreated back out the door.

She'd just taken a sip when Sandra let out an excited whoosh of air. Startled, Alyssa jerked back, spilling hot coffee on her hand.

Sandra's finger drummed the screen. 'Is that... Elizabeth Monroe?'

Cord hit pause. Due to the dim lighting of the restaurant and the poor video quality, the picture was dark, but the woman sitting alone three tables away from the Kensingtons was most certainly Elizabeth Monroe.

'Rewind ten seconds and hit play,' Alyssa instructed, scooting to the edge of her seat in an effort to get a closer look.

A tall, lean man entered, his steps faltering when he spotted Gabriel and Lydia, but when Elizabeth waved one slim arm in the air, he strode over and kissed the cheek she offered before sliding into the seat across from her. Clasping one of her hands between both of his, he brought it to his lips.

'Well, I'll be damned,' Alyssa said. 'Unless Ms. Monroe has an identical twin somewhere, that is definitely her.' Instantly, she recalled the strange look that had flitted across Elizabeth's face yesterday when she'd told them about the message Gabriel had left for her. She turned to Cord. 'When we interviewed Elizabeth, she didn't mention being at the same restaurant at the same time.

Why is that? And who is that man with her?' There was something familiar about him, but she couldn't pin her finger on what it was.

'She hasn't looked in the Kensingtons' direction,' said Cord, 'so, it's possible she didn't see him.'

Her partner had a point, even if Alyssa found it difficult to believe.

Five, ten, then fifteen minutes passed, and aside from appetizers being brought out and drinks refreshed, nothing happened. If either party was aware of the other's presence, they made no noticeable gestures to indicate such.

The three of them continued to watch the video in silence. It was not only beyond tedious such that Alyssa had to force her heavy eyes to remain open and vigilant, but it also succeeded in reminding her she was hungry. And the buttery garlic aroma of the kitchen wafting through the vents only made matters worse. On cue, her belly grumbled loudly. One palm moved to cover her abdomen while the other covered a yawn.

Suddenly Cord slapped his hand on the pause button. 'Huh. Tell me who you see now.'

Another man whose profile wasn't clearly visible due to the way he was turned to the side approached the maître d', and after exchanging a few words, the maître d' picked up the phone and spoke briefly into it. The way the man held himself while he waited didn't set off alarms in Alyssa's mind; it set off a series of gongs. Could it really be? 'Is that—is that *Mack* Kensington?'

'Sure looks like it to me,' Cord said. 'In fact, I'd bet a month's salary that it's him.'

Immediately, Alyssa knew what had been making her neck itch last night just before Holly had arrived. Barbara

Carpenter, the flamboyant neighbor who'd been out walking her lavender-colored dog the day Gabriel and Lydia were murdered, said she'd seen 'a tall man about Cord's height with dark brown hair *like Gabriel's* and driving a fancy car.' Though her pulse doubled in speed, her voice was level as she told Cord and Sandra what she was thinking. 'Mack Kensington has hair coloring just like his brother's, is close to your height, Cord, and drives an Escalade. Need I say more?'

'Hot damn,' Sandra breathed out. 'This case just became deeper than a game of Clue. My prediction is the shady criminal defense attorney killed his family in the kitchen with a rolling pin and a nine-millimeter before kidnapping his niece and her best friend.' When neither Alyssa nor Cord joined in her amusement, her laughter died off, and she muttered an apology.

On the video, Mack's gaze drifted down to his watch as he leaned against the maître d's podium, straightening again when a well-dressed gentleman walked out. The two shook hands and exchanged a few words, and then that was it. Even as the probably-Mack walked out, Alyssa noticed he'd never once glanced back in Gabriel's direction. And as Cord had suggested in Elizabeth's case, she had to admit to the possibility that Mack really hadn't known his brother was there.

But even if that were true, if her hunch was correct, and he was indeed the person Ms. Carpenter had spotted with Gabriel Thursday afternoon, it still left her with the question as to why he hadn't mentioned that he'd seen his brother earlier in the day. If they'd been arguing, as Ms. Carpenter had suggested, the obvious answer was that Mack was a lawyer and would know better than to implicate himself. On the other hand, his decision to keep silent placed him on the top of her pitiably short list of suspects.

'So, um…' Alyssa and Cord directed their attention away from the screen and over to Sandra when she hesitated.

'Um, what?' Alyssa encouraged.

'What are the chances that Mack, who lives nearly five hours away, just happened to be in Albuquerque *and* just happened to be at the same restaurant as his brother hours before the man was killed? That's a little too coincidental in my book.'

Cord chewed on the inside of his cheek the way he did when he was mulling something over. 'Could be coincidence. Could be something else. But the man's a big-shot attorney, so if he is somehow involved in fratricide, I can't imagine he'd be so sloppy as to knowingly be seen at the same place as his brother on the night the man was killed. Just doesn't make sense.'

Trying not to let her dislike of the man skew her perception, Alyssa considered the possibility that Mack was involved, that he'd murdered his brother and sister-in-law and kidnapped Addis and Emerson. But why? Something didn't add up. Like the man himself had pointed out, he was smart, and it showed in the way he'd gotten most of his guilty clients acquitted. 'I tend to agree with Cord. Mack knows the ropes, so it stands to reason he'd never be this sloppy.'

Almost as if he was discussing the weather and not a murder case, Cord said, 'On the other hand, remember what Mack said Friday morning about "not all killers being evil"? Like he was trying to defend the person responsible for murdering his brother and sister-in-law and kidnapping his niece and her best friend?'

Sandra shot out of her seat and began to pace. 'Of course! Mack might *normally* be more cautious if he's involved. But think about the crime scene: the ferocity with which Gabriel Kensington was slaughtered painted a picture of someone in a passionate furor, so it's possible he *wasn't* thinking clearly.'

Sandra was so excited, Alyssa hated to burst her bubble by playing devil's advocate. 'I see what you're saying,' she said, 'but there's one problem with that theory – Dr. Sharp mentioned Gabriel was killed by someone of short stature.' She tipped her head at the surveillance footage. 'That description most definitely doesn't fit Mack Kensington. Which isn't to say he's not involved, but with his occupation, we need to tread lightly.'

'Not to mention we don't have a motive yet,' Cord added.

The photograph of a smiling Addis and Emerson standing knee-deep in the Rio Grande, arms around each other, flashed briefly in Alyssa's mind. If it turned out Mack did have the girls, he'd have no choice but to get rid of them. He couldn't afford to do anything else.

As if she'd pulled the thoughts straight from her head, Sandra voiced aloud what Alyssa was thinking. 'If Mack's involved, Addis and Emerson are as good as dead.' She sucked in a deep breath and released it slowly before forging ahead. 'He'd have no choice but to kill them because they'd ruin him.'

Her gaze lit on Cord's face before immediately darting away. 'I don't think he could even risk' – she cleared her throat – 'selling them.' Cord's head snapped around, and Sandra apologized. 'I'm sorry. I'm just thinking out loud. If he does *anything* except kill them, there's always a possibility that they could escape.'

'And then life as he knows it is over,' Cord finished.

A blanket of silence drifted down while they each grappled with what Mack's possible involvement might mean in terms of their investigation. And even though it took quite a bit of willpower not to forego watching the rest of the video in favor of speeding over to Mack's house to demand answers, Alyssa managed. 'Let's finish watching this. Maybe we'll see something else that will tell us we're looking in the right direction.'

Cord reached out and hit resume. At a few minutes after eight, Gabriel pulled out his phone, glanced down, and then typed something before putting it away again. Though Alyssa couldn't hear what Lydia was saying, the tight, pinched look on her face made it clear that she wasn't happy. 'I'm guessing Gabriel just told Lydia about Addis's request to stay with Emerson,' she said.

'The timing fits,' Cord said as Sandra nodded her agreement.

A few minutes later, Gabriel and Lydia paid their tab and headed out, and Alyssa watched Elizabeth Monroe follow their movements. So, she had noticed Gabriel's presence after all. If that was the case, why hadn't she mentioned it last night?

Shortly after the Kensingtons left the restaurant, Elizabeth removed several bills from her clutch and tossed them onto the table before she and her partner headed out. They disappeared from view of the cameras shortly after exiting the building and heading in the opposite direction of the parking lot.

An undercurrent of *WTF?*, as the kids liked to say, had Alyssa's nerves zinging almost painfully as an unpleasant thought entered her mind and refused to budge. Could Mack Kensington and Elizabeth Monroe both be involved? It didn't make sense, but she couldn't discount the idea altogether.

'So, naïve question maybe, but can we get a search warrant for Mack's house and vehicle?' Sandra's question distracted Alyssa from her own unvoiced concern.

Cord was already shaking his head. 'Based on what? That he was at a restaurant the same night his brother was killed? That he fits the general description of someone Gabriel was seen arguing with hours before his murder? No way we'll secure a search warrant on anything as flimsy as that. The man's a Class A criminal defense attorney. He'll have that blocked before we finish uttering the words. Circumstantial "evidence" might be piling up, but it's not enough for a warrant. We're going to need a hell of a lot more to go on – not to mention a motive, as I said earlier – before we'll get any judge to issue even the most minor of warrants.'

Abruptly, Alyssa shoved her chair back and strode to the door. 'I'm going to grab the manager to see if he recognizes the gentleman with Elizabeth or the man I'm certain is Mack.'

'While he's in here, we might as well find out if he knows who Mack was talking to, as well,' Cord said to Alyssa's retreating back. She waved her hand in the air to let him know she'd heard.

A minute later, she returned with Christopher in tow, glad to see Cord had already rewound the video. 'Do you recognize any of these people?'

Christopher stepped closer and bent at the waist, studying the individuals frozen on the screen. 'Well, that's the restaurant's owner.' A manicured fingernail tapped the screen on the face of the man who had come out to speak to Mack. 'But as for the other two, nope. Don't recall ever having seen either one of them before, but that doesn't mean they've never been here. They're just not regulars. In fact, if I didn't know Mr. Kensington and his wife were already seated at their favorite table, I might actually mistake this one for Gabriel.'

'*Dark hair like Gabriel's*' and '*I might actually mistake this one for Gabriel*' may not be the strongest connections Alyssa had ever had, but they were worth pursuing, if for no other reason than to cross Mack off her list of suspects. Besides, her gut wouldn't let go of the idea that both Mack Kensington and Elizabeth Monroe knew far more than either of them was admitting. One way or another, she intended to find out what that was.

Because Addis and Emerson's lives could hinge on unearthing the truth – and fast.

Chapter Eighteen

Saturday, October 5

At some point during the night, the girls drifted into another heavy sleep brought about by the effects of the drug still lingering in their systems. Addis didn't even remember closing her eyes when she was suddenly startled to alertness by Emerson's jerky thrashing and horrified cries as she tried to dislodge whatever scampered across her chest.

'Oh God, Get it off me! Get it off me!'

In her effort to avoid whatever was attacking Em, Addis realized her best friend was hallucinating. 'There's nothing there. Nothing's on you, Emerson.' She pushed the assurance past a tongue swollen from horrid dry mouth and through the tightness in her throat.

Before Addis's words could penetrate the panic, Em banged herself against the wall, shifting back and forth like she was trying to saw her body in half. At the same time, her legs seemed to come alive with a mind of their own as they began kicking and shaking.

Pain swelled in Addis's chest as she watched, helpless. 'Em, what is it? Oh my God, what's wrong?' If Emerson was even aware of her presence, it didn't show as she continued thrashing around like the young girl in *The Exorcist*.

'Ah, God, I itch everywhere.' Em's wails were amplified in the cramped space.

Magically, as if the word itself could transfer the symptom to her, every nerve beneath Addis's skin tingled like she'd been bitten by a thousand mosquitoes all at once. At the same time, nausea churned through her gut.

'What's happening?' She couldn't be certain she'd asked the question out loud, or if it had joined the silent screams in her head.

Addis Penn Kensington, you need to take a deep breath and calm down. The voice might've belonged to Aunt Grace or her father, but it didn't matter because it managed to stab through the splintering grip of terror that had wormed its way into the very center of her being. She sucked in a steady breath through her nose and exhaled through dry, chapped lips the way Aunt Grace had always taught her to do.

In a brief snap of clarity, she recognized she and Em were likely suffering the side effects of whatever drug they'd been given, but understanding that offered no relief.

'How long can a person survive without food?' Addis was so swamped in her own misery that she wasn't even aware Em had stopped thrashing about.

The mere mention of food was enough to induce the sharp spasms that snaked their way across her digestive tract. Hunger and thirst warred for first place, so in a last-ditch effort to retain her tenuous hold on sanity, she forced herself to think back to her biology class. 'Mr. St. Peters said the average person can survive without food for thirty days, possibly forty, as long as they're well-hydrated.'

'What's well-hydrated?' Emerson's scratchy throat was getting worse.

'We're not. That's all I know,' Addis said. No use denying it. 'And since we can't manage to stay awake, there's no telling how long we've even been here. It could be days already.' Through the sudden silence, she was sure she could hear the *lub dub* of both hers and Emerson's thumping hearts.

'Do you still have that piece of glass or whatever?'

As soon as Em asked, Addis realized she'd forgotten all about it. Somewhere between hearing the vehicle they were convinced belonged to their kidnapper bumping along the road and conking out again, she'd dropped it, and now the uncomfortable bump beneath her thigh nudged her, almost as if it were telling her it had hidden itself. It took some maneuvering, but she finally managed to squeeze her fingers around it.

Behind her, Emerson wriggled, grunting as she adjusted her body. 'Hand it to me. I'll free you first – don't argue; we don't know how much time we have.'

Addis couldn't stop the crooked curve that bent her lips up. Even mired in the depths of a nightmare, her best friend could still read her mind. It took some dexterity to convince her stiff fingers to cooperate as she passed the shard of glass over.

She sank her teeth deep into her bottom lip as Em awkwardly sawed, jiggled, yanked, and pulled at the rope binding her arms to her sides. With each tug, the old rope rubbed and burned her sensitive skin to the point she no longer felt the itchiness, her hunger, or her thirst.

'Sorry, sorry,' Emerson cried each time Addis twitched.

Even though she spoke through clenched teeth, she muttered. 'It's okay.'

Em's panting grew louder and more labored as she seesawed the glass back and forth. Suddenly, her movements slowed. 'Ad? Do you suddenly have four fuzzy arms?'

If Em's words hadn't been uttered in a drunken slur, Addis would've thought she was kidding. Electric shock zipped along her skin. 'What's wrong?'

'Um, I think I need a second. I'm super dizzy, and I don't want to accidentally turn your appendages into one.'

'Here, I'll work on—'

'No, can't,' Em mumbled. 'Lips numb. Fingers tingle.' Emerson's head dropped to Addis's shoulder.

'Em!'

'I'm 'kay. Just… second.'

In an effort to keep calm, Addis recited the alphabet in English and Spanish, forwards and backwards and then practiced counting to one hundred in Spanish, as well. Just as she reached eighty-seven, Emerson's head lifted enough to lean against Addis's temple, and then the determined yanking resumed.

An interminable amount of excruciating tugging later, Addis was seconds away from begging Em to stop, admitting that she could no longer endure the blistering, agonizing burn. Instead, she held her breath, knowing deep in her soul that her best friend felt her pain as surely as if it were her own skin being tortured.

To distract herself – or to add to the torment – she closed her eyes and imagined a juicy cheeseburger piled high with green chile, pickles, and tomatoes and did her best to garner even the tiniest bit of spit for the sake of giving herself any amount of moisture to alleviate her gnawing thirst.

It wasn't until the warped wooden door scraped against the floor, followed by heavy footsteps plodding across the room that Addis realized she hadn't been hallucinating moments earlier when she thought she'd heard tires crunching over gravel.

Both girls froze when the door lifted, letting in a gloomy kind of light. Their kidnapper's eyes flickered over the two of them as, without a word, he produced more of the white pills and one bottle of water which he uncapped.

Then he lowered himself to his knees, and with muffled grunting, gripped Addis's ankle and dragged her forward. A howl of pain and fear burst from a primal place inside of her that she wasn't even aware she had. Twisting her body back and forth, she tried to loosen his grip, and in doing so managed to kick his chin before knocking over the bottle of water.

Rage, swift and fierce, engulfed the man as he released Addis's leg in favor of backhanding her across the face and snagging a handful of hair before she could fall back. Stars swimming in a person's vision was a real thing, she learned.

Engorged purple veins throbbed on the side of his face as he screamed in hers. 'Is that how you repay me for not letting Alex kill you?' Spraying spittle flew from his mouth. Yank. 'Are you listening to me? One word, and you'll both be dead! Is that what you want? And it won't be my fault this time.' He thrust her away from him and pushed himself to his feet, marching a yard one way and then back again, deep breaths sawing in and out as he wrenched handfuls of his own hair.

Abruptly, he stopped, legs spread over her. Squeezing her eyes tight, Addis prayed, selfishly, that if they had to die, she'd go first because she couldn't bear to witness her best friend's murder. When the expected blows never arrived, she risked peeking.

Sweat peppered the man's face as he towered above her, his eyes searching for something on the floor. Unable to stop herself, she traced the crevices along with him. She spotted it the same time he did – two white pills winking in one of the cracks. His glare promised retribution if she dared do anything, and Addis believed him. She willed herself to be still as he retrieved them.

'Open!' Not bothering to wipe the dirt, hair, and other foreign objects off, he placed a tablet on her tongue and tipped the now nearly empty water bottle just enough for the moisture to wet her tongue and throat so she could swallow. She gagged as the pill dissolved in her still dry mouth. At the same time, the droplet of water sent spasms shooting painfully through her stomach as her thirst was reawakened.

'Get over here.' It took Addis a moment to comprehend the order was directed at Emerson.

Tears and snot trickled down her face as she cricked her neck in an effort to send any strength she might have to her best friend, but Em's wide-eyed gaze never wavered from the floor as she awkwardly scooted out of the crawl space.

Her head had barely cleared when the man leaned over and with one hand yanked Em's head back while the other squeezed her jaw until her mouth opened. Then he dropped the pill to the back of her throat, growling when it appeared Em might vomit. He tipped the remaining water, but from what Addis could see, most of it hit Em's lips.

Rising back to his full height, he swiped one hand across the back of his neck before cradling his head like a vise. Then out of the blue, one booted foot kicked out, landing squarely on Addis's thigh, eliciting a muted, choked cry of pain.

'Not my fault. Not my fault. Your fault!' The muttered but frenzied claim was recited like a bad song stuck on the same lyric.

More than she'd ever wanted anything, Addis wished she could reach out and hold Emerson's hand. That was until a sudden strong breeze blew across her face, and she realized the front door was open. The urge to run gnawed like a dog with a bone, but she knew she'd never make it five steps, and there was no way she'd abandon her best friend anyway.

Instead, she stared longingly, seeing nothing but a forest of trees beyond the front stoop, telling her that they were in a mountainous area – which, actually, told her absolutely nothing.

The sudden silence that knocked Addis away from the dream of escaping was replaced by the grating sound of the man's booted feet scratching against the floor. Shivers ran a marathon up her spine and settled at the base of her neck, the tiny hairs there standing out.

The scraping stopped in front of the crawl space. 'Get in,' he ordered.

Unaware she was going to do it, Addis found herself pleading for something more to drink. 'Please, water,' she managed to croak out through her fear.

What she thought was a shadow of regret shaded the man's eyes, but she knew it was more likely anger at her for having spilled most of what he'd brought. Just when she thought he'd deny them, he picked up the discarded bottle from the floor and retreated around the corner. Rattling pipes creaked, and then he was back. Addis did her best to ignore the cloudy color, as well as the bits of debris floating in the water, as the man knelt before her and waited for her to tip her head back so he could allow her to drink. He only allowed her half before giving the rest to Emerson.

Once again, he rose to his full height and discarded the empty water bottle by tossing it somewhere behind him. Pointing, he ordered, 'Time to go back in.'

As they inched themselves backwards, Addis was aware that whereas the crawl space was at first the place of her nightmares, she much preferred it to being out in the open with the unpredictability of a crazed killer.

Before shuttering them back into darkness, he said, 'Don't worry; I gave you more fentanyl, so you'll be zoned pretty soon.' The door dropped back into place with a boom.

Addis drew her legs up. With each *tick-tock* of time passing, her brain and body betrayed her desire to stay awake and alert. She wanted to move, but her limbs were glued to the ground. How was it possible to feel both sluggish and like her heart was about to explode from her chest? Just before unwillingly tumbling back down the rabbit hole, her jumbled mind drifted from 'Who's Alex?' back to the assembly on drugs the student body was forced to attend every year.

The keynote speaker's voice had endlessly droned on about how fentanyl was fifty times more potent than morphine, the side effects could be more intense and last longer, and the craving for more could quickly eat at their every waking moment.

All of which begged the question: would this be the time she and Em would be out for good? Would they die before Aunt Grace could save them?

Chapter Nineteen

Not even eleven in the morning, and Alyssa was already feeling like she'd worked a twelve-hour shift. Trapped in the knowledge of the horrible things humans were capable of doing to others, she tried unsuccessfully not to imagine the various types of hell Addis and Emerson could be experiencing right this moment. In what she recognized as a twisted kind of logic, she also fervently prayed they were still alive, even if it meant they were suffering.

Images of Jersey Andrews, Rachel Otis, and all the other victims she'd encountered over her years on the force flitted unfettered through her memory. It took Cord's hand on her arm to bring her back out of her head.

'Lys, you okay?' His voice was low, as if Sandra couldn't hear the question from the back seat.

Mildly embarrassed though she knew she had no reason to be, Alyssa assured her partner she was fine. 'Yep, just playing with the angles of this case, trying to see which paths will lead to a common road.'

Since neither Elizabeth nor Rosalyn had yet to return their calls, nor had they answered when Cord had tried again, Alyssa had made the decision to confront Mack. Years of experience and dealing with all types of person- alities told her not to let him know in advance that they were coming which is why she'd stopped Cord when he'd pulled out his phone to do just that. Stopping in front of a Spanish-style home with vine-shrouded pergolas, she eyed the red RAV4 parked in the driveway.

Cord pointed. 'Isn't that Grace's car?'

'Sure is. This ought to be fun.' Predicting the volatility of what was to come, considering why they were here, as well as the contentious relationship between the siblings, Alyssa's voice dripped with sarcasm.

Steps away from the front door, she could already hear Grace and Mack shouting over one another, adding credence to her prediction. Stilling Cord's hand when he lifted it to knock, she shook her head, openly eavesdropping.

'I mean it, Mack! I want to know what the hell you thought you were doing going over to Gabe's office?' Grace growled.

'I already told you I didn't take anything.' In contrast with Grace's heated tone, Mack's voice was cold and calm.

'A technicality based on the virtue of the search warrant served. What right did you have?'

In Grace's most passionate discourses during trials, Alyssa had never heard such venom and frustration from the district attorney.

'I don't owe you any kind of explanation, *sister*. And please, allow me to point out the obvious – Gabe and I were *real* brothers. You were just a toss-in to the family.'

'Ouch. That was brutal,' Alyssa murmured at the same time Sandra gasped. 'I think it's time to announce our presence before we witness a crime ourselves.'

Cord rang the bell.

Steam was practically spiraling from Mack when he flung the door open. But it was the hope mingling with fear dancing across Grace's face when she saw them that Alyssa zeroed in on.

'Addis? Emerson?'

'Not yet.' Two words, but guilt burrowed deep inside her as devastated helplessness stretched from Grace's mouth to her eyes. Alyssa shifted her attention to Mack. 'Mr. Kensington, something's come to our attention, and we're hoping you'll be able to clear things up.'

Mack crossed his arms across his chest and curled his lips into a sneer. Remaining silent, he arched one brow and waited.

Cord kicked the questioning off with a statement. 'You were in town Thursday when your brother and his wife were murdered.'

'I already told you that.' Slowly, Mack lifted his glare from Alyssa to Cord with a brief pause on Sandra hovering behind them.

'When did you get to town, and where did you have dinner that night?'

A split second of confusion marred Mack's good looks before he realized where this impromptu interview was headed. He leveled a narrow glower at Cord. 'Are you seriously insinuating that I had something to do with my brother's murder simply because your department is incapable of doing its damned job?'

Cord didn't so much as blink beneath the snarling tirade, and Mack turned his wrath toward Alyssa. 'Gabriel and Lydia were slaughtered in their home, my niece and her best friend have been missing since Thursday night, and you have done damned near nothing to solve this case and bring them home. I thought you were supposed to be the best! Clearly, Albuquerque's version of *best* is a pretty low standard of achievement.'

Partly because she understood where his anger stemmed from and partly because he was right about them getting nowhere, Alyssa allowed the personal attack.

Behind him, Grace's voice was tired more than demanding. 'Christ, Mack, just answer the question.'

Her brother spared one quick disgusted leer over his shoulder before facing Alyssa once more. 'You forget, Detectives, that I'm one of the greatest criminal defense attorneys this state has ever had, so I deal with your kind day in and day out. I know how this works. You fail to do what the good citizens pay you to do and so you find a scapegoat to pin the crime on. Well, it won't work for you this time, I can promise you that.'

Alyssa arched her brows. She was willing to let some things go, but this wasn't one of them. 'You know, Mr. Kensington, what I noticed is that nowhere in that god-like status you've created in your own mind regarding your abilities was an answer to the question. Why is that? Were you hoping to deflect?' The heat of his anger nearly singed her when he stepped into her space.

'Back up,' Cord's tone was a warning that the defense attorney must have decided was one worth heeding because he actually obeyed the command.

'I had dinner at Antiquity with a former client. I'll be happy to give you her information so you can verify that. And just to prove she's not giving me a false alibi, I still have the receipt to prove it.' He was already whipping his wallet out of his pocket so he could thumb through slips of paper until he found the receipt in question and thrust it at Cord, thumping him in the chest with it as he did.

Cord peeked at the date and time, nodding at Alyssa as he handed it back. 'Now, what about the Ranch Steakhouse? What were you doing there Thursday night?'

The shock on Mack's face was either genuine or he really was a master actor. 'How do you know about that?'

Alyssa sidestepped his question with one of her own. 'Were you aware Gabriel and Lydia were there that night?'

'No, I wasn't. I was there to speak to the owner, and I was there less than five minutes. Something tells me you already know that, though, and you're simply harassing me. That being said, don't bother asking what business I had because it has no bearing on this investigation.'

Mack squared his shoulders. 'Now, if you're finished quasi-interrogating me, then maybe you can get on with finding the person actually responsible. And while you're at it, maybe you can find Addis and Emerson before it's too late for them, too. If it isn't already.' Aside from a narrowing of his eyes, he gave no indication he'd heard Grace's horrified gasp.

'Mr. Kensington, we're not interrogating anyone, quasi or otherwise. We're trying to get some answers, and sometimes that means asking the hard questions. I'd think you, of all people, would get that. After all, don't you want us to arrest the *right* culprit?' Alyssa countered in a tone as even as Mack's was confrontational.

Her comment was greeted with a derisive snort.

Whereas Sandra had stood back and observed, Grace waded into the fray by stepping around her brother. Eyes shimmering, she said, 'Do what you need to do, Detectives, just do it fast, and bring the girls home to us.'

'On that we can finally agree,' Mack said as he made to close the door.

Alyssa stopped it with her foot. 'One more thing, Mr. Kensington. What were you and Gabriel arguing about in his driveway on Thursday?' Considering they didn't really know it had been Mack that Barbara Carpenter had seen that afternoon, she asked the question on a hunch.

For all his bluster, Mack was unable to hide an expression of shock. 'If you have any further questions for me, Detectives, you can talk to *my* attorney.' With that, he shut the door in their faces.

—

They'd just left Mack's when Rosalyn Benson finally returned Cord's call. While her response could be described as anything but enthusiastic, she still agreed to meet with them that afternoon. After settling on a time, Alyssa drove through a fast-food restaurant and bought green chile cheeseburgers and fries for everyone. While they were waiting for their food, Sandra offered a suggestion.

'Since you have a little time before you head out to Ms. Benson's, you could drop me off at the precinct so I can help Joe and Hal. That way, I can continue trying to reach Elizabeth Monroe. And if I do happen to get ahold of her, Joe and I can go together to reinterview her. She's already met me, so she might be more comfortable if I'm there, too. But that's just an idea.'

'I like that plan.' Pride crept into Alyssa's voice, and she shared a smile with Cord, knowing from his expression that he, too, was pleased at how Sandra seemed to fit in so seamlessly with their tight-knit group. She had no doubt the young officer would be a huge asset to whatever team she ended up with, even theirs.

At quarter to two, after dropping Sandra off, Alyssa and Cord pulled up to a rambling ranch in Del Luna, NM, a small farming community forty miles to the south of Albuquerque that touted more barns and tractors than houses or people. A curtain flicked to the side, and a towheaded boy's face popped into view, followed by a younger, female version of him from the other side of the window.

Where the boy scowled, a look of distrust already present in his youthful features, the little girl's smile was bright and orange-stained. She waved until the boy turned and said something that caused her grin to droop into a frown before she disappeared out of view.

'Well, maybe at least one of them will be happy to see us,' Alyssa quipped as they made their way up the worn gravel path, avoiding a bicycle, a Big-Wheel, and various other items in what resembled a bizarre obstacle course to the front door.

Just as Alyssa raised her hand to knock, a frazzled woman carting a toddler on her hip opened the door. Chewing on a pacifier, the child wound a hand through the woman's thick hair as her bright blue eyes studied the strangers at the door.

'You must be Detectives Wyatt and Roberts. I'm Rosalyn, but you can call me Ros. Please, come in but excuse the mess.' Then twisting halfway around, she changed her mind. 'On second thought, let's talk out here on the porch. My house resembles an F-5 tornado or category three hurricane, take your pick.'

Cord chuckled as he stepped back out of the way, giving Rosalyn room to maneuver enough to close the front door after yelling to the kids not to kill each other or draw blood while she was outside. 'Looks like you definitely have your hands full with three little ones.'

'Yes, I do. Thank God one of them goes home later this afternoon.' She tilted her head to the toddler attached to her hip. 'I'm babysitting for a friend. I forgot how fascinating little ones find every single thing. And how anything they touch can turn into their idea of art. Like a can of mousse sprayed all over the toilet or a brand-new tube of lipstick used on the wall to draw me a picture of what I'm fairly certain she called a doll.' She smiled indulgently at the little girl as she bent and kissed the soft wisps of hair plastered to the child's head.

'But you're here to speak about Hayden's disappearance. And I'm rambling because it's been quite some time, and my family's gotten so used to everyone insisting he ran off. And now my mother's health is failing, and I'm afraid of what this will do to her...' She inhaled deeply, releasing a shaky breath. 'And I'm rambling again.' She waved one hand to two chairs opposite a porch swing, which she sat in. 'Please sit. It'll make me far less nervous. I think. Or maybe it won't.'

Perching on the edge of the water-stained cushions, Alyssa couldn't help but think that, to her eyes and ears, Rosalyn Benson didn't read like the type of person who wouldn't want to explore any and every avenue of her brother's disappearance.

No sooner had Cord situated himself beside her, than the toddler flopped forward as she held her tiny little arms out to him. Pushing her pacifier to the side, she said, 'Hode!'

Rosalyn pulled her back even as Cord's hands automatically reached out to catch the little one. 'She wants you to hold her. Bobbie Jo, stay here with Auntie.'

'Down. Hode!' Bobbie Jo insisted.

Whether it was because he wanted to get down to business or because he thought the tyke was too adorable to resist, Cord said, 'I don't mind holding her while we speak, as long as you're okay with it.'

After a second of consideration, Rosalyn sighed and released the little girl, helping as she flipped onto her belly and slid off the swing, toddling over to Cord with outstretched arms. 'Hode,' she demanded again.

He is so toast when his twins arrive, Alyssa thought as she watched her partner bounce the little girl on his leg and smile down at her efforts to play peek-a-boo. Turning back to Hayden's sister, she said, 'Why don't you begin by telling us what you remember about your brother's disappearance.'

Rosalyn's eyes shifted to a wall of trees separating her yard from a neighboring field. With a faraway look and a moccasin-clad foot pushing the swing into a gentle sway, she began. 'It was a Friday. April thirteenth.' A laugh that fell far short of humorous drifted off with the breeze. 'The irony, of course, is exactly how much Hayden loved his horror flicks. I can't tell you how often he dressed up as Freddy or Jason or Michael for Halloween, as a child or even as a teenager staying home to hand out candy. It's like there were never any other options out there.'

Happiness, love, and indulgence shone through her words as she relayed her memory of that night, holding even the wiggly toddler captivated.

'All I know for sure is he ran out to put gas in his car and run a couple errands before he picked Beck – sorry, Elizabeth – up. It wasn't until later we learned that the two of them were planning on taking off to hide out until she turned eighteen on May first so they could elope. When he left, I asked him to bring me back a strawberry Charleston Chew because I knew he thought they were disgusting. He shouted back, "Gross," and that was the last anyone ever saw or heard from him again.' One knuckle reached up to dab away the dampness from her eyes.

'No one really thought much of him not coming back right away because, for all of my brother's wonderful traits, he flat-out sucked at being on time for anything but his sports-related events. We just assumed time slipped away while he was out running errands and he'd decided not to come home before his date. It wasn't until Beck called us – you'd think I'd remember what time it was since it was the moment our lives changed, but I don't. She asked if we knew where he was because he never showed up at the library where they were supposed to meet. Later, when I replayed that conversation in my head, I think she was scared he'd changed his mind.'

Rosalyn's gaze narrowed into tiny slits, shifting the lines from around her mouth up to her eyes. 'If she'd told me then what they were planning, I could've told her Hayden took his responsibilities very seriously, and that there was no way he'd ever skip out on her and their child. As it turns out, that's exactly what the police decided.'

A glower so full of heat Alyssa could almost feel the burn was one more thing that didn't paint the portrait of a woman who would simply let her brother's disappearance fall by the wayside.

'Seven years later, I'm still stunned how quickly the police blew us off, insisting Hayden just vanished. After the police searched his room and spotted a half-packed suitcase, my parents noticed two more suitcases missing, along with most of Hayden's clothes. The police asked if he had any reason to run off, and we told them absolutely not. Then when we told them about Beck, they drove over to her house and questioned her. She confessed she was pregnant and that they were planning on running away, and after a thirty-second, rudimentary "search" for his phone and car, they closed the case, saying he wasn't a runaway since he was eighteen, but labeling him a guy capable of abandoning his family and the girlfriend carrying his child.' Her voice was steady and assured as she said, 'I promise you: that was not who my brother was. Even when he got into trouble as a little boy, he never tried to wriggle his way out of it.'

Alyssa was curious about something. 'You said your brother's suitcases were gone and another half-packed, and the police still closed the case as a willful disappearance. Did any of the authorities question why he would've walked away without the final suitcase, at least?'

'Pfft. Not only did they not question it, they refused to listen when we brought it to their attention. They actually looked my parents in the eye and suggested that we hire a private investigator if we were so unhappy with their findings. Like it was the movies. There was no way we could afford to hire anyone, much less a private someone. Stupid, uneducated assholes.' The words muttered under her breath were still loud enough for Alyssa and Cord to hear. 'I'm so sorry. I didn't mean that as an insult to you. I'm, it's just, Del Luna's police force has more than a little something to be desired.'

Alyssa must've missed the memo that came out stating today was *Bash the Authorities Day*. 'No offense taken. Speaking of private investigators, why don't you tell us about your meeting with Gabriel Kensington and why you weren't thrilled when Elizabeth hired him?'

Either Rosalyn Benson was an Academy Award-worthy actress, or she had no idea what Alyssa was talking about, which shot all kinds of holes in her theory that the

Benson family was somehow involved in the murders or Addis and Emerson's kidnapping.

'I never met with Mr. Kensington. He left a message indicating he wanted to, but it never happened. And then I saw on the news—And why would I not be thrilled that Beck was having someone open the investigation into Hayden's disappearance? That makes absolutely no sense. I'm not sure where she even got that idea. Maybe she was projecting what she *thought* or what she was afraid of?'

'You did seem hesitant, though, when I asked about meeting with you today,' Cord pointed out.

Rosalyn's feet pushed the swing back into a gentle sway. 'Ah, yes, that much is true.' She lifted her chin and met Cord's steady gaze. 'That's because I wasn't sure if my mother would be here. Right now, she's in an assisted living facility, and sometimes, in her more lucid moments she enjoys hanging out at the house with me and the kids.

'My whole life, that woman was the definition of rock solid – until Hayden vanished. Then her mental and physical stability nosedived, especially after Brandon was born. Even as a baby, he looked so much like his father, our hearts felt like they were being crushed in a vise anytime we got to see him. One day after Elizabeth had brought him by for a few hours, I found Mom curled up in her closet, clutching a picture of Hayden. The grief pouring out of her – as long as I live, I'll never forget that piercing animal howl. She just kept repeating, "I can't do it. I can't." Later, she confessed she'd frightened herself because she'd gotten angry that Brandon wasn't Hayden. She was terrified she'd lose her mind and hurt him.'

Rosalyn pulled a tissue from her pocket and wiped her eyes, then her nose. 'I used to judge her for that because the very reason she couldn't bear to be around Brandon was the reason I *needed* to be. My dad's death a year later exacerbated Mom's decline in health, and I finally began to understand. I'm telling you all this because, had today been one of those days when she wanted to hang out, well, yes, I was hesitant to meet with you because I was afraid of dragging her through it all again.'

That type of reasoning, that level of protection for one's family, tapped into Alyssa's wheelhouse of understanding. Without a doubt, she would've reacted the same way. 'What about your older brother? How can we get ahold of him?'

She hadn't even finished the question before Rosalyn nearly gave herself whiplash shaking her head no. 'You're a day late. He was in town for a couple of days, but he left yesterday on a hunting expedition, and he'll be gone for two weeks. No cell service.'

'What do you do in case of an emergency?' Cord pried the hair curling around his ears from Bobbie Jo's sticky fingers. She promptly popped her pacifier back in her mouth and burrowed her downy head in the crook of his neck.

Tiny butterflies danced inside Alyssa's chest when he kissed the top of Bobbie Jo's head, the warmth from his smile enough to heat a small room.

'Nothing. He finds out when he returns,' Rosalyn said in response to Cord's question.

Talking about Rosalyn's brother reminded Alyssa of the mystery man they'd seen on the video at the Ranch Steakhouse. 'Do you know if Elizabeth was dating anyone?'

Rosalyn didn't miss a beat. 'If she was, she didn't mention it to me. But we don't really have that kind of friendship. If it weren't for the mini-Hayden known as Brandon, I doubt we'd be in contact at all.'

'We're almost finished here, but before we go, could you tell us a little about Hayden's friends? Elizabeth said she didn't know them well.'

'She didn't. She was always so paranoid her parents would discover she was dating Hayden that she even hated hanging out here with us. When they did, they rarely left his room. And *friends* is a loose interpretation for the few people Hayden associated with. For as popular and athletic as he was, he didn't particularly gel with the arrogant attitudes of the other guys. His best friend was Marcel Gutierrez, and he died just over three years ago from cancer. Aside from that, it was a few stragglers here and there.'

'What about girlfriends?' Cord asked.

Rosalyn shook her head. 'He dated, but until Beck, never anyone even remotely serious. It was more about having a fun time with someone he also happened to kiss – or more. His "relationships" generally lasted about a couple weeks, and after the inevitable break-up, he always managed to stay friends with the girls. It was the wildest thing.'

She knocked on the window behind her. When her son's head popped up, she waved him outside. He was still wearing the same scowl when he poked his head out the door, waiting.

'Would you grab the picture I put on the coffee table a while ago and bring it to me, please?'

'Why?'

Rosalyn narrowed her eyes. 'Because I want it, and you're right next to it.'

'Fine.' He disappeared, reappearing again a few seconds later when he cracked the screen open and stretched his arm as far as it would go so he wouldn't have to actually step foot outside.

'Thank you.' She rolled her eyes and snapped the picture out of his small hand and offered it to Alyssa.

The youngster retreated back inside the house without a word, and Alyssa decided that must've been his way of saying, 'You're welcome.'

Rosalyn pointed at the picture. 'I had a brief stint where I was digging photography as a career choice, and that was one of my favorite pics. I have another copy, so you can have that one, if you'd like.'

A field of flowers just beginning to bloom, along with the way the trees in the background were still growing their new leaves, indicated the picture had been taken some time in the spring. Elizabeth was cradled into Hayden, smiling up at him with something akin to, yes, hero worship. In turn, he was gazing down at her, the pure joy of young love pouring from his eyes. His hand rested protectively against her stomach, so they must've known by then that she was pregnant. But Elizabeth was correct. The clothes she wore made it extremely difficult, if not outright impossible, to know there was another life growing inside her.

A frail-looking teenager stood off to the right, and Alyssa guessed by his sickly pallor that it was Marcel. But it was the person standing behind a tree, face shrouded in shadow, not really part of the picture, but not separate from it either that stole her attention. 'Who's this?' She flipped the photo around for Rosalyn to see, holding her finger near the person in question.

'Oh. That's Al.'

–

Armed with the names of the initial investigating officers, a copy of the police report, and the picture Rosalyn Benson had given them, Alyssa waited for a tractor to pass so she could pull onto the main road, chugging oh-so-slowly behind the monstrous green farm machine.

Grinning, she cast a sideways peek at her partner. 'You know you are sunk when the twins are born, right?'

Both hands shoveled through the hair on top of his head, leaving it uncharacteristically disheveled as he craned his neck back and stared at the ceiling of the Tahoe. 'Man, don't I know it.' Without lifting his head, it was his turn to peek at her. 'I'm freaking terrified of breaking them or scarring them for life by doing something stupid or…'

Alyssa's insides did somersaults even as she chuckled. 'Then you'll be fine. I think a lot of parents go through that. You're going to be great. I know it.'

'What if I'm not? Also, I can't imagine you ever feeling that way. You're a natural.'

The laughter that bubbled out of her was so swift, Alyssa was attacked by a coughing fit. 'You didn't know me when I was pregnant with Holly. I hate to say it, but I was less terrified of my service weapon than I was of holding my own child.'

'Really?'

'Yes, really.' As she passed in front of a small ranch that backed up to the highway, she turned serious. 'Al Greene. Too bad—' She stopped midsentence when Cord's phone vibrated in his pocket. She sensed the physical change in him as he retrieved his cell, issuing an audible sigh of relief that immediately assured Alyssa the call had nothing to do with Sara or the babies.

'Officer Falwin, what can I do for you?'

Alyssa cocked her head in his direction, curious as to why Sandra would ring Cord instead of her.

'I called you in case Alyssa was driving, and then after the phone started ringing, I remembered she had the Bluetooth, but by then it seemed silly to hang up, and—'

'Sandra, it's okay,' Cord interrupted. 'Why don't you just tell me what's up?'

Because Sandra spoke loudly, Alyssa could easily hear the conversation, but she still appreciated that Cord placed her on speakerphone anyway.

'Could be nothing, but a call came in a few minutes ago about an abandoned car.' Alyssa thought it was a strange comment until Sandra added, 'Didn't Elizabeth Monroe drive a brown BMW?'

Alyssa's stomach clenched, as if Sandra had physically punched her. 'Yes, she did.'

'That's what I thought. Should Joe and I go check it out in case it turns out to be nothing?'

It was hard to miss the eagerness and hope in Sandra's voice, but Alyssa was going to have to dash the young officer's excitement this time. 'Text Cord the address. We'll check it out. In the meantime, I need you to do a little research on someone else. Have a pen?'

'Yep, sure do.' Her response sounded a little less like cartwheels in a meadow and more like a field hand relegated to pulling weeds.

'Al Greene.'

Cord filled her in while Alyssa headed for the abandoned vehicle that she fervently prayed did not belong to Elizabeth Monroe.

Chapter Twenty

The tract of land that had once housed a bustling outdoor mall was now an enormous parking lot, cracked and over-flowing with weeds.

'Got to love the apocalyptic vibe,' Cord mused as Alyssa stopped her SUV next to two patrol units blocking off a brown BMW.

'You're not kidding.' Alyssa swept the area with one careful pass as she shut off the ignition. 'Not exactly the best place to leave a clunker, much less a Beemer.' She nodded to both officers, addressing the one she recognized. 'Phillip.'

The twenty-year veteran of the department tipped his head in greeting. 'Alyssa. Cord. Captain Hammond radioed that you were headed this way. One of the clerks' – he hitched his thumb over his shoulder to indicate the convenience store located across the street – 'spotted the Beemer when she got off work late last night. Car was still here when she arrived for today's shift, said something didn't feel right about it, and she called it in because it was better to be safe than sorry.'

Careful to avoid what appeared to be droplets of blood on both the side of the car and the ground, Alyssa poked her head inside the partially open driver's side door. On the seat was a navy-blue Michael Kors handbag, which Alyssa could name simply because she recognized the MK emblem stamped into the front. A red leather wallet peeked out while it appeared that a lipstick, a travel-size perfume, and several cough drops had rolled and lodged into the crevice of the seat. What she didn't see was a phone, at least not anywhere visible, either inside or outside the vehicle. Even though it was possible it was somewhere inside the car, Alyssa wasn't holding her breath.

Steeling herself against that sinking feeling she so hated, she craned her neck so she could see Cord who was speaking to Phillip. 'I recognize both the car and the handbag, and they definitely belong to Elizabeth. But just in case I'm wrong...' She donned a pair of gloves, and using a pen, opened the wallet to the plastic sleeve that held the owner's driver's license. Even though she'd expected it, she still cursed. 'Damn it all to hell.'

Backing out of the vehicle, she rotated in a slow circle, her eyes following a broken pile of brush that someone long ago had forged into a trail. She knew just beyond the path was a quick jaunt that led to the Rio Grande. She dropped her gaze to the ground, running her eyes along the rough blacktop.

'Searching for signs of a struggle?' Cord asked as he, too, made note of their surroundings.

Instead of answering Cord's rhetorical question, she posed one of her own, though it was more to herself than to her partner. 'What were you doing out here, Elizabeth, and where are you now?' Still searching the ground, she headed toward the trees. Cord joined her, slowing his long strides to match hers. She appreciated that he knew her well enough to remain silent while she tried to ascertain not only what had happened, but how it might tie into the Kensington case because more and more of her gut told her it did.

'Already checked that area,' Phillip called out. 'Nothing there but overgrown brush, trash, and remnants of partygoers.'

Alyssa waved one arm in the air to indicate she'd heard, but otherwise continued on, wanting to see for herself. But a few steps in, it was exactly as the officer said. Waist-high weeds proved this trail was no longer used with any regularity. Still, she performed a three-sixty, her eyes drifting high into the trees in search of anything out of the ordinary.

Finally, Cord said, 'Doesn't look like there's anything here to see. What say you and I mosey over to chat with the clerk?'

'Before we do, I'm going to ask Phillip to dispatch the tow company out here so our technicians can go over it.'

'Already made the request.'

Alyssa bumped him with her shoulder as they headed toward the parking lot across the street. 'You're okay, Cord Roberts. I don't care what others say about you.'

At the store, a jingling chime above the door announced their entrance, and the attendant behind the counter squeaked and clapped a hand over her heart when she whirled around.

A warm smile replaced Alyssa's all-business expression when she recognized who the woman was. 'Lorna Price. You're looking well. How are you doing?'

Alyssa knew Lorna from her last major case. She had worked as the night receptionist at the rundown hotel that was the pickup point of the drugged girls kidnapped for the sex trafficking ring. And despite her absolute fear that someone would discover she was the one who'd gone to the police with what she knew, she had still snuck out of the hotel lobby one night to snap a picture of one of the suspects before placing a frantic – and crucial – call to Alyssa, helping her team rescue the girls.

Lorna returned Alyssa's smile. 'Detective Wyatt, what a surprise, though I suppose it shouldn't be.' She nodded her head towards the parking lot across the street. 'But to answer your question, I'm better, thanks. After everything that happened at The Hotel Camino... Every time I walked in the door, I couldn't shake what had happened.'

'It's good you got out of there then.' Alyssa stretched her hand over the sticky counter where someone had spilled their drink.

Lorna met her halfway with a firm handshake. 'I'm putting myself through business school now.'

Overwhelming pride filled Alyssa, especially considering what a skittish and anxious-ridden woman Lorna had been the first time she'd come to the precinct. 'That's great! I'd love to chat more some time, but for now, did you call about the BMW out there?'

'Yes, ma'am. It just didn't seem right that a fancy car like that would be parked there during the light of day, much less all night. I didn't want to make the same mistake as before and wait, just in case something bad had happened.'

'You did the right thing. Did you happen to notice anyone in the area, either with or outside the vehicle?'

'No. Just that it was there when I left here last night about eleven, and it hadn't moved when I arrived today.' Her eyes skated toward the back of the store while she chewed the corner off one of her fingernails. 'We have security cameras if you want to have a look.'

'Are you allowed to give us permission?' Cord asked.

Lorna was already coming around the counter so she could lead them to the office. 'I'll call and make sure it's okay, just so you'll feel better, but I already know it's fine.' She stopped near a pair of crooked swinging doors and hollered to someone they couldn't see. 'Lars, I'll be in the office. I need you to cover the registers until I get back.'

'Fine,' a disgruntled voice yelled back.

'Lazy jerk,' Lorna muttered. Then, as they passed by the freezer section, she waved her hand upward where a camera was positioned. 'That one never works. And more than half the time, the one outside doesn't either. But even when it does, it's difficult to tell what's on the video. To be honest, Detective Wyatt' – she shot a disgusted look over her shoulder – 'it's more of a hopeful visual deterrent to would-be criminals. But let's be real – its presence does nothing. If someone wants to do something bad, a camera, working or not, isn't going to stop a thing.'

–

Within a few minutes, Lorna tucked Alyssa and Cord into a miniscule office space that barely had room for one person to breathe, much less three. Even with the cooler air coming in from the cracked window set high up on the wall, the room was horrifically stuffy.

Having no desire to experience the claustrophobic sensation of being locked in a closet, Alyssa asked Lorna if she could leave the door open. Then she turned to Cord, 'Oh yippee, I can't wait to once again get embroiled in the eye-burning drudgery of watching grainy footage.'

She watched Elizabeth pull into the lot shortly after nine and wait inside her car for nearly five minutes until an older truck, maybe from the seventies, traveling from the south, drove up and parked perpendicular to the BMW. A dark cover obscured the truck's license plate. When the driver climbed out of the car, Elizabeth followed suit. Unfortunately, because of the baggy hoody concealing the face, all they could tell was that the person was slightly shorter than Elizabeth.

For the next four minutes, even with the poor quality of the camera, it was clear to Alyssa that Elizabeth and the mystery person were engaged in an animated discussion. A point proved when Elizabeth Monroe tossed her hands into the air and turned to climb back into her BMW. The other person reached into a pocket and pointed something at Elizabeth's back. An electric arc flashed.

'A Taser?' she and Cord said at the same time.

On the way to the ground, Elizabeth's head slammed against her window and bounced off her door.

Her assailant checked left and right, then pocketed the Taser before walking over to Elizabeth and offering two swift kicks to the head that, to Alyssa's eyes, seemed forceful enough to be lethal. Elizabeth's assailant knelt down, grabbed her chin and yanked her head back and forth, presumably making sure she was out before reaching beneath her arms and dragging her to the passenger side of the truck where she was promptly dropped back to the ground until the assailant could open the door. After several failed attempts, the person finally managed to wrestle and heave Elizabeth into the cab.

Alyssa swore. 'Well, damn it, there goes any hope of technicians finding any fingerprints on Elizabeth's vehicle.' She tapped the screen where the footage clearly showed Elizabeth's attacker wearing a pair of gloves.

Cord shrugged. 'Doesn't look like the assailant ever touched the car anyway, so it probably wouldn't have mattered.'

Even though her partner was correct, frustration still bubbled in Alyssa as they watched the individual scour the ground around both vehicles before climbing in the truck, leaving a cloud of dust from the exhaust and a thicker cloud of black as the driver burned rubber peeling out of the parking lot.

'Dr. Sharp mentioned that whoever murdered Gabriel Kensington was possibly female or even a short male. How tall would you say that person is?'

Cord swept his gaze over Alyssa's form then focused back on the screen, hitting rewind until the truck pulled into the lot and Elizabeth's attacker climbed out. 'From this angle, I'm going to guess between five-five and five-seven, maybe?'

Alyssa shook her head. 'Take it from someone who's height-challenged. That person isn't five-seven. I'll agree with five-five, maybe even go five-four.'

'So, what do you think? Could we be looking at Gabriel and Lydia's killer?' Cord asked.

'Possibly, but more importantly, does this person know where Addis and Emerson are?' As soon as she said it, she thought of Brandon. 'Alert the team that we need to add Elizabeth Monroe to our list of missing persons. And while we're at it, we need to find out where her son is.'

Cord rubbed two fingers along his temples. 'I really hope we're not looking for a corpse.'

'We can't think that way,' Alyssa said, even though she'd thought the same thing.

The two of them pushed back from the desk, and as Alyssa scooted in front of Cord out the door, she heard him say, 'Is it just me, or do we need to be actively searching for a common thread that ties the Kensington case to Elizabeth Monroe's apparent kidnapping *and* Hayden Benson's mysterious disappearance?'

'It's not just you.'

Chapter Twenty-One

It felt like a thousand horses were trying to drag Addis's heart from her chest as she and Emerson did their utmost to ignore the idea that other living creatures of the many-legged variety were crawling around them as they lay flat in the dirt and rocks beneath the house, shivering as much from fear as the bone-chilling drop in temperature.

Earlier, after forcing her sluggish brain to rise above the dregs of another drug-induced slumber in which fang-clad demons were ripping into the flesh of her neck, she used her shoulder to juggle Emerson's head up and down until she finally woke.

Without knowing if they were alone or if their kidnapper was outside the crawl space, Addis breathed into Em's ear, 'We need to get these ropes off and get out of here.'

'What if he's out there?'

Addis chose her next words carefully. 'If he's out there, well, I prefer to go out fighting – even if I know I'm going to lose.' She ignored the tears stinging her eyes when her mind immediately conjured up a glowing Aunt Grace, fist pumping in the air, cheering her on. 'That's my girl.'

Emerson replied by sucking in great gulping breaths of air. 'Me, too.'

It had taken a few hours longer than forever, but the second Addis felt slack in the rope, she'd slipped her wrists through. The relief of being free was instantly replaced by a stinging sensation as the blood rushed back into her fingers. She took only a second to cradle and rub her wrists before turning to help Em.

Heart pounding, ears ringing, and listening to the whispered chants of 'Hurry, hurry, hurry,' she'd tugged and yanked and cut until Emerson's hands were also free.

Then it was no longer the ropes holding them captive; it was the uncertainty of what they'd find once they left the confines of their enclosure. Addis ignored the scrapes of splintered wood against her skin and pressed her left ear against the door, frustrated she couldn't tell if the noise she heard came from their captor in the living room or her hammering heart. Her palm skated across the wood in search of a handle or something. Her veins filled with icicles, and she knew she was stalling. For all her brave words of wanting to go down fighting, she knew she wasn't some heroine in an action-packed thriller.

Knowing she couldn't put it off any longer – they hadn't come this far just to come this far – she drank in a lungful of air and said, 'I'll go first.'

Em's hand spider-crawled down her arm until she could link their fingers together, squeezing tight enough that Addis cringed. 'No, we go together. On the count of three. One. Two. Three.' Her voice pitched an octave higher on the last word.

Shaking like a ceiling fan on its highest setting, they carefully, inch by painfully slow inch, pushed out on the door, relieved to see it lifting and not locked. It was difficult to know when the door was completely opened because all that greeted them was the thickest darkness Addis had ever experienced. A painful ache spread throughout her chest as she fruitlessly prayed for her dad to materialize so he could wrap her in his arms and tell her she was safe. She needed to hear it from him just one more time.

But no matter how fervently she wished for that fantasy, it wasn't going to happen, so she would just have to force herself to believe that she and Emerson could do this on their own.

Outside the crawl space, they stopped, their bodies jerking at every cricket's chirp, every tree limb scraping along the side of the cabin.

Addis repeated Emerson's earlier words. 'On the count of three, we stand. One. Two. Three.' Except their first attempt made it clear their muscles weren't as cooperative. Not willing to give up now, when the possibility of escape peeked on the horizon, she used the wall for support until she managed to get upright. While Em did the same, she trained her eyes in what she believed was the direction of the door, blocking out any thoughts of what was beyond. One step at a time was her motto right now, so they'd just deal with what came next when they reached that point.

An interminable amount of time passed as they felt their way along the wall, cringing with each creak and crying out when Addis's hand sliced across a protruding nail. After making one nerve-wracking, gut-turning stop in the kitchen for a tepid drink of rust-flavored water from the old pipes, Addis's fingers encountered the door. Blood pulsing so loudly it was difficult to hear, she tapped her fingers up and down until she felt the lock, wincing when a splinter shot beneath her fingernail. Then, leaning her forehead against their barrier to freedom, she released the bolt. Emerson's hand slid down her arm, and together, they turned the knob, flinching at the screeching sound as the bottom of the door rubbed against the floor.

Outside on the porch, it was still pitch black even with the sliver of shrouded moon casting a dim glow. Disoriented, Addis lifted her gaze to the dark clouds that were responsible for the starless night. 'Which way do we go? Without the stars, I don't know which way is north. What good is an interest in astronomy if I can't use it when I most need it?'

The low hum of an engine and the unmistakable sounds of a vehicle crunching its way over a rocky path sent her heart into a Kentucky Derby race. Together, she and Emerson froze like the proverbial deer, unsure which way to scamper to safety. Even as a pair of headlights came closer into view, Addis felt rooted to her spot.

The crackling sound of brush behind them finally galvanized Addis out of her stiffened state of inaction, and she clutched onto Em, her fingernails digging in as they shuffled sideways until they'd scooted off the far end of the porch. Keeping to the house, they edged their way to the back.

Suddenly, Addis's left foot dipped into a small indentation in the ground, and she fell, inadvertently dragging Emerson down with her. When she tried to rise back to her feet, her hand disappeared into nothingness, and she realized there was a crawlway beneath the cabin. Leaning close, she cupped her hands around Em's ears, and whispered, 'Under the house.'

Emerson jerked back, expelling her breath in one crackling gasp. 'No, I can't, Ad. Snakes.'

'We have to. It'll be okay; it's too cold for snakes right now.' And even if it wasn't, they'd be safer there than facing the alternative.

With the sound of the car drawing closer and the headlights casting just enough of a glow to outline the forest beyond, Emerson moaned but agreed, performing the sign of the cross before interlocking her fingers with Addis's.

Addis couldn't tell who squeezed tighter. 'Together,' they whispered through scratchy throats as they crawled beneath the cabin.

'Ouch. Something's poking me.' The sounds of a second vehicle bumping down the road shifted Addis's attention away from the pile of sharp sticks jabbing into her.

Too soon the engine shut off, and a car door opened and closed on the second vehicle. It wasn't until the voice of their kidnapper, muffled but distinct, trickled down through the floor that Addis realized she could hear the individuals inside.

'Why couldn't you just let me handle it?' Addis could barely hear, but she was sure she didn't recognize that voice.

'What the hell are you doing here, Alex?' The man's voice sounded more frightened than angry.

–

The outside temperature had nothing on the ice that flooded Addis's insides at the other person's response, and not only because the two people inside were discussing her parents' brutal murders.

No. The horror came from realizing that *Alex* was female. A woman was responsible for the staggering nightmare that had become her life.

Chapter Twenty-Two

Anger gnawed at Alex as she drove past the Balloon Field where hundreds of pilots blasted their burners inside the hot air balloons, setting the night aglow with color. Until he had stupidly kidnapped those girls and hidden them away, Adam had always gone to contortionist extremes to please her. She didn't care that he acted more out of fear of retribution from her than of blind obedience. It had made manipulating him as easy as bending a plastic straw.

Alex banged both fists on the steering wheel, ceasing only when a crackling sound pierced her fog of fury, the jagged break across her dashboard a perfect representation of her disintegrating control over Adam. She'd had a plan, had everything under control until Adam had gone and royally screwed everything up, and now they were one misstep away from being caught. Not one to lie to herself, she admitted what had been speeding her direction for a while: Adam had become a liability, one she needed to eliminate before things got even worse. Inside the cab of her vehicle, she howled out her rage.

A maze of zigzagging lightning strikes zinged across the sky over the Sandias, nearly blinding her. Mountain weather was so often notoriously unpredictable with its out-of-nowhere thunderstorms and hard, driving rains, but where Alex thrived on the volatility, Adam dreaded it.

Just like that, she knew where he'd taken the girls. In fact, it was so obvious, she was surprised it had taken her this long to figure it out. Not considering the traffic around her, she jerked her steering wheel to the left and reversed course, ignoring the angry horns of drivers forced to slam on their brakes to avoid hitting her.

Getting to them this late would be tricky, but every second those girls were left alive was another second she risked exposure.

As she rocketed down the highway, she felt like she could float away. With the girls dead, she'd have tied up every loose end except Adam. But that was okay because she had big plans for him.

–

More than ninety minutes later, Alex bumped along a mountainous road, cursing each rut. A deer bounded in front of her, but she didn't bother swerving to miss it, a little surprised it managed to escape her front bumper.

It took her a little longer than she'd expected since it had been so long since she'd last come here, so when she finally turned onto the correct primitive trail, she'd been relieved. She hadn't quite believed she'd be able to locate it in the dark, and there was no way she was waiting until morning. Not now, when she was so close she could taste satisfaction.

Soon, all her problems would be solved.

Except that when she climbed out of the truck and up the steps to the dilapidated old cabin, she found Adam standing inside the open door. It took only a second to understand the implications of the pile of ropes mocking them both with their emptiness.

'Why couldn't you just let me handle it?' Alex hissed.

Clearly unaware of her presence until she spoke, Adam whirled around. 'What the hell are you doing here, Alex?'

'What do you think?' She made a grand show of tossing her arms out to the side and rotating in a full circle. 'I'm here to save us – again – to do what needs to be done – again.' She closed in on him, backing him against a wall. 'You know what this means, right? If they make it to safety, they'll turn you in. You. And you can kiss your precious NFL career goodbye. You should've let me take care of them like I did the Kensingtons.'

Alex spoke through gritted teeth as she moved back to the door. 'It's late, it's dark, and I can't be out here all night searching. So, either find them, or I'll kill you where you stand. And Adam? Don't even think about running because I'll hunt you down like a wild boar and slaughter you like the stupid pig you are.'

There was no emotion behind her words, just a cold truth. And they both knew it.

Chapter Twenty-Three

Sunday, October 6

The overpowering stench of rotten meat, potatoes, and God knows what else burned into Alyssa's eyes as she maneuvered her way between the menagerie of flashing lights already on scene at a dumpster located outside a derelict apartment complex that she wasn't entirely sure was still legally habitable.

A group of tenants had already amassed, openly gawking as the officers on scene busied themselves keeping the onlookers from destroying or contaminating evidence. Those who weren't gathered stood in their doorways or at the railing of the second story. Every screech of the metal as the tenants leaned against it sent a jolt of fear through her that someone would lean too far, and the entire structure would crumble.

One of the responding officers – Lee Montague – walked up. 'Detective.' Eyebrows kneaded together, he peered around her, obviously searching for Cord. Being sports fanatics of opposing teams, the two liked to razz each other whenever they found themselves on the same case.

Alyssa didn't make him ask. 'He's with his wife, so I'm on my own for now.' The look of disappointment was almost comical. 'Walk me through what you know,' she said as she moved toward the dumpster where a woman had been found tossed inside, piles of black garbage bags thrown in on top of her.

Montague pointed in the direction of a young boy whose clearly malnourished form made it difficult for Alyssa to determine if his age was closer to five or ten. 'Kid was taking out the trash when he discovered the body hidden in the dumpster, got understandably freaked out, screamed until one of the neighbors came to see what all the commotion was about, and called it in.'

The boy whom Montague referred to wore dirty, rumpled clothing with more holes than fabric, and his hair was clumped together in dreadlocks made from having gone too long without a bath or brush. Draped around his shoulders was a threadbare blanket, the tattered and torn ends flapping in the wind. Alyssa had a sneaky suspicion he hadn't been taking out the trash but searching through it for his next meal. A fissure opened inside her chest, and she had to force her attention away so she could listen to Montague.

'One of the bags closest to our vic's body was spilled open showing a few receipts dated Friday, October fourth. According to the tenants, garbage is emptied here early – as in six a.m. – Friday mornings. We heard you might be looking for a woman who'd gone missing after nine Friday night, so we gave you a shout.'

He was, of course, referring to Elizabeth Monroe, Alyssa knew. A sudden flurry of motion and someone shrieking in a high-pitched squawk stole her attention.

'She's moving.' The girl belonging to the shrill voice waved her hand frantically in the air as she pointed down.

Alyssa snapped her head in Montague's direction, growling, 'I thought you said she was dead!'

'Swear to God, Detective, there was no pulse when we first arrived on scene. I checked it myself.'

Even though it happened more frequently than people might realize, Alyssa wasn't feeling charitable. What if those precious wasted moments resulted in the woman's actual death? Without bothering to be gentle about it, she elbowed her way in and peered over the top of the dumpster to stare down at the person everyone believed to have been dead. A woman's jean-clad legs were visible, one short-heeled black shoe on her left foot, the other bare. Alyssa could see, even through the woman's pants, that her right knee was positioned strangely in relation to the rest of her leg, as if someone had taken a sledgehammer to the side of it. Even her fingers were clenched into unnatural positions.

The woman's left eye was swollen while the right was slit open in a grotesque wink. And in case that wasn't enough for Alyssa's stomach to threaten an embarrassing revolt, she watched as flies and other insects invaded what appeared to be stab wounds to the chest and neck area. Still, despite all the damage and the ragged chunk of pony-tail that had been lobbed off, it was immediately obvious that the woman tossed in with the trash was none other than Elizabeth Monroe.

One of the paramedics who had climbed inside the dumpster shouted above the chaos of the onlookers. 'We've got a faint pulse.' Alyssa was jostled aside as a team of rescue workers struggled to lift Elizabeth out while still continuing frantic efforts to keep her breathing.

'Holy shit,' Alyssa breathed when Elizabeth's body was lowered onto a stretcher, the violent destruction to her torso on display. *How in the hell had she survived with that much damage, especially if she'd really been inside this bacteria-infested environment since Friday night?* She turned to Montague. 'How is it possible no one noticed a body inside a dumpster until this morning?'

'Wish I had an answer for you,' he said.

Alyssa studied each gawker's expression, instinctively searching for someone matching the description of the friend hiding in the background of the photograph Rosalyn Benson had shown them.

Instead of helping put the pieces of the puzzle in place, this case grew more convoluted with each new development, but what tied Alyssa's intestines into knots was the unfettered violence evident on Elizabeth's body. Combined with the savagery of the Kensington murders, she was afraid of what they'd find when they finally located Addis and Emerson.

Because despite the seemingly unconnected puzzle pieces, she was no longer uncertain as to whether or not Hayden Benson's disappearance seven years ago was tied into Gabriel and Lydia's murders.

Chapter Twenty-Four

Sunday, October 6

Alyssa found herself on automatic pilot as she headed to Elizabeth Monroe's neighborhood for the third time since Friday evening. Though she'd been relieved to learn last night that Elizabeth's neighbor had Brandon Monroe, she wasn't looking forward to conducting this interview, knowing it was all too real a possibility that the young boy could lose his mother.

Thankfully, the captain had already dispatched Joe to pace the hospital corridors in her place, along with strict instructions to contact Alyssa immediately with any updates. For the dozenth time, she wished Cord could've been with her this morning, but Sara and the babies had to come first. With Tony still out, she could've called Joe or even Sandra to meet her at the apartment complex where Elizabeth had been found, but she'd been too impatient to take the few seconds it would've taken to call either one.

The entire twenty-five-minute drive to Elizabeth's subdivision, she'd kicked herself for her inability to find that one tiny thread that, untangled, would lead her to a vicious killer, thus hopefully leading her to Addis and Emerson. So far, they'd received no results regarding any possible DNA from the crime scene, nor had they heard back regarding any fingerprints, despite Hal regularly breathing down the necks of the technicians responsible for getting the information to the team. This case may be like no other she'd ever worked on, but that was still no excuse not to have some answers by now. If only real-life crimes could be solved as quickly as the ones on television. As a result of her mounting frustration, Alyssa was a bundled coil of nerves by the time she pulled up to the neighbor's house.

It was a feeling that only intensified when the door flew open and Brandon's little form filled the entryway, tears sparkling in his eyes. Directly behind him was a rather nondescript woman, yelling for him to wait. At the same time, another little boy squeezed himself into the space between the door jamb and his friend, reaching out and gripping Brandon's hand in his own.

Alyssa's heart dissolved into a puddle on the wooden slats beneath her feet. Both boys bravely stood there wearing their Superman capes and Spiderman shirts, blinking rapidly, reminding her of Isaac and Trevor when they were this age and demanded for two full weeks that they be called by their favorite superheroes' names.

Even as Nate's mom opened her mouth to speak, Brandon, his lower lip quivering, beat her to it. 'Tessa won't take me to see my mom.' He straightened his back and planted his little feet apart. 'When I find out who hurt her, I'm going to beat him up. I'll be fast like Thor and use my hammer so he can't hurt anyone ever again.' One little fist reached up and swiped across his nose.

Beside him, Nate's neck bobbed up and down in solidarity.

Alyssa didn't know if Brandon's proclamation and determination made her want to laugh or cry. So instead, she lowered herself to his height and spoke directly to him. 'Brandon, I'm Detective Wyatt. I met you the other night when I came over to speak to your mom. Do you remember?'

'Yes.'

'Good. And do you know what my job is?'

Suspicion filled his wet eyes as he stared at her, trying to decide if she was trying to trick him. Finally, he stuttered, 'You re… re… 'rest the bad guys.'

Alyssa nodded. 'Yes, that's right. I arrest the bad guys. And I have a whole team of police officers who help me. But sometimes it makes our job harder when someone else – even if it's Thor – tries to do our job for us. And I know you wouldn't want that to happen because you want us to catch the person who hurt your mom, right?'

Still looking suspicious, Brandon jerked his head down once in agreement.

Leaning in just a fraction of an inch, she lowered her voice into a conspiratorial whisper. 'So, I'm wondering if I could ask you a pretty big favor. Would you mind giving me and my team a chance to find the bad guy first?'

Brandon turned to Nate. For several seconds, neither blinked nor spoke as they stood there staring at each other. Whatever silent communication passed between the two of them must've been clearly understood because when he faced Alyssa once more, his head dipped up and down decisively. 'Okay. I have a magnifying glass. You can borrow it for when you need to look for clues.'

The urge to wrap him in a hug was powerful. 'I tell you what. I'll keep that very generous offer in mind, and I'll let you know if I need it, okay?' Alyssa waited for Brandon's nod before she rose back to her full height. 'Now, I need to speak with Nate's mom if that's okay with you.'

Instead of answering Alyssa, he twisted around to Nate's mom. 'Do you promise not to keep any secrets from me?'

Tessa offered a broken smile as she curled her hand into a fist, pinky extended. 'Pinky swear. Now, you and Nate run back to the kitchen and finish your cookies. I'm just going to sit outside so I can speak to Detective Wyatt.' She waited for the boys to disappear before stepping onto the porch and closing the door behind her.

Instead of doing as instructed, both boys poked their heads through the sun-stained blinds. Tessa shook her head and pointed to one of three Adirondack chairs with small tables placed in between each. 'Please sit,' she offered. 'That Brandon's like a forty-year-old man in a seven-year-old body. Elizabeth has always said he reminds her so much of his father whenever he was in one of his serious moods, which she claimed was rather rare.'

'About that, did Elizabeth speak to you a lot about Hayden? About what might've happened that night?'

Tessa's gaze locked on a squirrel racing up the willow tree in her yard. 'Just that he disappeared the night they were supposed to run away together and that she never agreed with the claim that he'd run off in order to shirk his responsibilities. And then about a month ago, we were sitting outside enjoying the fall weather and a glass of wine when, out of the blue, she announced she was hiring a private investigator to find out what really happened. I guess Brandon had started noticing he was the only one of his friends without a father and was beginning to ask a lot of questions she didn't know how to answer.'

'What was Elizabeth's reaction when she learned about Mr. Kensington's murder?'

Tessa's forehead wrinkled. 'Well, when she saw it on the news, she called to tell me Gabriel was the investigator she'd hired, so I guess you could say she was understandably horrified. If you're asking if I thought her reaction was in any way out of the norm, then I'd have to say no, definitely not.'

Alyssa thought back to her interview with Elizabeth and how she'd insisted her son not get himself invited over for fish sticks Friday. 'I'm curious about something. When one of my officers stopped by last night, you said Brandon had been with you since Friday night. Was that planned or sudden?'

'Sudden.'

'And you didn't find that odd?'

'Not really. As much as she loves that boy, Elizabeth still sometimes needed a break, especially if she'd been working long hours.' The lines around Tessa's face deepened. 'I guess I should've suspected something when she called just before nine and asked if we'd mind keeping Brandon for a couple nights.'

A flush of adrenaline sent a wave of heat through Alyssa. 'Did she say why or indicate she was meeting someone?'

'No, and playing Monday morning quarterback, I realize now I probably should've asked.' Tessa used her fingernail to scrape at the loose paint on the table. 'If I had, maybe Elizabeth would be home, safe now instead of fighting for her life.'

Alyssa cut her off. 'I know it's not easy, but you can't allow yourself to think that way.'

Tessa waved her comment away. 'Much easier said than done. When she didn't call to check in on Brandon, and I didn't see her car yesterday, I began to worry, but my husband told me not to overreact because she'd asked us to watch Brandon for a couple nights, and it had only been less than twenty-four hours.' She snorted. 'I knew I should've trusted my gut that something was wrong.'

Alyssa wasn't sure calling the police yesterday would've produced different results, but even if it had, there was no rewind button for a do-over. So, instead of dwelling on what couldn't be changed, she redirected the conversation back to the Bensons. 'I want to return to the topic of Hayden. Did Elizabeth ever talk about his family or even her own?'

'Definitely not her own. Apparently, when they learned she was pregnant after Hayden disappeared, they screamed at her for being an ungrateful whore who was going straight to the fiery pits of hell with her unborn bastard.' Her mouth twisted into a grimace as a muscle near her eye pulsed rapidly. 'That night Elizabeth took what she already had packed and never looked back. All these years later, she said they've never tried to reach out to her, and she wouldn't risk putting her son in such a poisonous, hateful situation anyway.'

'Did she have any siblings?'

'Not that she's ever mentioned to me.'

'And what about Hayden's family?' Alyssa prodded.

'I can't really say how much contact she had with them. But I do know she tried to keep in contact with his sister. Rose or Ramona' – she snapped her fingers – 'Rosalyn, that's it! But she never really said much about her. I've seen her a couple of times when she's stopped by to visit Brandon. She's always seemed so absolutely in love with that little guy. And she always invites Nate to go with them on their little explorations.'

Alyssa's phone chimed with a text. She glanced down and saw Joe's name. 'Excuse me,' she said while she read the message.

> Monroe is out of surgery. She'd lost an awful lot of blood, so might be some brain damage. Won't know for sure until she's awake, but for now anyway, they're keeping her in a medical coma. Sorry.

Alyssa had to swallow past a sudden lump as she thought about the seven-year-old boy wearing superhero clothes and offering her his magnifying glass who was far too young to lose his mother, mentally or physically. She fired off her response.

> Thanks for the update. You may as well take off since there's nothing you can do but wait. I'll swing by the hospital when I finish up here.

She put her phone away and broke the news to Tessa. Together, they went inside to tell Brandon his mom was out of surgery but was still not awake. Then Alyssa hunkered down so she could look into the eyes of this little guy who'd managed to worm his way into the center of her heart. 'Does that offer to borrow your magnifying glass still stand? I have a feeling it's going to help my team catch the bad guy.' She couldn't explain the compulsion to ask, but when he raced to the kitchen and returned with the magnifying glass in hand, proudly presenting it to her, she knew she'd done the right thing.

Afterwards, she thanked Tessa for her time and said bye to the boys, appreciating how she'd been more unnerved at the idea of facing two seven-year-old superhero-clad youngsters than she was at the prospect of staring down an armed suspect.

On the way back to the hospital, she called Brock to let him know she'd be later than expected.

Chapter Twenty-Five

Sunday, October, 6

Alex scraped her hair back into a ponytail, securing it before coiling it into a tight bun at the nape of her neck. When a few loose strands managed to elude the rubber band, she threw her brush into the sink and yanked them out, roots and all.

After tossing them into the toilet and flushing them away, she studied herself in the mirror. Things were unraveling, and she seemed unable to stop the speeding train wreck barreling her way.

In the back of her mind, she'd always known Adam would be too weak to deal with this. She'd known it, and she'd used him anyway because she also knew that once her plan was set in motion, she'd no longer have any use for him, and so he'd never live long enough to implicate her.

Moving into her bedroom, Alex opened her night-stand drawer and pulled out the worn photograph she kept tucked away. Lifting it to her lips, she softly kissed the smiling image of Hayden Benson before running her fingertips along his face as if he were there in the flesh. It had all started when he'd come to her in a dream, pleading for her forgiveness. He'd realized he'd made a horrible mistake in choosing Elizabeth over her. To prove it, he'd outlined his plan.

Alex would steal Brandon away and raise him as her own – hers and Hayden's, the way it always should've been. Elizabeth didn't deserve the little boy anyway.

Waking the next morning, the dream had seemed so real. Propping herself up against her headboard, she'd been surprised to see herself tightly clutching the photograph she'd always kept carefully hidden away. In that moment, she'd known it hadn't been a dream at all; it had been a vision. And she'd known exactly what she needed to do because Hayden had told her.

She started by tracking down Elizabeth's address – not at all difficult in this day and age – and then she'd begun following her, carefully noting her daily routines. And the more she watched Brandon, the spitting image of his father, the more anxious she was to have him. He belonged to her.

Impatience burned bright, but every time it did, Hayden would whisper in her ear: 'Just wait. The right time will come.' And she'd believed him.

Right up until the day she'd watched as that stupid bitch met with Gabriel Kensington. There was only one reason Alex could think of that would explain why Elizabeth had hired a private investigator – she'd never accepted that Hayden would willingly abandon her and their unborn child. Sitting a table away and listening to Elizabeth drone on about how much Hayden had loved her and how they'd planned to run away had sent Alex into a blind rage, but that wasn't even the worst part. It was *who* Elizabeth had chosen to hire to dig up the past.

Like everyone else in Albuquerque, Alex knew that, love them or hate them, the Kensingtons were powerful and influential people. Add to that the knowledge that Gabriel was rumored to be the best private investigator in the state, and Alex knew she had a problem.

She'd raced home to ask Hayden what she should do, but he'd remained stubbornly quiet, and that was when she'd realized he'd tricked her. He hadn't wanted her forgiveness; he'd wanted her to be captured, and his traitorous betrayal had her fury scaling new heights. She'd show him. She'd show them all.

But first she'd need to know what Gabriel had discovered. Her plan was to go to Kensington Investigations and break in after everyone had gone home. But the day she'd gone, Gabriel had rushed out of his office, phone pressed to his ear as he left a message for Elizabeth urging her to call him back immediately, that he had photographs she needed to see. She'd heard him mention Hayden's name. And then before she could react, he was in his vehicle and driving away.

The compulsion to follow him home, to kill him immediately nearly drove her insane. But she was smarter than that. She forced herself to regroup. And then it had come to her.

Thursday night, she'd grabbed Adam and gone to Gabriel's house and introduced herself, claiming Elizabeth had confided in her that she'd hired a private investigator to look into Hayden's disappearance. She pretended she had information that would help him, but then not only had he recognized her, despite her disguise, he'd spotted the gloves on her hand. Unwisely, he had the unmitigated gall to threaten to call the police if she didn't leave. From the fear in his eyes, she'd known he'd found something incriminating. She needed to know where that evidence was, and she wasn't leaving without it, so using the gun and Adam's intimidating bulk, she'd shoved her way inside.

And then that haughty wife of his had to come into the kitchen, that ugly mouth of hers twisted into that 'I'm better than you'll ever hope to be' sneer, and so she'd shot her, more to wipe that judgmental look off her face than anything else. Gabriel had wasted no time turning to run, and she'd just reacted, shooting him in the back. With Adam screeching behind her and Gabriel still standing, a frenzied rage had overtaken her, so she'd grabbed a rolling pin and bashed him in the skull with it. If a bullet wouldn't take him down, then she'd do it another way.

But even shot and half his brain exposed from the gaping hole in his head, he'd still refused to die. If she was being completely honest, she hadn't even been aware of standing to grab the butcher knife until she was towering above him again. But then she'd dropped to her knees, straddling him as she thrust the knife into his chest over and over again.

Only when she was physically spent did she stop. From the horrified expression on Adam's face, she knew she must resemble Carrie in the epic pig-blood scene from Stephen King's novel. Grinning and feeling lighter than she had in years, she rose and grabbed a towel, wiping her face with it before shoving it into her back pocket so as not to accidentally leave any DNA around. Reaching up, she'd adjusted her wig and then moved over to the sink to wash the blood from her gloved hands. Mesmerized, she watched the red and pink swirl together before disappearing down the drain. When she finished, she grabbed a handful of paper towels and thoroughly dried the sink, before also shoving those into her pocket.

Then she clapped her hands in front of Adam's face and ordered him to follow her to Gabriel's office – not so much because she wanted or needed his help but because she didn't fully trust him not to do something stupid. After hacking into Gabriel's security system to erase any evidence of her presence, she'd upended that room and had found nothing, not even the keys to his private practice. Pissed, she'd continued her reign of destruction in the bedroom for no other reason than she wanted to.

Back in the kitchen, she'd rotated in a circle, her eyes searching high and low for anything that might implicate her. That was when she'd spotted Gabriel's and Lydia's phones lying near their bodies. Careful to avoid the blood, she snatched both up, powered them down, and shoved them into her front pocket. And then she'd squeezed her grip around a still-stunned Adam and dragged him outside where she proceeded to shove him into the cab of her truck. When she was sure he wasn't going to bolt back out, she moved around to the driver's side, climbed in, and then meandered the streets until she came across a ditch bank. Without even slowing, she lobbed both phones out the window and into the water. She knew the last place they'd ping would be the Kensington house, so the chances of locating them now were slim to none. She had no idea what kind of information he'd had on that device, and she couldn't risk finding out the hard way.

Throughout it all, Adam rocked slowly back and forth, mumbling, ripping handfuls of his hair out. For the most part, she'd tuned him out. That is, until he said, 'What if we left something behind, something that proves you killed them?'

She'd slammed on her brakes, jerking them both forward as they lurched to a dead stop. His face paled to an impressive shade of white she'd never before seen. In her most cajoling tone, she said, 'Don't I always take care of everything, Adam? All you need to do right now is go home, take a shower, and get some sleep. Leave the rest up to me.'

After making sure he was safely inside his house, she left, already scheming his 'accidental' demise.

But before she could set her new plan in motion, he'd gone and screwed everything to hell and back. Elizabeth Monroe may have been the impetus that started this ball rolling, but Adam had made it infinitely worse.

And now it was time for her to adjust her strategy. She picked up the object she'd recently 'borrowed,' and threw her head back, laughing.

This would almost be worth Adam's screw-up.

Almost.

Chapter Twenty-Six

Sunday, October 6

Echoes of rushing water filtered through the continuous stream of trees, but from where it came was a mystery because Addis and Emerson hadn't been able to locate it, no matter how many times they'd circled the endless, woven, interlocked paths. 'We have to be close. It has to be right around here,' Addis said for what felt like the hundredth time.

'But it's not,' came Emerson's tearful reply as she dropped to the ground.

Weary to the point of just wanting to give up, Addis was unsure what to say. Aunt Grace would know. She always had the exact perfect words for every situation. But she wasn't Aunt Grace; she was just a terrified, seventeen-year-old girl trying to avoid a murderer. Or two. Before settling herself next to Em, she used her foot to brush away some pinecones and then reached down and pulled two twigs that were snagged in her friend's greasy, scraggly hair.

She didn't need a mirror to know she looked just as bad, if not worse. And from the throbbing in her face, she knew she probably had a bruise or two from being hit. But overshadowing everything else was a relentless, driving thirst. They'd braved chewing on a few leaves that were still clinging to their green, but it wasn't nearly enough. And she was well beyond hungry. At this point, she knew with certainty she would devour anything placed in front of her, even her gag-worthy foods: beets, cottage cheese, oatmeal, grits, liver and onions. Hell, if she knew what to do, she'd try to catch one of the cute squirrels or chipmunks scampering around the forest floor.

But then images of her parents' bloody, lifeless bodies twisted through her mind, and she knew, starving or not, she would find it difficult to kill anything.

Alex and Adam. Those were the names of the monsters responsible for her parents' murders. Lying under the cabin, listening to the coldness of the woman's anger, Addis had buckled in grief, muffling her sobs with the crook of her elbow. Now she stared down at the pocketknife clutched in her hand.

Afraid Addis's cries would give away their location, Emerson had wrapped herself around her, nestling the two of them together until they were closer than cups in a cupboard. It was then Addis had felt something jab her painfully in the hip, and she'd reached down to move the object, only to realize it was a knife. Useless as a weapon perhaps, but having it made her – both of them – feel better, so they'd kept it.

In the light of day, they'd noticed someone's engraved name had worn off over the years. A picture of a bear and the letters A and E were all that were left visible, along with what appeared to be a date.

Emerson leaned her body into Addis. 'Do you remember when we talked our dads into taking us camping? How old were we?'

'Nine.' Addis closed her eyes and let the memory wash over her, hoping that remembering the gut-clenching laughter and the hiccups that followed would somehow help her hold onto her father a little longer, like she could pretend he was still alive, just waiting with Aunt Grace for her to come home. Of course, her mother's death devastated her, too, but the truth was they had fought constantly, due in great part to her mom's endless jealousy and false accusations. She was good at that, accusing people of things. What she was bad at was accusing the *right* people of the *right* things. But the unbreakable bond Addis had shared with her father – well, the loss of him was a punch felt all the way to her soul.

Em's broken chuckle sounded more like a smoker's cough, hauling Addis back from the edge of collapsing under the weight of her loss. 'God, our dads were as clueless about being in the woods as we were.' She searched for Addis's hand, squeezing tightly. 'Thank goodness for those cute boys who were camping nearby, otherwise we never would've gotten our tents up or a fire going.'

'Or food,' Addis added. Remembering it, she could almost taste the charred hot dog slathered in ketchup and mustard, could savor the hot sweetness of burnt marshmallows and melted chocolate on graham crackers. 'And then the next day, when they got us lost on the way back from the stream—'

Emerson picked up the memory where Addis left off. 'Only to realize we were right next to camp all along.'

'If nothing else, that was an adventure, even if it lasted only one night.'

The camping conversation exhausted, the heaviness of their predicament once more took center stage in their minds. Addis leaned her head back against the bark of the tree, wondering if they should just curl up together and let whatever may come just happen. If their fate was to die, they would; if their fate was to find help, they would. She just didn't know if she could keep going on. But saying that to Emerson seemed like the ultimate betrayal.

As if her best friend had logged in to her private thoughts, Em whispered, 'I'm so tired, Ad. I don't know if I can keep going.'

Addis opened her mouth to offer encouragement, but nothing came out. No words of wisdom, no declarations of *Hey, we've got this*, not even a steadfast agreement of *Yes, let's just lie down right where we are and wait for the wildlife to eat us*.

Because the unshakeable, unchangeable truth of the matter was this: what did she really have to live for anyway? Her parents were dead, slaughtered in their kitchen, and it wasn't like her life could return to any semblance of normalcy. In fact, if she was being completely honest, if she and Em somehow survived this, all she could see in front of her was the emptiness of her future.

Addis was ripped away from her misery by the sound of water, only this time, it came in an absolute sudden, drenching downpour that rained down to intermingle with her streaming tears. Every other thought was shoved aside as she tilted her head back and opened her mouth wide as she allowed the rain to flow down her throat.

Only when she began to choke did she stop. And in that moment, watching Emerson quench her thirst as well, Addis remembered what she had to live for. If she gave up, so would Em. And she couldn't have that.

A clear picture of Aunt Grace cheering from the sidelines of her track meets, yelling out encouragement to dig deep and fight on gave her that little extra boost of the mental strength she desperately needed to cling to if she and Em were to survive.

Somehow, someway, they would find their way out of this nightmare.

They had to.

Chapter Twenty-Seven

Sunday, October 6

It was after ten when Alyssa finally got home, tired and cranky and unable to shake it even when she realized Holly was there. And now her less than stellar mood was on display as she scowled at the way Isaac crammed his index fingers into his ears, dramatically singing 'La-la-la-la' as loudly and as off-key as he could safely get away with. In the meantime, Holly rolled her eyes at her brother.

'Oh, grow up,' she muttered.

Alyssa snapped her fingers in front of Isaac's face. That, along with the glare she shot his way, effectively cut off his last *la*. 'No one invited you to be a part of this conversation, so if you don't want to hear what your sister has to say, then grab what you need and get out of the kitchen.'

Armed with a family-size bag of Cheetos, a jar of salsa to dip them in – a combination Alyssa found repulsive – and a sports drink, Isaac bounded back upstairs, leaving her alone with Holly once more. Since she was more concerned with what was going on with her daughter, she chose to ignore her son's late-night snacking.

'As you were saying before your brother derailed you, you and Nick had a late dinner, and afterwards, he walked you to the door and kissed you goodnight.' Her heart smiled at the notion of her daughter's boyfriend chivalrously seeing her safely inside.

'Right.' Holly reached over and retrieved a white envelope from her oversized bag that doubled as a purse and a backpack. Toying with the corners, she expelled a deep breath and then dropped it onto the table, nudging it closer to Alyssa while pressing her hand down on it to prevent her from opening it.

'Am I supposed to guess what's in there?'

Holly sighed and released her hold even as she avoided her mother's knowing, penetrating stare. 'Everyone – Nick, Sophie, and especially Rachel and Jersey – said I'd be dumb to wait to show you this, so that's why I'm here so late.'

Alyssa's skin prickled with unease. *Especially Rachel and Jersey?* Though she could push it to the back of her mind from time to time, it was impossible to forget that Holly had narrowly missed being one of the victims of the sex trafficking ring that had devastated too many lives.

'This was peeking out from beneath the porch swing cushion, and I didn't think much of it, to be honest,' Holly continued. 'So, Nick had already taken off by the time I opened it.'

Using her fingernail, Alyssa opened the flap, tipping out three photographs as she did. Staring back at her were images of Holly and Nick at one of their favorite restaurants, another of Holly laughing down at Nick as she cuddled onto his lap, and a final one taken in one of the parking lots of UNM as Holly, Sophie, Jersey, and Rachel climbed into Holly's car.

'What time exactly did you receive these?' she demanded, not caring that her voice was edgy and angry.

That happened when she felt one of her children was being targeted.

Holly's skin took on the appearance of an overripe tomato as she pushed back her chair, standing so she could bounce on the balls of her feet, one of her biggest tells that she was more nervous than she was letting on. 'I don't know what time it was placed there, but it was a little before nine when I opened it.' She rolled her eyes at herself. 'And yes, I debated for a long time whether or not I should show you because I didn't know what it meant.'

The vein in Alyssa's temple twitched. 'I don't suppose anyone saw who dropped it off.'

'Sophie, Jersey, and Rachel were all home, but they didn't see or hear anyone.'

'You should've called me right away.'

'You were still working, so I don't know what good it would've done. It just would've distracted you from your real job.' Her voice tapered off at the withering glare Alyssa focused on her.

'That is quite possibly the weakest excuse you've ever invented.'

Holly shrugged. 'It was spur of the moment, so it was all I had.'

Alyssa cupped Holly's cheek in her hand. 'There is nothing, absolutely nothing, more important to me than this family. Furthermore, you know that.'

'I know. That's why I'm here. Even though I don't know what this is supposed to mean.'

'We'll find out, but for now, I'll take these with me to work tomorrow and see if we're lucky enough to lift any prints off of them.' Alyssa shifted her gaze down the hall to her husband's closed office door. 'And we're going to need to tell Dad.'

Holly frowned. 'I know.' With her fingers tapping a staccato rhythm against the counter behind her back, she sucked in a lungful of oxygen through her nose before slowly releasing it in a low whistle through pursed lips. 'But he's going to get all weird and insist I move back home.' Her lips flattened, and she stiffened her spine in a move that was one hundred percent Alyssa. 'I won't do it. I'm staying at the duplex.'

'I don't doubt it for a second,' Alyssa said, even if secretly she backed her husband's stance on this topic.

Chapter Twenty-Eight

The sky was still dark when Alyssa pulled into the precinct at quarter to six Monday morning, consumed with thoughts of the contents of the envelope delivered to Holly. To her detective's mind, it was meant to send the clear message that her daughter was being watched. And as suspected, when they'd told Brock, he'd demanded his 'baby girl' move home that night, and Alyssa had found herself the buffer between two pieces of dynamite ready to detonate because neither her husband nor her daughter was about to budge. On one hand, she was filled with an immense sense of pride at Holly's fierce independence, but on the other, she was firmly in the court of playing mama bear so she could more easily protect her cubs. But for now anyway, Holly's obstinance had won out, much to both Alyssa and Brock's dismay.

She was still replaying the scene in her mind when she spotted Cord sitting inside his vehicle, head pressed against the headrest, rubbing his temples, and basically looking like death warmed over. Though he'd called last night to tell her he'd be in, that Sara was fine, and the early labor scare had been nothing but a false alarm, she was having second thoughts as to the wisdom of his choice to work today.

She rapped her knuckles on the window, and Cord jerked upright, his hand automatically going to the weapon in his holster before realizing it was her. He unwound his tall frame from the car, lobbing a rare scowl of displeasure her direction.

'Are you trying to give me a heart attack or just get yourself shot?'

His grumpiness wasn't really aimed at her, so Alyssa wasn't bothered by his tone or his words. 'Not sure yet. Can I get back to you?'

He shook his head, mumbled under his breath, and then proceeded to lead the way into the station. They nodded to Hal, who was sitting at the front desk discussing something with Ruby. He wasn't out there much longer before joining her and Cord in the conference room.

Alyssa peeked over her shoulder as Hal rolled in. Grinning, she said, 'So, what was that about?'

Hal returned her grin. 'Oh, nothing.'

Alyssa's grin grew wider. 'In other words, you're still trying to butter her up. How's that working out for you?'

It was an ongoing goal of Hal's to make the grumpy secretary laugh. To date, he'd been unsuccessful. There were two pools going – one for when he succeeded and one for when she grew tired of the game and clobbered him upside the head. The pot with the most amount of money was the second one. Alyssa herself had tossed in twenty.

'It's gonna happen, oh ye of little faith,' Hal said.

The rest of the conversation was cut off when Sandra strolled in, giggling at something Joe was saying.

'Care to share?' Hal asked.

'Nothing you haven't heard before,' Joe said. 'Just regaling our new teammie here with some of Tony's hunting adventures. Remember when he woke up in that hunting blind to find a bear had climbed the tree and was watching him sleep? He told us he almost peed himself.'

It had happened just last year when Tony was still Tony. Alyssa recalled how he'd shared the story with them, and how they'd all laughed so hard, they'd cried. She missed her teammate, and she knew the others did, too, but none more than Joe. Watching him settle himself next to Sandra, she wondered if he'd subconsciously paired himself with her because he missed the camaraderie with his best friend.

Alyssa cleared her throat to get everyone's attention, then gave an update on Elizabeth Monroe's condition which was unchanged from last night. The jovial mood of moments ago morphed into instant sobriety.

Sandra raised her hand. 'I asked Hal to help me check into that name you gave me. Alexandra Greene, aka Al, lived next door to the Bensons and attended Anasazi High School in Del Luna from 2009-2012. A couple weeks after Hayden Benson disappeared, Alexandra's mother, Helen Ross, put their house on the market and moved away. In July 2012, Helen Ross was killed in a single-car rollover accident on I-40.'

A soft knock on the door interrupted Sandra.

Alyssa peered up just as Ruby poked her head in. Missing was the usual scowl. In its place was a mixture of anxiety and pity – which was the first thing that sent Alyssa's blood pressure soaring to the ceiling. It crashed through the roof when, in a voice far from her normal growl, the secretary said, 'Detective, your daughter and her friends need to speak with you.'

Maybe it was Ruby's delivery or maybe it was the way Alyssa shot out of her seat and across the room like it was on fire, but she sensed her entire team on her heels with Cord directly behind her. One look at her daughter's pale face and the way her friends surrounded her was all it took for her to latch onto Holly's arm and corral everyone into an empty interrogation room, grateful that Cord joined them without her having to ask.

Holly fell, rather than sat, in the first chair she came to. Her elbows were pressed tightly into her sides as her body rocked almost imperceptibly. Nick, who would be in Holly's lap if he stood any closer, rubbed his palm briskly up and down her arm.

On the other side of her, Sophie, pale-faced, eyes glassy with moisture, perched on the very edge of her seat, Holly's left hand gripped between the two of hers. Across from the three of them sat Rachel and Jersey. Jersey's eyes darted rapidly around the room before focusing on the door as if cataloguing her only available escape route. Of all of them, Rachel was the least active, but Alyssa could tell by the way she stared down at her upturned palms as if they held all the answers to the questions plaguing them that she was far more affected than she appeared.

Teetering on the edge of losing her cool, Alyssa's voice was a little gruffer than she intended. 'What happened?'

From beneath lowered lids, Holly cast a glance in Cord's direction before averting her gaze and opening the satchel bag clutched between her hands. Her face lost all its remaining color as she placed another photograph on the table, using the tip of her fingernail to scoot it toward her mom.

Her voice was flat and inflectionless when she spoke. 'I was woken this morning by the doorbell. When I got to the door, no one was there. But this was stuck in the screen. There's a message on the back.' Nick squeezed Holly's shoulder as she shivered.

A pair of latex gloves appeared out of nowhere, and Alyssa was grateful Cord had thought of it. Her hands shook as she donned the gloves and pinched the photograph between two fingers. She read the message on the back first, not even minding when Cord read the uneven script over her shoulder. *We can get to you anytime, anywhere.*

A red haze obscured Alyssa's vision, but she forced herself to flip the image over. All the blood in her body drained down to pool at her feet. The image in her hand scared the hell out of her far more than any crime scene ever had.

She'd seen this photograph before – well, the unaltered version of it. It was one of hundreds that evidence technicians had taken when the trafficked girls had been located back in May. But how would someone outside of law enforcement have access to this photograph? In the original, Jersey and three other girls stared out of their cell as they waited for someone to unlock their cage and rescue them from their nightmare. Jersey had collapsed against the metal bars that day, crying out when she recognized Alyssa had come for her.

In this photo, however, three of the faces were scratched out, and superimposed over Jersey's was Holly's. The explicit threat was chilling in its own right, but it was the implicit threat that had Alyssa wanting to snatch Holly up right this second and lock her away in a convent. She didn't know how it was possible to be both numb and boiling over with rage, but she was.

'What the hell! Someone better start explaining.' The tic of Cord's pulse was clearly visible in the tendons bulging in his neck.

Four pairs of eyes darted back and forth between Holly and Alyssa, but Alyssa was focused on her daughter. Like her mother, Holly kept her real emotions safely under wraps, afraid of 'being a burden' or worrying everyone more than they already were. But this situation was different than some minor incident like denting the car or failing an exam; this was her daughter's life.

The uncomfortable, awkward silence grew thicker the longer it stretched out. Finally, Nick, in an admirably controlled voice and never taking his eyes off Holly, filled Cord in.

As Nick finished explaining the best he could, Alyssa turned to see her partner and friend firing daggers of barely suppressed anger in her direction. It took her a split second to grasp why he was so pissed at her – she'd failed to mention the first set of photographs last night when he'd called, and he was taking it as a personal affront. She opened her mouth to explain, but he stopped her with one growled word through clenched teeth: 'Later.'

–

Later was going to have to wait because after Holly and her friends left, Alyssa had one foot dangerously dangling off the ledge of losing her cool entirely, and she knew if she didn't get five minutes to herself, her wrath was going to rain down on a lot of undeserving people.

When Alyssa had suggested Holly explain her situation to her professors and ask for a few days off, she had flat-out refused to listen to reason. Exasperation swirled with fear for her daughter's safety, and so she'd called her daughter pigheaded and stubborn.

Holly had tipped her head to the side and pursed her lips, pointing at Alyssa, 'Pot' – she directed the finger at herself – 'kettle.'

Not amused, Alyssa aimed low. 'Fine. I'll call your dad and have him escort you to all your classes.' It was only a mild threat.

In the end, Cord had ended their stalemate by offering a compromise. Holly would text someone when her classes were out, and she wouldn't go anywhere alone for any reason. Period. Alyssa knew her firstborn's acquiescence came more from the terrified expressions on her friends' faces than anything else. Even the *thought* that she might be kidnapped and forced to endure the same horrors they had was more than just unimaginable.

Now, instead of heading back to the conference room to rejoin the rest of her team, Alyssa turned in the direction of her and Cord's shared miniscule closet of an office space. When Cord stalked after her, she held up her palm to stave him off, knowing he knew her well enough to read between the lines. 'I'm going to call Lynn to see if she has anything new on the Kensington case.'

Like she knew he would, he stopped. The same way she knew he was going to demand that explanation as to why she had held back on informing him of the first set of photographs.

Alone in her office, she dropped her head into her hands and allowed herself a moment before retrieving her phone from her pocket and dialing the medical examiner. As Sandra had pointed out the day they left Elizabeth Monroe's home after interviewing her, it was no secret that Alyssa's family came first. However, that didn't mean she didn't have a case to solve and two teenage girls to bring home. Recognizing that it still wasn't yet seven, she placed the call anyway, knowing Lynn would be in since she preferred the stillness of the early morning hours, much like Alyssa did.

Lynn answered on the fourth ring, out of breath as if she'd been running to get to the phone on time. 'Detective Wyatt. I'm guessing you're calling for an update, and I'm sorry I have nothing to report for you, other than finding a smear of blood in Addis's phone case. I've sent it off to the lab, but it'll be a while yet until I even know if it's usable. I know that's not what you wanted to hear, but I'm working as fast as I can. I know what's at stake here.'

Deflated but not surprised, Alyssa thanked Lynn and headed back to her teammates, making a quick detour for the sludge the department called coffee. It tasted like a mud puddle, but it was black and strong and that was all she cared about for the moment. Well, that and the fact that it gave her a few more precious moments before she had to face her disappointed partner.

Except Cord was sitting in the break room, his left ankle resting on his right knee, arms crossed, expecting her.

Ignoring her partner's disapproving glare, she sipped her coffee before saying, 'I didn't tell you last night when you called because, for one, you're cradling a lot as it is with Sara and the babies, and for two, I remember how difficult it was for you back in May what with the anniversary of your sister's death, and frankly, I didn't want to put your mind back in that place. That doesn't mean I trust you any less, not with my life or my family's.'

Cord said nothing at first. Then slowly, he uncrossed his legs and leaned forward until his elbows rested on the table, hands clasped together. 'Let me get this straight; you trust me, but you're operating on a double standard.'

'That's not—'

'I'm not finished. You realize that if I had treated *you* with kid gloves after the Evan Bishop case, you would've handed me my ass on a platter.' It was a bald statement with no room for argument. 'It's a double standard, no matter how you spin it, and to be candid, Lys, it pisses me off.'

Alyssa winced. He was right. 'I know, and—'

He cut her off again. 'This partnership of ours works because we trust each other personally and professionally, and we have each other's backs, no matter what. But if you start breaking down that system, then I gotta start thinking like maybe you don't think I'm quite as capable of performing my job, which means our well-oiled system is going to splinter.'

When Cord pushed to his feet, Alyssa thought he was finished, but he still had more. This time, the hurt in her partner's voice was clear. 'If I'd known confiding in you about what happened with Shelley would result in this, I would've kept it to myself.'

Alyssa felt her partner's words like a punch to the gut. 'Cord, everything you said is one hundred percent on the nose. And I'm sorry. I really am. You don't deserve that, and for the record, I have *never* doubted your ability to do your job or have my back. Ever. I want to be clear on that. It doesn't excuse what I've done, even if my heart was in the right place. All I can offer is my apology and hope you'll accept it.'

Cord cocked his head to the side. 'Does that mean you're going to let the team help? Because, you know, Hal, Joe, Tony, and even Ruby have watched Holly grow from a wobbly toddler playing with tape dispensers and highlighters into the dedicated, determined, strong, independent woman you and Brock raised her to be.'

'I promise.'

'Good because I already told them, so it's in the past and already forgotten.' At Alyssa's wide-eyed stare, he shrugged. 'I was pissed and worried. It came out. I'd apologize, but I'm not sorry. Besides, I want to find out who's terrorizing your girl, too. What kind of guy would I be if I didn't look out for the girl who's been "secretly" crushing out on me for years?' he joked.

Alyssa chuckled. 'You've got a point there.'

'Then let's go talk to the team in so we can put our heads together. On the way, you can tell me what Lynn had to say.'

'That'll be a short conversation. Nothing.'

Cord sighed. 'Well, before I came to check on you, Joe was on the phone with Hedge, so maybe he'll have some news from the crime scene.'

Chapter Twenty-Nine

Shivering, crying, and desperately trying not to give up, Addis slid down the tree trunk, pressing her back into the rough bark. The glowing orange of the sunrise might've shown them which direction they were heading, but that was where its assistance ended. Its heat didn't even offer a reprieve from the biting cold wind.

Yesterday, in the light of day and after having spent the most terror-filled night of their existence lost in the darkness, they'd decided that if they walked in a straight line without making any turns, they'd eventually emerge from this endless array of trails and trees. It had all sounded so simple. Scary, yes, but it was a solid plan, or so they'd thought. Except, at least three times, they had been forced to turn in a new direction. And twice, they'd found themselves back at their place of captivity.

The second time, Emerson had collapsed to her knees, smothering her sobs against the ground. And for a moment in time, Addis had considered giving up, crawling back inside, and hiding inside the niche in the wall. After all, there would be no reason their kidnapper and his accomplice would have to look for them there. And while the shack was far from warm, it couldn't be colder than it was out in the elements. Not to mention they'd be safer from the wild animals stalking the night, howling out their presence.

Ultimately, she knew there was no way she was going to be able to convince her own head and heart to willingly go back inside that place. Instead, she'd hugged the pocketknife in her palm, allowing a false sense of security to calm her. It may have offered no real protection, but it was all they had.

And then night had once again enveloped them in its entirety, forcing them to scale new heights of what Addis was sure Aunt Grace would call bravery, but which she called a losing battle to survive. And now with another day approaching, she nestled closer to her best friend and burrowed her head into the crook of Em's neck.

'Do you remember that time when Josie Martins and Brenda Mosley dared us to go through that haunted house?' Em's hoarse, scratchy voice was probably caused as much from her many spells of jagged crying as from the cold and fear.

Addis's pulse spiked at the mere mention of the memory. It hadn't been her finest moment. 'Yes.'

'Neither of us wanted to do it, but I mean, it was Josie and Brenda, our sworn enemies since the fourth grade.'

Addis loved Em, but exhaustion, starvation, and this hellish ordeal made her want to lash out to get to the point already. Because forcing her to relive that experience was *not* helping boost her confidence level by any stretch of the imagination. Besides, *that* had been fake. *This* was real.

'Well, even though we wanted to give up, we stuck it out. Together. And we got out of there. We puked afterwards, but we did it.' Emerson lifted her shoulder until Addis raised her head and stared at her. 'And we're going to do this, too. We have to. Because this time, we don't have a choice. This time, we can't say no and walk away. Because this time, if we don't do it, we're going to die. And I don't know about you, but I'm not ready to meet my maker just yet. We have too many plans. And since we're stronger together, I know we can do this.'

Addis wanted to believe her, but her penchant for positivity had run out somewhere between walking into her kitchen to discover her parents' murdered bodies and their daring yet foolish escape that had turned into nothing more than a colder version of captivity. 'What if you're wrong? What if we can't?'

Emerson cupped Addis's chin, forcing her to look at her. 'That night in the haunted house? You're the one who kept reminding me to stop thinking that way. It was one step in front of the other. This time our lives actually depend on our success, so we're going to do the same thing. Every time we hit one of those false exits, we're going to backtrack until we find the correct path.' Em closed her eyes and leaned her forehead against Addis's. 'You with me?'

What could Addis do but agree? After all, if Em could dig deep enough to convince herself to keep going, she could, too. Sheer grit and determination forced her to her feet. Wobbling on her weak legs, she locked her knees in place before extending her hand to pull Em up beside her. 'I'm with you.'

Chapter Thirty

Monday, October, 7

Walking back into the conference room, feeling the stares of her teammates, old and new, Alyssa did her best to ignore the pulsing headache quickly migrating to the front and sides, making her head feel like it had doubled in size and was now on the verge of exploding. Everyone locked their worried eyes on her. Even Sandra's face was draped in concern.

For now, she ignored the trepidation that cloaked them like a well-worn shawl because, as Cord had said, Joe was on the phone with one of their technicians, Bill Hedge. Even if Cord hadn't told her, she would've known because Hedge had a booming voice that could probably be heard from space, and so hearing him from across the room was no problem, especially as Joe was partially holding his cell away from his ear so as not to go deaf.

Raising his hand, he held his index finger and thumb close together in a gesture generally understood to mean *a little bit*, but which her team had come to recognize as Joe meaning *give me just another minute*.

While she waited, she tried to read Joe's expression. His eyes were wide, pupils dilated, and his skin was flushed, which generally meant he was either fatigued or excited. Could that mean they might have finally found one thread to tug at that would unravel this whole sordid mess and lead them to Addis and Emerson?

Hal drew her attention away by rolling his chair over to her and touching her hand. 'Don't shoot the messenger, but you look like hell, Lys.'

'Gee, that's so sweet of you to mention,' she snarled.

Hal's smile gave him a childish, cherubic appearance. But then he became serious again. 'You know I'm kidding, but Cord gave us a brief rundown on what's going on with that girl of yours, and I know you'll tell us more when you can, but for now I want to remind you that Brock, Holly, and Isaac aren't your only family. Don't shut us out.'

Embarrassingly, tears clouded her vision and threatened to spill over. Thankfully, she was saved from making a complete fool of herself by Joe's announcement as he hung up and sprang to his feet.

'This is it, folks, our first real break. Bad news first: Hedge was able to lift a fingerprint from Addis Kensington's phone, but as we expected, it turns out it belonged to her, so no help there. However, the good news is that the bullets retrieved from the scene were traced back to a twenty-two caliber Glock 19.' Joe was practically bouncing up and down. 'Are you ready for this? Of course, you are. The weapon used to kill Lydia Kensington and incapacitate Gabriel is registered to one Alexander Greene of Creede, Colorado.'

Instantly, an excited energy buzzed around the room.

'Did you say Alexan-*der* Greene?' Cord asked.

'Indeed, I did.' Joe's grin was contagious.

Hal and Sandra wore identical expressions of disbelief. Alyssa locked eyes with Cord before the two of them bolted out the door in search of Captain Hammond. Her impatience was palpable as she waited for the captain to wrap up the call he was on. It took a Herculean effort not to jerk the receiver from his ear and slam it down. Wise man that he was, he sensed their news was more urgent than his phone call and hung up with a barked, 'What?'

'We have a promising lead, but we're going to need your approval for a road trip.' Alyssa explained what Joe had learned.

When she finished, Hammond studied Cord. 'Do you feel comfortable heading out of the state with all that's going on with Sara? Because if you don't, I'll tag Joe or Sandra to accompany Alyssa.'

'I appreciate it, Captain, but one of Sara's friends, another nurse, is staying with us now, so I should be good to go.'

While Alyssa felt a tremendous sense of relief both because Sara wasn't alone and that Cord wanted to accompany her, she felt obligated to point out an important factor. 'It's nearly a five-hour drive. What if something happens?' The side-eyed look combined with the pursed lips was more than enough for her to know Cord was just as concerned about her leaving Holly right now as she was about him leaving Sara. But they both had jobs to do, and besides, there were plenty of people who would step in and up to protect her daughter. Except for a few friends, Cord was all Sara had, as her parents were out of the country until Thanksgiving a month and a half away.

'I tell you both what, I'll talk to Sara and see how she feels about me going. But I can already tell you she'll probably be relieved not to have me hovering over her all night' – a half-smile tipped one corner of his mouth as he repeated his earlier claim – 'even if I don't hover. I predict she'll have my bag packed and at the front door before I get off the phone.'

Even Hammond offered up one of his rare smiles at Cord's prediction.

'All right then. You make your call while I let Brock know, and let's see if we can be on the road in the next thirty minutes.'

Forty-two minutes later, after stopping first at Alyssa's and then Cord's – where Sara did indeed have his bag packed and ready for him at the door – they hit the interstate heading north.

'Sara looks better than I expected,' Alyssa admitted.

'Yeah, especially considering the babies have been kicking the hell out of her kidneys and bladder lately.' Cord winced and pressed the heel of his palm against his side as if he were experiencing sympathy pains.

Alyssa laughed. 'That crap hurts, so I'm glad she can smile through it.' They drove for a while in silence, and then she said, 'Fingers crossed and God willing that Alexander Greene can give us the answers we need.'

'Amen to that.'

Alyssa's foot pressed down a little harder on the gas, shooting up to fifteen miles past the posted speed limit signs. She promised herself she'd slow again at the New Mexico/Colorado border.

Chapter Thirty-One

Tuesday, October 8

Once a bustling hub known for its mining history, the tiny town of Creede, Colorado, now boasted a population of around three hundred. And it was the type of place where everybody knew everyone else's business, something Alyssa and Cord learned while eating dinner on the heated patio of the only café, where they were informed by no fewer than four locals that Alexander Greene wasn't expected back from his weekend camping trip until sometime after midnight. It hadn't taken long to guess that someone – or maybe a few someones – had seen them knocking on Mr. Greene's door earlier in the day.

Which is why they found themselves early Tuesday morning once again standing on the front stoop of the quaint house with the brilliant red door and purple siding built into the mountainside. Zipping her jacket and wrapping the softest, warmest scarf she'd ever purchased around her neck, Alyssa knocked on the door. She wasn't sure what she was expecting, but it definitely wasn't what she was seeing.

Haunted was the first descriptor that popped into her mind when she saw the man who answered the door. Instead of the late forties she knew him to be, thanks to

Hal's research, the man in front of them looked to be in his early sixties. 'Mr. Greene?'

'Yeah, that's me.' He kept one hand on the doorknob while the other pulled at the salt and pepper beard that still held a hint of the red his hair had once been. 'Tamara at the Snowshoe Lodge warned me two "city cops" were headed my way. Then Marcie at the gas station called right after Walter from the coffee shop did and clarified it was two *Albuquerque* detectives who needed to speak with me.' He rubbed his palm briskly over his balding head. 'I reckon since I didn't give them much to go on, they'll already be starting up the gossip mill to get things juiced up and going for the real deal. Before you leave town, the truth won't even matter.'

'Small-town living, right?' Cord said.

'Like most things in life, there's something to be said for and against it, I suppose. But I suspect that's not what you drove all the way from New Mexico to talk to me about, so why don't you both come on in?' He waved his arm toward a living area that held more rocks and mountain gear than it did furniture or photos. In the corner was an old-fashioned woodstove that reminded Alyssa of the one her father used to keep in the basement of their Indiana home. Sitting atop it was an old cast iron skillet, along with an ancient coffee percolator. 'Have a seat, why don't you?'

Alyssa and Cord settled onto a well-worn but comfortable sofa while Mr. Greene opened some curtains, the natural light neutralizing the dark gloom of the house. Within seconds, he eased himself into a La-Z-Boy recliner across from them.

Alyssa wasted no time diving right in. 'Mr. Greene, I appreciate you taking the time to meet with us, so I'll get straight to the heart of the matter. Last Thursday, we were called out to a double homicide where we discovered two teenage girls had also been kidnapped. Yesterday, we discovered one of the weapons used, a twenty-two caliber Glock 19, is registered to you. Can you explain that?'

Alexander Greene paled under her announcement, and he wiped one hand across his face. 'That gun went missing years ago when I left New Mexico after my divorce.'

'Did you report it stolen?'

'No ma'am because I knew my ex-wife had likely squirreled it away because it was the one she most preferred of the guns I had.'

'And your ex-wife is…?'

'Helen Ross.'

'When's the last time you spoke with Helen?' Cord showed no reaction to hearing the name.

'Seven years ago. July fourth. It was her favorite holiday what with all the fireworks lighting up the sky. She called to tell me she and' – he hesitated, closing his eyes before continuing – 'my daughter, Alexandra, had moved from their home in Del Luna. She – Helen – was killed in a car accident a week later. One of her front tires blew out going around a curve in the canyon. I found out when an old buddy read about it in the paper and called me.'

Sadness crept in, emphasizing the lines on his face, and Alyssa guessed that, divorced or not, Alexander Greene still loved his ex-wife.

'And what about your daughter, Mr. Greene? Are you in contact with Alexandra?'

The sorrow of moments earlier was replaced with a cold mask of indifference. 'No, I'm afraid not. Frankly, she's the reason I left New Mexico in the first place.' His hands tightened into fists that he pressed against his thighs.

'If anyone had told me on the day she was born – I didn't know a man could *feel* so much love – that one day my own daughter would scare the hell out of me, I would've laughed in that person's face.

'When Alexandra was a toddler, she was the epitome of a daddy's girl. She followed me everywhere and would've gone to work in the fields with me if I'd let her. From the time she was five, she went fishing and hunting with me as often as she was allowed. All that changed when she turned seven.'

'What happened when she was seven?' Alyssa prompted.

'I'm not sure I know how to explain. Alexandra was always so used to being the center of attention. It was pretty common for everyone to gush over her and compliment her perfect manners. And then a new little girl – Sasha – moved just down the road from us. They hit it off right away, but a few weeks later, when school started back up, things changed.' His fingers moved to drum on the arm of the chair, sending little dust motes to float in the air between them.

'The teachers loved Sasha. Everyone did, including the other kids. The boys, the girls, just everyone. It took about a week before I noticed the way Alex would go silent or grow inexplicably angry anytime Sasha's name was brought up. But then about a month into their school year, Alexandra asked if Sasha could sleep over. Of course, Helen and I agreed.

'The next morning, when the girls woke, Sasha had a huge bald spot where her hair had been sheared off. It was so bad, the only way to fix it was for her parents to buy her a wig or shave her head.'

Immediately, the image of Elizabeth's shorn ponytail popped into Alyssa's mind.

'Alex insisted Sasha must've been sleepwalking, but I will swear to the day I die that there was something dark in my daughter's eyes when she said it. Later that day when Sasha went out to feed her new bunnies that they kept in the barn... I'll spare you the details and just assure you they were no longer alive.'

Alyssa's gaze flickered over to Cord to gauge his reaction, but he was busy jotting notes in his tablet.

Alexander continued. 'That evening, I was throwing in some laundry and discovered so much blood on Alex's pajamas, it looked like she'd bathed in it. When I questioned her, she denied knowing what had happened. Let me just skip the rest and cut to the end scene. Over time, I began to fear for my life, as well as my wife's, but Helen was afraid of what people might think if we sent our own very young daughter away for help. Especially since I'd been doing some research. Now, I'm not what one might call experienced on the internet – never found a real need for it – but what I found out was that, while it might be exceedingly rare for a prepubescent child to be diagnosed with a severe psychosis, it was still possible.

'Then one evening, after Alex got in trouble for something, Helen grounded her and sent her to bed early. The next morning, both my wife's cockatiels were floating in the bathtub with broken necks. Helen and I got into a heated fight which ended with me pleading for her to wake up before something worse happened. Later that night I woke to Alexandra standing at my bedside...' Sweat not caused by the heat of the woodburning stove glistened over Mr. Greene's skin as his eyes darted around the room. 'One of my hunting knives was clutched in

233

both her hands. I remember thinking she was too tiny for something so large, that it looked more like a sword. But when my brain finally accepted what I was seeing, I realized that my seven-year-old daughter had the business end of a knife aimed just above my chest, waving it back and forth from my head to my heart as if deciding where she wanted to stab me first.'

Alexander uncapped the water bottle beside his chair and guzzled the contents before crinkling the plastic and tossing it into a trashcan a few feet away. 'Even then, Helen wouldn't relent. I'm not proud of it, but while she was at the grocery store, I packed my things and threw them in my truck. She came home before I could take off. She said she was hurt but understood.'

'What did you do regarding custody of Alexandra?' Alyssa asked.

'I didn't fight her, nor did she expect me to. I offered financial assistance, but she declined. I continued pleading with her to at least get Alex in to see a therapist, but she not only refused, she started shutting me down whenever I brought it up.' His right hand scrubbed at the top of his head. 'She was a good woman, Detectives, but she was the very definition of *pride goeth before the fall*, if you know what I mean.'

'Mr. Greene, you said the last time you spoke to your ex-wife was in 2012. Did that mean you also spoke to your daughter once in a while?'

'Absolutely not. At first I tried to stay on friendly terms with Helen, but she remarried quite quickly, and I kind of melted into the background. I'll admit I was actually relieved because, even hundreds of miles and a state away, I, a grown man, a veteran of the armed forces, was still terrified of my own child, and if there's anything that can make a man feel more pathetic, I sure don't know what it is.'

'You wouldn't happen to know the name of Helen's new husband would you?' Cord asked.

Alexander used his thumb and forefinger to smooth his beard, snapping them together when he remembered. 'Campbell was the last name. Couldn't say for sure about the first. But that marriage didn't last much longer after her son was born.'

'Son?'

'Yes, sir. One day out of the blue, Helen called to tell me she'd had a baby, a little boy. I never even asked his name. It was less than a year after I left, and I guess it hit me the wrong way—'

'What do you mean by the wrong way?' Alyssa asked.

Mr. Greene's chin bent toward his chest, putting his pink-tinged ears on full display. 'I suppose it would be safe to say I got a tidge jealous. Anyhow, I got maudlin and nostalgic, ended up getting drunk, and so I poured my heart into a letter that would've made Hallmark proud and mailed it off. It wasn't too long before I received a package with some pretty disturbing pictures printed off the computer. Things like a knife through a heart, dripping with blood, a decapitated animal, that type of thing. It was only the one time, and I've never gotten another thing.'

Alyssa sat up straighter. 'Do you still have them?'

Alexander shook his head. 'Nope. I actually took them to the police station one day to file a report, but they told me there was no way to prove they came from Alexandra and that, unless she did something overt, there wasn't much they could do. I figured if she ever chose the *overt* route, I'd be dead, and by then it would be too late.

Thought about calling Helen, but I'll tell ya, I just wasn't up for fighting that fruitless battle anymore. Maybe that makes me weak, but that's the God's honest truth.'

'If you didn't try to keep in touch after Helen remarried and had another child, how did you know she was divorced again?' Alyssa asked.

Alexander's eyes shifted to a mounted elk head on the wall. The long stretch of silence held more meaning than his words. 'Helen called one night, weeping like she'd lost everything. It's pretty shameful that my immediate thought was that our daughter had done something horrible. But when I finally got Helen calmed down a bit, she explained that, like me, her new husband had packed up and moved out, but this time, he'd taken their baby. Turns out I wasn't the only one who felt terrorized by Alexandra. But even after all that, Helen refused to seek help, but I don't know if that had more to do with her fear of how she'd be judged or if she herself was terrified of Alexandra's retaliation and didn't want to admit it.'

The detective in Alyssa shook her head at a person's ability to turn a blind eye to danger, but the mother in her understood that fierce drive to protect her child no matter the cost. 'Mr. Greene, do you have any idea where Alexandra lives now?'

'No, ma'am, and as long as it's far away from me, I don't care to know. Now, I've answered your questions, so I have a few of my own. You mentioned a double homicide and kidnapped teenagers. Can I take that to mean you believe my—Alexandra—is somehow involved?'

It was Cord who fielded this answer. 'We're still trying to figure that out ourselves.'

On a whim, Alyssa raised another question. 'Do you know anything about your ex-wife's neighbors in Del Luna?'

'No. Should I?'

'I was just curious. What about Mack or Gabriel Kensington – either of those ring a bell?'

It was Cord's turn to shoot a sideways glance in her direction, but she ignored him, not wanting to miss any telling looks on Mr. Greene's face, but it didn't matter because aside from crinkling his forehead as he rolled the names over in his mental Rolodex, it was clear the Kensington name meant nothing to him.

He confirmed her suspicion with a decided, 'No again. Sorry.'

Tossing out her last real hope, Alyssa said, 'I suppose it would be too much to hope you've got any photographs of Alexandra or your wife lying around.'

'Burned the lot of them one night in a drunken pity party for myself.'

Discouraged, Alyssa pushed to her feet, retrieving a business card as she did. Handing it over, she said, 'Mr. Greene, we appreciate you taking the time to speak with us. If there's anything else you can think of, please don't hesitate to call.'

Coming to his feet, Alexander ripped off a sheet of paper from a nearby notepad and scribbled something on it before handing it to Cord. 'Here's my number if you need to get ahold of me for any reason. I don't relish ever coming face to face with my daughter again, mind you, but if there's something I can help with, I'd like to do it.' He turned his head away from them. 'Maybe then I won't feel such a burden of guilt for abandoning my wife.'

Staring at the back of Mr. Greene's head gave Alyssa an idea. It was a long shot, perhaps, but worth it. 'Do you mind if we take a strand of your hair for DNA purposes, just in case?'

Without hesitation, Alexander reached up and yanked out several strands of his beard. 'Let me grab a sandwich bag for you,' he said, disappearing into the kitchen and handing it over when he returned.

At the door, Alyssa thanked him again. Then partway down the steps, he stopped them with words that carried the weight of failure. 'God help you, Detectives, if Alexandra had anything to do with these killings and kidnappings.' And then he turned on his heel and headed back inside.

Back in the car and headed for Albuquerque, Alyssa said, 'I don't know what you're thinking, but I'm of the opinion that Alexandra Greene has just moved her way up to the number one spot on my list of suspects.'

'One hundred percent with you,' Cord agreed.

Chapter Thirty-Two

The exploding fragments of her perfect plan sent Alex into a frenzy of crazed destruction. She couldn't believe that after all she'd done for Adam, he'd gone and changed the locks to his house, which meant he probably suspected he would never make it to the NFL because dead people couldn't play football.

A disappointment, really, considering all she'd done to ensure his success in that department. At seventeen, when he'd been distraught over the possibility that his high school rival was getting more traction and attention from the college scouts, she'd sliced the guy's brake lines and forced him off the road, effectively ending his football career before it could get off the ground. Because it wasn't only dead guys who couldn't play in the NFL; neither could those who were paralyzed from the waist down.

And what about the sixteen-year-old kid who'd heckled him mercilessly online after Adam had fumbled the ball that resulted in his team losing the state championship? For days, Adam had fallen into a deep depression about it. A week later, when that kid was found facedown in the river with his throat slit and his tongue removed, Adam had come to her, demanding to know if she was responsible. She'd smiled and shrugged, and though he insisted he was angry, that he'd never wanted that, it hadn't taken long for him to pull out of his funk.

Hell, she'd even snapped the neck of his ex-girlfriend's cat after it had scratched him and caused such an awful infection, he hadn't been able to play the sport he loved for two weeks.

After all that, he had the audacity to try to lock *her* out, to choose the lives of two stupid, insipid teenagers over her? That treachery alone was worthy of his death.

But that would have to wait because he hadn't returned home last night, and so she'd been forced to head up to the mountains herself to track Addis Kensington and Emerson Childress. She knew they were still out there because if they'd somehow miraculously found their way to safety, it would've been all over the news. So, they'd either been killed by the wildlife or they were still stumbling around hoping for a savior to come along and rescue them. And didn't she look like a savior?

However, when hours of tracking the rugged terrain produced no evidence of any possible trails, she'd barely managed to suppress the guttural roar that had been building up inside her. Consumed with a burning rage, she'd hiked back to her truck and headed down the mountain. If she couldn't take care of the girls – yet – she'd just have to go deal with the other issue that threatened to topple her house of cards – Elizabeth Monroe.

But before this day was over, she vowed, all her problems would be solved once and for all, including Adam.

Chapter Thirty-Three

Pareidolia. The phenomenon where a person saw shapes in everyday objects – like the rusted metal grate sitting cockeyed above Addis's head and currently mocking her with its smirky smile as it dripped moisture into the shallow hole she and Em had agreed would be their best option for 'refuge' for the night. Now peeking over at Emerson's restless, shivering, semi-sleeping form, she began to wonder about the intelligence of their choice.

As yet another night had fallen, leaving them once again lost in the literal darkness of this nightmare and a forest filled with the eerie calls of wildlife, Emerson had tripped and fallen onto a metal grate, wrenching her wrist in the process. Too weak to help her up, Addis had collapsed next to her, where the two had clung to each other, neither wanting to admit they could no longer go on.

It was only when the clouds veiling the meager light from the moon lifted that Addis finally saw what Em had tripped over. 'A cattle guard,' she whispered. She may not know much about the not-so-great outdoors, but she did know that, supposedly anyway, these were meant to stop livestock and wildlife from crossing. Her heart thumped painfully inside her chest. If there were cattle guards, there might be ranchers nearby.

As quickly as the excitement ignited, it fizzled out. Even if they did magically stagger upon another living soul in the inky blackness of the night, how would they know who they could trust, especially since they'd never seen their kidnapper's accomplice? Logically, she knew they would eventually have to trust someone, but for some reason, the thought of doing so in the dark was something every fiber of her being shied away from.

When she spotted the broken gap in the cattle guard, a wisp of an idea shaped itself into an action. If they crawled into the space beneath the metal, they would be better hidden as well as protected from hungry animals.

'What if – what if we squeeze down there' – Addis jabbed her finger toward the hole – 'and shelter for the night? I mean, it won't protect us from the weather, but it'll help keep the animals away.'

Emerson hesitated. 'How far down does it go?'

Lying on her stomach, Addis peeked through the slats in the grate, trying to keep the lump of terror lodged in her throat from escaping. A better question would be: what kinds of things currently claimed this space as their habitat? Gagging, she scooted forward until her upper body rested on the still secure bars and then dangled her left arm into the black abyss, doing her best to tune out Emerson's frantic *what are you doings* as she tried to convince her brain that nothing was crawling on her skin, that no legendary monster was at this moment about to latch onto her arm and drag her down to its lair.

'I can't tell how deep it is, but I can't feel the bottom. It might be a tight squeeze, but I think we have to try, Em. It's dark, so what else can we do?'

For the longest time, the only answer came from the mysterious sounds of nature before Emerson finally agreed. 'You're right; it might be our best option.'

The width of the gap had been deceptive, and so it hadn't been quite as simple slipping between the open bars as they'd thought. Addis had shimmied in first, bearing the brunt of the serrated edges of broken metal scraping against her skin because she'd been able to guide Emerson away from the worst of it. At least the drop wasn't as bad as she was afraid it might be since it turned out the hole was only approximately two feet deep. It meant they'd have to lie down, but that couldn't be any worse than what they'd already been through. At least that was what she tried to tell herself even as the stench of rotting trash and God-knows-what-else seemed to seep into her nostrils and every inch of exposed skin.

And now, in the dawning light of day, Addis wondered if she had the strength or even desire to drag herself back up. It wasn't that the distance was so great, or at least it wouldn't have been if she wasn't fatigued and oh-so-cold, but the very real notion that they had to *trust* someone out there to help them was simply too much for her overtaxed mind and body.

Beside her, Emerson was beginning to stir from her not-quite sleeping, not-quite awake state, and Addis reached out to rub warmth into her best friend's arm. When Em spoke, her throat was scratchy and raw, changing the natural cadence of her voice.

'God, Ad, what are we going to do? There's no way we can keep going like this.' Moisture trickled down her cheeks as the first round of tears for the day released. 'I don't *want* to do this anymore,' she cried.

Addis didn't have a response anyway, but that ceased to matter when the rumble of an engine broke through the sounds of nature. Friend or foe? There was only one way to find out, but could she do it? Was she brave enough?

Guessing Addis's intention, Emerson's fingernails sliced into her arm, dragging her back when she moved to poke her head through the gap. 'Wait until it passes. Please. It might be *them*.'

Or it might not be. Even so, Addis hunkered back down with her friend a breath before a truck thundered over them, knocking debris and mud onto their heads, forcing them to release each other in an effort to shield their eyes.

Only when the truck passed, and Addis had counted to ten did she risk sitting up again, the top of her head grazing the bars. Then slowly, she crawled back to the gap and rose until she could peer out. It was like a hundred hammers slamming against her ribcage when she realized the vehicle was backing up, the driver's eyes staring right at her through the rearview mirror.

Muffling a scream, she dropped back down, ignoring the scorching pain brought about by a piece of metal gouging across her cheekbone and scuttling back with hands and feet as she subconsciously sheltered Emerson's body with her own.

'What is it? What did you see? Is it them?'

Addis couldn't speak because her vocal cords were frozen upon hearing the echoes of a car door opening followed by crackling sticks and leaves as the person in the truck approached the refuge that had inadvertently become their new prison.

The crunching sounds of booted footsteps stopped, casting a shadow into the hole, and Addis screamed at the pasty face looming from above and peering down.

Chapter Thirty-Four

It was close to three o'clock when Joe called. They'd just passed into Albuquerque's city limits, and Alyssa was just realizing how famished she was since neither she nor Cord had wanted to stop for more than a small bag of chips and a soda when they stopped to fill up for gas.

'Hey, Joe. What's up?'

Anger sizzled over the line. 'Where are you?'

A thick layer of apprehension coated the oxygen in the air. 'Just drove back into town. We should be at the precinct in thirty minutes or so. What's going on?'

'Apparently, Elizabeth Monroe went into cardiac arrest today.'

Alyssa recognized the tight control of Joe's voice; it was the tone he used when he'd neared the edges of restraint. What she didn't understand was why. This might be bad news, but it wasn't the kind that warranted this type of reaction. 'What aren't you telling us, Joe?'

'The guard responsible for watching Monroe's room slipped away to use the restroom. He insists he was gone less than two minutes, and that when he returned, he poked his head in, made sure all was still kosher, and then about five minutes later, the alarms inside the room went off. Someone yelled out a code blue, doctors and nurses raced in, and he caught sight of one of the nurses doing chest compressions while another one grabbed the AED. Then he was closed out of the action. He tried to find the nurse who'd checked on her earlier, but apparently she'd already gone off shift.'

The image of Brandon Monroe standing on his friend's porch trying to be so brave while vowing to find the person who hurt his mom breached the edges of Alyssa's memory, and she felt a fist squeeze around her heart.

'Have you been able to personally speak to any of the medical staff?' Cord asked.

'Actually, yes. Do you remember Dr. Homa?'

'The doctor who treated Callie McCormick. Yeah, of course, I remember her.'

'Well, believe it or not, she's Elizabeth's doctor, as well. As soon as I explained there might be a link between Monroe and two missing teenagers, one whose parents had been murdered, she cut me off and told me she'd be happy to speak with the two of you. She left her personal number.'

Like Cord, Alyssa remembered Dr. Homa from the Evan Bishop case. Compassionate and passionate, she'd been as devastated as the detectives at what had happened to Callie. 'Can you text me the number? Also, would you mind updating Captain Hammond?'

'Hal's doing that as we speak. Sandra and I are combing through old yearbooks from Anasazi High School, but aside from class photos that prove she attended the same school as Hayden Benson, there's nothing much to tie Alexandra Greene to him, apart from her living next door to the Bensons, that is. We're still digging, but the girl's like a ghost. No digital footprint – not even any credit cards

247

that are tied to her name, at least none that we've found. Was your road trip successful?'

'Yes and no. Alexander Greene is Alexandra's father, but he left the family when she was seven. We'll fill the team in on that development as soon as we get back to the station. We confirmed what Sandra already told us, that Helen Ross died in a car accident July 2012. According to Mr. Greene, though, after their divorce, Helen remarried and had another child, a boy. He never asked the name, but he also mentioned they, too, divorced, which I assume is why Helen reverted back to her maiden name.'

Similar to the effects the sound of crunching glass mixing with metal had on her, the sound of lead scratching across paper sent shivers tingling along Alyssa's spine as Joe scribbled notes on what she'd said.

'I'll get on this right away and see what else I can dig up.' There was a light thud as if Joe had tapped his fist or dropped the pencil, and then he released a heavy sigh.

Alyssa and Cord exchanged identical looks of concern. 'What is it? There's clearly something else on your mind.'

'Look, Tony hasn't been answering his phone, and when I went to his house last night to check on him, the mailbox was stuffed, and several issues of the *Albuquerque Journal* dating back to Saturday were still lying in the driveway.'

'Maybe he's up at his hunting cabin?' Because she knew him so well, Alyssa heard the apprehension in Cord's voice, just as she knew he was trying to stay positive for Joe.

'Already considered that, but have you ever known Tony not to hit me up to check on his mail or get his paper out of the drive? You know how paranoid he is about that kind of thing.'

'I know you're worried about him, Joe. All of us are. Let's put our heads together later and see if we can come up with a plan to reach him.' Even as the words passed her mouth, Alyssa was thinking that Tony was more than just a great cop; he was a skilled hunter and tracker, and an avid survivalist on top of that, so if he didn't want to be found, he wouldn't be.

Chapter Thirty-Five

Tuesday, October 8

It was the dampness of the ground seeping into her clothes, as well as the setting sun filtering through the leaves and shining into her eyes that once again dragged Addis back to semi-consciousness beneath a barely-there canopy of trees. Squinting as much to avoid being blinded as to stop the brightness from setting her brain on fire, she carefully inched her head to the left and then to the right.

'Em? Emerson, please, please, please.' Even if she hadn't already known that her best friend wouldn't respond, Addis couldn't stop herself from crying out her name. And just like the dozen other times, silence met her pleas.

She had no idea exactly how long she'd been blinking in and out of awareness, but she knew that each time she'd willed her eyes to open, the sun's position had shifted. The drop in temperature, along with the fading light, was enough to tell her she'd lost the entire day.

Exhausted, starving, her body and mind battered, Addis knew she no longer had any fight left in her. But worse than that was the fact that she had finally accepted that she had nothing, and no one, left to hang on for. Picturing Aunt Grace's face when she realized Addis would never be coming home again, she burrowed under a heavy blanket of guilt that she was giving up. She wished she had the will to go on, but she just didn't.

Emerson.

Her best friend's name was a whispered cry that eked its way past the balloon of grief in her chest. She squeezed her eyes tight against the memory of being pulled from the space below the cattle guard, her screams mingling with Emerson's, watching her best friend's wild-eyed panic as she'd shaken her head in denial and reached up as if by sheer will she could save Addis.

At that exact moment, Addis had known that her death was unavoidable, but that it didn't have to be the end for Emerson, that in fact, this could be her friend's best chance to truly escape.

An incredible pressure had built inside her as she mouthed *I love you*. Then, shutting out Emerson's terrified screeching, she'd allowed her body to go limp as she was hauled up. She'd waited until her captor practically dropped her and turned back for Emerson before putting what remained of her waning energy into an earnest struggle, kicking, biting, and scratching until she'd spotted her best friend clawing her way out between the gap in the metal.

Run, Em, run. She'd pleaded with her eyes when Emerson wavered, her horrified stare trained on what was unfolding in front of her.

A rough voice had growled as two weathered hands clasped onto Addis and yanked her up, but the words had been lost in the violence of her struggle because she knew – she was no longer fighting for her own life; she was fighting for the friend who'd stood beside her through all life's ups and downs. Even if the price was her death, she owed it to Em to try.

The last sounds she'd heard from Emerson were her soft, muffled whimpers a second before she'd slipped into the shadows of the trees. There had been a string of curses, and then Addis's head had snapped back as pain exploded in her left jaw and radiated up into her temple, sending a burning sensation flashing across her entire face.

And then there had been nothing but darkness.

Until she'd woken up with the sun dipping into nothingness, and a few scattered stars beginning to peek through the fragmented clouds.

A blast of breaking branches announced the presence of someone trampling through the brush. She watched as a man stepped into the small clearing, a wicked knife gripped in one hand, another hiding in a sheath strapped to his leg, a rifle secured across his back, and a dark smile dancing around his eyes as he held one finger up against his lips, shaking his head back and forth in warning.

Sobs ripped from her throat, and she closed her eyes so she wouldn't have to see the knife, praying her death would be quick and easy. She didn't want to go like her father. *Please, just shoot me.*

She had no idea if her plea was only in her head or if she uttered it out loud.

Chapter Thirty-Six

Tuesday, October 8

The day had been interminably long already, and it wasn't over yet. Alyssa rubbed her tired eyes and squinted at the clock, only mildly surprised that the time had already bumped past seven and was climbing closer to seven-forty. It hardly seemed possible that only this morning, she and Cord were in Creede, Colorado.

She shoved guilt aside and sent a message to Brock that she wouldn't be home until late. He responded with his usual:

> Don't forget to eat. If I'm asleep when you get home, wake me. I love you.

She shot off a quick reply:

> Love you back. Promise to make it up to you and Isaac when things settle.

She added a heart emoji, hit send, and then set her phone aside. Before texting Brock, she'd called Holly to check in and to see if she'd received any more threatening notes.

She hadn't, but Alyssa's tension didn't ease at the sickening thought that someone twisted, possibly from *The Toybox* case, was currently targeting her daughter. But right now, Holly was safe, surrounded by friends, and so, at least for this moment, she pushed aside her fear so she could concentrate on the grave matter of locating Addis and Emerson.

Transferring her focus to the sea of evidence, crime scene photos, and interview records, she willed them to unlock their secrets and reveal the link that would bust this case wide open so she could bring the girls home.

The one-week mark was biting at their heels, reminding her that she and her team still had no viable leads and no real suspects aside from a woman who had seemingly beamed herself off the planet following Hayden Benson's disappearance, which in and of itself sent up enough red flags to lift a ship. Just thinking about how the Del Luna police department handled – or didn't handle – the Benson case made her want to spit nails. Disgusted, she thrust an open file away from her, causing dozens of loose pages to flutter in the air and land haphazardly on the floor and table.

'I just got back, so I know that anger's not directed at me,' Cord said as he stepped into the room.

Alyssa whirled around. 'How's Sara?' Earlier, he'd called to see how she was doing, and something in her voice had prompted him to run home to check on her.

The word *pride* may as well have been written in glowing letters on his forehead. 'That woman is a warrior. I don't know how she does it.'

'You know if you need to go be with her—'

Cord sealed her argument with the one thing he knew she wouldn't rebut. 'If that were Isaac or Holly out there, how would you feel if all hands weren't on deck? And Sara really is fine at the moment, and she's not alone, either. Now' – he waved his arm dramatically over the mess Alyssa had made – 'want to tell me what this is all about?'

'Rosalyn Benson was right – the Del Luna PD of 2012 was inept at best and outright criminal in their negligence to follow up on Hayden's disappearance. They ruled him as an eighteen-year-old kid who skipped out on his responsibilities and left us with nothing but a half-assed attempt at a police report to go on. No witness statements, no efforts of even the most rudimentary search in case they were mistaken. Because clearly, if there's no vehicle and no phone, then there must be no crime. What police academy did they attend?' Had those officers been under her – or Captain Hammond's – supervision, there would've been hell to pay.

Shoveling her fingers through her hair, she stared at the diagram Joe and Sandra had created while she and Cord were in Colorado. Gabriel, Lydia, Addis, Emerson, Elizabeth, Grace, Mack, Rosalyn, Hayden, Helen, Alexander, and now Alexandra Greene's names were scrawled along the top. Alyssa had added *Campbell (?)* to the end. 'It seems to me that half the names listed up there circle back to Alexandra Greene. So, where is she now?'

'I wish the lab would hurry up with that DNA analysis of the blood found in Addis's phone case,' Cord said. 'Wouldn't it put a pretty bow on things if it came back as belonging to Alexandra?'

'It would, but that still wouldn't tell us where the girls are.'

'What wouldn't tell us where the girls are?' Sandra walked in and set down a coffee brew box and two dozen doughnuts on the table. 'I know it's a cliché, but I figured we'd need copious amounts of both sugar and caffeine for the all-nighter I suspect we're about to pull. By the way, Joe and Hal are right behind me.'

'I'm ready to rock and roll,' Joe said around a yawn, followed by a mile-wide grin when he spotted the coffee and doughnuts. 'Whoever brought these, you're my hero.'

Sandra chuckled as she handed Joe a Styrofoam cup along with a paper plate and napkin. 'I've always wanted to be someone's hero.'

When everyone was finally settled, Alyssa and Cord brought Joe, Hal, and Sandra up to speed regarding their visit with Alexander Greene.

'So,' Sandra said, 'what you're saying, or at least what I'm hearing, is that you don't just believe this Alexandra fits into the bigger picture, you believe she *is* the bigger picture?'

Before Alyssa could answer, an exhausted Lynn Sharp poked her head in. 'Thought I might find you all in here. The DNA results from the blood found in Addis Kensington's phone came back as a match for an Adam Campbell.'

Helen Ross's second ex-husband's surname was Campbell. But that wasn't what caused the electric jolt. That name sounded familiar. She turned to Cord, but both he and Hal wore almost identical comical expressions. 'What?' she demanded.

Hal pulled at his earlobe. 'There's a football player by that name over at UNM who's got all sorts of NFL scouts salivating at the mouth for their shot at him.'

Cord nodded. 'Guy might only be a sophomore, but his arm's a damn torpedo on the field.'

The way Joe shifted in his chair and wrinkled his forehead was enough to tell Alyssa that whatever he was about to share, she wasn't going to like. 'His arm's not the only reason you might remember his name.' His gaze shifted from Cord to Alyssa. 'Two years ago, he was one of six individuals whose DNA was collected when police were investigating a date rape case on campus. For the record, Campbell was cleared in that incident.'

While she noticed the disgust that skated across Sandra's face, what Alyssa heard was rape, UNM, and football, and not only because she remembered now why the name was familiar to her. Isaac idolized the Lobos football star. Thinking back, she could clearly recall how devastated he'd been when the news of Campbell's possible involvement broke in that rape case, and the utter relief he'd shown when Adam was cleared.

But it was the image of Holly's face superimposed over Jersey's that froze in her memory. Beau Cambridge was Jersey's ass of an ex-boyfriend and also played football at the university. Her neck twisted to the left as she stared at the whiteboard where she'd written *Campbell (?)*. Her hand hit something, and she heard a crash and a murmur of voices, but it was all white noise as her entire skeletal system turned into jelly.

Unaware she was doing it, Alyssa picked up a marker and jotted Holly's name with a dotted line connecting to Campbell. But the hits didn't end there. When she turned back to face her team, she saw Hal rubbing at his brow as if he was trying to wipe it off his suddenly ashen face. And she knew, whatever he was thinking was worse than bad. 'You've obviously got something to share, Hal. Just spit it out. No matter what it is, we have to know if we're going to find Addis and Emerson.' *And protect Holly*, she thought to herself.

'When Adam Campbell was eight, he played for the Albuquerque Bandits' junior pee-wee league.'

All the oxygen seemed to be sucked from the room. Except for Sandra, the entire team was immobilized by this information. Almost reluctantly, their newest member asked, 'What does that mean?'

The monotone quietness of Joe's response masked an underlying current of shock. 'Tony helped coach the Albuquerque Bandits for about five years – around the time Adam Campbell would've been eight years old. Tony was so excited when Adam announced his intent to play for the Lobos that it was all he talked about for a week.'

Nausea burned a hole in Alyssa's stomach. Part of processing *The Toybox* house of horrors had included recordings of the crime scene, as well as hundreds, if not thousands, of still pictures. *Four terrified girls locked in a cell, shivering, and sobbing as they waited to be rescued. Jersey clinging to the bars as Alyssa unlocked their prison door.* That particular photograph, the same one that had been altered to include Holly's face, Alyssa knew, had been one of many placed into a box of evidence. Only someone close to the investigation would've known about it. Someone like Tony. Had she been so unwilling to see the truth of what was right in front of her that she'd refused to see how he was sewn into the tapestry of this story?

The throb behind her eyes exploded into a full-swinging sledgehammer that pounded deep into the center of her brain.

Because the alternative was unimaginable, she wanted to believe this was one time the details had to be nothing more than coincidence. But there were things glaringly obvious that she couldn't ignore. Such as the fact that Tony had returned early from a hunting trip, scratches on his face and arms, and he was at the Kensington crime scene. And then he'd conveniently abandoned the team at the onset of this case.

But more importantly, not only did he have access to evidence from *The Toybox* case, he knew the lengths to which Alyssa would go to protect her family – and he'd know the best way to distract her would be to go after one of her children.

But why?

The touch of Cord's hand on her forearm snapped her back. Barely hanging on to her composure, she turned to Hal. 'I need you to dig up Adam Campbell's address two minutes ago.'

Hal's fingers flew over his keyboard. 'Done. Should be showing up on your phone any second now.'

He was still speaking when her phone chimed. 'You're the best.'

'I know, but it's good to hear other people admit it once in a while.'

The weak attempt at humor glided right over Alyssa's head. She didn't know how, or even if, the photos sent to Holly could be linked back to Tony, Adam Campbell, the Kensington murders, or the girls' disappearance, but she'd move heaven and earth to figure it out.

Snatching her phone off the table, she headed for the door. 'Cord, Joe, come with me. Hal, Sandra, I need you to find out everything you can about this guy. Something tells me we're going to find out he's Alexandra Greene's half-brother.'

The hair at the back of Alyssa's nape lifted. Along with the fact that Adam Campbell's DNA had been discovered at the crime scene was Lynn's theory that Gabriel's murderer might have been female or a short male, leading her to the unshakeable realization that they may be looking for two killers.

And while that might answer some of her questions, it didn't explain how Tony fit into the puzzle. But even worse was knowing that Addis and Emerson could be in the clutches of *two* psychotic individuals who were clearly unafraid of using violence as a means to an end.

–

The realization that Adam Campbell's house was less than a quarter mile from where Holly and her friends lived made Alyssa lightheaded. But she shoved that aside as she climbed the porch. All the blinds were closed, and there was no evidence of lights on anywhere. Her fist hovered in the air as Cord took up residence near a window layered in years of dirt and grime while Joe waited at the side of the house in case someone exited out the back. When everyone was in position, she knocked.

'Albuquerque Police. Open up!' she yelled, startling at least one neighbor's yappy dog into a frenzied bark. Soon after, several others joined in the chorus, causing the hair at the nape of her neck to stand up. She was glad Ghost wasn't a barker. When he sensed his version of danger, he'd stand in a rigid protective stance until it was gone. Only once had she witnessed him growl deep in his throat and bare his teeth, and that was at a man who'd been at the park watching a group of unsupervised children. Ghost's reaction had been so strange and unexpected that Alyssa had stayed and watched until the man finally left, and the children ran into a house in the adjacent neighborhood.

'Excuse me. If you're looking for Adam, he left just before you got here. Said he was heading out of town for the week.'

Alyssa shifted so that she could see both the person speaking as well as the front door. A young woman was struggling to control a huge, growling Rottweiler currently trying to escape the grip she had on its leash. She was a little surprised the muscular animal hadn't yanked the girl's arms right out of their sockets.

'Did he say where he was going?'

'Nope, just that he needed to get out of the city for a while.'

'Are the two of you friends?'

Adam's neighbor actually snorted. 'Pfft, no. I know he plays on the football team and that he's very quiet for an athlete. I've tried a few times to engage him in conversation, but while he's not unkind, he's pretty standoffish. Which is kind of why it surprised me that he mentioned he was leaving at all, especially since it's football season.' Her dog had finally quieted and plopped himself down as he leaned his thick body into his owner's legs, almost knocking her off-balance. She patted the top of his head and when she looked back up, she said. 'Am I allowed to ask if everything's okay? Is he in trouble for something?'

Alyssa ignored the question. 'What's your name?'

'Emilia Martinez. I live two doors down.' Emilia pointed behind her.

'Did you ever see him with his sister?' Alyssa asked the question out of pure instinct.

'Um, I'm not sure?' Emilia's answer was posed as a question. 'He didn't really have many visitors, which I always thought was a little strange for a football player, but what do I know? I'm not a fan of the sport. But on occasion, I did see the same girl come visit him. It was always dark, and so I never really got a good look at her.'

'I don't suppose you happened to see what kind of vehicle this girl drove, did you?' Every cell in Alyssa's body was beginning to vibrate. With each new discovery, they were close to getting answers; she could feel it.

'A truck, that's all I can tell you. I don't even know what color. Sorry.' With each response, Emilia's voice grew heavier with concern.

'That's okay. You've been very helpful.' Alyssa pulled a business card out of her pocket and started to hand it over before she noticed the way the Rottweiler's body tensed as he growled low in warning. Thinking better of it, she set the card down on the railing and backed away. 'Would you mind giving me a call if you see Adam, the girl, or the truck?'

'Sure, no problem.'

Despite the horrifying implication that one of her cherished team members might somehow be involved, as well as the frustration at being unable to question Adam Campbell, Alyssa felt a zing of excitement. She sensed that they'd finally found the link that might break this case wide open.

'I'm going to call Holly and see if the name Adam Campbell means anything to her or the others,' she said as she climbed back into her Tahoe and pulled away from the curb. A tornado of emotions swirled through her – excitement that they may finally be getting closer to solving this case, as well as fear of what might be revealed when their questions were finally answered. When they found Addis and Emerson, would they still be alive? Or would her team be moving in to recover two more corpses?

Not caring that Cord and Joe were listening, she whispered, 'Keep fighting, girls. Don't give up. We're going to find you.' She refused to believe she was speaking to their ghosts.

Failure was not an option.

Chapter Thirty-Seven

Like a crab evading the net, Addis scrambled backwards and away from the man as he fumbled in his knapsack. Through swollen eyes, she watched him waving something thin and black in front of her. His mouth moved, but the roaring in her ears turned his words into little more than a series of vibrations in the air.

She didn't recognize this man, not like she'd recognized the kidnapper who'd taken them from her house. She desperately wanted to ask him what he'd done with Emerson because she knew he must've gone after her after knocking her unconscious. But she also knew she was terrified of the answer.

If she didn't know, then she could pretend Em had escaped, that she was on her way to finding help. Of course, the possibility of Em ever being able to lead rescuers back to her was less than slim, especially since Em could get lost going around the block.

'Come on, stand up.'

Because Addis had sunk so deeply into the fantasy of believing Em had escaped, the man's gruff, gravelly voice had the same effect as an ice bucket of water being splashed over her. Her muscles were beyond weak from lack of food or water, not to mention the all-too-paralyzing numbness of her situation, but too frightened to do anything else, she nonetheless did her best to obey.

But it was a fruitless effort as she lost against gravity once, twice, then three times. As her legs collapsed beneath her yet again, something shifted inside her, and it took her a second to recognize it as fury. Why was she giving up? Why was she acting as if her death was a foregone conclusion? Where had her will to survive gone? *You're stronger than you know, Addis Penn Kensington.* Aunt Grace's consistent advice anytime Addis came to her with one of her struggles filtered through the white noise of the wind through the trees, giving her a renewed strength, mentally at least.

Fortified with fresh resolve, she hugged one of the trees and used it to help her stay upright. But even as her knees locked into place, she knew as soon as she released the trunk, she would be kissing the damp earth once more. She managed a few shuffling steps before she tripped over her own two feet and went sprawling forward, just barely managing to catch the brunt of the fall with her arms instead of her face. Battling against the scream building in her throat, Addis realized her will to continue fighting for survival had been short-lived.

Get up, Addis. Right now. Keep fighting.

Aunt Grace's voice was more muffled in her memory this time, so Addis told it to shut up. Grief mixed with anger as she told her aunt she had nothing left. *If you really wanted me to keep fighting, you would've found a way to save me already. But you didn't, and I'm too tired and too weak to care anymore, so just leave me alone and let me die.*

One minute she was giving up, and the next, the man was squatting in front of her so he could swoop her up into his arms. Her terrified scream was muffled when the man shoved her face against his shoulder so hard that her teeth cut into her lips.

'Quiet!' His abrupt order was full of menace. They'd only gone a few steps when he stumbled. His arms tightened as he toppled forward, and Addis knew she was about to hit the ground again; only this time, it would be with the full brunt of this man's weight bearing down on her.

As he fought to regain his balance, he juggled to keep her in his grip. While he concentrated on keeping the two of them upright, something shifted inside her, and Addis lifted her hand to gouge his neck, wanting to embed as many of his skin cells under her fingernails as she could. That way, when they found her body, they'd hopefully be able to track down her killer. It would be her message from the grave.

'Son of a bitch! Knock it off,' the man snarled, almost flinging her from him in an effort to remove her nails from his skin.

Somewhat astonished to find herself still cradled in his arms as opposed to being tossed on the ground like forgotten trash, Addis released her grip.

And started crying. It was really over. After she and Emerson had managed to escape, she'd actually started to believe she'd get to see her Aunt Grace again, but who was she kidding? This wasn't a movie where the heroine gets rescued at the end. There wasn't a knight in shining armor who would be riding to her rescue, no guns blazing, no grand, last-minute reprieve. She was going to die, like her mother, her father, and most likely, Emerson.

Chapter Thirty-Eight

Adam's hands were a mess of gashed skin and blood. Embedded in one particularly deep slice near his wrist was an array of tiny crystals of crushed rock where he'd repeatedly smashed it against the ground.

If only he'd been brave enough to go to the police all those years ago when Alex had slashed that kid who'd been hassling him about losing the big game, he wouldn't be in this situation. Not that he hadn't considered it, but she was like a demon who could read his mind even when she wasn't with him. A couple days after he'd confronted her, demanding to know if she was the one responsible for the kid's murder and insisting he'd never wanted that, she'd asked him over, a smile beaming from her face when she'd answered the door. Then she'd grabbed both his hands and twirled him around in an awkward little circle before tugging him inside. Her bubbly attitude was not only rare, it was also contagious, and he'd found himself grinning along with her, though he had no idea why.

But then the door had clicked behind them.

And he'd watched Alex put on a performance worthy of an Academy Award or Oscar or whatever. The glee from moments earlier evaporated as she collapsed to the ground, hugging her knees to her chest. Rocking back and forth, sobbing into her hands, her hysteria grew in volume, nearly robbing her of breath as she cried:

I thought I could save him, be the mother Adam never had. I begged him not to do it, that the kid was just being a kid. But he was just so angry. And then after, he came to my house, and he threatened to... to gut me like a pig if I told anyone, if I turned him in. I wanted to, but I was so scared. I mean, he had pictures that he forced me to look at. Oh God, I don't want to go to prison. I know I should've been brave enough to call the authorities, but... Oh, please, don't let this be happening.

Then she'd lifted her head, all evidence of tears erased, and sneered. 'Just in case you're toying with the idea of going to the police, who do you think they'll believe, you or me? And just for the record, I *will* gut you.' With each promise, she'd tossed a Polaroid photograph of the boy in various stages of his torturous death.

Afterwards, Adam had run from her house wanting nothing more than to confide in and seek advice from his father, but that would've meant he'd have to confess that he'd secretly been in touch with his sister for the past few years, that he had neglected to heed the warning that Alex was dangerous.

But his father was gravely ill, and Adam was too frightened the truth would do what his failing heart hadn't yet managed. And so, he'd kept his secret, only whispering the truth to the closed casket that held the withered remains of the bravest man he'd ever known. That was two days before Adam's eighteenth birthday, and his shame had kept him from ever visiting his father's grave again.

On his worst days, he would play the *what if* game. What if he'd never discovered that photograph in his father's closet when he was five? What if his father hadn't sat him on his lap and told him that the infant in the picture was him, that the woman was his birth mother, and that the young girl was his half-sister? Adam vividly remembered the fear in his fearless father's eyes, the way his arms had tightened protectively when he'd uttered Alexandra's name as he explained that taking Adam away was what was best for all of them. That haunted expression had stayed with his father for days, and that was enough to convince Adam's young mind that Alex was a monster, complete with Satan's horns and a tail to boot. Because nothing ever frightened his father, not even the boogey man.

But that was all in the past, and he couldn't change the path of destruction he'd chosen that led him to where he was today – waiting for Alex's instructions on how to fix this current mess. Because he knew she was right, that he'd screwed up by going back to the Kensington house that night, by kidnapping the two girls, and then by hiding them in a misguided, useless attempt to save their lives. What made it all worse was that he'd found his beanie under his bed earlier today. Still, that changed nothing. What was done was done.

And regardless of how much he didn't want to admit it, he knew Alex could make all of his problems go away, just like she always had. But then she *should* because it was her fault he was in this disastrous situation at all.

Howling, he pummeled his fists against his head over and over. What had Alex expected? He wasn't a criminal. He was a football player.

Which was why, this morning, he'd done the only thing he could do. He'd called her, admitting that he'd watched in numbed shock as a hunter had pulled the girls from a cattle guard.

Even though Alex hadn't been able to see him, he'd shrunk under her explosive rage, sniveling and crying as she berated him for his stupidity. Only when she'd depleted her laundry list of everything he'd ruined and told him all the ways he was worthless did she calm down.

'Listen to me. Do exactly as I say, and I'll take care of everything.'

'You promise?' He hated how she'd reduced him to a simpering child.

'I promise. Now, close all your blinds and turn off your lights. If anyone knocks, don't answer the door. Leave the key for the new locks under the bush in the front yard, and I'll let myself in.'

Several hours of wearing his carpet thin slipped away before Alex's words finally tunneled to the forefront of his mind. She'd told him to leave the key for the new locks, but he'd never told her he'd changed the locks because he knew she'd demand to know why. And it wasn't like he could very well tell her the truth – that he had nightmares about her disemboweling him for screwing up. After all, he'd known her to kill for lesser reasons.

There was only one way she could know. She'd been by the house, and she hadn't told him. Because she was going to take care of him, too?

An ominous text dragged him back from the brink of insanity, making him suddenly aware of the destruction he'd caused. His eyes strayed from the pink insulation winking out at him from the exposed wooden beams that made up the inner frame of his house, to the message making his eyes burn.

Torn, indecisive, he ended up doing the only thing that made sense to him. He ran.

Chapter Thirty-Nine

Wednesday, October 9

In a foul mood because they'd been forced to wait until morning to secure a search warrant for Adam Campbell's residence, Alyssa had crawled into bed Tuesday night, but instead of getting some much-needed shuteye, she'd tossed and turned until her even-tempered husband had growled at her. She'd just dragged herself out of bed and plodded down to the kitchen when Nick called. At four-fifteen in the morning, it couldn't be good news so, heart knocking against her ribs, she answered.

'There's another envelope that wasn't here when I left last night just before ten-thirty. And in case you're wondering why I'm here this early, it's because I've been camping out since Holly got that last picture. But last night, I had to go home for a while, and I fell asleep.' Guilt crept into his voice. 'As soon as I woke, I raced back over here. That's when I saw it, and I called you right away. Holly's still asleep and doesn't know yet.'

Alyssa was already in her bedroom, throwing on some clothes. A shower and brushing her teeth would have to wait. She ordered Nick to stay put, shook Brock until he jerked upright in the bed, told him what was going on, and then flew out the door. She briefly toyed with the idea of waiting until she saw Cord in a few hours to tell him, too, but bearing in mind their last chat, she quickly nixed the idea and called.

After getting the rundown, he agreed to meet her at Holly's. When she pulled up, Nick was sitting on the porch cradling his head. 'Where is it?'

He pointed to one of the two rocking chairs perched on either side of the window. A white envelope decorated with yellow smiling-face stickers spelling out *HOLLY* peeked beneath one of the legs. Whoever had placed it there could've done it without ever stepping foot on the porch. A car door slammed, and she twisted around to see Cord sprinting in her direction. His phone was already out, camera ready, and with the muscles in his clenched jaw ticcing furiously, he took several photos from different angles before snapping on a pair of gloves to retrieve the envelope and open it.

The dark, evil threat lurking below the surface of the photograph of Holly, Sophie, Rachel, and Jersey was enough to lodge Alyssa's heart in her throat every single time her eyes landed on it. The girls were lounging on the field near the dormitories, heads thrown back in laughter. A caption had been placed above Jersey and Rachel's image: *The Toybox misses you.* And above Holly and Sophie's: *The Toybox wants you.*

The thought of *anyone* having to endure that twisted den of sexual deviancy was enough to send Alyssa into a mental tailspin, but the idea that it could be her daughter... she couldn't allow her head to go there. Whoever was threatening Holly – immediately, and against her will, Tony flashed into her mind – would have to go through her and her entire team first, not to mention Brock, Mabel, Nick, and even Isaac and probably Trevor.

She was fighting the internal battle between waiting for or waking Holly when her daughter snatched the decision from her by jerking open the door. Standing there with bedhead, in sweats, fuzzy socks, and a sweatshirt, she barely glanced at Nick before focusing on her mother. 'What the hell is going on?' And then her eyes drifted down to the envelope clutched in Cord's hand, and she knew.

Yet her stubborn, mule-headed daughter still refused to pack up her bag and come home until they got to the bottom of things. Not wanting to leave her friends was her first excuse, and Alyssa told her they could go, too. In the end, she couldn't force Holly to do what she didn't want to do, but that didn't mean Alyssa had to be happy about it, either. Which is why she shot laser-sharp glares over her shoulder until Holly closed and bolted the door behind her.

'I've gotta tell you, Cord, I'm pretty sick and tired of people targeting my kids.'

'You and me both.' Together, they stood on the sidewalk, hesitant to leave until Cord suddenly stiffened. 'Look.' He pointed to a security camera across the street on one of the other houses.

Without considering the time, the two of them raced to the house and pounded on the door until a groggy man with glasses askew answered. Alyssa flashed her badge and asked if the man's camera worked, explaining the urgent need to check it out. She was relieved when he ushered them in and brought up the footage on his computer.

The clock in the corner flashed the date and time. It was six minutes past eleven when an old truck parked three houses down, and someone with a baggy hoody obscuring his face snuck onto the side of Holly's house and secured the envelope beneath the rocking chair.

'What. The.' Cord exploded from his chair as Alyssa went from frozen to numb in a matter of seconds. It was the same vehicle they'd seen on the video with Elizabeth Monroe across from the convenience store.

'Last night, Emilia Martinez mentioned the woman who occasionally visited Adam drove a truck. We need to find out if she recognizes that' – she pointed to the screen – 'as the same one.' Alyssa forced the chilling words past her lips. 'If it *is* the same truck, it's possible we're watching Alexandra Greene in action.'

Goosebumps peppered her skin as an unsettling thought burrowed deep. According to Alexander Greene, both he and Helen Ross's second husband had abandoned their families because they feared Alexandra. If she was that disturbing at such a young age, Alyssa was afraid to think about how much worse she could be as an adult. And now, in a way Alyssa had not yet figured out, Alexandra seemed to be embroiled in both the Kensington case, as well as whatever was happening with Holly.

Unable to erase the savagery of Gabriel Kensington's murder from her mind, Alyssa flushed with a burning anger at herself for not having thought earlier of checking the security cameras in Holly's neighborhood. If she had—She stopped the thought before it could gain traction because, right now, she needed to focus her energy on locating Addis and Emerson.

At this moment, Holly was safe, and she'd stay that way, even if it meant Alyssa had to have Brock hog-tie her and drag her home against her will. She'd be spitting nails, but at least she'd be safe while she was doing it.

274

At five minutes to six and with varying degrees of exhaustion, the rest of the team strolled into the conference room, and Alyssa placed the photograph back in the envelope. Like she had the others, she would take it over to Bill Hedge and see if any fingerprints could possibly be lifted from it.

'Lys?'

Looking over at Hal, Alyssa was surprised to see everyone staring at her as if they were waiting for a response. 'I'm sorry. My mind was elsewhere. Can you repeat what you said?'

Hal tipped his head to the side as he studied her, but if he had anything to say about her lack of attention, he kept it to himself. 'I was telling everyone I did a little digging into Adam Campbell's history last night after I got home. He was born to Barry, who died two years ago of heart failure, and Helen Campbell, neé Ross, which definitely makes him the half-brother to Alexandra Greene.'

Cord snapped his fingers. 'That's right. I remember when Adam signed with the Lobos. The media focused on portraying him as the "phoenix that rose from the ashes" because he'd grown up without a mother and had lost his father two days before his eighteenth birthday.' His gaze shifted between both Hal and Joe. 'Do you remember that?'

Both men nodded while Joe added, 'When Tony read Barry Campbell's obituary in the paper, he was concerned with how Adam was holding up. He even considered trying to reach out, but decided that would be awkward, especially if Adam didn't remember him.'

Even though she'd expected that Adam and Alexandra were related, Alyssa still felt a rush of adrenaline at having her suspicions confirmed. Before she could respond to Hal or the others, Bill Hedge poked his head in.

'Got a second?' He forged ahead without waiting for a response. 'Found one usable print on that set of photos you gave me. Prints belong to Adam Campbell.'

A hazy cloud of red and purple stole Alyssa's vision, and she gouged the soft fabric of the chair she was gripping in an effort to keep herself from reeling through the room like a tornado of destruction. 'Are you absolutely positive?' She didn't even attempt to mask her fury.

'One hundred percent. Hope that helps. Listen, I've got to run.' Hedge backed out of the room, completely unaware of – or at least wise enough not to mention – the hurricane of emotion he'd unleashed.

'Lys.' Hal's voice came at her like he was miles away underwater – or she was. Finally, he clapped his hands, the sharp sound snapping her back.

Afraid she'd not be able to rein herself in if she lost her cool now, Alyssa's voice was even as she said, 'I don't care how many judges you have to wake, I want that search warrant for Adam Campbell's residence yesterday.'

Slapping down the urgent need to race back to her daughter's house to act as a watchdog, she reminded herself that Holly had promised to stay home behind locked doors with Nick, Sophie, Rachel, and Jersey. Right now, Alyssa had to focus on the fact that there were two teenage girls out there who desperately needed to be found. Wherever they were, they had to be terrified, and she knew she and her team would do whatever it took to bring them home.

Chapter Forty

Dawn was just beginning to push the night out when Addis opened her eyes. Though she'd fought against sleep with every fiber of energy she had left, exhaustion had finally won out. Sitting up, her eyes landed on the table where a water bottle sat with a note secured beneath it. Beside it was a wickedly sharp hunting knife. Leaning forward, she grabbed the water and then placed the knife beside her before reading the note.

> *Out searching. Drink. Stay hydrated. Food's in the fridge. Help yourself. Cabin's locked. Stay inside. You'll be safe.*

Addis blinked. So, last night had been real; she hadn't just dreamed it up. Uncapping the water bottle, she forced herself to take small sips, replaying yesterday's events in her mind.

—

Call it self-preservation, call it instinct, call it whatever, but Addis wasn't letting her guard down, no matter what this guy claimed.

'So, you're really not going to hurt me?' As much as she tried to put bravado behind her tone, her words still came out as a timid squeak.

The man's grip on her arm tightened. 'No.'

'Then what's your name?'

'Tony.'

'And you're a cop?' The black wallet he'd been waving in front of her made sense now. If he was telling the truth, which the jury was still out on.

'Yes.'

'Do you know my Aunt Grace? She's the district—'

'Yes.'

'Did you know where we were? Is that why you're here?'

'No.'

His flat, one-word responses did nothing to ease her anxiety or boost her trust. 'Where are we? Do you know where Emerson is?'

'The Pecos.' His voice lowered to a gruff whisper. 'And no.'

Crushing grief sawed away at her pretense of bravery, but she forced her next question through quivering lips. 'Have the police arrested the people who killed my dad and mom?'

Tony jerked to a stop. 'People?'

Her tears didn't fall, but they did cloud her vision as she recalled her kidnapper and his unexpected visitor calmly and coldly discussing her parents' murders as if the act had held no more significance than cleaning a fish. Addis nodded yes, and then told Tony about their escape and hiding beneath the cabin when they'd seen the cars' headlights and adding that both she and Emerson had recognized the guy who'd kidnapped them, but neither could remember where they'd seen him before.

When she finished, she repeated her question, 'If you didn't know two people were involved, then they're still out there somewhere, right?'

Tony hesitated before offering a soft, 'Yes.' Almost as an afterthought, he added, 'I'm sorry. And it might not help much right now, but I know the detective working on it, and trust me, if there's a more kickass, determined gal out there, I've yet to meet her.'

A cold breeze blew across Addis's face, and she shivered, grateful for the camouflage jacket he'd tossed at her earlier with the brusque, barked command, 'Put it on.' When she'd made no move to obey, he'd shrugged. 'Or freeze to death. Your call.' Now, she caressed the pocketknife she'd transferred to one of the pockets, taking comfort in its nearness.

'If you're really one of the good guys, why did you knock me out?' As desperately as Addis wanted to believe this man, after everything she'd been through, she was having a few trust issues.

Tony pulled at his bottom lip before puffing out an aggravated breath. 'I didn't have time to think. Someone was coming down the road, I didn't know who it was, and I needed to quiet you down and get you out of the open before you were spotted. After your friend slipped away, I had to make a decision to go after her or try to get you to safety first. That was the first solution that came to mind. In hindsight, it might've not been the best.'

Emerson. Had she escaped to safety, or had she run directly back into the arms of a murderer? Addis made a fist out of her right hand and pressed her knuckles into her chest as if that would ease the ache of unknowing. 'Why didn't you just tell me you were there to help us?'

Tony jerked to a stop and turned her toward him, though his face stayed shrouded in darkness. 'I tried, but you were already screaming. Besides, would you have believed me?'

Stubbornness and fear made her want to argue that yes, she would've, but in light of those trust issues, they both knew it would've been a lie. 'No, I suppose not.'

Something large crashed in the forest, sending a cascade of animals scrambling for cover. Addis staggered as she watched an eerie cast of shadows flickering in and out of focus somewhere off in the distance. Her heart did backflips and somersaults as every twig snapping convinced her she'd been shot at, every bird that startled from the trees was her kidnapper pouncing on her from above. Only when she spotted the truck camouflaged ten feet in front of them did she realize they'd never stopped moving forward.

Wheezing gasps slipped past her lips as her fingernails dug into Tony's skin.

Crouching so that he was eye level to her, Tony grabbed her shoulders. 'Addis, it's okay. That's my truck. Look at me.' He shifted one hand to cup her chin, forcing her wide eyes from the vehicle to him. 'It's okay,' he repeated.

Pulse pounding loudly in her ears, Addis nodded numbly, even as her gaze darted left and right in search of an escape route, knowing she wouldn't make it three steps before this man tackled her to the ground. Why had she trusted him when her instincts had screamed 'Danger'?

His mouth was moving, so she knew he was still speaking, but renewed fear drowned out whatever he was saying. Then finally, with his voice blending in with the whistling wind, something he said got through. 'I'm going to get you somewhere safe – something I should've done earlier and would have, if I'd been thinking clearly – before I head back out to search for your friend.' One by one and using a gentler touch than the situation probably warranted, he removed her fingernails from his skin and scurried over to the truck.

Addis stood with her feet cemented to the ground. Could – should – she really trust this guy? He had a badge. He was a cop. And she had to trust someone. The sound of a rifle being cocked broke the cricketing silence of the night, and she slapped her hand over her mouth to muffle her cry.

An eternity later, Tony was back and urging her forward. At the truck, he quietly opened the driver's side door and helped her inside which was a good thing since she was too weak to do it on her own. On the bench seat was a scratchy blanket that smelled old and mildewy, but it was warm and dry, and Addis found herself huddling beneath it as Tony ordered her to hunker down on the floorboard and to keep her head down.

She didn't ask why; she just obeyed. With her cheek pressed against the vinyl seat, she watched as Tony reached behind it and pulled out a thermos and an insulated bag. The Velcro ripping open was unexpected and oh so loud. But then he shoved a bottle into her hand along with a sandwich stuffed into a plastic baggy, and every single thought except drinking and eating – and Emerson – dissipated into the cold air.

'Drink slowly; you don't want to get sick, so small sips, small bites. It's not much, but you'll need your strength if we're going to locate your friend.'

In the cab of the truck, his voice was different, and Addis realized it was because he was finally speaking in a normal cadence, not a whisper or an urgent plea.

After swallowing a bite of the peanut butter and apricot jelly sandwich and washing it down her parched throat with three slow but satisfying sips, she asked. 'How are we going to find Em? Do you have a phone? Can't we just call that cop you told me about?'

With pinched lips, Tony patted the front of the seat where a caddy was attached, fumbling around until he retrieved his phone. He pressed his thumb against it to unlock it before sliding it across the seat hard enough that it would've clocked her on the nose if she hadn't shifted to the side. 'No signal. But feel free to try yourself if you don't believe me. And it'll take at least two hours, maybe more in the dark, to get somewhere with even a minimum signal strength. And then I'll have to wait for help to come, and even if they allowed me to leave again which they wouldn't because they'd need to interrogate me, it would take me at least another couple hours to get back up here.' His eyes bored into hers. 'We could do that – but your friend may not have that much time.'

The fear that she'd driven Emerson back into danger overrode the lure of safety, and Addis shook her head. She couldn't live with herself if she was whisked away while her best friend continued fighting for her life, either against their kidnapper or against the elements.

The letdown drained the remainder of her earlier adrenaline rush, and without her permission, her body betrayed her by crashing down. She put up a valiant struggle to keep her eyes open, but aside from propping them open with toothpicks, the battle was lost. Her muscles liquefied until she pretzeled herself into a warped fetal position within the cocoon of the blanket. One word ran like a ticker tape across her mind as she drifted off: Emerson.

At the sensation of flying through the air, she bolted upright – or at least she tried to – but found herself securely fastened in someone's arms. Disoriented, confused, she struggled to figure out where she was, what was happening. Seemingly out of nowhere, yet another cabin popped into view.

She was carried up the porch steps, and as the door swung inward, her struggles doubled in effort. Twisting her neck to the side, she sank her teeth into a muscular bicep. Like a dog fighting to keep his bone, she snarled and swung her head back and forth, fighting the gag reflex when blood coated her lips as she broke through skin.

The next thing she knew she was flying through the air as she was unceremoniously tossed onto a leather couch. She bolted upright and planted her feet in the direction of the door. But three steps in, her path was blocked, and she was enveloped in a bear hug with her feet dangling off the ground.

'Damn it, calm the eff down, would you! Christ Almighty and Mother Mary, Peter, and Joseph. You're safe. I promise. I'm Tony, remember. This is my hunting cabin. I have to get some supplies and regroup. You'll be safe here while I go search for Emerson. Don't you want me to find her?'

It was Emerson's name that penetrated the shield of terror, and just like that, her struggles ceased.

'If I release you, are you going to try to bolt again, or can I trust you?'

'You can trust me.'

'Okay, listen. Are you listening?' His tone indicated he didn't necessarily trust her. Instead of speaking, she nodded against his shoulder. 'Okay. Wiggle your left hand.' She did, freezing when she touched the hilt of a knife. 'I'm going to set you back down on the ground, and then I want you to take that knife from the sheath, okay? Slowly now.'

With the knife squeezed tightly between both hands, she centered it in front of her chest with the pointy side up, watching as Tony suspended both arms in the air and backed up. 'That's for you to hold onto. Now, would I give you a lethal weapon to use against me if I was going to harm you?'

Panting and out of breath, she croaked out a hoarse, 'No.'

'Okay. I'm going to put my arms down now, so don't go stabbing me.'

Addis didn't smile. She was exhausted and tired of being scared and she wanted Emerson to be safe and she wanted to go home and she wanted her Aunt Grace and she wanted her mom and dad to not be slaughtered and she wanted to rewind the clock so that none of this had ever happened and she wanted to wake up and call her best friend and tell her about this insane nightmare she'd had and she wanted to giggle about it as they pretended they would make a movie out of it. But they didn't need to make a movie because this was real life.

Her tears blurred out Tony's movements, and then the knife clattered onto a table as she greeted the floor with her knees and covered her face, sobs coursing through her trembling body before Tony lifted her up and placed her back on the sofa where he left her huddled while he moved about the cabin.

For a guilt-ridden moment, Addis wanted to change her mind, to beg him to take her home, to haul her off to safety. But she knew she couldn't do that. No, she wouldn't. Because more than anything, she wanted to find Emerson. She'd never forgive herself if she survived and Em didn't.

–

Unaware she'd drifted back into sleep, the thundering click of a bolt unlocking jolted Addis awake and had her springing to her feet, clutching the hunting knife in both hands as she prepared to fight for her life.

In the doorway, Tony froze with his hands in the air. Speaking softly, he said, 'I'm sorry. I didn't mean to startle you. You can put the knife down – or hold onto it if you feel safer.' Though he moved farther into the room, he was careful to keep his distance.

But it wasn't his words or his movement that Addis focused on. It was the fact that he'd returned – without Emerson. Without warning, the knife tumbled from her hands, and her knees buckled as an avalanche of guilt threatened to bury her.

In her efforts to save her best friend, had she inadvertently gotten her killed instead?

Unable to live with the thought, Addis curled herself into a tight ball on the floor as her cries echoed off the walls around her.

Chapter Forty-One

Wednesday, October 9

Had Adam been standing in front of her when he confessed yesterday that a hunter had located the girls, Alex would've wasted no time in impaling him through the throat with the scissors she'd been gripping in her hand.

Only when no news came of the girls being rescued overnight did her fury descend from a full boil to a slow simmer. From the beginning, Adam had always known the price for crossing her, and from the moment he made that disastrous decision to return to the Kensingtons, everything he'd done to 'rectify it' had been nothing but one giant recipe of failure. And she was tired of cleaning up his messes.

From afar, she watched the officers pounding on his door. They could knock as long and as loudly as they wanted. Adam wouldn't be answering. No, they might not find Adam – not yet anyway – but she'd made sure they'd find something else.

When a locksmith van parked in the driveway, and the door was finally kicked in, Alex left. There were still several things to do to ensure Adam took the fall. But she had no intention of ending it there. Failure chewed at the edges of her mind, and if there was one thing she wouldn't abide, it was that.

There was only one remedy. Addis Kensington, Emerson Childress, and now their hunter savior had to die. And she'd take pleasure in being the one to do it. It was just a small matter of hunting them down. But she could be patient. To a point.

–

The Wells Fargo stagecoach, Darth Vader, and the Kissing Bees, Alyssa's favorite balloons, drifted just above the trees on the horizon, but she didn't notice as she and Cord waited for Joe to record evidence of the interior of Adam Campbell's house before they began their search. Outside, Duke City's Lock and Key waited in their van so they could secure the house after her team finished serving the warrant.

Sandra was off canvassing the Kensington neighborhood once more to ask if anyone recognized or remembered seeing the truck that had been present at both the location of Elizabeth Monroe's assault and the delivery of the photographs to Holly's house. In the meantime, Hal was busy checking registration records to see who the truck was registered to. Every answer led them one step closer to locating Addis and Emerson.

Impatiently waiting, Alyssa's eyes wandered the room until Joe called from the back of the house. 'Whoa! Wait until you get a look at this.'

She made her way down the hall and poked her head in. Pink fiberglass covered everything from the bed to the red beanie beneath it to the overturned night tables to the lamp partially buried in the wall near the closet, making it appear as if an insulation factory had exploded. Someone had gone on a rampage.

But that wasn't what stole her attention. Three envelopes decorated with yellow smiley stickers spelling out HOLLY grinned up at her. Beside the envelopes were three stacks of photographs numbered four through six. To Alyssa that meant that Adam Campbell had been planning on terrorizing her daughter at least three more times and she found herself squeezing and releasing her fists as she fought to retain control of her temper.

'Joe, have you recorded this yet?' Alyssa pointed to the photographs.

'Yes, ma'am.'

'I can see a handwriting imprint on that top photograph, so I'm going to flip it over. Please keep the recording going.' She snapped on a pair of gloves and turned the bile-rising image over where it revealed what appeared to be a hastily written note. She read it aloud for Cord, Joe, and the recording.

Doesn't this look like fun? Why don't you ask your friends how much they enjoyed it?

Jaw locked and teeth clenched, Alyssa turned to Joe. 'Was Tony ever alone when we processed the crime scene up in Placitas?'

'No, absolutely not. The two of us were always together. And aside from witnessing the room itself, neither of us processed it.'

Alyssa was being toyed with; she knew it. What she didn't know was why – or really, by whom – and it pissed her off.

'Lys, look.' Cord pointed down at a piece of paper.

Puzzled, she twisted around to face her partner. 'It's a grocery list.'

'Yeah, it's a grocery list. How often do you have a guest write down your grocery list?' Cord asked her.

'I'm confused. So, instead of playing this little game, why don't you just spit out what you obviously think I need to be seeing?'

'The handwriting's different.' He nodded between the grocery list on the floor and the photographs on the bed. 'I'm no expert, but even I can see these were written by two different people. The *f*'s on those' – he pointed to the picture – 'have a tail. Compared to the *f* there' – he shifted to the grocery list – 'which is almost chopped off.'

Joe leaned over Alyssa's shoulder, zooming in slowly to make note of the handwriting samples. 'I see what you mean. The notes on the photographs were written by a left-handed person. As a leftie myself, I recognize that lean. Whoever wrote the grocery list is right-handed.'

Now that Cord and Joe pointed it out, it was plain as day. So why weren't there two sets of fingerprints on the photographs? Unless whoever wrote the threatening notes was smart enough to wear gloves. She forced herself to think it: Tony would know to do that.

'Tony's not left-handed,' Joe said as if he could read Alyssa's mind.

'So, who gave these pictures to Adam to deliver to Holly?' Her gaze lifted to the bedroom window. Somewhere out there, someone was watching; she could feel it.

–

More than an hour later, the team had bagged up the grocery list, the photographs, Adam's laptop, a pair of worn Converse sneakers, a pair of jeans with muddy hems found in an overflowing trash can between the washer and dryer – in an almost staged display, Alyssa had thought when she'd first seen them – and a hairbrush containing long strands of hair.

As they waited for Duke's to secure the residence, Joe broached the subject none of them wanted to discuss. 'I want to go on record that I don't believe for a second Tony's caught up in this. He's my best friend, and hell, he's watched Holly grow up just like most of us, and he just wouldn't do that to you, Lys. There's a logical explanation. That being said, we can't keep this from Hammond; we're going to have to tell him.'

Alyssa knew he was right, but she didn't relish having that conversation because she'd never wanted to be more wrong about something than she did about the evidence pointing to Tony's involvement. She'd learned long ago that just because she willed something not to be true, she couldn't ignore what was in front of her.

'I'll tell him,' she said, her voice low and full of sadness.

'We'll tell him,' Cord and Joe said together.

Chapter Forty-Two

Wednesday, October 9

As she'd been doing since Tony had picked her up off the floor and calmed her, Addis followed him around his cabin. Unlike their kidnapper's place where the coffin-like walls were covered in cheap, dark wood paneling with fungus seeping through the cracks, this one was old but still more modern – and almost obsessively clean, at least in Addis's limited opinion of what a hunting refuge should look like.

Every wall in every room was decorated with various hunting trophies and garish animal heads of all shapes and sizes, the largest being that of a bear, its face forever frozen in an angry snarl. And regardless of where she stood, the eyes of each displayed animal followed her, almost as if accusing her of being the predator to its prey.

It might be a taxidermist's dream place, but to her, it sprang well past the creepy-as-all-hell vibe, which spoke volumes considering all she'd been through. Frankly, she was done with creepy. On the other hand, Uncle Mack, an enthusiastic hunter, would salivate over this place. Addis tugged at the ripped collar of her shirt and shivered inside the bulky oversized camouflage jacket she still wore. All these dead animals shrank the space around her, making it far more suffocating.

Ignoring the mounted head and shoulders of the mountain lion leering down at her like she was his lunch, she continued shadowing Tony as he amassed piles of supplies, shoving them into his already bloated knapsack. Fighting back a shiver and the urge to peek behind her to make sure the sleek cat wasn't about to leap off the wall and latch onto to her jugular, she continued the argument she'd started ten minutes earlier. 'You can't make me stay here. I'm awake now, and I'll just follow you if you try.'

'Oomph,' was the only response he offered as he set his bag down with a thunk and lifted a framed photograph of a magnificent Mexican grey wolf, tall, proud, and partially hidden in the midst of a stand of trees, off the wall. Like all the other animals, stuffed or photographed, its yellow eyes followed her as she watched Tony open a panel that, at first glance, looked like nothing more than a fuse box, and place his finger against a scanner until a whispered series of clicks revealed a hidden door that opened to a massive safe.

Tony shifted to block her view, but Addis leaned to the side and peeked around him. She wasn't sure what she was expecting, but it definitely wasn't what she saw. Lightheaded from a sudden lack of oxygen, she stumbled backwards. 'What are all those?' she breathed.

Tony reached in and grabbed a rifle and two smaller guns. 'Bows, various rifles, muzzleloaders, other hunting gear.' His voice was clipped, almost angry.

'Why do you have so many?' Her decision to blindly trust this stranger suddenly seemed like a very bad idea. Who needed that many weapons to hunt an animal?

Exasperated, Tony spun around. 'What I use depends on what I'm hunting. Sometimes I use a bow, sometimes a rifle, sometimes a muzzleloader. Sometimes I hunt bear, sometimes elk or deer, sometimes something else. I keep them all up here, secure, so they don't get into the wrong hands. Are you finished with your twenty questions now?'

Addis gulped back the important one that sprang to the tip of her tongue: *What do you use to hunt people?* But she figured she had her answer with the three weapons he set down on the floor before reaching back in and grabbing ammo.

'How many of those do you need?'

His hand hovered in mid-air as he peered over his shoulder and fixed her with his steady stare. 'Enough to get the job done.' The coldness that seeped into his voice sent shivers racing along her skin. He closed the safe, reset the panel, replaced the wolf photo, and then brushed past her as he stepped into the small restroom off the hallway where he opened a medicine cabinet and grabbed a first-aid kit before emptying most of the rest of the contents in with the rest of the plethora of stuff.

Finished there, he headed back to the kitchen with Addis practically glued to his heels. From the counter, he opened a medium-sized insulated cooler and set it down in front of the refrigerator where he grabbed several bottles of water, some type of lunch meat, and on the very top, he secured a plastic container filled with bread.

Snagging a blanket off the back of a chair, he added it to the pile he'd set on the kitchen table. Then, hands on hips, he swept his gaze around, probably trying to determine what he might've forgotten.

'Were you hunting when you found us?'

'Actually, I was tracking…' A curly wave of hair fell into his eyes when he shook his head. 'Never mind. It's not important. What's important is that I came across you and your friend when I did.'

An onslaught of tears threatened to spill over when a picture of Emerson being tracked by a crazed killer replaced that of the cute little animal Addis envisioned had been injured by Tony. An explosion of fiery pain in her chest robbed her of breath. When she could speak again, she said, 'I'm going—'

Tony placed both hands on her shoulders, cutting her off. 'Look at me.' He waited until she obeyed. 'You look like a smart kid, and I'm betting that you want to find your friend more than you want pride to stand in the way. Like I mentioned earlier, if time and the possibility of me being detained weren't factors, I'd get you to safety first, but this is the best option we have to work with. You're still weak from malnutrition, and you'll only slow me down. Our best option for success is if you stay put.'

Addis didn't bother to tell him she would've fought him anyway if he'd insisted on getting her to safety before they'd found Emerson. She did her best to tamp down on the ache in her heart that whispered they might not find her alive when they did locate her – *if* they located her at all.

Tony released her long enough to retrieve the gun he'd shoved into the back of his jeans. 'Do you know how to shoot a gun?'

Addis whipped her head back and forth, retreating until she tripped over a wooden stool, barely catching herself before she went sprawling to the floor. 'No, no, I can't.'

Tony bent his knees until he was eye level with her. 'Listen, remember what I said about knocking you out to find Emerson? There was someone else out there. Now, I've been hunting since I was old enough to point a rifle without toppling over, and the fact that I didn't find her scares me. She was as weak and worn out as you, so unless she got extremely lucky, someone else may have found her first. Or worse, two someones. And if they did, I can't be worried about you, her, and them. Now, take this gun. It's better to be safe than sorry, as the saying goes. Hopefully, you won't even have to use it. But in case you do, just point and shoot.'

A thundering wave of noise rushed through Addis's ears, and she saw Tony's mouth moving, but what he said was lost in the whoosh of panic threatening to drop her. Only when he set the gun down and guided her into a chair far away from it did her nerves begin to settle back into place.

Perched on the edge of the coffee table, Tony gripped her hands in his larger, warmer ones. 'Addis, I need you to listen. Unless Emerson got extremely lucky, she's in danger out there. If she didn't get to shelter, and I don't see how she could've, she's already spent another night in the freezing temps up here. Or worse. I know I don't have to spell out what that means. It's lighter outside now, and I can move faster and cover more ground. In order for me to have the best possibility of success here, I'm going to have to leave you with the best protection I can. And I'm sorry, but that's a gun. If by some chance the people who killed your parents and kidnapped you stumble upon this place, you have to shoot first.'

'I can't,' she whispered as a fresh cascade of tears dripped into her ears and tickled her cheeks. 'Let me come with you. I promise I can keep up, and I'll stay out of your way.' And then something occurred to her, her ace in the hole, so to speak. 'If Emerson *is* out there, if she did manage to escape, and she spots you before you spot her, she'll recognize you, but she won't know you've come to help, and she won't believe you if you tell her. And you know I'm right because you even said so yourself when I asked why you didn't just tell us right away. But if I'm with you, I can convince her.'

From the look on Tony's face, she knew she'd won even if he still wanted to argue. 'Please, you know I'm right, and you already said it – we can't waste any more time. Emerson could be out there hurt – or worse.' She slapped down on the word dead because it was easier to accept that her best friend was out there lost, alone, hungry, weak, and cold. Outside, off in the distance, either a coyote or a wolf howled before a chorus of others joined in, their excited yips followed by the terrified screeches of a trapped animal.

Tony's voice was gruff when he agreed. 'I don't like it.' He hooked his knapsack over his shoulder, grabbed the cooler, and jerked his chin up to indicate the blanket. 'Grab that.'

Please God, don't let us be too late.

The engine roaring to life carried her prayer off into the wind, and Addis hoped it was on its way to Emerson.

Chapter Forty-Three

The conference room was filled with a palpable, weighty silence brought on by waves of anger and denial. Even though Tony's potential involvement was linked to circumstantial incidents, Alyssa knew the team couldn't just ignore what they didn't want to believe.

Captain Hammond had taken the news far worse than any of them had expected, and they'd expected it to be bad. Not wanting to wait until they reached the precinct, they'd made the call on the drive back. She, Cord, and Joe had tag-teamed telling him. Alyssa had no way of knowing what was thrown, but the resultant splintering crash was deafening enough that she might as well have been standing right next to him.

Afterwards, Alyssa tried Holly again to find out what she could tell her about Adam Campbell. The phone barely rang once before she answered.

'Hey, Mom.' The crack in her daughter's voice betrayed her anxiety.

'Hi sweetie. Got a couple minutes?'

'Yes. Sorry I couldn't call you back last night. That migraine came out of nowhere, and I was down for the count. But it's gone now, so that's good.'

'No worries. Sophie told me you'd gone to bed. And your headache wasn't out of nowhere, honey. You've been clobbered with a stressful situation, and it all manifested itself in the form of a migraine. Which is kind of the reason I'm calling now. What can you tell me about Adam Campbell?' Given the reason she was asking, even uttering the football player's name left a bitter taste in Alyssa's mouth, and she found herself reaching for the drink in her cupholder.

Confusion was evident in Holly's tone. 'Not much. We don't have any classes together, though I see him from time to time on campus. I can tell you he's the quarterback, and there are rumors about the NFL wanting to sign him. Probably better to ask Isaac. He could probably give you his height, weight, statistics, last girlfriend, and the guy's favorite food.'

'His fingerprints were on at least one of the pictures you received – and we found more envelopes addressed to you with additional photos in his house today.' The temperature in the cab of the Tahoe plummeted as she dropped the bombshell on Holly.

'But why?' her daughter finally managed to ask.

'I don't know, but we're going to find out. I promise.'

'Mom, do I need to be more worried than I already am?'

The tremble in her daughter's voice made Alyssa want to hit something. Anger at the person responsible for putting it there bubbled inside, threatening to spill over. Because she didn't want Holly to be so frightened, she was tempted to lie, but keeping her in the dark wouldn't keep her safe. 'I don't know how to answer that question, honey. But I'd feel better if you'd go hang out with Dad and Grandma tonight.'

'Nick's still here, and we thought we'd all just stay in, order some Chinese, and watch movies tonight.'

Alyssa dug in. 'Invite them. Tell Dad I said he could spring for pizza. Or Chinese. I'm sure he'd love to see *all* of you – and he'd grow fewer gray hairs if he could see for himself that you were safe with him.'

A soft chuckle tinkered into the air. 'Liar. He wouldn't be excited to see Nick at all. Isaac, now, that's another story.'

'Your dad's still getting used to seeing another guy monopolize his little girl's time. He'll adjust.' It didn't do her a bit of good to deny that 'excited' might not exactly be the opposite of how Brock felt about Nick, but it was pretty close.

'Nick wants to keep me as safe as you and Dad. Maybe he'd like my boyfriend better if he knew that.' Holly turned serious. 'And I know you're right, that Dad would feel better if I was under the same roof as him. But, Mom, I just hate the idea of disrupting my life and giving this person more power.'

God, why did her daughter have to be so much like her? 'First, your dad likes Nick just fine. But even dads can be a little green with envy when they're replaced by another guy. And what better way to show him that Nick wants to keep you safe than by all of you hanging out with Dad tonight?'

Alyssa knew the decision was made when Holly brightened. 'Hey, do you think he'd make lasagna if I called now and asked?'

'Sweetheart, he'd try to wrangle the moon out of the sky if you asked him to, so, yeah, I'm sure it's a pretty safe bet that he'll say yes. And Holly, until you get there, will you check in throughout the day, just so I won't be more worried than I already am?'

'Sure,' Holly said.

'Thank you.'

Now, in the conference room surrounded by mounds of evidence, Tony's absence was felt like a throbbing thumb.

Alyssa was jostled out of her thoughts when Sandra raced into the room, eyes shimmering with barely constrained excitement. 'I know where he took the girls. Adam Campbell. I figured it out! At least, I think I did!' Their newest teammate's announcement may have come out of the blue, but it succeeded in grabbing everyone's attention.

'Adam's grandfather was Jeremiah Campbell. He died in 2004. But before his death, he'd applied for a slew of permits to build a hunting cabin up in the Pecos. There's no address on any of the permits, but there is a location: Unit One, Block Twenty-seven, Lot One in San Miguel County. I typed that information into Google Maps and was able to zero in on the cabin. It's barely standing, and one stiff wind could end its life for good, but it *is* still erect.'

An electric buzz passed between Alyssa and Cord and then Joe and Alyssa. Tony's hunting cabin was in the Pecos, giving yet another tenuous but definite link between Adam and him.

Chapter Forty-Four

Addis's feet hurt, as did the rest of her, after having spent the past several hours glued to Tony's side. The sun had long since peaked high in the sky and was now eking its way into its western descent, winking in and out above the tree line. But she pushed that and the dip in temperature to the back of her mind as they tracked what they hoped, once again, was Emerson's trail.

After the second trail they'd explored had turned out to be another bust, Tony had released a string of curses under his breath before turning to Addis and apologizing. 'I'm really sorry. I don't know what I was thinking. I should've taken the risk to get you to safety and get a real rescue team in here. It's no excuse, but I'm a damned good tracker, and I just thought I had a better chance of finding her before Search and Rescue got set up.'

The tortured expression on Tony's face almost managed to send Addis into another bout of bawling. Swallowing several times, she waited until she was positive she wouldn't once again turn into a blubbering mess before she touched his arm and told him the truth. 'I would've fought you all the way. I know you would've won out in the end because you're stronger, but I would've resented you for it.' Emotion clogged her throat as she added, 'I couldn't live with myself knowing I was safe while my best friend is out there somewhere probably fighting for her life, if she's even alive, especially knowing she wouldn't be in this situation at all if—'

Tony jerked his head up. 'Listen to me; you are *not* at fault. The people who killed your parents and kidnapped you are the *only* ones responsible.' Addis opened her mouth to contradict him, but he cut her off. 'Are we going to stand here and argue or go find Emerson?'

Addis sniffled. 'Find Em.'

And now here they were on their fourth possible trail, and it had been Addis who noticed the trampled, broken brush that led to what appeared to be a circular path. As they passed it, she pointed out the passenger window. 'Is that a trail?'

Using his rear-view mirror, Tony had scanned the area and then reversed. Shifting into park, he leapt out, leaving the truck idling. 'Stay here while I check.' When he climbed back in, there was an edge of excitement in his voice. 'Hop out.' While he hid his truck in brush so thick even she had trouble believing there was a vehicle there, she studied the terrain, proud that she'd picked up on some of the little things just by observing Tony. She also annoyed him with endless questions, such as why he always camouflaged his truck. 'In case anyone's lurking about' had been his flat response. By *anyone*, she knew he meant her and Emerson's kidnappers.

Without conscious thought, her feet guided her toward the path. The closer she got, the faster her heart pumped. She hadn't even realized she'd veered off and away until she heard a crashing behind her. Her mouth went dirt dry as Tony came hurtling around the corner, face so beet red he looked to be on the verge of a cardiac arrest, hissing,

'What the hell do you think you're doing! Are you trying to give me a freaking heart attack?'

She couldn't stop it; she buried her head in her hands and fell to pieces, not because he was berating her, but because he reminded her of her father the time she'd gone off exploring on her own at an outdoor market.

She'd been six, and he'd turned his back for a moment to speak with a vendor about some classic records or cars or something. She'd spotted a man walking the cutest puppy, and without thinking, she'd followed, wanting so badly to pet the dog. But then that man had rounded a corner, and a huge playhouse caught her eye. Before she knew it, she was darting in and out of that. One thing led to another, and she'd been having quite the adventure, never realizing her father had been searching for her for nearly thirty minutes.

Unlike that day in the market with her father, who'd scolded her all the way back to the car and all the way home, Tony stopped mid-rant. 'Shit. Don't cry. Damn it. You scared me, that's all. I'm not going to hurt you. Damn it! I didn't… please stop crying.'

Addis wiped her arm across her runny nose and mumbled, 'Sorry.' Then she pointed down to the soft, worn patch of red and orange leaves scattered on the ground, lifting her finger and rotating it in a slow circle. 'Em and I always joke that she's so directionally challenged that she could get lost going around the block. I guess this forest is a little different, but—'

To her surprise, Tony didn't make fun of her. Instead, he followed her finger and then planted himself firmly in front of her, his arm extended as if to shield her. From what, she was afraid to ask.

'Does any of this look familiar to you?' Tony whispered in a low, hushed voice.

'No. Why?'

A strange look crossed his face, and she poked his side. 'Tony, why?' Her voice pitched high in fear.

'We're just a short distance from where I first spotted you and Emerson.'

The crackers he'd forced her to eat not long ago swelled in her stomach, and she breathed in through her nose and out through her mouth the way he'd ordered her to do the first time she almost hurled on him – right after she tripped over a half-gnawed carcass of a cow. When she was fairly sure she wasn't going to humiliate herself, she latched her fingers into the straps of Tony's knapsack. 'I'm ready when you are,' she said with more bravado than she truly felt. Aunt Grace's most consistent advice rang through her head: *If all else fails, fake it 'til you make it.*

Five minutes later, she practically tripped over her best friend's feet sticking out from between two juniper bushes. It wasn't even her foot that snagged Addis's attention; it was the way the pink glitter toenail polish, now cracked and caked with dirt and blood glistened in the short shaft of sunlight trickling between the branches of the aspen trees.

Barely swallowing her scream, she jerked Tony to a stop. The fingers of one hand bit into her palm to hold back the terror of finding her friend dead while the other waved up and down in the direction of Emerson's feet.

Tony whirled around, took one look at her wide-eyed expression, and followed her finger to the discovery. Tossing his knapsack to the ground, he growled out his order, 'Stay. Put.' Then he grabbed hold of several branches, breaking them off before finally dropping to his knees and crawling inside the bushes with Em.

Two lifetimes later, he edged back out cradling Emerson in his arms. Her face was ashen, her hair was a tangled mop of twigs and leaves, and Addis would swear her lips were blue.

'She's alive, Addis, but she needs help. Now. I need the first aid kit. Get my bag.' When she didn't move, his voice shifted to a no-nonsense, militaristic tone. 'Do it now,' he demanded.

Shuffling backwards and kneeling to heft the heavy bag onto her shoulders, all without taking her eyes off Emerson, Addis finally gave up, sat on the ground, and using her feet, shoved the bag in front of her until Tony could reach it. She watched as he gently set Em back onto the ground, careful to keep her on her side, probably because of the blooming knot the size of a grapefruit decorating the back of her skull.

Tears streaked Addis's face as she crawled over to her best friend, running her knuckles along Em's cheeks, whispering apologies and imploring her to please be okay. 'You can do this, Em. Remember, we're in this together. And we have help now, so don't you give up. We're going to go home. You just have to wake up now. Please…'

Emerson groaned low in her throat and cracked one eye open, her tongue snaking out to lick at her chapped lips. Blinking rapidly, she finally croaked out, 'Ad, are you real, or am I dead?'

Before Addis could answer, Emerson spotted Tony – or rather, she noticed his presence looming above them, and she opened her mouth in a horrified *o*, eyes widening in terror when Addis clapped her hand down before her best friend could release the scream building up.

Leaning close to Em's ear, she reassured her, 'He's safe; he saved me; he's going to save us. It's okay, Em. It's okay. I promise.' When she showed no signs of believing or even hearing her, Addis shook her until Em finally allowed her attention to be dragged away from Tony.

'It's okay, Em, I promise. We're getting out of here. Together. It's okay.'

Chapter Forty-Five

Electric energy sizzled in the room as the team formed a semicircle around the table to study the set of maps for San Miguel County and the Pecos so they could outline their game plan to search for Addis and Emerson.

'You did good work here, Sandra.' Cord patted her shoulder as he moved past her. It seemed every few minutes, someone on the team praised her.

The sparkle of excitement in Sandra's eyes was difficult to miss, and Alyssa remembered what that rush, that sense of pride, was like the first time she'd found the key element in a missing person's case.

Concerned that he was a too-tight coil about to spring, Alyssa watched Joe clamp the lid of a yellow highlighter between his teeth as he studied the map grid. 'There!' He spit out the cap and drew two circles, connecting them with a roughly drawn line. Tapping the pages in an angry rhythm, his grip on the highlighter tightened until his brown hands paled to white. 'Tony's cabin's here. Adam's here. Not close, but relatively speaking, close enough.'

Alyssa stilled Joe's thumping with a palm over his hand. 'Remember, we don't know for certain Tony's involved. We just have to make sure we look at every branch of information, not simply the ones we want to see.' Even

306

though she'd said it to him, she knew she was voicing the words as much for her benefit as for Joe's.

'You're right. This could all be a huge ass coincidence. It wouldn't be the first time we've been wrong.' He made eye contact with each member of the team. 'Remember, there's little to no cell service up where we're headed, and what is available at the base is only when you first head in, and it's spotty at best. Keep your walkie talkies handy.'

As if the two of them had coordinated the script, Cord reached into a box and tossed a radio unit to everyone, save Hal, who sat with a gloomy expression Alyssa hadn't witnessed since the days he'd first learned he'd be confined to a wheelchair the rest of his life. It was that look that sent the weight of anticipating what they might learn once they were up there in the mountains crashing down on her.

'I got ahold of Mountain Search and Rescue. They agreed to meet you at the Glorieta turn-off so they can lead you in.' Hal's even tone did little to hide the hurt and guilt of all that haunted his mind. His gaze shifted to the darkening shadows of the room. 'Sun sets early this time of year, and it's going to be dark before you ever get there, so be careful. You have more than just mountain lions and bears to worry about.'

Hal's warning immediately triggered the memory of Isaac's harrowing mountain escape, sending Alyssa's heart racing. Concern stained the faces of her teammates, and she knew everyone had guessed where her head had gone. But she didn't have time to dwell on that. Isaac was safe. Addis and Emerson were not. Shaking it off, she began issuing orders.

'Sandra, you'll be with Joe. Cord's with me. Hal, keep shoveling until we learn everything we can about Adam

307

Campbell. I want to know what his favorite childhood food was, his first pet's name, his first girlfriend, and everything in between and after. And find out if there's anything else outside the little league team linking him and Tony.' The air in the room swelled with tension, and she didn't miss the way everyone stiffened. Making the demand in and of itself seemed like a betrayal, but it had to be done.

Alyssa's eyes drifted over to the labyrinth of crime scene photos that now included the pictures delivered to Holly. 'Same goes for Alexandra Greene. We need to find out what part she plays in all of this and *where* she is.' Her gaze swung to the chart on the whiteboard. 'Wherever she is, it can't be far. Just because the truck wasn't registered at all doesn't mean it doesn't belong to her or Adam.'

As frustrated as she was when Hal told her that whoever was driving the truck was doing so illegally, it was nothing compared to how she felt when Sandra then informed her that no one in the Kensington neighborhood recognized or recalled seeing the truck in the area, either on Thursday or in the days just before or after.

'Keep me posted on anything you find out, and we'll do the same.' With that, Alyssa clapped her hands, and the team rolled out.

–

Despite the cold air, Alyssa's skin was tight and clammy as the eeriness of yips and yelps from coyotes shimmered around them. By the time her team reached Glorieta, the search and rescue team were already circulating, and nighttime had swept dusk out and ushered in the absolutely impenetrable dark. With no city lights to break up the sinister shadows, she felt every inch of the chilling terror, knowing it paled in comparison to what the girls must be feeling, what they must've felt all along.

Squinting to see beyond the tree line, she made a vow to herself. One way or another, come hell, high water, or sudden torrential flooding of biblical proportions, she was bringing Addis and Emerson home tonight – even if it meant combing every inch of these woods alone.

Together, her team approached the tent SAR had assembled as a temporary home base. Half a dozen flood-lights cast mystic shadows onto the ground where four men and three women hunched over a table. They were within a few feet of the congregants when one of the women straightened, said something to the man beside her, and then pumped Alyssa's hand with one firm shake.

'Alyssa?'

'That's me.'

'Victoria. Nice to meet you. My team is scoping out the best way to go in. With the four of you, there'll be eleven of us. Two of our guys will stay behind to man the station.' She walked as she talked. 'You have your radio units?' When Alyssa nodded, Victoria continued. 'Great.'

At the table, she pointed a finger and offered lightning-fast introductions. Already Alyssa liked this woman who didn't feel the need to waste anyone's time with idle chitchat that didn't apply to the urgent situation at hand.

'Listen,' Victoria addressed everyone in a direct, commanding tone, 'we'll need to work together, combine my team's mountain rescue specialty with your team's criminal tracking knowledge in order to have the best chance of bringing these girls out safely. So, we'll lead your team insofar as the search aspect goes, and we'll follow your lead on the best way to extract – what are their names?'

'Addis and Emerson,' Cord offered.

'Right. Addis and Emerson. Is everyone good with this?'

Save for one man who stood there stiffly with arms crossed and lips turned down in a half pout, half sneer, everyone acknowledged their agreement. Alyssa hoped he was one of the ones sticking behind because not only did she not have time to coddle some guy's bruised ego, she didn't care a whit about his self-esteem when she was this close to rescuing the girls.

'We all know what's at stake here and the inherent danger we may be up against, both man and nature-made, so if everyone's questions and concerns have been addressed, let's roll out,' Alyssa said.

Five minutes later as they caravanned up the mountain trail, the shadow figures created by bouncing headlights sent a shiver ricocheting along Alyssa's spine, especially when it was accompanied by a high-pitched squeal from an animal she couldn't name. *Please let the girls be here. Please don't let it be too late; let them still be alive.*

Chapter Forty-Six

Wednesday, October 9

While Tony checked Emerson's injuries in the midst of emerging shadows, Addis kept up a running litany of the things the two of them were going to do when they finally got back home, trying not to choke on the crushing reminder of what she was returning home to. She had a lifetime to find a way to come to terms with the tormenting loss of her parents' murders.

'After we fill up on chips and salsa, we'll spring for some froyo. You can even choose where we go.'

At the mention of food, Em's eyes drifted back to the sandwich Tony had ordered Addis to dig out of the cooler earlier.

'Are you ready for another bite?'

'Yes, please.'

Supporting Em's neck, Addis fed her a bite and then helped her with the water bottle. While her friend sipped slowly, Addis whispered to Tony. 'Are you sure she doesn't have serious head trauma or brain damage or something?'

Not looking up from the gash he was cleaning near Em's wrist, he said, 'If she had serious head trauma, she likely wouldn't be able to communicate at all. She probably has a *very* minor concussion from hitting her head. But other than that, she's dehydrated, hungry, and her body's been through a lot. Just keep feeding her the sand-wich and helping her drink.'

Addis didn't know if she believed him entirely, but what he said made sense, so she tried to trust he was telling the truth and not just saying what she wanted to hear.

After using butterfly bandages to close the gap in Emerson's skin, Tony pointed to her shoulder. 'This is going to hurt. I'm sorry. On the count of three. One. Two…'

Emerson's howl echoed off the canyon walls when Tony stopped counting at two and popped her dislocated shoulder back into place. Streams of moisture spilled down her cheeks.

Too bad Tony couldn't fix her best friend's right ankle as easily. Addis's eyes drifted down, wincing at the black and blue swollen joint that was easily twice its normal size. The way Emerson explained it, it wasn't the tripping and falling over a rock that caused the snap; it was when the rest of her body decided to go the opposite direction as she flailed to the ground. As a result, her foot had become wedged.

When she'd finally untangled herself, she'd thought she might have a sprain, but when she tried to stand, even the slightest pressure sent her reeling back down. She said her biggest worry at that moment was not the broken ankle, but the fact that she had struggled to stave off the waves of dizziness so she wouldn't faint.

'If you fell over there,' – Tony hitched his thumb over his shoulder – 'then how did you end up all the way over here?'

'Well, I couldn't stay out in the open, so I dragged myself over and between these bushes because they seemed to offer the best shelter.' Because Addis knew Em as well as she knew herself, she detected the faint tone of pride in her voice.

The wind shifted, ushering in the foul stench of rotting insides from a dead animal they, thankfully, couldn't see. 'And then I passed out from the pain – you know, after I got dehydrated from eating those leaves that had me purging every meal I've ever eaten in my entire life.' She peeked up at Addis. 'Don't all those wilderness shows tell you that you can survive on that kind of stuff?'

'How should I know any better than you?'

'Well, just so you both know, they freaking lied!' Emerson mumbled.

'Well, we'll definitely have to warn my dad for the next—' Addis stopped cold when she realized what she'd been about to say. She released Em's hand as the devastating reminder robbed her of air. Never again would she be able to share hers and Em's adventures with her dad. Never again would he wipe her tears and force her to laugh over some stupid boy who she'd convinced herself was her soulmate for life. He wouldn't be there to insist she was the most stunning girl on the Homecoming court, he would never grill her prom date, watch her graduate, or one day, far down the road, walk her down the aisle, or bounce his grandchildren on his knees while sneaking them chocolate candies before bedtime like he'd always done with her.

Addis wasn't aware she'd begun hyperventilating until Tony was suddenly beside her, shoving her head between her knees, ordering her to listen, to breathe with him.

By the time she finally pulled herself together again, it had grown even darker and colder. But it wasn't the cold draft washing over the back of her neck that stole her attention from her meltdown, it was the way Em's serrated fingernails gouged into the top of her hand. Afraid of what she would find, Addis slowly traced the path Em's eyes followed.

What she spotted might not have been quite as chilling as their kidnapper, but it ran a close second. 'Bear,' she managed to rasp out.

Tony whirled around, and Addis fought the urge to yell at him. Her nerves were already a tangled yarn of anxiety. Was he *trying* to draw attention to them? They'd watched the movie *Grizzly*. No way had she and Em survived this long only to go out as that thing's tasty dinner.

'Stay still,' Tony warned as the bear reared up on its hind legs. 'It's just as curious about us as we are of him.'

'Um, I think *terrified* is the word you're looking for, not curious,' Addis hissed with an embarrassingly high squeak.

Finally, after one of the longest minutes in an infinite line of long minutes this week, the bear grew bored and ambled off, peering back at them only once before disappearing over a small bluff. Addis loudly expelled the breath she'd been holding.

'Was that a grizzly?' Still gaping in the direction where she spotted the bear, Emerson wheezed out the question, the hand she'd reclaimed from Addis pressed tightly against her chest.

Tiny lines crinkled in the corners of Tony's eyes.

Addis was insulted that he was amused by her friend. 'Hey, that's a legitimate question.'

The effort to fight back his laughter transformed his face, making him appear far less threatening than he had when he'd found them.

'No,' he answered now, chortling as he did. 'It was only a black bear.'

'*Only*,' Addis scoffed even as Emerson grumbled, '*Only*.'

After shooting amused grins at both of them, Tony switched off his humor, turning serious once again. 'Time to head to the truck.' Reaching into his knapsack, he pulled out two more water bottles, handing one to Emerson and one to Addis. Then he zipped the bag shut and hefted it onto his back.

How he didn't topple over face first into the dirt with the weight of it, Addis couldn't understand. Especially when he squatted low, tucked one arm beneath Emerson's knees and fitted the other around her back before rising back to his feet with a 'Here we go,' and nary a lost breath.

A deeper shade of red in Emerson, Addis had never seen. Not even when the love poem she'd penned for the boy she'd crushed out on two years ago fell out of her backpack only to be discovered by the meanest couple in school.

'I can hobble along if you help,' Emerson piped out shrilly.

Without slowing, Tony brushed her comment off. 'You can't, and we don't have time to discuss it.' He lifted his chin and peered over Emerson's body, capturing Addis's eyes. 'You jog ahead and lead the way. I'll—'

'What? I can't… I don't… I'll get us lost,' she stuttered.

If the expression he wore on his face was an accurate depiction of how he felt, Tony had finally reached the point of exasperation. '*You're* the one holding the flashlight. I need you to help watch out for rocks and sticks and potholes. If I fall and twist *my* ankle, the three of us are fu— screwed.' His pasty complexion abruptly morphed into the color of a third-degree sunburn.

'Oh. Okay, I can do that,' Addis said, stepping out in front of him and waving the light back and forth to illuminate the path. As she placed one careful foot in front of the other, she allowed herself the pretense that her dad, not Tony, was behind her, escorting them to safety. Once she and Emerson were out of danger, the avalanche of reality would be back in force, but for now, she would let the fantasy wash over and warm her.

Chapter Forty-Seven

Wednesday, October 9

Alex knew what she was doing was riskier than anything she'd done before, but that only heightened the anticipation, notching up her adrenaline as she trekked through the mountains in search of the girls. Adam had already been dealt with – the pathetic look on his face as he'd pleaded for mercy would forever be etched in her memory. She'd thought she might feel a little bit of regret or sadness ending her brother's life, but when it was done, it had felt like accomplishing any other tasteless task. All that was left now was to kill the girls – and the hunter. And then she'd be in the clear once again.

If only Elizabeth Monroe had left well enough alone, none of this would've had to happen, but she'd been a problem from the very moment she'd sashayed into Hayden's life, stealing all his attention away from her.

Alex shut her eyes and allowed herself to be transported back to the day everything had changed. Because she'd concocted a last-minute story about needing him to come by and help her fix her lawn mower, she hadn't been surprised to see Hayden pull up outside her barn. He'd always been dependable that way. What she hadn't expected was for him to confide in her that he couldn't stay long.

Initially, he'd been cagey and refused to tell her why, but she'd been persistent, and so he'd relented, but only after making her swear on her life that she wouldn't tell a soul. As it turned out, it hadn't been her life he should've been concerned about. She'd pursed her lips and mimicked turning a key in a lock.

He'd breathed out a sigh of relief, and she'd known he hadn't really wanted to keep it a secret from her. And then he'd confessed that he and Elizabeth were planning on running away that very night because he'd knocked her up and wanted to do the responsible thing. But they had to keep it quiet, he'd said, because poor little Elizabeth was scared of what her parents might do to her if they found out. Alex had covered her mouth and giggled, thinking it was a joke, but when she realized he was dead serious, she'd seen her future slipping away, and she couldn't have that happen.

Desperate, she'd latched onto his arm and tried reasoning with him, to make him see how *she*, not Elizabeth, was the one who was meant to be by his side forever. When he'd shaken her off and stepped back, telling her he didn't reciprocate her feelings because he loved Elizabeth and his unborn child, she'd been hit by a rage so blinding, everything except the driving need to shut him up fell away.

To this day, she still wasn't sure if she'd picked up that shovel with the intention of killing him, but her intent didn't matter because once the metal hit his skull, she couldn't be stopped until his chest no longer rose and fell. And he definitely hadn't been talking anymore, so she'd succeeded in her goal.

After she'd killed him, she'd driven his car into the old barn and then dragged his body over and wrestled him into his trunk. Then, she'd grabbed a hose from outside and cleaned up the mess before moving inside and taking a shower. Hours later, Rosalyn Benson had called to see if she'd seen her brother, and Alex assured her she had not and suggested trying Elizabeth. Later that night, the police had stopped by, and she'd repeated the same story.

It had taken planning and patience, but later, she'd managed to rid herself of all evidence that Hayden had ever been to her house. If only freeing her mind of him had been as easy—

Lights and voices effectively snapped Alex back, and for several seconds, she had to fight to get her breathing back under control as her heart knocked against her ribs.

A zinging pain shot up her arm, and she glanced down, realizing she'd clenched her hands into such tight fists that her fingernails had dug through her skin. Opening her palms, she wiped them on her pants and looked around. It was time to stop living in the past and concentrate on why she was here – to kill the girls, wherever they were and whatever it took.

Chapter Forty-Eight

The hike back to Tony's truck had been rife with tension, primarily because Addis couldn't be swayed from the belief that they were being followed, that the three of them weren't out there alone. Each snap of a twig convinced her they were currently being stalked. She'd even persuaded herself that the soft breeze blowing across her face was actually their kidnapper breathing against her cheek. Not even when she, Emerson, and Tony were safely locked inside his truck did she let down her guard, scooting over as far from the passenger window as she could, even though it meant crowding Emerson, who didn't seem to mind as she wrapped her arm around Addis's shoulder.

Now, with the only illumination invading the inky blackness of the heavily wooded area coming from Tony's bright headlights, it was still all too easy for Addis's imagination to twist the shadows cast into the night into monsters equally as real and frightening as the one who'd kidnapped her and Emerson. Because she was freaking herself out, she sat facing forward, no longer staring out the side window. Bending her elbow and tucking her forearm under Em's chin, she patted the side of her friend's face that wasn't currently burrowed into the crook of her neck.

Despite the countless ways driving this fast could end badly, the truck continued bumping along at a speed indicative of someone attempting to win the Indy 500, a sport her dad had obsessed over watching. Each rut in the road elicited a moaning whimper from both girls, reminding Addis that their road to recovery would be long. Without fail, Tony cursed and muttered an apology after each one. Addis wanted to tell him he didn't need to keep saying he was sorry, but she was too afraid she'd distract him. She was so close to being reunited with her Aunt Grace that she didn't want to risk the chance that Tony would take his eyes off the terrain and thus be unable to avoid slamming into a wild animal – the bear they'd spotted earlier came to mind – or a tree, or going off any of the sheer cliffs they'd come across. Dropping her gaze to her lap where she cradled Tony's phone, she once again pressed a button, illuminating the screen, fighting back disappointment even though she'd expected it. 'Still no signal.'

'Son of a—' At first, Addis thought he was reacting to her comment, but then Tony's right arm snaked out and shoved them both forward so forcefully, they almost slammed their heads into their knees, and that was only after narrowly missing the dashboard. 'Stay down,' he ordered.

The tension in his voice was second only to the knot of terror gnawing its way out of her as Tony decreased his acceleration by a fraction.

Through the thundering in her ears and over the sound of the engine, his words finally penetrated. 'There are headlights up ahead. It could be nothing, but I need you to listen to me carefully. Are you listening?' He waited for their shuddering yeses. 'I'll do my best to go around whoever's out there, but if I can't, if I have to stop the truck… if things look like they're going to head south, I'll jump out, and then you'll need to climb behind the wheel and floor it. Do you understand? Don't wait for me. Punch the gas and run over anything – or anyone – in your way.'

The guttural sound of near defeat sent chills skittering along Addis's spine as much as his demand. Because she knew when Tony said, 'if things look like they're going to head south,' what he really meant was if he was somehow incapacitated – or worse, killed.

'Please, Daddy, if you could be my guardian angel right now, we could really use your help.' She wasn't aware she'd whispered the plea out loud until Emerson breathed a hushed 'amen' into her ear.

And then all pleas and prayers flew out into the night when the truck fishtailed as Tony slammed on the brakes. This time, Addis knew her scream wasn't only in her head.

Heart thudding, breaths panting heavily, fear tingling along her nerve endings, Addis gripped Emerson tighter when Tony's door opened, and he leaped down from the cab, depressing the locks before slamming the door behind him with an urgent, 'Remember, go fast and run over anything in your way.'

Too late, Addis wished she'd asked how long they should wait for a sign before leaving him behind.

Chapter Forty-Nine

Wednesday, October 9

Aside from Cord's startled, 'Jesus' when the four-wheel drive they were travelling in skirted the edge of a cliff on one side with the rock mountain on the other with less than a foot to spare, and the grunts and muffled 'oomphs' when they hit a rut, the team was quiet as they bounced along the rough terrain.

'There wasn't a less piss-my-pants way we could've gone?' Cord muttered when they finally cleared the cliffs.

In the driver's seat, Victoria chuckled. 'Maybe, but this was by far the fastest approach.' She peeked in the rearview mirror to catch Cord's eyes. 'We shaved off a good seventy-five to ninety minutes this way.'

Almost half an hour later, the brake lights of the lead vehicle carrying Joe and Sandra illuminated the night with bright red. Shortly after, the distorted, vibrating timbre of Joe's voice crackled over the staticky mic. 'This is the turn-off to Tony's cabin.'

The queue of SUVs stopped, their idling engines breaking through the rhythm of hooting owls and scampering woodland creatures. Communicating silently, Alyssa and Cord both climbed out of the Range Rover, walking side by side to meet Joe and Sandra who they'd agreed would take up a post near the turn-off to Tony's just in case. None of them had verbalized what *just in case* might mean. Two members of the search team would stay behind with them, again, just in case.

'We'll radio as soon as we locate Campbell's place. In the meantime, if anything—'

Joe's face was a mottled shade of discoloration, made all the more unnerving by the shadows cast upon it from the headlights, as he waved away Alyssa's words. 'I'll let you know. Now, go find the girls.'

There was nothing she could do to ease the ache of possible betrayal, so she offered a terse nod before she jogged back to the Range Rover and used the running board to help haul herself inside, slamming the door harder than was necessary. As soon as Cord was buckled in behind Victoria, she gestured out the windshield that they were ready to continue up the mountain.

The deeper they drove into the pines and aspens, oaks and maples, the faster the kinked knot of dread grew until she was little more than a five-foot-three tightly controlled mass of nerves. *Please let the girls be there. Please let them be alive.* It had become her silent mantra throughout this entire trek into the mountains.

A flash of light up ahead nearly blinded Alyssa a split second before Victoria hit the brakes, while the crackle of the mic broke through, announcing, 'We've got an approaching vehicle, moving at a high rate of speed. Stand by.'

'That's Tony's truck.' Cord's voice was full of the shocked disbelief Alyssa felt.

What happened next was a swirl of motion as the inside of Tony's cab was lit up by the floodlights Victoria had flipped on. Alyssa barely registered her teammate's pinched expression as he leaped down from his truck, slamming the door behind him. His words didn't carry back to her, but it was clear he'd spoken to someone she couldn't see.

Pumped up on adrenaline, Alyssa shoved aside the eruption of anger and betrayal and reached for her weapon as she, too, opened her door and climbed down. However, unlike Tony, she left hers ajar, using it as a shield if it should come to that. Damn it all to hell. She so badly had wanted to be proven wrong, to know that there was a reasonable explanation for all the coincidences, and that there was no way possible her teammate was involved.

Tuned in to a dozen things at once, Alyssa registered Cord's mirrored stance.

Over the next few seconds, Alyssa was prepared for many things to happen – except the grin and shouted exclamation of what sounded like sincere relief that erupted from Tony. Nor did she expect him to pound on the driver window and holler inside, 'It's okay. You're safe.'

Until she realized he had no idea they were onto him. When she spotted the gun gripped in his hands, she shouted, 'Place your weapon on the ground, Tony, and put your hands in the air where we can see them.'

Tony's eyebrows shot up onto his forehead, an action she'd grown accustomed to over the years. 'Setting the gun down,' he yelled over the idling engines, extending one arm into the air while bending low to set his firearm on a pile of leaves. 'What's going on, here, Lys?'

Her answer was ignored as soon as the passenger door of Tony's truck opened, and Addis Kensington carefully slid down until her feet hit the ground. Then, moving in front of the vehicle where she was backlit by headlights, she opened her mouth to speak, but all that came out was a squeak before her knees buckled, and she started to crumble to the earth. Tony's frightened eyes darted between both weapons trained on him even as he dived forward, catching her before her face could hit.

And then there was movement everywhere, but it was the way Addis sobbed into Tony's chest as he soothed her, rubbing small circles into her back, his words flitting through the breeze and over to Alyssa that convinced her there was more to this story than she was seeing. She couldn't stop the flutter of hope that she was somehow wrong, that there was no possible way her friend and teammate was in any way involved.

'It's okay,' Tony said. 'You're going to be safe now. Remember that kickass lady I told you I work with, the one who knows your Aunt Grace? That's her, right there. I told you she wouldn't give up until she found you.'

Still reassuring Addis, Tony lifted his gaze to meet Alyssa's and cocked his head once toward his truck where Emerson Childress still sat in the cab, her body visibly trembling. Both hands covered her mouth, and from the dome light shining down on her, Alyssa could clearly see the tears that fell like a late October rainfall down her face.

Holstering their weapons, Alyssa and Cord approached as understanding warred with relief that there was no way Tony would've risked telling the girls about them unless he had been the one to rescue them. Had he known all along where they were? Was that why he'd skipped out this past week? Or could this be a rare case of true coincidence? Though the guilt of doubting him was like ingesting spoiled food, the question of the threatening photographs delivered to Holly – photographs that Tony had access to – kept Alyssa from entirely trusting him. But for now, she was forced to set that aside because the truth was, she needed his help.

Victoria, along with the other members of the search and rescue team, scurried over to Tony's truck. 'Looks like a bad sprain or possibly a broken ankle,' she yelled.

If all they had to contend with in the way of physical injuries was a bad ankle, Alyssa would count herself lucky.

A chorus of organized chaos erupted all around them as Victoria and her team readied Addis and Emerson for transport back to the Glorieta home base where she'd radioed ahead for an ambulance to meet them.

After an abbreviated explanation from Tony on how he'd found the girls – noting that he said nothing as to his reasons for mysteriously taking off in the midst of their case – Alyssa excused herself to speak to Addis and Emerson, who both shared matching stories corroborating Tony's version of events.

Afterwards, Cord reached out to Joe. 'We're this close, so Lys, Tony, and I will be continuing on to Campbell's cabin. Alyssa wants you and Sandra to accompany Addis and Emerson to the hospital and contact Grace as soon as you have a signal. Tell her we'll be in touch as soon as we can. Search and Rescue are rolling out now, so they should reach you in about thirty to forty minutes. And Joe, the girls mentioned two names: Adam and Alex. They never saw Alex, but see if you can gather some photos that include Campbell, see if they can identify him that way.'

Standing shoulder to shoulder with Tony, Alyssa unrolled the map onto the hood of his truck. 'Of the three of us, you know the Pecos the best. Do you think you can find this?' She tapped the circled area where they believed Campbell's cabin was.

Head bent low as he ran the flashlight over the map, Tony muttered under his breath, his finger tracing first one path then another before lifting his head and darting his eyes around the woods surrounding them. 'I think so. It won't be easy in the dark, though,' he warned.

'But it can be done? You're sure?' Alyssa wasn't reassured by Tony's shrug any more than she was by his statement.

'As sure as I can be.' Glancing back down at the map, Tony whistled low. 'They really hadn't gotten far when I came across them hiding beneath the cattle guard.' His words held a heightened sense of urgency, and Alyssa had a feeling it had to do with the fact he no longer had control over protecting the girls as they were being whisked off to safety.

'You understand you're going to have to explain how you ended up here at all, right?' She held her gaze steady on the teammate she physically ached to trust again.

Tony's eyes shifted away, then drifted back down to the map. 'Yeah. I'm sorry you guys are doubting me. Does Joe—never mind, I don't need to hear that answer. I don't like it, but it makes sense.' There was no censure in his tone, just a sad acceptance that his teammates had suspected him at all. 'It was my fault. It never occurred to me… but why would it have? None of us knew where the girls were.' Abruptly, he straightened and folded up the map. 'But we'll deal with all that after we find this guy.'

'Tony, the guy is Adam Campbell.' Alyssa didn't blink as she watched for Tony's reaction.

He took two stumbling steps back, shaking his head. 'Adam Campbell, the Lobo football player half the NFL teams want? The same Adam that I helped—' His eyes widened as understanding dawned. 'That I helped coach.' One hand wiped down his face, and then he whirled around and kicked his booted foot into his wheel well. 'Damn it! Shit. Damn it. Sonofa—' His final curse turned to a howl of frustration.

When his rage simmered to a more manageable level, he directed an unwavering scowl at Alyssa. 'It's beginning to make more sense. Because I helped coach Adam Campbell once long ago, and then I take a little time off to get my head together because I've got a lot of personal shit going on in my life, things none of you know—'

'Whose fault is that?' Alyssa interrupted.

'That's not the point. I had nothing to do with whatever this is. You'll either have to trust me or send me on my way. Or hell, arrest me if you need to. But I *can* help you find this cabin.'

For several seconds, Alyssa regarded her teammate before confronting him with the one question she had to have answered. 'What about the photographs from the sex trafficking case that have been delivered to Holly, along with threatening notes?'

There was no way Tony could fake the color that drained from his face. He had no idea what she was talking about.

That he was incredibly hurt that she could ever suspect he'd harm or target her family, especially one of her children, was evident in the way his voice broke when he asked, 'What are you talking about, Alyssa? What photographs, and what threatening notes? Is Holly okay?'

She didn't get a chance to answer because, having finished outlining instructions to Joe, Cord walked up. 'Are we ready to roll out?' When no one answered, Cord touched Alyssa's arm, asking in a tightly controlled voice while shifting his gaze over to Tony. 'Lys? What's going on?'

Tony stared at her, one eyebrow lifted in question. The move was hers. Her answer was to open the back door of Tony's truck, leaving the front passenger seat open for Cord, since his legs were so much longer than hers. 'Let's do this.'

-

Through a cloud of red, Alex scrambled to adjust as her entire plan crumbled before her eyes. For a moment, she considered cutting off the vehicle carrying those stupid girls down the mountain, but then it would be her against a virtual army, and she knew she couldn't kill them all before she was killed.

No, she would have to regroup. Wait. Maybe it was time to send more images to Holly Wyatt. Or maybe more drastic measures needed to be taken.

Heading back down the mountain, she allowed herself the fantasy of forcing the rescue team off one of the cliffs, of hearing the satisfying crunch, the screams of agony and pleas for help, but she had other things to tend to for now, other plans to make. Only with her death would she be out of this game. Because that was what this had become – a game she had no intention of losing.

Chapter Fifty

Wednesday, October 9

Alyssa snapped the hair tie secured around her wrist, ignoring the sting, as they trekked their way up the winding, off-road trail. Nearly forty-five minutes had passed since entrusting Addis and Emerson's care to Joe, Sandra, and the search and rescue team, and the bubbles of anxiety, of not knowing where or how they were caused her stomach to hurt – even if she tried to blame it on the rough ruts. For the dozenth time, she considered calling off the search for Campbell's cabin until first light and then heading back out, but like she had every time before, she dismissed it.

Tony hit the brakes, jolting her forward so that she had to throw out her hands to protect herself from faceplanting into the back of the front seat. 'Let me see that map again.'

Cord unfolded the map while Tony flipped on the dome light. He hummed as he ran his finger down the paper, then bent forward to peer around Cord before glancing outside his own window. He pointed to an obscure trail faintly illuminated by his taillights, then threw the truck into reverse and backed down the hill, seeming to hit every single hole in the road along the way. Alyssa was really beginning to hate the topography of this mountain.

When Tony stopped again, he stared straight ahead at the nearly invisible turn-off leading to Campbell's cabin. 'Yep, this is it.' He twisted around and showed Alyssa and Cord the landmarks he'd noted. He tipped his head to indicate where they were heading. 'At a guess, I'd say we're a ten-minute hike away, assuming we don't want to drive up and alert him to our presence.'

Blocking out the hint of sadness that betrayed Tony's true feelings, Alyssa put her jacket back on and secured her flashlight as she scooted across the back seat so she could climb out. 'What are we waiting for? Let's go.'

An avid runner, Alyssa was in shape. Even so, her chest heaved in and out as they climbed the ever-steeper terrain that was nearly a thousand feet above Albuquerque's altitude. And then, appearing seemingly out of thin air, she spotted the cabin. Or, a more accurate description might be a 'wooden hovel.' Somehow, it had appeared less slovenly on Google Earth. The three of them switched off their flashlights, casting them into total darkness until their eyes adjusted to what little light the moon and stars offered.

'No sign of a vehicle,' Cord whispered.

Tony waved his hand over the ground. 'But one's definitely been here recently. You can tell by the tire tracks that they're a few days old, at best.'

Both men turned to Alyssa. 'What's the play, boss?'

'From the air photos, it appeared there was only a front door and that window there as possible means of escape. So, Tony you take the back, Cord, you take this side, and I'll go in the front. If he's here, he's not getting through us.'

Everyone checked their weapons before moving over to their assigned posts. Ignoring the sudden chorus of high-pitched, howling coyotes, Alyssa waited until the guys were in place before ducking low and heading to the front door, careful not to put her foot through the rotting steps. Listening for any sound of movement, she moved in closer to the door, sucked in a deep breath before expelling it, and then used the side of her fist to pound loudly on the door. Her heart skipped a beat when it screeched open, revealing someone's leg.

She took several calming breaths in and out before switching on her flashlight and slowly peeking around the splintered doorframe. When her eyes adjusted, she released a string of curses, and while she didn't holster her weapon, she did switch the safety back on before carefully navigating through a pile of rubbish to the end of the porch where she called out to Cord and Tony. 'He's here. But we won't be taking him in, at least not in the way we'd hoped.'

Inside, Tony located a light switch that operated a solitary bulb suspended from a broken light fixture. On, it cast a small amount of flickering light into the room.

There in front of them with his back against what appeared to be a stack of milk crates, legs bent crookedly beneath him as if he'd been kneeling before his death, was Adam Campbell, mouth agape, eyes bulging open, part of his face missing, brain matter spattered onto the walls and floors around him, arms flung out to his sides. His right hand still gripped a gun.

Closing her eyes, Alyssa rubbed the middle of her forehead. Adam Campbell was supposed to be her key to getting some answers, but more importantly, if not a little selfishly, she needed to know why he'd targeted her daughter, how he'd come to be in possession of photographs from a sex trafficking ring shut down five months ago.

Opening her eyes again, her gaze ping-ponged from the insects already taking up residence in the gore that had once housed a human over to Tony, who seemed unable to look away from the grotesque display in front of them.

Alyssa liked to think of herself as a good judge of character, but the last year had sorely tested that theory, and as much as she wanted to believe Tony's expression was nothing more than sadness for a once-promising athlete he'd helped coach, she couldn't help trying to decipher if there was more to it.

Which was why she found herself studying Tony's hands, searching for any evidence of a recent struggle, or even powder burns. As if he knew what she was doing, he flashed her both hands before shoving them into his front pockets and walking out into the chilly night, avoiding more of both her and Cord's close scrutiny.

Chapter Fifty-One

Instead of lying in the hospital bed, Emerson Childress reclined on an extremely uncomfortable-looking plastic two-seater chair crammed into a tiny corner. One leg was drawn up to her chin with her arm wrapped around the knee while the other rested on the doctor's rolling chair. Her ankle was wrapped in a medical bandage, and a row of black stitches stretched partway down the length of her calf with a matching set near her wrist. Hannah sat beside her, rubbing her sister's back.

Across from them and perched on the edge of Emerson's bed was Addis, her face and arms covered in colorful bruises and angry scratches, and her dangling feet covered in red hospital booties. When Alyssa had dropped by late last night to check on them, Grace, after ensuring Addis was asleep, had stepped into the corridor, her composure rattled as she relayed how Addis had disintegrated when her Uncle Mack had shown up at the hospital. Mack and Gabriel, she'd explained, looked so much alike that when they were younger, they sometimes were mistaken for twins.

Addis had been understandably inconsolable at the knowledge that she'd never again see her father or the mother that had driven her crazy more than anything else.

She'd soaked Grace's shirt as she'd begged her to bring them back. Even Mack had been shaken to his unshakeable core.

This morning, Grace and Mrs. Childress hovered nearby while Mr. Childress sat in a chair with both his hands extended in a way that reminded Alyssa of an umpire waiting for the pitch of the baseball.

'Looks like a full house in here,' Alyssa greeted everyone as she and Cord stepped into the room.

Grace peeked over her shoulder, the sadness in her eyes so deep and piercing, it threatened to penetrate the shield Alyssa had erected in order to steel herself for hearing the girls' story. Mr. and Mrs. Childress kept their eyes glued on their daughter, but Mr. Childress did offer up a 'Good morning, Detectives.'

Alyssa was empathetic to their situation. After Isaac's ordeal, the thought of allowing him out of her sight for even a second had her edgy and anxious. Even today, if he was more than a couple of minutes late returning home from school or other activities, she perched on pins and needles until he was home again.

'I'm glad everyone's here,' she said, hesitating when Addis, with Grace's help, slid off the bed and walked over to her. The hug was unexpected and shredded some of Alyssa's self-control as her arms automatically engulfed the teenager in return. Voice choking, Addis whispered a soft thank you.

Then, she stepped back and, sounding like she was speaking around a golf ball, addressed both Alyssa and Cord. 'Most of my wounds are superficial.' Her fingers hovered over the jagged cut crisscrossing her cheek that would likely become a permanent visual reminder of the trauma she and Emerson had endured. 'The doctors say

I'll be good as new, physically speaking, as soon as I'm properly hydrated.' Guilt flashed in her eyes as she peered at Emerson. When she turned back, she whispered, 'Tony said you wouldn't give up.' This time, Addis collapsed into Grace's arms, her sobs ricocheting off the walls of the room.

It was several minutes before Hannah, red-eyed, stood and gently cupped Addis's elbow so she could escort her to Emerson's side. Immediately, their hands found each other and joined together, offering the silent support only best friends and those with shared nightmares could do. Alyssa's heart constricted at the movement that so much reminded her of Holly, Sophie, Rachel, and Jersey.

'It was my fault Emerson was kidnapped.' Addis's announcement, so sudden and unexpected, sucked all noise from the room.

Emerson was the first to break the silence. Gripping Addis's chin, she forced her to look at her. 'It's not.'

'It is, and you know it. If I hadn't gotten so mad at my mom and gone to your house—'

Mrs. Childress cut her off. 'Then there's a strong possibility we'd be mourning your death, too. Of course, you'd come to our home when you're upset. When have you two girls ever done anything differently? What matters in this moment is that you're both safe now. And I believe that's because you had each other to stay strong for.'

Alyssa hated to break the moment, but she and Cord still had a job to do. 'I know this won't be easy, but we need you to walk us through what happened that night.'

Emerson's gaze flickered from her mother to her sister and back again. 'I think you or Daddy should take Hannah to the cafeteria to grab a bite to eat.'

337

Hannah started to protest, but Mrs. Childress silenced her youngest daughter with a warning look.

'Let's go, pumpkin. I'll buy you an ice cream.' Mr. Childress reached out to engulf Hannah's much smaller hand in his own. 'We'll come right back after the detectives finish.'

With a huff of frustration, Hannah turned eyes full of hurt on Emerson.

'I'm sorry, Hannah. I know you want to stay with me, but it'll be easier to get through this if you're not in the room.' Emerson's voice cracked as she begged her sister to understand.

Hannah sniffled and ran her forearm across her nose, nodding once, before shuffling out. The door closed quietly behind her, but it didn't drown out her heart-breaking sobs.

The tension in the room mounted the moment Addis began to recount the tragic events of the worst night of her seventeen years. 'I'd barely gotten through the door after I got home from school when my mom came flying down the hall from her bedroom, accusing me of stealing her designer make-up – as if we even shared the same style. But she was *always* accusing me of something, and it was getting worse. Even after she'd find something she insisted I stole, she wouldn't apologize or acknowledge that she was wrong, saying I probably had snuck it back when she wasn't looking.

'Anyway, I was already on edge because, well, it seems silly now, but I was upset because the guy I thought was going to ask me to Homecoming asked someone else. And then my mom just blindsided me.'

Emerson snorted, her lip curling in disgust as she mumbled under her breath. 'Asshat.'

'Emerson,' Mrs. Childress warned.

Alyssa almost chuckled at Cord's expression when he realized Emerson was referring to the boy who'd hurt her best friend's feelings. She could tell from his face that he wasn't sure which emotion he should be expressing. He was in for a wild ride if his and Sara's twins were girls.

'What? He was. Is.' Emerson released Addis's hand and crossed her arms over her chest, and Alyssa couldn't help it this time – she chuckled. Not that it would be easy, but she had a feeling these two would find a way to navigate through the events of this last week as long as they did it together.

Still grimacing with disgust at this 'asshat,' Emerson picked up where Addis left off. 'After Addis came over, we hung out in my room while we bi—complained about boys and crappy parenting' – she caught her mom's eyes – 'not you and Daddy – and then we decided to grab a bite from Little Anita's.'

In a seamless transition, Addis picked up the thread of the story. 'Over nachos, we decided it might be better if I just stayed at Em's for a while. I cleared it with my dad while Em cleared it with her parents, and then we headed back to my house to pick up some clothes.'

Emerson shook her head. 'Well, first we drove around, remember? We were trying to wait until nine-thirty because that's when your mom usually locks herself in her room to watch her shows.'

Addis nodded, her gaze shifting from her best friend to Alyssa. 'That's right. I figured there was less of a chance of running into her' – her voice broke – 'and getting into another shouting match.'

Both girls leaned into each other as together, they relived the nightmare of discovering Addis's parents had been murdered.

Mrs. Childress wrapped one arm around Emerson while Grace hunkered down beside the chair and stroked her niece's hair, whispering assurances that she was okay now, that she was safe, and promising she'd be there to help her get through.

A tear betrayed the impact this interview was having on Cord, and he turned slightly as he tried, surreptitiously, to wipe the traitor away. But his compassion, his ability to emotionally connect with victims, was one of the things Alyssa most admired and respected about him, what made him the best partner she'd ever had.

'It was the smell that hit us right away.' Addis kept her eyes closed as she spoke through a scratchy throat.

Emerson nodded, whispering, 'I'll never forget it, though I don't even know how to describe it.'

'I knew right away my mom had been shot, but she just looked asleep. And then Em spotted m... m... my dad.' Without warning, Addis shot up and shoved between Alyssa and Cord, barely making it into the bathroom before her breakfast greeted the toilet. Grace rose to her feet and followed, closing the door behind the two of them.

The sound of dry heaves followed by more retching filtered back into the room, turning Alyssa's own stomach sour, not because of the act, but because her job required her to force these girls into reliving that night. Never again would they feel the freedom of innocence they'd shared before the fateful night of Thursday, October third.

Nearly ten minutes later, they reemerged, with Grace pressing a damp washcloth against the back of Addis's neck. After Addis settled back down beside Emerson, Grace snatched the blanket off the hospital bed and draped it over both girls. Emerson dropped her head onto Addis's shoulder. Addis, in turn, rested her cheek on the top of Emerson's head.

Alyssa hated to push the girls, but she needed more information. 'Do you think you're okay to go on?'

Together they whispered 'yes,' and for the next twenty minutes, Alyssa and Cord listened as they recounted the horrible events of that fateful night.

'Okay, I know this has been a lot, but tell us about the night you and Emerson escaped.'

Alyssa was surprised to see Addis and Emerson share a smile. Then Addis's hand emerged from beneath the blanket holding something in her palm. 'We found a shard of glass in the crawl space, and we used that to help saw through the ropes.' Light pink suddenly stained Addis's cheeks as she showed Alyssa what she held. 'We found this under the cabin, and I know it wasn't much in the way of real protection, but it was like our good luck charm, and so I kept it.'

'Do you mind if I take a look at that?' Alyssa asked.

'Sure.'

Examining it, Alyssa knew Addis was correct in her assumption that the personalized gift-shop knife would've offered no assistance since its rusted blade was far from sharp. Most of the lettering had worn off, but she could make out an *A* and an *E*. Alex? Something stirred inside her. Careful to keep her tone even, she said, 'Addis, Cord and I are going to need to hold onto this for a bit, okay?'

If Addis was confused, she didn't show it.

'What made you crawl under the cabin the night you escaped?' Cord asked.

'We'd just gotten to the porch when we saw headlights. It was too dark to see where it was safe to go, so we decided to hide beside the house, and that's when Addis fell and realized we could crawl under it, so we did.'

'It was stupid dark under there, and it didn't help that something sharp kept poking us.' Addis shuddered. 'The guy who kidnapped us sounded angry at the other person.'

'What did he say that makes you think that?' Alyssa asked when Addis hesitated.

The girls looked at each other before Addis shrugged. 'Um, I think it's because he said, "What the hell are you doing here, Alex" or something like that, anyway.'

Even beneath the hospital blanket, it was easy to see the girls trembling, and Alyssa wondered if either of them was aware that they'd simultaneously inched closer to each other as, whispering, Emerson repeated Alex's threat. 'Alex was the one who said they had to kill us like they killed Ad's mom and dad.' A knock on the door distracted everyone. When Mrs. Childress called for the visitor to enter, Tony and Sandra walked in together.

'Hey. I was in the neighborhood and thought I'd come and see for myself how the two of you are doing.' The girls wore matching smiles at Tony's greeting.

But as quickly as her smile emerged, Emerson's faded. Face flushing, she took a sudden interest in one of the many cuts on her finger. Alyssa and Cord exchanged puzzled expressions. Then, Emerson spoke into her lap in a voice so soft and quiet that Alyssa had to move forward in order to hear.

'It felt like I'd been running for a really long time, and everything looked the same, like I was just going in circles. I was really scared because I was lost and alone and feeling guilty because Ad' – she tilted her head just a bit and offered a sad smile at her friend – 'because Ad—Well, you know. I thought she'd given up her life to save me.' Tears leaked from the corners of her eyes, and she used her knuckles to brush them away, wiping them on the blanket before continuing. 'Addis said you told her you were a good tracker.'

At the way Cord's eyes immediately shifted from the girls to Tony, Alyssa knew he'd also noted the hint of accusation in Emerson's tone.

Tony's head bobbed up and down, seeming to understand what Emerson was getting at. 'You're wondering why I never found you?'

With her eyes still cast down, Emerson shrugged even as she whispered, 'Yeah, I guess.'

'Well, I did search for you in that area, so I can only guess that it was probably afterwards that you hid in the spot where we found you.' Tony shuffled forward until he could squat down in front of her. 'Hey, can you look at me for a second?' He waited for Emerson to lift her head. 'Even if you had been there when I searched, you should be proud of yourself, and do you know why?'

'Why?'

'Because you did the right thing in hiding yourself, and even hurt and disoriented, you managed to stay hidden until Addis' – he tipped his head toward her best friend – 'found the trail that led us to you.' Tony's eyes shimmered when Emerson's neck snapped in Addis's direction.

'What? You didn't tell me that.'

Alyssa missed Addis's response because her phone vibrated. Not wanting to disturb the girls while they were speaking, she'd turned the ringer as low as it could go without actually turning it off before she'd come in to interview them. She glanced down. It was Dr. Homa,

343

and if she was calling, it had to be regarding Elizabeth
Monroe. 'Excuse me. I have to take this.'

Chapter Fifty-Two

Thursday, October 10

Alyssa answered her phone just as Cord joined her in the hallway. 'Detective Wyatt speaking.'

'Detective Wyatt, this is Dr. Homa over at the University of New Mexico Hospital. I'm calling about Elizabeth Monroe. Do you have a few minutes?'

The last time Dr. Homa had called her unexpectedly, it had been to offer grave news, almost literally, so Alyssa's muscles tensed in anticipation.

'First, it's been all over the news that you and your team rescued Addis Kensington and Emerson Childress, so nice work. But that's not the point of this call. Late last night, Elizabeth's situation was upgraded from critical to serious, and I suspect before long, we'll be elevating that status to stable. She's doing remarkably well – actually, no, that's not quite accurate – her recovery is nothing short of miraculous. That's the good news.'

'That is good news, Dr. Homa, so now hit me with the bad.' Alyssa watched Cord's eyebrows shoot upward as he studied her face.

The doctor sighed before diving in. 'Because of Ms. Monroe's cardiac episode, I wanted to run some tests. Now, on the surface, her heart strain is understandable considering the amount of trauma she suffered, as well as somehow managing to survive the bacterial infections she received from being in that dumpster. However, Ms. Monroe's heart was near poster perfect. I'll cut to the chase: the lab found high levels of nifedipine in Elizabeth's blood.'

'Nifedipine?' Alyssa asked.

'It's a blood pressure medication that comes in capsule or pills but can also, in rare circumstances, be ordered as a liquid. Though a few doctors will still prescribe an extended-release version of the medicine, many of us in the medical field no longer prescribe nifedipine due to its tendency to drop a person's blood pressure unpredictably and rapidly, raising the risk of a cardiac episode,' Dr. Homa explained.

'Such as Elizabeth Monroe's.'

'Such as Ms. Monroe's. But there's more. I had my nurses pull the IV line and send it to the lab as well for testing. Detective Wyatt, someone introduced an elevated level of nifedipine into Elizabeth's IV line. Her cardiac arrest was not caused by her injuries.'

Alyssa was sure Cord could hear the thumping of her heart. 'Dr. Homa, if Detective Roberts and I swing by, what are the chances we can speak with Elizabeth and take a look at the hospital security cameras?'

'Well, there are privacy laws to consider, but I think the chances are high on both counts. Have me paged when you arrive, and I'll see what I can do to smooth the way for you.'

'Thank you, Dr. Homa. I appreciate it.'

'One more thing, Detective. I do want to warn you that Ms. Monroe, at this time, has no recollection of the attack. All she knows is what she's been told, so if you're hoping she'll hand you the smoking gun that tells you who her assailant is, I'm afraid you're out of luck there. And just to be clear, it's quite possible she'll never recover that part of her memory.'

Though deflated by the news, Alyssa wasn't surprised. 'I understand, and again, thank you.'

She ended the call and pulled Cord to the side. After she filled him in, his first question was, 'What do you want to do about our interview with Addis and Emerson?'

Alyssa chewed her bottom lip and then huffed out a frustrated breath. 'Listen, I watched the girls' reactions when Tony came in, and they're clearly not frightened of him. We *could* theoretically ask him and Sandra to take over. Or, we've got enough for now, so we could always return in a little bit. If we go that route, we'd also be able to check on them again.'

'I vote for the second option.' What neither Alyssa nor Cord said aloud was that, while it may no longer be a matter of trust, they still needed some answers from Tony.

Before heading to the parking garage, they returned to Emerson's room. Ignoring Grace's, Tony's, and Sandra's scrutinizing stares, Alyssa thanked the girls and assured them that she and Cord would pop back in tomorrow to see how they were holding up.

'It's too bad Elizabeth's not housed here in the same hospital as Addis and Emerson. That would've been convenient,' Cord said a few minutes later as he climbed into the Tahoe.

'But when does the universe ever cooperate that way for us?'

'It doesn't, of course.'

'Of course.' Alyssa waited for a trailer stacked high with wrecked cars to pass before pulling out into traffic. 'But at least now, more pieces of the puzzle are starting to shift into place. Hopefully, Elizabeth will be able to shed enough light to expose the remaining pieces we're still missing.'

Cord flipped open his notebook. 'Okay, let's talk this out while you drive. So far, we've been able to piece together that Adam Campbell and Alexandra Greene are half-siblings. Adam's fingerprints on the photographs delivered to Holly' – there was a slight tightening in Cord's tone – 'and his DNA at the Kensington crime scene, prove his involvement in both cases.'

'Both girls instantly and positively identified him as their kidnapper when Joe showed them the photographic lineup of UNM's football team last night,' Alyssa threw in.

Cord nodded, continuing, 'The girls heard Adam refer to his visitor as "Alex," a female, who then admitted to killing Gabriel and Lydia.'

'According to Adam's neighbor,' Alyssa said, 'he often had a female visitor who drove a truck. The person who attacked Elizabeth drove a truck – the same one which was present when the latest photographs were delivered to Holly – and, though we couldn't see a face, the driver was much shorter than Adam, which coincides with Dr. Sharp's theory that whoever killed Gabriel was female or a shorter male.'

'Don't shoot the messenger, but playing devil's advocate, that truck's not registered, and so we can't definitively tie it to Alexandra Greene, which is the assumption here.' Cord clicked his pen while he spoke, stopping only when Alyssa shot him an irritated glare. 'Sorry.'

'Yet,' she corrected. 'We can't tie her to the truck yet – but I feel safe in assuming that, even if it doesn't belong to her, she's the one driving it. And since we can now connect her to everyone, beginning with Hayden Benson,

Alexandra Greene remains my number one suspect.' She drummed her fingers on the steering wheel. 'My theory is that somehow Alexandra discovered Elizabeth hired Gabriel to look into Hayden's disappearance. I don't think it's a far leap of logic to assume he's dead, quite probably by Alexandra's hands.'

'But how did she find out? And why Lydia?'

At a red light, Alyssa darted a quick look at her partner. 'What I want to know is why did Adam target Holly, and how did he get those photos from *The Toybox* case? And did Alexandra know what was in those envelopes she was delivering to my daughter?' Alyssa's blood pressure shot up, and she had to force herself to take several calming breaths.

Cord spoke quietly. 'My guess is when we finally locate Alexandra Greene, we're going to find out she's also left-handed, just like the person who wrote those notes to Holly.'

Alyssa didn't have an answer because she had a feeling her partner was right, and only by tracking down Alexandra would they be able to find out *why*. For the next mile, the two of them rode in silence, broken only when Cord suddenly pulled out his phone.

'I just want to check on Sara real quick before we get to the hospital. She swears she was feeling fine this morning before I left, but she was looking a little piqued.'

Though his voice gave nothing away, Alyssa could tell by the way he drummed his fingers on his thighs that Cord was on pins and needles as he waited for his wife to answer. 'Tell her I said hi.'

When Sara finally picked up, he released a relieved breath, and Alyssa felt her own muscles unclench.

'Hey baby, I'm just checking on you and my babies. Yeah? That's good. All right. Rest. Oh, and Lys says hi. Okay. Love you, babe. See you later.'

Stuffing his phone back into his pocket, he said, 'She says hi back.'

–

Alyssa paced outside the room while nurses cleaned and changed Elizabeth's bandages. The clasp of closure on this case was within her reach, and though she tried not to get her hopes up, it was difficult – especially now that Addis and Emerson had been located and were safe. To cover all her bases, she crossed her fingers, prayed, and performed the sign of the cross in the hope that Elizabeth would provide some much-needed answers.

'You know pacing isn't going to get you in there any quicker, so here's a thought: stop.' Cord grabbed her arm and tugged her out of the way of a patient who'd been doing laps around the nurses' station since they'd arrived.

Alyssa ignored her partner's comment. 'Whoever did this to Elizabeth – and again, I'm going with the elusive ghost Alexandra Greene – must have some sort of medical background in order to have access to the nifedipine.' Her eyes studied the nurses, technicians, and all the other readily available staff that had access to patients. 'Maybe she works here.'

Like he was wont to do, Cord poked a hole in her theory. 'Don't you think that if Alexandra had regular access to her intended victim, Elizabeth Monroe would be dead right now instead of being upgraded from critical to serious with hopes of moving up to stable?'

Alyssa narrowed her eyes. 'Your desire to consistently counteract the things I say with reason and logic is not your most admirable trait, I'll have you know.'

Cord was unmoved, as his chuckle proved. But their conversation ended when two nurses piled out of Elizabeth's room. The matronly one wearing puppy dog scrubs and a nametag that read *Michaela* greeted them. 'We just gave her a pain pill – orally. She didn't want it administered intravenously because she wants to speak with you. She's pretty worn out, so it's difficult to say how much time you'll actually have. Good luck.'

'Thank you,' Alyssa said, already opening the door.

Lying in the hospital bed, her skin mottled in yellows, greens, and garish blues, Elizabeth Monroe looked much smaller and weaker than the woman Alyssa had interviewed for the first time nearly a week ago. 'Miss Monroe, it's good to see you awake.' She jabbed her thumb in Cord's direction. 'This is my partner, Detective Roberts. Thanks for agreeing to see us.'

Elizabeth grimaced as she fought with elevating her bed so she wasn't lying flat. 'Detective, Tessa told me you've checked in on Brandon a couple of times just to see how he's doing, and I'd like to thank you for that. I know that's above and beyond your job requirements, and I want you to know I appreciate it.' Her voice was rough, like she had a bad case of bronchitis and laryngitis all wrapped up in one miserable package.

Alyssa smiled. 'Your son is very protective of his mom and is doing quite well, all things considered. I understand Rosalyn offered to take him until you were fully recovered and out of the hospital, but after she and Tessa spoke, the two of them decided Brandon would be more comfortable staying with his best friend and closer to home. The last time I checked in, the boys were busy drawing you get well cards and planning their futures as superheroes or cops. Apparently, there was a pretty lively debate on whether or not they were allowed to do both or had to choose one over the other.' A warm tug pulled at Alyssa's heart, picturing Brandon's passion for superheroes.

Elizabeth's grin came off as more of a grimace. 'Tessa did tell me that when she called.' With a loving, indulgent chuckle, she pointed to several drawings propped on the windowsill. 'She dropped those off when I was still in a coma. Superheroes and cops are probably a safer bet because I don't think either of them are quite ready to be enrolled in art school just yet.'

Where she was smiling seconds ago, tears now filled Elizabeth's eyes. 'His father would've been so proud.' Then sobering again, she said, 'There's been lots of talk that you rescued Gabriel Kensington's daughter and her friend. Is it true they actually escaped first? Or are you not allowed to tell me?'

'It's been on the news, so I can tell you at least that much. They were being held in a crawl space in a cabin up in the Pecos. They managed to get loose and escape, and as they were hiding, they found what they decided later was their good luck charm.' Alyssa wasn't sure why she did it, but she pulled out the pocketknife she'd placed in an evidence baggie and dangled it in front of Elizabeth's face so she could see.

It took several seconds for her to realize Elizabeth was no longer listening. Her gaze was locked on the pocketknife, but before Alyssa could ask what was wrong, Elizabeth's eyes rolled back in her head, and the alarms in her room started blaring.

Chapter Fifty-Three

Thursday, October 10

Alyssa was two steps behind Cord as they raced out of the hospital, but that was only because she was trying to place a call at the same time. It rang four times before going to voicemail. Again. Panting less from exertion than tension, she fought the desire to hurl her phone against one of the concrete pillars as she passed, for no other reason than to release some of the blistering rage stirring in her gut.

The decision to wait until they reached the Tahoe before trying again was made for her when she peeked down at her screen to make sure her finger hit the correct number, and she almost rammed into a fire hydrant, barely skirting around it in time. Apparently, her multitasking skills didn't stretch to include running and dialing at the same time, something Cord pointed out as soon as the SUV was in sight.

Unlocking the doors, she shot him a withering glare. She'd just turned the key in the ignition when Hal's incoming call blasted through the speakers. She answered with: 'I've been trying to reach you.'

'As evidenced by the half dozen missed calls,' Hal said drily. 'I was in the restroom, and since I prefer to piss in peace, I left my phone behind.'

'Too much information, Hal.'

'Sorry. What's up?'

'Long story shorter: Addis and Emerson discovered a pocketknife beneath the cabin where they hid and decided it was an amulet of sorts. I showed it to Elizabeth Monroe, and her reaction sent her into a medical episode. But once she was stable again, she demanded to speak to Cord and me. Turns out that pocketknife was a gift from her to Hayden Benson the day before his disappearance. She said she'd seen it in a gift shop, and since it had his name, she saw it as a sign and purchased it for him. Most of the lettering is worn off, but it makes sense. There are lots of possible explanations for why this knife was found in a remote cabin in the woods, but most of them lead back to the same thing: it places Hayden with either Adam Campbell or Alexandra Greene shortly before he was never seen again.'

When Alyssa stopped to catch her breath, Cord filled Hal in on what they'd seen on the hospital's security cameras.

Hal was unnaturally quiet for so long that Alyssa had to check to make sure they hadn't dropped the call. 'You still there?'

'Yeah, I'm here. Listen, I have some news to share with you, as well. First, Dr. Sharp dropped in. Her preliminary finding on Adam Campbell is that he didn't commit suicide as the gun gripped in his hand suggested. Someone hammered his skull in before he died, so she's ruling his death a homicide. Using his body temperature as a gauge, as well as the rigor mortis that had set in, she estimates his death occurred somewhere over twenty-four hours ago but less than seventy-two.'

Alyssa's mind immediately flashed to Adam's neighbor. 'According to Emilia Martinez, she saw Campbell leaving

354

his house Tuesday night, so we know he was alive then.' From the corner of her eye, she saw Cord nodding his head in agreement. 'Now, you said, "first." Does that mean there's more?' she asked.

'I'm afraid so. Last night and this morning, I've been trying to unearth as much information as I could regarding Adam Campbell and Alexandra Greene. In the process, I came across one of Gabriel's electronic files labeled "D.P.," and when I clicked on it, several photos and articles came up.' A heavy sigh came over the line. 'I've got a name and an address for someone I think you're going to want to talk to.'

For the next few minutes, Hal filled them in on what he'd discovered, and just as he'd been stunned with Alyssa and Cord's news, they were with his. It was all starting to make sense.

At the next intersection, Alyssa flipped the car around and headed east on I-40 on their way to Cedar Crest. After hanging up, Hal had forwarded several links to her phone, so with luck, the person they were racing to see would help put the final piece of the puzzle in place.

Chapter Fifty-Four

The DJ on the radio droned on and on about Addis and Emerson's miraculous escape from their mad captor, how they'd used a stupid piece of broken glass to help loosen their ropes, and the more he lauded their heroism, the more fiercely Alex fought the urge to turn the car around and head to the hospital where they would remain under observation for at least another twenty-four hours.

Her world had suddenly turned into the graviton ride at the state fair, except instead of staying safely glued to the side, she was being sucked down into the vortex with no hope of clawing her way out.

When she reached her house, she crawled into the attic and dragged out several large trunks and suitcases. Next, she went to her bedroom to retrieve her treasured assault rifle, the one she only used for target practice – on unsuspecting animals – out in the middle of nowhere. But tonight, it would be her insurance policy. She would not be cornered or captured, but if she was, she'd make widows, widowers, and orphans out of as many people as she could, and she'd do it laughing the entire way.

But first, she needed to finish what she'd started, what she should've done seven years ago after she'd killed Hayden. This time, she'd make sure Elizabeth Monroe did not survive the night. And neither would her son. The anticipation of getting the precious 'Beck' to cower and beg for her son's life filled her with excitement and adrenaline.

Just a few more hours, and it would all be over.

Chapter Fifty-Five

Thursday, October 10

Alyssa pulled to a stop in front of a cute little blue house surrounded by the quintessential white picket fence. In a nearby corral were a pony and a horse, and running around in the yard were two young children. The little girl was maybe three years old and dressed up like a pirate complete with eye-patch while the boy, perhaps four or five, romped around the yard with a too-large cowboy hat threatening to topple from his head as he used a broken broomstick handle as his makeshift horse.

A twenty-something man stood when he saw the two of them approaching. He turned and said something to the kids who groaned but obeyed whatever he'd told them to do, which apparently was to go inside.

'Darren Pease?' Alyssa said as she neared the white gate.

'Yes, ma'am. Who's asking?'

'I'm Detective Wyatt with the Albuquerque Police Department. This is Detective Roberts. We have a few questions we'd like to ask you about Alexandra Greene.'

Darren twisted around when he heard the front door close behind his children, and when he turned back to face them again, Alyssa thought a marble statue in the middle of a frozen tundra would be less cold.

A tic in his jaw contorted the dimple in his cheek. 'Haven't heard her name for a while. I don't suppose you've come to tell me she's dead?'

'No, afraid not.'

Darren shrugged. 'That's too bad. I'd've enjoyed the opportunity to dance on her grave.'

Damn. That was harsh, Alyssa thought.

'No, she's very much alive and well.' She opened one of the links Hal had sent, clicked on an image, and passed her phone over. 'Look familiar?'

Darren's eyebrows stretched for his hairline. 'That's not Alex.' He handed her phone back.

'Are you sure?'

'It's not the Alexandra Greene I knew.'

Alyssa used her thumb and index finger to enlarge the photo and passed it back to him. 'Why don't you look a little closer.'

The way Darren pursed his lips before taking the phone again told Alyssa he was humoring her more than anything else. But a moment later, his spine stiffened, and he cocked his head to the side before drawing the image closer to his face. Then he tapped on a mole located just below Alexandra's ear on her neck. 'I'll be damned. It is her.' His shocked expression bounced between Alyssa and Cord. 'You said you're here to talk to me about her, but clearly, I haven't seen her in some time, not since the accident anyway. I didn't even recognize her.'

'Can you tell us a little bit about that accident?' Cord asked.

Darren twisted around and waved to his daughter as she tapped her palm against the window, her arm flying back and forth as she yelled hello from inside the house. Two seconds later, his wife appeared, wearing exhaustion like a comfortable piece of clothing as she mouthed 'Sorry' and carted the little girl away.

Darren unlocked the gate and swung it inward. 'May as well come have a seat on the porch. This might take some time.'

As he spoke, a stiff breeze kicked the warmth of the day out, but even with the chillier air, sweat trailed down the sides of Darren Pease's face, dripping into the collar of his shirt, staining it a darker blue.

'I met Alex at Regal Cinema where we both worked. She was usually fairly quiet, more observant, I guess. As a former geek who got picked on, I felt bad that the rest of the staff treated her like Rudolph the Red-Nosed Reindeer, and I made it a point to include her or sit with her at lunch breaks or whatnot.' He rubbed the back of his neck, twisting it from side to side as he did.

'Then one day, she blurted out that she liked me. I didn't want to lead her on, so I told her I didn't reciprocate those feelings, that I had a girlfriend' – he tipped his head back toward the house – 'who's now my wife. Anyway, she was clearly sad, but she said she understood. I was afraid things were going to be awkward, but the next day, everything seemed normal. Then about a week later, she approached me for a ride home, and I said sure.'

Darren stopped speaking long enough to reach down and open the lid to a cooler at his feet that Alyssa hadn't noticed. He pulled out a beer, guzzled half, and set it down. 'Um, I'd offer you one, but I have a feeling you'd decline seeing as how you're on duty.'

'Appreciate the thought, man,' Cord said.

'Listen, I can't prove what I'm about to say, but I will go to my grave knowing in my gut that Alex tinkered with my brakes.'

'What caused the accident?' Alyssa asked.

Instantly, his entire face flushed a deep red, and he averted his gaze as he cleared his throat. 'Uh, um, Alex said something like she'd rather us die together than see me with someone else. Then she, uh, told me she could, uh, do things for me. One second she was in the passenger seat, and the next, her head was in my lap, and my pants were undone, and all I remember next is swerving into the path of a semi on the interstate. I managed to avoid the crash, but when I jerked the steering wheel, I overcorrected and started to careen off into the canyon. I hit the brakes, but nothing happened. We were both thrown from the car. I have to admit, I was surprised either of us survived. Both my legs were broken, I suffered a lot of internal damage, and one of my ribs punctured my lung, but Alex had it worse. In addition to all her other injuries, the bones in her face were shattered, and I heard it took a lot of plastic surgery to fix her up.'

Half an hour later, armed with more information and a new understanding of Alexandra Greene, Alyssa and Cord shook Darren's hand, thanking him.

Just as they stepped off the porch, he stopped them. 'Can I ask what Alexandra's done? I assume it's something pretty bad if you're out here talking to me.'

Because she saw no need to hide the truth from him, Alyssa said, 'She's a suspect in at least four murders, and three attempted murders.'

Back in the car, she started the engine and turned the heat on low, hoping to ease the ache of cold. When the temperature dropped in the mountains, it dropped fast.

'Well,' she said, pulling away from the curb. 'You ready for our next stop?'

Cord clicked his seatbelt into place. 'No, but let's go anyway.'

Chapter Fifty-Six

Thursday, October 10

While Alyssa headed back into Albuquerque, Cord called Captain Hammond with an update, then he called the rest of the team in.

Adrift in the mire of their own thoughts, it was a quiet ride back to the precinct. Only when Alyssa parked the SUV and turned the ignition off, did Cord break the silence.

'Stop it,' he said.

'Stop what?'

'Stop blaming yourself.'

Alyssa grunted. 'No offense, Cord, but it's my daughter who was threatened, and if I'd seen what seems so obvious now... did I tell you Isaac called me this morning, pissed at me for not telling him myself what was going on? He wanted to know how *he* was supposed to protect his big sister if he was kept in the dark? My fourteen-year-old son felt the need to yell at his mother, a detective, for God's sake, about protecting Holly. So, yes, if you don't mind, I think I will blame myself.'

Instead of responding, Cord shook his head. She knew him well enough to know it wasn't because he agreed with her; he just knew she'd have a comeback for anything he said.

Just inside the doors to the precinct, they bumped into Tony whose expression was a combination of anger, hurt, and betrayal. He knew. 'Liz just got here, so now that's everyone.' They'd found out earlier that she'd finished her work in Las Cruces Tuesday night, and so they'd asked her to join them.

Alyssa didn't answer because there was nothing to say. Less than five minutes after entering the conference room, the entire team was assembled, including Captain Hammond who stood back in the corner in a failed attempt to be as unobtrusive as possible.

As soon as the room quieted, Alyssa began. 'It took longer than I would've liked – than any of us would've – but we finally have some answers. This isn't going to be easy to hear, but—' She nodded to Cord.

All eyes swiveled his way. 'Sandra Falwin, you're under arrest for suspicion of murder and kidnapping—'

That was as far as he got before the room exploded in action with Sandra shoving to her feet, a look of alarm on her face, her hand inching toward her belt. Alyssa had no idea if she was going for her service weapon, but none of them were taking the chance as five guns were immediately trained on her.

'Don't even think about it!'

'Keep your hands where we can see them!'

'Don't move!'

'What the—'

Everyone shouted at the same time until Hammond whistled for silence. Sandra's eyes shot wildly around the room, landing on Alyssa. 'I don't understand what's going on. Would someone please explain?'

Her gaze unwavering, devoid of any warmth or affection for this woman she'd hoped to mentor, Alyssa waited as Cord was able to cuff a distracted Sandra's hands behind her back while reading her the Miranda Rights. 'Do you know what's sad,' she finally said. 'The fact that the potential for you to become one of us, to become one of the best, was really and truly there.' She tried unsuccessfully to keep the pain of Sandra's duplicity from creeping into her voice. And she knew she wasn't the only one feeling it.

'Here's what we know. Feel free to fill in the blanks for us. At seven years old, your father – Alexander Greene – woke to you holding a knife over him, and that incident, along with others, forced him into leaving the family. Three months later, your mother remarried when she realized she was pregnant. Shortly after your brother was born, Barry Campbell also learned to fear you, and so, he, too, divorced your mother, who gave up her parental rights to Adam Campbell, your half-brother.'

Still trying to remove Cord's grip, Sandra's posture drooped, and her head swung around the room as she tried to make eye contact with the rest of the team. In a wobbly voice, she said, 'I told Lys that I had a baby brother who died from SIDs.'

Alyssa waved her comment off. 'Everything you told me about your family was nothing more than a story you concocted in an effort to "connect" with me. The only truthful element to that fabrication was how you weren't close to your parents.'

Sandra stopped struggling, but remained quiet, and Alyssa couldn't decipher if the expression on her face was curiosity or something else. She continued. 'After you killed Hayden Benson, you and your mother left Del Luna, and shortly after, you were able to track down your brother using social media. Somehow, you managed to convince Adam to give you a chance. But at some point, he had to have realized how dangerous you really were, so I was confused as to how you managed to convince him to keep you around. That is until Hal uncovered some interesting information in Adam's past, specifically his high school days. It would seem that there was one accident and one rather gruesome murder, and incidentally, both boys had somehow threatened Adam. My guess is when we reopen those cases, we'll learn that they have your fingerprints all over them. Maybe Adam was your accomplice then, too, or maybe he was simply aware of what you'd done, but either way, that's the hold you had over him, so you probably had no trouble manipulating him into doing your bidding.'

A gleam of admiration, probably for herself, appeared in Sandra's eyes.

This was where the story became a little murky, but Alyssa forged ahead as if her hunch was fact. 'Somehow you discovered that Elizabeth Monroe had hired Gabriel Kensington, and you had to stop him before he discovered the truth. But you were too late, weren't you?'

The calculated expression that settled onto Sandra's face was almost as good as a blatant confession, as far as Alyssa was concerned.

'In hindsight, I guess I probably should've suspected you sooner, especially after you called to inform us Elizabeth's vehicle had been located. You said, "*Didn't* she own a BMW?" Past tense, of course, because you thought you'd killed her.'

Sandra's lips tightened, and a veil of anger dropped into place. In that moment, Alyssa could easily sense the evil that had driven Alexander Greene and Barry Campbell away. And she had to admit, she couldn't blame them.

Ignoring the hatred shooting from Sandra's glare, Alyssa kept her eyes trained on the young officer. 'Knowing what you're capable of, Adam, perhaps in a misguided attempt to protect the girls, kidnaps them and stows them away so you don't also murder them.'

Adopting a look that reminded Alyssa of a kicked puppy, Sandra's gaze darted around the room. 'This is crazy. You all realize that, don't you? She's finally lost her mind. You've all seen it coming after what happened with her brother.'

Cord yanked on Sandra's arms, eliciting a squeal out of her. 'This would be a good time to shut your mouth,' he warned.

'In the meantime,' Alyssa went on as if Sandra hadn't spoken, 'you insinuated yourself into the investigation by showing up at the crime scene – with wet hair, as I recall, so fresh from cleaning yourself up – and then, realizing what a perfect opportunity it was for you to stay up to date with the case, you somehow managed to manipulate Captain Hammond into inviting you to work with my team, and we were happy to welcome you on board.

'But let's back up a moment, shall we? When we were finally able to fit the pieces of this puzzle together, I had to stop and ask myself, how in the hell could a sociopath like you pass the psych exam for joining the police force? But recent events reminded me how frighteningly simple it is for someone like you to fool the system.'

This time Sandra rolled her eyes. 'You sound like a lunatic, you know that? You can't prove any of this, and do you know why? Because you're wrong. And you know it. I guess Mack Kensington was right after all when he accused you of finding a scapegoat to take the fall for your inability to solve a crime.' She craned her neck until she could see Captain Hammond. 'Are you really going to stand there and let her get away with this? Is she so *valuable* that you're going to let her make this shit up? Is that how all your cases get wrapped up so prettily?'

Hammond matched her glare for glare, but aside from the clenched jaw and the flared nostrils, gave no indication he'd even heard.

'When things first started to unravel, you concocted a plan that involved Holly.'

Tony's neck snapped in Alyssa's direction so fast that she actually heard it pop. At the same time, Joe breathed out his understanding. 'The pictures, the threats. It was a ploy to distract you, throw you off your game. And she had access to the evidence room. You were right, Lys. Not a bad idea knowing how protective you—'

Beside him, Hal's hiss and blistering glare directed his way caused Joe to throw his hands up in the air. 'Whoa, keep your weapon holstered, man. I didn't say I agreed with or liked it.'

Hal snarled something unintelligible in a tone completely at odds with his usual charming personality.

This was hard enough on her team as it was, and Alyssa didn't need their anger directed at each other, so she drew Sandra's attention back to her. 'Things really started falling apart after Adam's DNA was linked to the crime scene, especially since Addis and Emerson had managed to escape. You warned Adam about our search warrant and told him to get out of the house and to meet you up at the cabin. After you left work that night, you drove up to the Pecos where you staged your own brother's suicide. Is that when you conceived the idea that it would throw us off if you were the one who then "discovered" where the cabin was?'

Alyssa didn't really expect a response, and she didn't get one. 'You must've been having quite the laugh before we came across Tony and the girls. My guess is you were hoping they were still wandering, lost in the woods, and you could return after we discovered Adam's body. You'd approach Addis and Emerson as a cop and get them to trust you. And then you were going to kill them and dispose of their bodies. Of course, the fact that Tony was in the picture meant you'd first have to take him out, as well.'

Tony finally chimed in. 'Even if you'd managed to get the jump on me without the girls realizing it, getting them to trust you wouldn't have worked because they would've recognized your voice, the same way they did in the hospital. That's why both of them suddenly became agitated and suddenly needed some rest right after Lys and Cord left.'

Eyes narrowed, Sandra spoke through gritted teeth. 'Are all of you forgetting the fact that my name is Sandra Falwin, and I look absolutely *nothing* like Alexandra Greene?'

Alyssa was about to mention that they'd sent Alexander Greene's beard hair off for a DNA analysis that would prove Sandra and Alexandra were one and the same, but Hal was already speaking.

'Funny you should mention that. I did some digging – it's amazing what you can find with just a hint in the right direction. Alexandra Greene met one Darren Pease at Regal Cinemas and began crushing on him. He didn't reciprocate. Cut through to the end, and you and Darren are in a nasty accident on I-40. Alex suffered multiple lacerations to her face which required extensive facial reconstruction. Over the next two years, you reinvented yourself, including the adaptation of your name. Alex-andra became Sandra, though your brother still called you by your childhood nickname, Alex.'

'But you couldn't really remain Sandra Greene,' Cord added. 'It was too obvious, so you cleverly took on your great-grandmother's name, Falwin. It's amazing what the internet can produce, isn't it?'

The chill from Sandra's voice could be felt in the room. 'Like I said, there's nothing here for you to prove. I was trying to humor you, but now I'm done listening to you invent stories.'

Hal rolled his chair over until he was directly in front of Sandra. 'You're one of us, you know.' By the expressions on everyone's faces and the way they sort of settled back, Alyssa knew her team had already guessed what Hal was up to. 'You know, it takes a lot less energy to tell the truth. Think about the weight that would finally lift. That feeling of being abandoned by both your father and your stepfather, not to mention the fact that Barry Campbell stole your brother from you, too, wouldn't be as heavy.' Hal clasped one of Sandra's hands between both of his and lowered his voice. 'I don't think you meant to kill Hayden at all. It was an accident, and then you tried to cover it up because you didn't think anyone would believe you.'

Alyssa watched Sandra's defensive posture begin to crumble under Hal's soothing tone. She'd witnessed firsthand how pointless it could be to resist falling under his spell; it was kind of like a flame trying to withstand a windstorm.

'You reinvented yourself,' Hal continued, 'but then Gabriel Kensington discovered who you really were and was going to destroy everything.' Without taking his eyes from Sandra, he dropped her hand and opened a laptop.

There in full color was an array of photographs and articles about Alexandra Greene and Darren Pease's accident. Hal clicked through to the last one where Alexandra was seen leaving the hospital after her final facial surgery. 'These were in a file on Gabriel's laptop.'

Next, he opened a document titled *Phone Interview with Dr. Rojas* dated Wednesday, October second. 'Dr. Rojas was the plastic surgeon responsible for doing the extensive work on putting you back together, so to speak, and Gabriel was able to track him down. Now, you knew you'd changed, but you also knew no one would listen when the truth came out. So, you went to Gabriel, hoping to appeal to his sense of right and wrong. But he declined to listen. You tried to show him, didn't you, how you'd evolved? But he refused to hear, refused to see. So, then you grew angry. What happened? Did you kill Gabriel and then have to kill Lydia to erase the potential for witnesses?'

'I shot her first.' A thunderous expression darkened Sandra's face. 'I found out with everyone else that the gun I used was actually registered to my father.' Alyssa flashed back to the look of utter shock that had crossed Sandra's face when the team had learned that bit of news. At the time, she hadn't thought much of it.

Almost as if she were speaking to herself, Sandra continued. 'When I confronted Adam about it, he told me all he knew was that he'd inherited it after his father died. So, I guess Barry Campbell stole more than my brother from me; he also stole my father's gun.'

The hissed confession was out, and no one moved a muscle, afraid if they so much as inhaled or exhaled, the spell would be broken.

'After I shot Gabriel, I hit him with the rolling pin, and then I don't know what overcame me. I just couldn't stop until it was done.'

The dark, faraway look in Sandra's eyes made Alyssa wonder if she was even aware of what she'd just admitted.

'When I went with Alyssa to interview Elizabeth, I was afraid there was a chance she'd recognize me, but she didn't, so I knew I was in the clear. But I couldn't be positive she never would, so I knew before I left that I was going to have to get rid of her, too. I'd always planned to, anyway.'

When Joe sneezed, the spell was broken, and a cold mask fell into place on Sandra's face. 'None of what I said can be used. I was under duress and forced into a false confession. So, as is my right, I'd like to insist on speaking to an attorney before this goes any further.' Unlike moments earlier when she hadn't seemed to realize she was even speaking, her voice was now full of informed arrogance.

A maze of fury, disappointment, and betrayal replaced Hammond's usual scowl as he stepped up. 'I've got her.' At the door, he turned back. 'Nice work, team.' And then he was pushing Sandra in front of him as he led her away.

For nearly a minute, the team sat speechless as they tried to process what had just happened. Finally, Joe, starting and stopping several stuttered attempts, managed to mutter, 'I've gotta say, I did *not* see that coming.'

It took another half hour to unravel the rest of the story, and by the time they were done, everyone looked as drained as they all felt. 'It's been a long day,' Alyssa said. 'Everyone, go home and get some rest. Come in late tomorrow because I'm going to head over to the hospital first thing to visit Grace and the girls and then Elizabeth.'

Liz stood and pushed her chair back, shaking her head as she headed for the door. 'I don't know whether to be sad or glad that I missed this one.'

Joe patted her on the shoulder. 'Be glad, pal. Be glad.'

One by one, the team filed out with Tony lingering behind. 'Lys, have you got another second?'

Alyssa watched Cord hesitate in the doorway as he cast a concerned gaze her direction before closing the door behind him. 'Yes.' She had a feeling Tony was about to explain his sudden disappearance, and she was right.

'You know my dad has been struggling with dementia for a few years now. I felt guilty putting him in a home, and I was doing okay with the day nurse coming by. But in the last month or so, he's become more violent. I actually didn't go hunting that week I took off because I wanted to stay close to Dad. Wednesday night, his neighbor called. Apparently, Dad had attacked his caretaker because he thought he was robbing him. By the time I got to the house, he was pretty much out of control, and he ended up attacking me for the same reason.

'I didn't want to do it, but I knew I had to get him committed right away, and it wasn't sitting well with me. Before my mom died, I promised her I'd always look after him, take care of him. Anyway, I knew I needed to distract myself, so I called Hammond and told him I'd gotten back from my "hunting trip" early, and so that's why I was there at the Kensington house Thursday night. But it became pretty clear to me pretty quickly that my head wasn't fully in the game. So, I decided to take off, telling myself that the team had Sandra now.' He snorted. 'Clearly, that went well.'

'Tony, why didn't you just share this with us? We're a team; we stick together. We might've been able to help you through it.'

'I know, and I know this is going to sound lame, but the truth is, I was embarrassed that my elderly, sick father had gotten the jump on me, and on top of everything else, I guess I didn't handle it right.'

'Tony, you kept the promise you made to your mom,' Alyssa said. 'You put your dad somewhere where he'd be safe, despite the hurt it caused you. You have no reason to feel shame.' She smiled gently up at him. 'Well, except for choosing not to share with the rest of your team, who could've helped you out.'

'I know.' Abruptly, Tony shoved to his feet, pacing from the table to the whiteboard and back again, raking his fingers through his hair as he did. 'But that's not everything.'

Tony's head dropped forward on his neck, and as much as Alyssa was compelled to go to him, she fought it, afraid he'd bolt. Considering he was finally opening up, she didn't want to risk it.

Just as suddenly as he'd begun pacing, he stopped and faced her, allowing her a glimpse of what she could only describe as a look of self-loathing.

'I knew one of the guys arrested in the *Toybox* sting. Back in high school, we played together on the baseball team.'

Feeling like she'd been sucker-punched, Alyssa gripped the back of a chair and waited for the rest.

Shadows filled Tony's eyes as he continued in a wobbly voice. 'Our senior year, there was a rumor that he'd raped a girl. I won't get into the nitty-gritty, but suffice it to say, the details floating around were awful similar to what we

374

uncovered up in Placitas.' He wiped one hand across his mouth. 'We weren't friends, and the rumor kept shifting and changing. In the end, I didn't do anything about it. I didn't report it. I didn't confront him or even ask the girl. I did what everyone else did. I swept it under the rug since it didn't have anything to do with me.'

'Tony,' Alyssa began, 'you can't—'

Tony's hand snapped up, palm out. 'Please, Lys, let me finish, or I'll never get through this. When I saw his name come up on that list of suspects in May, I nearly lost my mind. Especially when I remembered that *room*, that *cage* those girls were held in. It makes me sick. I failed. No, I wasn't a cop then, but I still could've done something.' His voice broke.

'Then one day Holly came in with Rachel and Jersey to see you, and it all came tumbling down on top of me. Everything I did was covered in layers of second and third guessing to the point I was afraid I was going to end up getting me or Joe killed. Me, I didn't care about, but Joe, I did. I tried talking to the counselor about it, but frankly, I was too ashamed, and I felt like it was her job to tell me none of it was my fault.'

'None of it *was* or *is* your fault, Tony,' Alyssa interrupted. 'You were a teenager. You reacted in a normal teenage way. Reporting that boy might've resulted in stopping *him*, but it wouldn't have changed the course of that trafficking ring being created. I hate to break it to you, friend, but you don't have that much control.' When he returned her lopsided half-smile, she had hope that things would be okay.

'But let's look at the bright side, shall we. Because of your hiatus, you were able to save Addis and Emerson. The universe works in mysterious ways, you know.'

Tony cleared his throat. 'Yeah, about that trip to the Pecos. I don't want you to think less of me, but I'll be honest. I pretty much hated everything about myself, and I was seriously considering ending it all. I'd gone out hunting that morning, and I spotted an elk, but I was distracted, and my aim was off, so I only managed to injure it. It was when I was tracking it that I realized I just couldn't do anything right anymore, so I felt like I might as well just put myself out of misery. But then by pure chance, I stumbled on the girls, and something shifted inside me. I was more determined than I ever remember being to save them.'

'Redemption, personal and professional,' Alyssa said softly. 'Not that I think you needed to redeem yourself, but that's what drove you. That and being the amazing person and law enforcement officer that you are. Maybe you couldn't save all the girls from *The Toybox*, but you damned well saved Addis and Emerson. Thank God you were in the right place at the right time. Ever wonder why that is?'

In answer, Tony blushed.

'Thank you for sharing all this with me, and while I'm not going to say anything to the others, I think *you* should, especially Joe. But that's for you to decide. Either way, I've got your back. But I do have one more question for you. Why *didn't* you tell us? It had to have been more than guilt.'

A rush of color exploded onto Tony's face. 'Honestly? Because of you.'

If he'd slapped her, Alyssa couldn't have been more stunned. 'Me?'

'Yes. After everything *you've* been through this year with both your kids being targets of some seriously crazed nutjobs and finding out you have a serial killer in your family… If you could come through all that, seemingly unscathed, what right did I have to feel trauma over not reporting something, you know?'

'No, I don't know. But do you want to know why I *seem* unscathed? Because I have the best people surrounding me, people who are my teammates *and* my friends. So, next time, you remember you can come to us. Any or all of us. You got it?'

Tony's eyes glassed over. 'Thanks, Lys. And thanks for understanding. I'll see you tomorrow.'

'There's nothing to understand.' Alyssa touched Tony's arm as he moved towards the door. 'And I'm going to encourage you to get back into counseling.' When he opened his mouth to protest, she cut him off. 'I can always sic Isaac on you. He'll give you a dissertation on the merits of talking to someone. You know I'll do it, too.' She was relieved when Tony chuckled.

'I'll think about it,' he promised.

'That's all I'm asking, at least for the moment,' she said, feeling a weight lifted now that she understood where her teammate's head had been. She followed him out the door. 'See you tomorrow.'

Chapter Fifty-Seven

Grace's brushed and darkened brows rose into perfect arches when she answered the door to Alyssa and Cord Friday afternoon.

'Addis is asleep upstairs, so if you need to speak with her again, it'll have to wait,' Grace said, inviting them inside.

'We're actually here to see you if you have a few minutes.'

Grace studied their faces. 'Of course. Would either of you like some coffee?' She smiled. 'Never mind. I know *you* would, Alyssa. Cord, would you?'

'No, thank you.'

'Suit yourself.' She set one mug in front of Alyssa before taking a seat at the kitchen table. 'Sugar is on the counter behind you, and the creamer's in the fridge – not that you need any of that, unless you've switched things up recently.'

'If I remember correctly, you take yours the same way.'

Grace lifted her mug to 'salute' Alyssa. 'So, what's going on?'

'We just finished visiting Elizabeth Monroe,' Alyssa began. 'Her status has been upgraded to stable and she's been moved to a private room. When we left, the neighbor who's been watching her son had just brought him in to visit.' Alyssa smiled as she remembered how Brandon, his Superman cape flying out behind him, had raced into the room just as they were finishing up, scooting between Alyssa and Cord instead of around them before clamoring onto the bed amidst Tessa's cries of, 'Be careful.'

Unmindful of her stitches and bruises, Elizabeth had clasped her son to her chest, weeping into his hair as she stroked his back, rocking him back and forth. With watery eyes, she'd peered up at Alyssa and Cord, choking out, 'I knew he wouldn't abandon us.'

Alyssa had smiled softly. 'Sometimes finding the truth takes a little more time, but I'm glad you were able to get your answers, that you never gave up on what you knew in your heart was the truth.'

It was then that Brandon had softly patted his mom's cheek to turn her attention back to him. With his chest puffed out, he'd poked himself and said, 'I let the police girl borrow my magnifying glass so she could catch the bad guy who hurt you.'

Love shimmering through her tears, Elizabeth had pulled her son down for another hug, whispering, 'Thank you. That was very thoughtful of you, my brave boy.' Though she still couldn't recall meeting Sandra the night of her attack, she had a fuzzy recollection of Sandra calling to ask a few more questions. Even so, Elizabeth had been stunned when she'd learned the officer's real identity was actually Hayden's friend, Alexandra Greene.

Now sitting in Grace's kitchen, Alyssa had a feeling the discovery would be worse for the district attorney, but before she could break the news to her, Grace beat her to it.

Lifting her cup to her lips but not drinking from it, she said, 'I'm guessing then that the two of you are here to tell me about Officer Falwin's arrest for Gabriel and Lydia's murders.'

Alyssa shook her head. They hadn't even released the information to the media yet. 'How did you—Never mind. You're the district attorney. Of course, someone told you. Who?'

Grace simply raised her brows. 'It explains the girls' reaction at the hospital. I knew something was wrong after Sandra and Tony left, but I think Addis and Emerson were too afraid to admit why, especially since Falwin was a cop. Now, I assume there's more and that you've come to fill in those gaps.' When Cord shifted in his seat, she glanced once in his direction before turning her attention back to Alyssa. 'Did Ms. Monroe ever explain why she agreed to meet Sandra in an abandoned parking lot? Didn't she find that to be just a bit of an odd request?'

Alyssa tilted her head to the side. 'Yes and no. Elizabeth remembers picking up her phone to call me so she could confess that she'd seen Gabriel at the Ranch Steakhouse the night of the murders. Because she was afraid she'd become a suspect, she didn't tell us when we were interviewing her. The guilt for holding that information back was too much, and so I'm guessing when Sandra called under the pretense of having follow-up questions, Elizabeth just wasn't thinking clearly.'

Grace's hands tightened on her coffee mug. 'Did she know Gabriel would be there?'

'No. Coincidentally, Hayden's brother was in town, and she went there to meet him. When she spotted Gabriel, she decided since Ted was with her, she might as well follow Gabriel out and ask if they could see the pictures he'd mentioned in his message. But by the time she and Ted got outside, it was too late. Gabriel and Lydia were already gone.'

As soon as Elizabeth had mentioned Hayden's brother, Alyssa and Cord had known why the man on the security feed at the Ranch Steakhouse had looked so familiar. Ted was the older version of Hayden.

'Then, when Elizabeth told us the knife Addis and Emerson found beneath the cabin was a gift to Hayden, that bit of the mystery began to clear, so now we have a crew up in the Pecos where we believe Sandra hid Benson's body,' Alyssa said. 'If any bones are discovered, then we'll have a forensic anthropologist examine them to determine if they belong to Hayden, which I suspect they will.

'We may never find out the truth behind his death, but based on Darren Pease's experience, coupled with her father's claim that Alex's metamorphosis came after a new girl moved into town and stole some of her adulation, I'm guessing she became enraged when Hayden told her he didn't return her feelings, and consumed by delusional fantasies of the two of them together, she snapped.'

'What about his phone, his car? No one ever found them, right?' Grace asked.

'Lots of places to toss a phone, and if our hunch is correct, and Hayden Benson's remains are somewhere near the cabin, we'll look into dredging the Pecos River. Lots of cars have gone there to die after being stripped of their parts,' Cord said.

Alyssa sighed. 'There's one more thing. I know you don't blame her, but Elizabeth asked if we'd please tell you she's so sorry. I tried to explain that, unfortunately, there was nothing to link the cases together until after the tragedies, but she still feels responsible for Gabriel and Lydia's deaths, as well as what happened with the girls.'

Grace's eyes suddenly widened as if she were caught in the middle of doing something wrong. Alyssa swung around and spotted Addis leaning against the wall. None of them had heard her come in.

'You know,' Addis's voice was just a wisp of a whisper, and Alyssa had to strain to hear her, 'in the last week, I've learned monsters are not ogres who hide beneath our beds or in our closets. They live in plain sight all around us. And two of them stole my life when they murdered my parents. So, you tell that lady that the guilt doesn't belong on her shoulders.' She did nothing to stem the flow of tears, but she did allow Grace to envelop her in her arms as she collapsed into wrenching sobs that ate at Alyssa's very soul. A few minutes later, Addis's cries slowed, and she pulled back from her aunt.

Feeling the need to give them space and having done what they'd come to do, Alyssa nodded to Cord, and together they stood. But she still had one more thing she needed to share. Because Addis was still standing there, Alyssa hesitated but then decided the teenager had been through worse and would hear about it anyway. She turned to Grace. 'Do you remember how Mack had wanted to go through Gabriel's office?'

'Yes.' Grace spoke in a monotone.

'Hal found some suspicious financial activity in one of Gabriel's charities – the one in which Mack was on the board. Since that was the only one he was involved with, and none of the other charities showed any discrepancies, I can say with relative confidence that Gabriel wasn't aware of any wrongdoing. Professional courtesy: there's going to be an embezzlement investigation.'

More than anger, Grace expressed disappointment. 'Sadly, I'm not surprised. I don't suppose you ever discovered why Mack was at the Ranch Steakhouse the night of the murders?'

It was Cord who answered. 'The business client he had dinner with later that night was the owner's sister, but that's as much as we were able to uncover, for now at least.'

The lines around Grace's mouth deepened, but whatever she was thinking, she kept to herself. Instead, she thanked Alyssa and Cord for stopping by. 'I know this is your job, and while it seems so ineffective, I'll never be able to thank you and your team enough for bringing Addis and Emerson back to us.' Her smile was warm even while her eyes showcased her sadness as she stared over at her niece.

'Of course.' Alyssa turned to Addis. 'You have an amazing role model here, but I'd still like to offer you a word of advice. Don't let anyone tell you how long it should take for you to heal. You and Emerson have survived a nightmare most people can't even begin to wrap their minds around. And don't be afraid to seek help.' She didn't say it, but she had a feeling that Tony, who had confided in the entire team this morning, would be there to help guide her and Emerson through some of their rough patches.

Addis sniffled. 'Yes, ma'am.'

Grace ruffled her niece's hair and then followed Alyssa and Cord to the courtyard. 'Detective, before you go, I do have one more thing I need to discuss with you.'

Alyssa and Cord exchanged puzzled looks.

'In light of your... connection... to the McCormick/Bishop case, I just wanted to let you know in advance that I'll be offering a plea deal to Rafe McCormick. I believe his actions were the result of temporary insanity brought about by the brutal murder of his wife and unborn child. I'm in no way condoning vigilantism, of course, but this case goes beyond that, I believe.'

Alyssa didn't allow herself to dwell on the reasons why she was relieved to know Mr. McCormick wouldn't spend the rest of his days rotting behind bars. Not quite trusting herself to speak around the sudden lump in her throat, she nodded to the district attorney, offering a brief wave to Addis who now stood in the doorway, her head leaning against the frame as she waited for Grace to come back in.

Back in the car, Alyssa turned to Cord and said, 'You know what? I'm taking the rest of the day off and I'm going to go spend it with my family. Brock called to say Holly and the gang showed up again for a late lunch, so everyone's at the house. And I haven't seen much of them lately, so…'

Cord grinned. 'Good, because I was planning on playing hooky as well and watching sappy rom-com movies with Sara while we gorge ourselves on burnt popcorn.'

Alyssa laughed. 'You, my friend, have some weird taste buds.'

'Hey, this one's on Sara. Those babies give her some strange cravings. Burnt popcorn, pickles and lemon juice, jellybeans and guacamole.'

Alyssa shuddered. 'Stop. That's so gross. That even beats Isaac's Cheetos and salsa combo.'

Cord's laughter cut off so quickly, it scared her. 'What? What's wrong? What did I miss?'

'It's a boy and a girl. We weren't going to say anything to anyone, but Sara and I discussed it, and we both wanted you to know. Besides, Sara's super stoked to be able to share it with *someone*.'

Alyssa's grin couldn't be any wider. 'Cord, that's great news! You and Sara are going to be amazing parents, I just know it. And I can't wait to meet them. In due time, of course,' she added, feeling superstitious about jinxing the babies to arrive too soon.

'We're still arguing over our son's name, but we're naming our daughter Shelley.' A tear trailed down his cheek, and that quick, Alyssa felt the golf ball bloom in her throat yet again.

'I think your sister would love that.'

A sad smile ghosted his face. 'Yeah, I think she would.'

–

After dropping Cord off at the precinct so he could get his own vehicle, Alyssa rolled her window down so she could savor the aroma of roasting green chiles wafting through the air while she drove home. When she walked in, her heart smiled at the lively card game being played at the kitchen table, grateful the kids were on fall break. Everyone was there: Brock, Holly, Isaac, Mabel, Nick, Rachel, Sophie, Jersey, and Trevor.

Strolling over to her husband, she bent down and kissed him. But before she could head upstairs to change her clothes, he stood and wrapped her in his arms. 'Missed you, baby. Glad you're home.'

Her heart couldn't possibly have held more love than it held at that moment.

Their attention for each other was dragged away when Isaac, Trevor, and Nick let out ear-splitting whoops, high-fived and fist-bumped over Holly's head, and danced around the kitchen like lunatics, drawing laughter from everyone.

She was wrong. The love and happiness for her family would never cease growing.

A letter from Charly

Well, I must admit that 2020 has been the craziest year on record in my lifetime, at least that I remember, and I imagine, a lot of you feel the same way. Luckily for me, Alyssa Wyatt had another crime to solve, and so I had a place to channel some of the stress and insanity, at least for periods of time.

Speaking of which, I'd like to tell all the readers out there how thrilled I've been at you reaching out to personally tell me how much you've enjoyed the Alyssa Wyatt series. It never ceases to put a huge smile on my face… especially when you tell me you've somehow connected with her or any of the other characters. Thank you, also, for sharing your love of Alyssa with all your friends and family. I'm so glad you've taken to her as much as I have. She embodies so much of the strength and compassion I admire in others.

Please continue reaching out by getting in touch with (or following) me in any of the ways listed below.

Sincerely,

Charly Cox

Charly's Chat: www.clcox-author.com
Email: charlycox@clcox-author.com
Twitter: www.twitter.com/charlylynncox
Facebook: www.facebook.com/charlycoxauthor

Instagram: www.instagram.com/charlycoxauthor
Goodreads: www.goodreads.com/author/show/19490745.Charly_
BookBub: www.bookbub.com/profile/charly-cox

Acknowledgments

As always, I have many people to thank for helping me along the way. So, I'll get straight to it.

A very special thank you goes to my incredible nephew Peter Romero, the most avid, enthusiastic hunter I know. As a vegetarian (or pescatarian every once in a while), I know less than nothing about the fine intricacies of hunting, and Peter spent a long *(long)* time answering my vast array of (probably strange) questions (sometimes the same ones) about when, what, where a person could go hunt at what time of year, what time of day was best, and what did a person use to hunt specific things... oh, and why did they use them, and what happens *after* the hunt. Then he spent even more time making sure I understood what he was saying. It was crazily fascinating stuff. Not only did I learn quite a bit, but it was also great fun listening to all his stories. I may not be ready to go hunting yet, but I think Officer Tony White and Peter would get along splendidly.

Another special thank you goes to Mary McAfee. From the hallways of DRMS, you've gone from co-worker to friend to someone I turn to when I just need a mother's advice. You are always ready with a hug, to lend an ear, and to share your words of wisdom and encouragement. Thank you for always continuing to support me.

I'd also like to thank Jennie Ayres, a most brilliant and incredibly talented person and editor, for all the considerable time, effort, and hard work she has put into helping me shape and fine tune not just this book, but all of the Alyssa Wyatt series. You have been absolutely invaluable.

As always, Keshini Naidoo (Hera Books) deserves a huge, massive thanks for always having her finger on the pulse of the story, for allowing me to bounce ideas off her, for calming my moments of madness, and at least a million other things. Alyssa Wyatt and her team would definitely not be the same without you.

Lindsey Mooney (Hera Books), for everything you do to get my stories into the world and into readers' hands and homes.

Kevin and Timothee (who was the inspiration behind Brandon's, Nate's, Isaac's, and Trevor's fascination with superheroes because, at the age of four, he insisted on being called Laser Black), for being with me every step of the way and just being the best support system a gal could ever want. I love you.

And to all my usual peeps who have never faltered in their ceaseless support and encouragement (you all know who you are), as well as those of you who willingly answer all my law enforcement and medical questions (I'm looking at you, Bud Wolfenbarger and Tracy Banghart). You ALL keep me going, and I can't imagine it any other way.